Tears of Like Souls

A Julie Madigan Thriller #2

Val Conrad

Black Rose Writing | Texas

ISBN: 978-1-935605-84-3
PUBLISHED BY BLACK ROSE WRITING
www.blackrosewriting.com

Printed in the United States of America
Suggested Retail Price (SRP) $20.95

Tears of Like Souls is printed in Times New Roman

*As a planet-friendly publisher, Black Rose Writing does its best to eliminate unnecessary waste to reduce paper usage and energy costs, while never compromising the reading experience. As a result, the final word count vs. page count may not meet common expectations.

Dedication: To my father – 1933 – 2010

My dad taught me reading, writing, and responsibility. If you know me at all, you know I got the first two down pat. But looking back at the last one, he was a responsible man – this is a trait not common today. To him, an issue was either right or wrong, and there was not any middle ground. He loved to fish, and though he didn't get to spend as much time fishing in his last years as he might have hoped, he never gave up the idea that a bad day fishing was better than a good day at most anything else. He loved flying and shooting, and he loved the ranch where he'd lived, both earlier in his life, and his last years. Baby calves, feeding, it never mattered to him – he did those tasks required there with the same meticulous responsibility he did everything else.

Except, I discovered, housework. After my mother died, Dad learned to do the things to keep a home running, but he didn't like it. Suddenly he couldn't imagine all the work his wife had done every day. There is a tiny saying on his refrigerator – *Doing housework never hurt anyone, but why take a chance?*

Many people influenced my father, but the words of one man, offered shortly after the death of my eight-year-old brother in 1966 were *be of good cheer*. Not a contrite greeting or farewell, it offered no luck, no vague wishes, no response to expectations of others about how to feel, but a way of presenting yourself to the world, regardless what happened. The same man offered me the same advice when I called to tell him about my father's passing, and I find it comforting. So while it's been a sad occasion to mourn the passing of a responsible man I called Dad, I offer to you those same words of advice – be of good cheer.

ACKNOWLEDGEMENTS:

To me, fiction is best set against a background of acceptable reality, so I've tried to maintain the most accurate geographical, medical and legal facts possible in this story. However, because the story is fiction, some of the information may have been altered to fit the plot and should in no way be seen as the fault of those generous people who provided me details. I'd like to thank Mike Oltersdorf, Leelanau County Sheriff (Michigan), and a Michigan Circuit Court Judge (who wishes to remain anonymous,) for their time in explaining the intricacies of Michigan law.

There are dozens of other people I'd like to thank for their support – including critique group members Caron Guillo, Travis Erwin and Vickie Schoen, who offered many questions and suggestions to make this a better read. Thanks also to Tonie Bolin and my sister Paula Hendrick, who offered to proofread, and Vickie Brobst, who read and proofed versions along the way and always encouraged me.

Most of all, I wish to say a gracious thanks to my husband Bill, who has offered me his friendship, his opinion and support, and most of all his love. We've not chosen the easiest of roads to travel, but the most worthwhile.

CHAPTER

1

September 25, 1995
El Paso, Texas

My soul had swirled down a drain into hell, and I slammed headfirst into a wall of physical and emotional exhaustion at the speed of insanity. Sleep, what little I'd had in the last three or four days – I'd lost count – would not keep me much longer from the collapse ahead.

Sitting outside the hospital, I was haunted by images that would not vanish. When I closed my eyes, visions of the last seventy-two hours – even events I'd only heard by phone – played in my head with stunning clarity of color, touch and smell, branded into my memory like burn-in on a video screen.

Twice in the last week, I'd listened helplessly on the phone as someone I cared for had been shot – three nights ago, when Zach had been on a Florida beach, and then only hours ago, when Anthony Bock opened fire in a St. Petersburg hospital room.

This last time, one man I loved survived. And one didn't.

Your life is screwed up, I thought, when your serial-killer half-brother is responsible for one of your lovers having to tell you the other is dead. Had things gone Anthony's way, I'm sure Jeremy McNeeley and Zach Samualson would both have died in Florida.

Anthony Bock had also kidnapped my mother, who'd escaped a bomb in a barn not far from Ruidoso, New Mexico, though I'd yet to find out how. Dehydrated and weak, she'd fled captivity. I'd ridden in the rescue helicopter that had delivered her to William Beaumont Army Medical Center in El Paso, where she was being treated. Now I sat outside, away from the doors, my back to a wall.

FBI Special Agent Nolan Forrester, who'd rallied many of the resources in the search for my mother, found me sitting outside the emergency department in the morning sun. It was warm for the last week of September, yet I was chilled to my aching bones.

Nolan sat down beside me and said nothing for a while. Maybe he gazed out over the shades of brown surrounding El Paso, wondering what my eyes seemed to focus on in the distance.

Knees pulled to my chest, I tried to hide the trembling muscles that might give away the fact I was little more than a human train wreck in slow motion, awaiting devastation yet to come. Still reeling from the news from Florida, I sometimes had to remind myself to breathe. Despite my initial meltdown after hearing the news that Anthony Bock hadn't died alone in a Florida hospital room, I was calm now. The overwhelming grief I was trying to control would not remain contained for long.

"Your mother has some army major backed into a corner, making him sign her release papers," Nolan said, breaking the silence. "The FBI jet just landed here and refueled. Where do you want to go?"

My brain lagged, needing time to make sense of his words, and I turned to him in blank confusion.

"I figured you might want to go to Florida," he clarified.

Gathering the energy to speak was like wading in wet concrete – slow and futile. "Has anyone notified his family?" I asked, trying to focus on the future for a moment instead of the disastrous past. "Could we stop in Atlanta? I'd like to tell Jeremy's parents, if you could make that happen."

"Julie, I know you were – I mean –" Nolan paused, finding no diplomatic way of stating the truth, so he ignored it and continued. "That's not a good enough reason for you to be the one to tell them."

"Having sex with him," I filled in his hesitation. "Let's not start being bashful now, Nolan. I owe his parents a personal explanation. And I don't need to tell Jeremy's wife because I feel guilty – she needs to know he was going home to her."

"Are you sure?" he asked.

Am I sure I don't feel guilty? Am I sure Jeremy was leaving me again? Or am I sure I want to face his family and tell them he's dead?

"When Jeremy saw me at the cabin in Michigan that last time, whatever he felt for me died right there – I saw it on his face. He left a note with Brandan before sneaking away, saying he was sorry – again." I took a deep breath. "He couldn't see beyond what I'd done, past the newest scars on my soul. Not anymore."

"You're not that broken, Julie Madigan," Nolan declared.

I turned to him, wondering what he saw when he looked at me, because I truly felt shattered, like a Christmas tree ornament.

He shrugged. "The plane is ready whenever your mother's finished."

An hour later, we were on the jet, headed east.

For the sake of the overall investigation, I spent the first part of the flight trying to explain Anthony Bock's lifelong murder spree, beginning when he witnessed his mother being killed by his stepfather, and ending with Jeremy McNeeley's death in the hospital room in Florida. The list of victims between, including Bock's stepfather and his biological father – my father – defied my ability to accurately count.

My mother sat speechless through most of the explanation. Behind her stone face, I had no idea what kind of reaction she hid. Still, she summarized the situation best, saying, "I'm astounded at the thread of evil he wove through our lives, nearly killing us both."

I didn't tell her that Bock wanted me to live, making me kill to prove I'd *enjoy* it. Picking up the pieces of this hateful chaos, I realized that the hardest part was knowing I'd survived. So many others had not.

In my mother's eyes, though, I watched her make connections about the man she thought she knew while I described the monster he hid inside. Bock had quietly drawn her in until it was time to make her a victim, and she lacked the iron walls to hold at bay the violence he'd unleashed.

I was glad she didn't have much to say because I had no idea how to listen to her facet of the story, much less know how to fix what had happened to her.

3

When the jet landed in Atlanta, a female agent brought a variety of garments on board so I'd look more presentable to see the McNeeleys. My mother helped me choose from several FBI-ish-looking suits that were almost too stark and formal to deliver a death notification, if such a thing is even possible. She picked a blouse, skirt, jacket, pantyhose, and sensible shoes. From a small makeup kit, I chose only a powder to dull the worn, ragged look I saw in the mirror. To finish, I pulled my hair into a low bun, which was all the energy I had.

Nolan tended to business outside with our greeting party while I changed, but when I came down the steps, my knees quivered as if gravity had doubled. My muscles could barely support my weight as I walked.

"This is Julie Madigan," Nolan said, introducing me to a pair of FBI agents. "She's the medical examiner investigator who helped with this case. With her assistance, we also managed to save one more victim last night – her mother."

We shook hands. Nolan might have told me their names, but this information didn't register if he did.

"Ms. Madigan, we had someone check ahead," one agent explained. "Dr. McNeeley's parents are home, but there is no sign of his wife at her own."

"He told her to go somewhere safe. His parents will probably know," I replied.

"Do you want me to go?" Nolan asked.

I nodded. "I don't know what they should or shouldn't be told – that's your department. I only know what I need to say."

From the backseat of a black sedan, the city passed outside as the agents drove us to the McNeeley's house, but the buildings and lights meant nothing to me.

I was unprepared for the two people who came to the door together. Time had changed them since we'd met, only once in Albuquerque, not long after Jeremy and I began dating. Fifteen years ago, I managed to count – not quite half my life.

Hannah McNeeley was a tall, elegant woman with sterling silver hair swept into a thick French braid, so beautiful it seemed like jewelry. Jeremy had inherited her caramel-colored eyes and golden skin that had not yet begun to reveal her age.

William, in contrast, was quite ordinary. Balding, grayish brown hair cut short. Hazel eyes. He seemed to have little throw to Jeremy's physical appearance, but I knew they'd shared an intense passion for medicine.

The McNeeleys sensed disaster when Nolan made his FBI introduction, but they invited us in to sit down.

Hannah said she remembered me. "Jeremy mentioned you went to work for the state police about the time he left to finish medical school."

After he broke off our engagement and walked away.

I nodded. Taking a breath, I began. "Now I work with a medical examiner's office in Michigan. A few weeks ago, we received an unusual microbiological sample, so I called the CDC for assistance."

William spoke up, "Oh yes. The *Bilharzia* from South Africa."

"Yes. Imagine my surprise when Jeremy arrived in my office the next morning to consult on the case," I said. The words I spoke only delayed the inevitable bad news, and I struggled to make the story make sense. "The killer also kidnapped my mother as a way to manipulate me, so I flew to New Mexico to find her yesterday morning. From what we put together, Jeremy left Michigan to come back to Atlanta. To come home."

I choked on the word.

Nolan continued for me. "We presume Dr. McNeeley saw the suspect in the airport in Traverse City or maybe in Chicago, and then he followed him to Florida. From the airport in Tampa, your son trailed him to a St. Petersburg hospital to where a friend of Julie's, a Drug Enforcement Agency officer who'd been shot a few days ago, was a patient."

"Jeremy went there to warn Zach," I said, "and he was still there when this man entered the room. When the shooting began, Jeremy was hit." I gulped air. "They couldn't save him."

I could only absorb more pain – there was no deflection left to protect myself.

Tears rolled down my face as I watched the McNeeleys' world shatter.

Hannah leaned against her husband and sobbed quietly for

several minutes.

After taking a deep breath, William spoke. "Jeremy called me from the airplane yesterday." He took his wife's hand. "He said he was on his way home, but there was something he needed to do on the way. He asked me not to call Deanna – said he'd be back in a day or two."

"I came to tell her, too," I said. "I owe her that much."

"She and Stephanie have been staying here with us since he called a week or so ago," Hannah said, looking at her watch. "They should be home any time. Deanna took Stephanie to her therapist."

"Jeremy told me about Stephanie's hyperlexia," I said. "It broke his heart he couldn't connect with her."

Hannah began to speak, but as if on cue, there was a soft knock on their door.

"That's Stephanie," Hannah said with a faint smile. "She doesn't like the doorbell."

"Why not?" I asked as William went to let them in.

"Because the door itself doesn't actually ring, and the sound is not a bell. It's a chime. She doesn't like things that aren't what they say they are."

William escorted in a woman and toddler. He made the brief introductions and asked Deanna to have a seat. He picked up Stephanie and was discussing a snack when they disappeared into the kitchen.

I took a deep breath. "Deanna, if I understood what Jeremy told me, you know who I am. I came here to tell you face to face he left Michigan on his way home to you."

Her eyes jumped from me to Hannah's somehow composed face and back to me, reading the warning signs of tragedy ahead.

Deanna wasn't physically the sort of woman I expected – I'd imagined a tall, magnificent woman, like Jeremy's mother. Instead, she was tiny and fragile. She wasn't going to be strong like Hannah. I could see hysteria building like the ground cracking in an earthquake.

Facing the other woman might have been tolerable, but Deanna knew whatever was going on here was more than that. It was too much.

"Mrs. McNeeley, Jeremy was fatally wounded when –" Nolan

said when the silence had stretched on too long. Like ripping off a bandage over a wound all at once.

Deanna turned to me and screamed, "No! You bitch, this is your fault!"

While Hannah tried to calm her down, I sat there with tears burning down my cheeks, letting her verbally attack me. Nothing she said was any worse than what I'd already told myself.

She called me names. She made angry but accurate allegations that I was sleeping with her husband. She blamed me for everything.

Finally she collapsed onto the sofa and looked at me. "Why? Tell me why he died," she said, rage deflating to agony. "Why you?"

"I loved Jeremy a very long time ago, but he broke off our engagement. When he came to Michigan for the CDC, I tried to be angry, to not feel anything, but the walls I put up fell," I said. "You're right. I did sleep with him, because he told me his marriage was over, which I assumed meant he was divorced. I was furious when I found out he wasn't."

Deanna listened, arms crossed over her chest like armor.

"Yesterday morning, after I escaped from a cabin with a dead man's blood on my hands, Jeremy realized he could never look at me again, knowing what I'd done. He didn't even say good-bye." I wiped my eyes and almost gagged at the smell of blood trapped in my memory. "When he left, we believed he was coming back here to you and Stephanie. No one knew he'd gone to Florida until it was over. But he went there to save someone else's life."

"Oh," she squeaked.

"You can never hate me as much as I hate myself that this happened to him or to all of you," I said. "If I could undo any moment to put him here with you now, I'd do it. I'd take his place if that were possible. You deserve him. Stephanie deserves him. And I'm eternally sorry I screwed it all up."

I stood up to leave, and Nolan followed my lead.

After a sigh, Deanna looked up at me with a much different expression. "I'm surprised you could say those things to me after I called you such names."

"I'm easy to hate because I'm alive. If it makes you feel better, hate me, but don't lose yourself in anger. You still have a beautiful child who needs all your love," I said. "Jeremy cried one night telling me about her."

We were at the door, ready to leave when William came in, carrying Stephanie, who ignored the two strangers in her grandparents' house.

Her eyes moved from William to her mother and her grandmother, then she asked, "Where's Daddy?"

It was all I could do to get out the door.

CHAPTER

2

An hour later, the FBI jet was again airborne, bound for Tampa.

What little energy I'd had drained out of me on the McNeeley's curb, hopefully hidden from a little girl who didn't need to see a stranger lose her sanity.

Someone had stowed dinner on board for us, but I had no appetite, even though I couldn't remember when or what I'd last eaten. I picked at the food only because I was sitting across from my mother, making her usual fuss – "You've got to eat something."

When she gave up on feeding me, I changed out of the FBI attire back into my dirty clothes, and then I pretended to doze.

I didn't like the images floating around in my head, and the thought of falling asleep chilled me. Sleep would lead to dreams. Dreams to nightmares. But I simply could not talk or listen about Bock any more.

Finally at the Raytheon terminal at Tampa International Airport, the jet engines whined down to welcomed silence. I packed the FBI clothes I'd worn and other items in my pack before I stood up. The FBI would not wait around to fly me to Michigan.

Nolan fussed with his laptop and papers, waiting for me to make my way forward.

"I've been a pain in the ass," I said as he stood up to face me. "I'm sorry. Thank you, for everything you did. I couldn't have located or rescued my mother without your help."

"Julie, we couldn't have done what we did without your help, either. You should come to the Bureau."

9

I shook my head. "You and I both know I couldn't pass an FBI evaluation."

"Despite what you think, you're not so physically or emotionally broken that I wouldn't work with you. Think about it. When the dust settles, we should talk."

I extended my hand, fighting tears. "Thanks for the wings, too. This wasn't necessary but was very much appreciated. I'll see you in Michigan in a few days?"

"We'll be waiting."

And then he did something I didn't expect – he pulled me close and hugged me.

"Take care of yourself, Julie," he whispered in my ear, "and your mother."

"I'll try. Thanks."

Standing at the top of the jet's steps, I looked down to see half a dozen people on the tarmac, most strangers.

One tall man stepped forward, surprising me. I dropped my bag and ran toward him, jumping into his open arms, trying to be careful of the bandage on his neck.

"Julie," he said between kisses. "You're really okay?"

"Yeah, I mean, no. Something's happened. When Kim and I –"

Zach Samualson put one finger over my lips to quiet me. "Listen to me. Dr. McNeeley told me what happened in the cabin. I'm sorry about what you had to do. I'm sorrier this guy killed so many people you cared about. The best I could do was to shoot the bastard for you."

"Is he really dead?" I whimpered like a lost child, hoping the monster was gone. "Anthony, I mean?"

"Yeah, he is," Zach said. "Between the three of us, we put ten rounds in him, Julie. I'm very sure he's dead. He can't ever hurt you again."

I wanted so much to believe him. "Take me where I don't have to think about people dying," I said, feeling those muscular arms holding me together.

Zach kissed me again. "We'll go. We both need some down time and there's a lot to talk about. We can take off for a new horizon tomorrow." He grinned and pointed to the bandage on his neck, covering the wound he suffered when he was shot. "Tonight, I better go back, though. I sort of snuck out of the hospital."

"Aren't you a bad boy?" I said, wrapping my arms around him tighter.

"Isn't that what you love most about me?" He laughed and kissed the top of my head, "I couldn't miss being here when you landed."

"I'm glad you came."

"Baby, I promise everything's going to be okay." He cupped my face in his hands and kissed me one more time.

Looking up into his eyes, I believed.

After introductions and thank-you's all around, Nolan said they were headed home to Michigan as soon as the fueling was complete and the crew changed.

Drug Enforcement Agents Pauly Brodenshot and Domino Hurley, who'd abetted and aided the escape of their partner from the hospital, loaded us all into a van for the ride over the bay to St. Pete.

Pleading exhaustion, Mom asked Dom to drop her at a hotel near the hospital. I went inside with her, and we each got a room. She told me she just wanted to shower and go to bed. She promised me she was all right, and that we could make plans the next day.

She might have really wanted to talk more, but whether it was hers or mine, the reluctance to share more details was too great – we both recognized that. I didn't want to leave her, but she insisted I go back to the hospital with Zach and his team.

Visiting hours were long over when we arrived, and I thought the charge nurse was going to strangle Zach with her stethoscope for leaving. The note he'd left to explain he had not been the victim of foul play might have satisfied security, but she was stomping mad.

"I mean no disrespect, Ma'am," Domino interrupted, stepping between her and Zach, "but each of us has either been shot at, shot, kidnapped or worse by the same gunman who tore up your hospital last night, so you might appreciate why we need a little time to debrief together. We could really use answers."

She changed tack and tried to get us to leave based on some medical logic, but Zach was having none of that, either. Resigned, she begged us to be quiet and closed the door behind her after she got her AWOL patient tucked into a bed and attached to as many devices as she could find.

Once she left, we all had pieces of the puzzle to share. I unthreaded the story in less detail than I had in the jet for Nolan. The biggest surprise to them was that Bock was my half-brother, born before my parents ever met. And of course, Zach and the other two agents had no idea what had been happening in New Mexico as I'd been searching for my mother.

"We were at the emergency room in El Paso when you called, Dom," I said.

Domino put his arm around my shoulder. "I didn't mean to scare you, but I wanted you to know it was over."

"Why didn't Zach just call me to start with?" I asked, flustered again at how the news had undone what little control I had left over my emotions at that moment.

He and Zach exchanged looks.

"Zach was busy trying not to bleed everywhere," Pauly announced, saying what neither of his partners would dare. "And Dom swore he wasn't about to tell you Z'd been shot again."

"Again?" I demanded.

"It's nothing really," Zach said. "I got grazed." He pointed to his right upper arm. "They were cleaning it up in the emergency room. You know, for liability's sake. Apparently it's bad PR when your patients get shot."

With that, we all laughed, and the tension eased.

Finally around 2 a.m., the order came for us to move out or else, so Pauly, Dom and I walked to the parking structure.

Domino drove Pauly home first.

"How's things with Pauly's foot?" I asked Dom as we watched his partner hobble on crutches to an apartment. "Zach said it might end his career."

"He won't know for a while, I guess. There's enough metal in there to set off the airport alarms right now. He's not even supposed to be up walking."

"I know what it's like to realize you'll never go back."

"Broken neck, huh?" Domino whistled.

"That's not what really ended my career with the New Mexico State Police," I said, twisting a wad of tissue. "Physically, they blamed the shattered shoulder since I could no longer pass the physical agility test – pull-ups, pushups, you know. But I suspect the state thought the emotional damage was what would keep me from doing the job. Zach helped me get past the injuries and on with living. I owe him a lot."

"You have no idea how good you've been for Zach. We've been partners a long time in agency years." Dom stopped at a red light. "He never explained what happened the night we picked you up at the bar or later at his mom's house, and I didn't ask," he said with mischievous brown eyes. "Do I want to know?"

Domino was referring to the night Zach had kidnapped me from a nightclub and proven to me that flirting with fate was still a form of suicide.

I shook my head. "Not tonight."

"All I know is how much it changed Zach," he concluded.

I smiled. "Changed us both. Someday I'll buy you a beer and tell you."

He pulled up to the hotel doors and stopped.

"I'm glad you're all okay. Thanks for everything, Dom." I hesitated before I opened the door. "Are you married?"

"Yes, ma'am. I'm a perfect exception to the blue rule. Veronica and I've been married nineteen years in July, and I've never been with another woman, before or after her. High school sweethearts. I swear, I don't know how Roni puts up with me or this job, but she's my world."

"Maybe love's enough to overcome anything, Dom." I leaned over and kissed him on the cheek. "See you tomorrow."

When I got to the perfectly anonymous hotel room, I peeled off the dirty clothes and fell onto the bed into an empty sleep. Tomorrow would begin a whole new direction, and my mind needed the rest to change gears.

My plan to sleep in was rudely interrupted by the phone. Not nearly enough sleep, I thought, and I deserved to be grumpy about it.

"Madigan," I said, regretting I couldn't manage to say "hello."

"Good morning, Blue Eyes," Zach said cheerfully. "Do you have a balcony facing east?"

"God, I hope not," I grumbled.

"Oh, you can sleep when you get old. Go look out the window at the sunrise."

I rolled off the bed and stretched the phone cord to the patio doors.

"Spectabulous, Zach. And what is it they say about red dawns?" I said, looking over Tampa Bay from the sixth story.

"We're not going sailing. It won't matter."

"Good, I haven't been on a boat in years," I said with a yawn.

"You live on Lake Michigan and you haven't been on the water?"

"Well, we watched the Cherry Festival Air Show last summer on the sheriff's deck boat," I said, "but we weren't on the ocean."

"Hmm, so you *will* lie to me. That's good to note. How about a Caribbean cruise?" he asked. "Or maybe a week or two in Jamaica?"

"It's not that I don't want to go far, far away with you, Zach, but there's a mess waiting for me in Michigan, I'm afraid."

He sighed. "Julie, I know you need time to sort out everything, but I can't take back those three words from the other night," he said then paused. "The doctor wrote my discharge orders, so I should be ready to go in a couple of hours. I'll have Domino pick you up and bring you to the hospital. Let's do something senseless – go to Disney World, Busch Gardens, Key West. We just need to be together."

Mindless entertainment sounded appealing.

"Or we could spend the day in your hotel room," he suggested in his sexiest voice.

As safe as I'd felt with him holding me last night, I wasn't ready to spend time alone with Zach, tangled in the sheets. Besides telling me he loved me, there was too much pain and death still rattling in my head – I couldn't let that in bed with us, though we'd shared a lot of our secrets and confessions there. Nor was I sure I could trust myself in public with all these emotions, orbiting like electrons about to reach critical mass. So while having his strong arms around me all day was inviting, I needed him with his clothes on, somewhere private.

Somewhere I can fall apart.

"Think you could find your way onto a beach or anywhere else in this county without a bulls-eye on your chest?" I finally managed to ask.

"Maybe." His voice said he really wasn't kidding.

"I don't want to wear my gun or vest today, so can you think of anywhere safe?" What might have been a joke sounded desperate.

"Julie," he said, "if I can make you feel you never have to wear them again, I'd be a happy man. I'll do whatever it takes to protect you as long as you'll let me. That's a promise."

"I believe you," I said, trying to bring back his morning smile. "Swear to me you won't ever go out like that without your gun again, or I'll shoot you myself."

"Deal."

We made plans to start the day. After a quick shower, I put on the only clean clothes I had – those provided by the FBI agent in Atlanta. They'd have to do, considering the way everything else smelled.

On my way past, I slipped a note under my mother's door, saying I'd gone to pick up Zach.

I didn't feel right about abandoning her all day, so my note said I'd come back to the hotel to have breakfast together before making any other plans.

Domino was waiting for me downstairs when I stepped off the elevator.

"Wow," he teased about the clothes. "You're spending way too much time with the feebs, Julie. You're starting to look like one of them."

"Clean counts for something," I said, not pointing out that he, too, was a federal officer, despite his baggy jeans and wild Hawaiian shirt. "I wanted to grab something more casual before we picked up Zach, but it's still too early."

"Did you try the gift shop here?"

Rainbow-colored t-shirts and shorts looked more comfy than what I had on, but the store wouldn't open for another two hours.

What the heck, we could shop later. I only looked like . . .

"FBI, Ma'am," the man in the suit and power-red tie said as we turned the corner to the lobby. Without lifting mirrored sunglasses that weren't necessary indoors, he flashed a badge in my face. "Are you Julie Madigan?"

"Not today," I said.

"Ma'am?" The answer wasn't what he expected.

15

No sense of humor at all, I thought, when he pulled down his glasses on his nose and eyed me over them.

"I have a warrant for your arrest, Ms. Madigan. . ."

Well, shit. . .

CHAPTER

3

". . . for the murder of Deputy Matthew Drake Shannaker. Turn around and place your hands behind your back," the agent said, dropping his shades back to his nose, droning as if bored with the script in a bad movie.

"You gotta be kidding!" Domino exclaimed, yanking out his own federal ID and shoving it in the guy's face. "What's the FBI got to do with this?"

"Dom, please. I'm not surprised," I said, though really I was. "I have a weapon, if you'd allow Agent Hurley to take possession of it?" I spread my arms for the agent to remove it and the holster, fighting a smirk as Domino snatched them from his hand. Then I asked if I could retrieve my room key for Dom, and the still-nameless agent let me fish it from my pocket before handcuffing me. "See what you can do about getting my mother and Zach to Michigan. And make sure Mom gets everything out of my room."

Domino Hurley looked flustered as he realized this time he'd be telling Zach the bad news about me.

♦

No private jet for the flight to Michigan – I was stuck on a commercial airliner, escorted by a deputy, handcuffs and all. However, we had three seats, providing more shoulder room.

Still I hate being stuck by the window.

Nolan Forrester met us at the airport in Traverse City, Michigan, the day after my federal arrest. "Julie, I'm sorry. I didn't think this would go down so quickly. The prosecutor is under a lot of pressure to make a pretrial examination immediately," he said, looking around and then lowering his voice. "Mrs. Shannaker's connections run deep in Leelanau County, I'm told."

I'd simply forgotten about Matt's mother until I sat alone in a cell the night before.

She deserved the whole truth about her dead son just like I'd owed the McNeeleys an explanation, but it appeared this apology might have an audience that included a judge and maybe even a jury.

I heard my name and looked around to see my boss jogging toward us, waving his ID to the man who'd flown with me. "I can't believe they've done this!" Dr. Gerald Katz said, appearing appalled at the handcuffs.

There was no chance to speak with him.

The deputy escorting me was a serious, humorless man who was unwilling to make time for me to talk to anyone. Not waiting for Zach and my mother to get off the jet, either, he clamped a hand around my arm and marched me through the concourse and outside to a media circus. I didn't duck or try to hide my face, but I tried not to look defiant, either. No need to blurt "No comment" statements – no one could have heard me over the shouts – stupid questions I couldn't believe were asked or that would dignify an answer.

The deputy shoved me into a government car and away we went.

The rest of the afternoon, I experienced the other side of due process. I was booked, pending arraignment Thursday morning for homicide and a several lesser crimes, including evasion of a federal officer. No way had I evaded Nolan Forrester in Florida, since he'd flown me there in the jet and let me out.

No big deal, but I wondered if the cumulative charges were designed to complicate the bigger picture, so there'd still be something to prosecute me for if the homicide charge fell.

If . . . what an if.

I was surprised no one had thought of child endangerment or adultery.

There's still plenty of time.

After the fingerprints and photos, the deputy put me into an interview room alone.

Half an hour later, Zach came in.

"I can't stay long. Here's what Forrester told me, if you care to give it credence," he said with sarcasm. "First, they won't let Nolan have any contact with you, in case you wonder why he doesn't. None of the cops can. Dr. Katz and I talked. I'll find out what I can."

I nodded, not knowing what else to say.

"Matthew's mother was married to –" he started to explain.

"I know about Carolyn Shannaker and her dead husband. She has a lot of sympathetic support in Leelanau County. I figured this would happen when –" I looked around, wondering if anyone was watching or recording us.

He followed my glance and shook his head. "I was told no. Professional courtesy, I guess, because I'm federal. Katz said the prosecutor apparently thinks this is bogus, but the law is the law. It could get thrown out at arraignment or end at pretrial. He told me the best lawyer around called him about taking your case. He'll be by to see you in the morning before the arraignment hearing."

"Did Gerald say who?" All day yesterday and last night to consider the facts and I hadn't thought about hiring an attorney. No wonder I was sitting in jail.

He shook his head. "I was asked to pass along the lawyer's request that you write out everything you remember about the case," he said, indicating two legal pads and a pen he'd dropped on the table.

Two hundred sheets of paper.

"I'll write small," I said, wondering if it was a task I was really up to, or if paper could contain so many catastrophic details of the last forty years of Anthony Bock's life, or even the last few weeks of my own.

"Is it okay if your mother and I go to your place?"

Although it seemed a courteous silly question, my answer stunned him. "No, the bomb squad needs to take a look. Don't eat anything or use anything Bock could have contaminated. In fact, get someone to clean it all out. Food, linens, furniture – everything. What a mess."

He looked at me like I had lost my mind.

I briefly explained Bock's uncanny ability to break into houses and poison people.

"I can't wait to hear the rest of this story, J'," he said, shaking his head in disbelief.

Yeah, me, too. I'd like to hear the G-rated happily-ever-after ending.

"Use my Suburban if you can find it," I said, wondering where it had wound up after Kim and I were kidnapped at the lakeshore in Traverse City. "After the bomb squad's done with it."

He nodded as if I'd mentioned getting an oil change. "So where do you want to go when this is done?"

"Somewhere warm and peaceful." I looked around at the pale gray walls. Almost anywhere else but jail would be an improvement.

He smiled. "How about the Bahamas for a month?"

"What about your job?" I asked. "You can't just –"

"Yes, I can. I'm on medical leave for now; I have tons of vacation time when that's done. As long as it takes, Julie."

I wanted to say he had to be crazy. Tell him to run before my life cratered around us both, but the only words that came out were, "I love you."

"Not the most romantic place to hear you say that the first time, but I'll take it," he said, pulling me out of my chair onto his lap and wrapping his strong arms around me. He pushed a strand of hair away from my face. "I love you, Julie. I'll tell you again, it's going to be okay, I promise."

♦

Time seemed to crawl as I alternated between writing down what had happened and staring at the walls, contemplating my situation – charged with killing a man.

How does one plead to this when there is no question whether it's true?

There was a witness. I had blood on my hands at the scene of the crime. My fingerprints were on the weapon, if it survived the fire or was even found. I'd even told law enforcement officers at the scene what I'd done and several more since.

Which leads to my belief that truth can be greater or less than the sum of its facts.

I scribbled the thought in a margin.

Not that I was unsympathetic to Mrs. Shannaker's intention to punish someone – I *had* held the knife, but I wasn't the person responsible for Matthew's death. He was doomed to die, no matter what. I'd cut his throat in an effort to save Kimberly Katz, but I wanted Matt to feel the hands of someone who cared about him as he died, like he'd held his dying father. I wonder if Carolyn ever suspected her son had shot her husband intentionally.

I couldn't deny that I'd cut Matt's throat, but it wasn't murder.

♦

They let Zach and my mother visit that evening, but I failed to reassure her I was really okay in the jail. She was beside herself, thinking about her only child behind bars, but at least I wasn't lying in a hospital. Or in a coffin.

I suggested she go back to Albuquerque. Her job waited, and the case wasn't likely to be settled in the next few days.

"Maybe I should. It's better than trying to do all that shopping for you," she kidded, referring to the news from Zach they'd need to replace all the food and other substances in my home that could have been contaminated.

"Mom, you should consider doing the same at your house. I can't imagine Bock didn't plan for an alternate ending," I said.

That didn't set well, but the point was a good one, and Zach said he'd make a call to Albuquerque to have someone search her house.

"There's no way he could have invaded my home," she argued.

"No, Mom, you invited him in," I stated, as ugly as it was.

Zach took a more convincing approach. "They tell me Bock broke in to his cousin's home in Arizona and contaminated a new bottle of nasal spray, killing both her and her daughter. They found a needle puncture in the bottom, sealed with a dab of white glue. The family didn't see where he'd cut the screen to get in while they were on vacation."

If it didn't bother my mother, that tidbit drove me over the edge of paranoia. I insisted Zach call a professional cleaning service to wash, steam, disinfect and otherwise decontaminate everything in the house and garage. "Or throw it out."

"Everything?" he'd asked.

"Think about it, Mr. DEA," I said. "What couldn't you soak LSD into – sheets, my sofa, towels?"

"But stuff in your garage, like your Harley?"

Okay, I didn't want to throw *that* out. "Get it to the dealership for an inspection."

He looked skeptical.

"Someone who came up with all those ways to kill would as likely turn loose a hundred black widow spiders in the bedroom as place a bomb on the back gate or under my truck."

Zach shuddered.

Spiders. That did the trick.

"Bock's last best crime from the grave," I said, "is to drive me out of my mind in fear. And you need to have someone find the surveillance equipment he used in my house, too. He mentioned watching me."

Zach agreed to take care of those details.

I suggested he take my Harley out after its safety inspection at the dealer. "No sense both of us being locked up and unable to enjoy the autumn colors," I said. "Take Mom for a ride."

She wasn't getting on any motorcycle, she informed us. "Horses are still safer, so I think I'll go home to New Mexico instead."

They finally left, and I returned to my cell and began to write again.

When my attention wandered later in the evening, I decided Zach's six-foot-six frame might look a little overgrown on my low-slung Heritage Softail, but he'd look good on a Road King. I imagined him with his ponytail flying in the wind. Maybe I could get him one for his birthday in May, if I got out of this legal mess I was in.

If.

My thoughts hung on Zach, with all the changed feelings I had. Okay, not changed exactly, but acknowledged. Stated aloud, face to face for the very first time.

After David Wesley's attack and a long recovery, Zach had proven to me that I didn't really want to die. He'd gone to great effort never to say how he really felt about me because I'd told him I didn't want someone to love me. That he did anyway was no secret to me, and he knew I knew it, too. It was a game we played, even when he showed up in Michigan – a game where he scared me just so I could experience the fear that made me feel alive sometimes, and he got to love me when I pretended I felt nothing.

But a few nights ago, as we talked on the phone about a DEA bust he'd been involved in, he realized he was about to be shot, and Zach said the three forbidden words of the last four years. And in that same moment, I realized the security and love I thought I'd felt for Jeremy before he walked away was really what I'd felt for Zach all along.

The problem with being in jail is there is too much time to think.

Think about Zach, who knew what I'd done to Matthew – every gory detail. Who had to know I'd been sleeping with Jeremy. Who was still with me, holding my hand.

Think about how my life crashed in a matter of weeks and what I had left.

Think about what I'd do after this whole murder charge thing was done.

And think about what I'd do if I went to trial and lost everything.

I resumed writing my statement for the attorney, in as much detail as I could muster. Starting at the very beginning was the best I could do, explaining who Anthony Bock really was and exactly how he came to be twisted in my life. Most of the story I wrote was either hearsay or obvious aftermath – lists of names, descriptions of dead bodies, x-rays of broken bones, scars, and the secrets no longer hidden.

Needing to be accurate, not flawless, the exercise left me feeling empty and wrung out. It must have been something like what I'd heard other people say about hitting the bottom – I had no more energy to muster positive emotions. But it was a totally different sense of depression than I'd had after I recovered from what David Wesley had done to me.

Only now I knew my husband had not been alone the day my

throat was slit – Anthony Bock was in the townhouse, too.

Although Bock was the epitome of evil in my mind, I could see how the monster had developed during his childhood, based on what he'd told me. Still, there was no excuse for killing at least seventeen people I counted by memory.

We would probably never know the final count for certain.

I explained how other people helped me piece together the story about Anthony, starting with our interview of K.C. Adams, the first patrolman on scene of Angela Bock's murder in Detroit when Anthony was seven years old. A decade later, one could presume it was Anthony who'd killed the man who had cut his mother's throat, but who knows what else happened until the murder of his biological father – my father – and then so many others?

Even though Anthony had flittered on the periphery of my life since killing my father, I hadn't known I was his victim again until the barn exploded several weeks ago, putting me in the hospital.

The state bomb expert was of the opinion that my injury in the explosion at the Tucker barn was an accident – because I wasn't supposed to have been there when first explosion took place. Perhaps I was supposed to have responded after both bombs had killed my coworkers, to pick up the pieces at the disaster. But Dr. Katz had asked Matthew Shannaker to call me to bring the laser equipment, and a chain reaction occurred in the very seconds after I'd seen the device under the barn's flooring, including the misfire of the second bomb, destroying the barn and its contents, and exposing secrets of many of the people I know and work with.

Secrets. . . Everyone hid something from someone, including me. Tracing Bock's murders backward, I believed his killing stemmed from one event – witnessing Robert Bock killing Angela, his mother. He discovered Bock wasn't his real father, and then he learned he wasn't my father's only child. Though I suspected my father didn't know about Anthony, perhaps that was the very first secret.

I had many secrets. Gerald Katz knew only pieces when he hired me – that I'd been injured in an assault, but not the specific details. When I was in the hospital after the barn bomb went off, he and Matthew Shannaker learned I'd been a New Mexico State Police sergeant. My career had ended with the injuries caused by David

Wesley, my husband, in an attack where I shot and killed him. Later Matt shared with me his secret that he'd pulled the trigger after his father had been diagnosed with a brain tumor and didn't want to face dying slowly. MaryAnne Katz, my boss's wife, had been revealing her secret to Gerald about the lump in her breast while their older daughter Kim and I were kidnapped. Then there were Jeremy McNeeley's nasty little secrets, including his daughter and a wife.

And there were many other secrets of Anthony Bock's, some we'd be learning for a long time, I suspected. Using an identity he'd stolen – probably from a man he killed – Bock had been "dating" my mother for almost a year, altering his appearance to make himself look closer to her age. As for Mom's secrets, I thought I'd let her keep the one about whether they'd been intimate. Knowing was something I could not face.

She said she never gave the age difference any thought, guessing the man she knew as Everett Lawson was five or six years younger. I couldn't say much since I'm seven years older than Zach.

Then I realized that during all our time together, Zach had been the one person who'd kept most of his secrets. Despite four years of phone calls and occasional nights or weekends together, I only knew bits and pieces of his life. Like the story about the drug bust and the children a week ago, I seldom got the whole story from him.

In comparison, Zach knew so much about me – things my mother didn't know (and I hoped she'd never find out). Was it because he didn't share them, or because I had never looked for his secrets, focusing instead on restacking the bricks I put up between my heart and his?

"Hell is where sadists have to be nice to masochists," Zach had quoted that night in the ranch house when I told him my past months of recovery from the injuries in the assault had been hell. "As easy as it would be to fall in love with you, we're both damned," he'd said.

I hadn't understood his words then, though I did now – he'd desperately wanted to love me, but he knew I wouldn't stand to be loved. Almost drowning in the hatred and resentment of what my now-dead husband had done to me, I didn't want anyone to be nice to me, much less to love me. But I'd desperately needed to know someone could want me, as broken and scarred as I felt. Zach had made love to me, showing me his desire was not just physical, and far beyond what words could ever have convinced me. Still, I pretended it wasn't love, even when he came back the next time, and the next.

When I moved from Albuquerque, I'd called and left my new home number in Zach's voice mail. I didn't expect to hear from him for weeks or months, which was typical. The second week after I'd moved in, I walked into the house I'd rented and found him in my shower.

From the phone number I'd provided, he'd managed to get an address and past two locks on my front door. It was the only time I ever caught him, because I came in two hours early. However, it wasn't the only time he'd surprised me. That was how we played the game – he loved me, and I hid in the castle until the next time he scaled the walls to find me.

Now when the walls I'd built had finally come down, there were bars and secrets to separate us.

CHAPTER

4

My new attorney, Crockett Vance, arrived the next morning at the jail at seven o'clock, insisting I have an opportunity to shower before the arraignment.

No argument from me.

Because I didn't trust anything at my house, Dr. Katz had sent clean clothes from my office stash. Or they looked like they were mine, but nothing fit due to the weight loss I had ignored the last few weeks.

Loose was still better than the smelly orange jumpsuit I'd been wearing.

When I had changed clothes, a deputy escorted me to the interview room where two associates of Mr. Vance's introduced themselves, Sharron Robertson and Tim Benjamin.

Sharron brought me a cup of coffee and presented a breakfast tray. I had a peach muffin and a banana, although eating was not on my mind.

Mr. Vance arrived ten minutes later. He had to be old enough to be my grandfather, but was a solid-built locomotive of a man with a full head of snowy hair. He wasn't as big as Zach in height or weight, but pound for pound, Vance looked just as intimidating. Reputation said a lot. I'd heard corporate cases had been dropped upon his mere entrance to the courtroom. Criminal law wasn't his specialty, but I suspected his next best would be good enough.

I started our conversation after he sat across the table from me. "My primary goal is to keep Kimberly Katz from having to testify.

Nothing personal, but I don't want lawyers chewing her up." Kim was the only one who could corroborate my story about not having any choice.

On the other hand, I doubted she realized that I killed a man to protect her, to gain her freedom.

Would I go to prison to do the same?

"That's not an issue we need to worry about today, Ms. Madigan. Trust I will not forget your concerns when the time comes." He scanned the handful of pages I'd written. "Very good," he said, tapping them into a neat pile and setting them aside in his leather briefcase. "I'll read these all carefully later. In court this morning, you are not going to enter a plea. In fact, you shouldn't say anything at all. If asked a direct question by the judge, I'll indicate whether or not you should answer. Not entering a plea for any of the charges forces the court to enter not guilty on your behalf, but this technically only applies to misdemeanor crimes."

I asked about the specific charges.

"These will be delineated at the arraignment as well. While there are several charges, the big one is homicide one, which is very good."

I shook my head, wondering what could be good about that.

"Ed Mecklenburg, the prosecutor, isn't shot-gunning you with either an open murder charge or even selected charges below homicide one with alternatives, just a single charge," he explained. "In a trial with charges filed for all levels, you are held over for the highest charge, but you could be convicted by the jury of any of them. Here, if the judge doesn't dismiss the case at arraignment, which I doubt will happen today, the preliminary examination will determine if there is evidence to try you on exactly this charge and nothing lower. Everything rides on murder in the first degree or we all go home after the prelim."

I nodded, presuming that the single charge had been intentional, but I didn't know why.

Mr. Vance leaned back and studied me. "Dr. Katz told me a bit about you. I assume you've been on the stand before, but this is different, being a defendant. We'll see how it goes this morning. The issue isn't whether you did this, but under what circumstances. This was not premeditated murder of a law enforcement officer, no matter what his mother thinks. Tell me what it was."

Having had many empty hours to consider this, I replied, "Cold-blooded manipulation by a multiple murderer to make me kill or else face even more evil consequences. I made the choice to take the life of a dying man who would have been tortured to death anyway, in hopes of saving the life of a teenage girl."

"So this wasn't a matter of saving yourself – it was solely defense of the child?"

I nodded.

"If it comes to that, I'll state how we wish not to cause further distress to a young girl who has already suffered enough. I think that will carry a lot of weight."

"Thank you. It means a lot to me. I'm not sure how much all this is going to cost, but –" I had money I'd never thought about spending like this.

"I didn't take this case for the money," he said. "This is one of those issues where the big dogs have to fight over what's really right. Ed and I agree on that under the table, but still he'll present his best case. I wouldn't expect anything less."

And so two hours later, I stood as Judge Randall Dodge Hiatt read the charges against me, which included murder in the first degree, fleeing the state to avoid prosecution, evasion, and mutilating a dead body.

"Your honor, the Defense asks that the charges of fleeing the state and evasion be dropped," Mr. Vance said. "My client flew with FBI Special Agent Nolan Forrester from here to New Mexico in urgent hopes of saving one more life left in jeopardy by the suspect – my client's mother."

"Your client did not return with the agent to Michigan with him," the judge countered.

"My client was *not under arrest* at that time, Your Honor. And this same FBI agent did voluntarily fly her from New Mexico to Florida and left her at the airport in Tampa with other federal officers, who were also victims of the same killer, with the understanding she intended to return, as she stated, and there is no evidence to the contrary. Less than twelve hours later, FBI agents arrested her based on these warrants, simply because she was out of state. She waived extradition to return here and face these charges."

"Mr. Mecklenburg?"

"The State has no objections, Your Honor."

The judge read the remaining charges, and bail was discussed.

My attorney asked for release on recognizance as I was a medical and legal professional with no previous criminal history, presented no danger to the community, and I presented no flight risk.

He hadn't even finished his last sentence when a voice screeched from the back of the courtroom, "She got away with killing her husband, too!"

I didn't have to turn around to know who it was.

For several minutes, the judge banged his gavel and threatened to empty the courtroom as Carolyn Shannaker blasted me, squirming in the grips of court officers who tried not to injure her, until two deputies finally steered her out into the hall.

Judge Hiatt finally asked Mr. Vance if he wished to address the issue.

In the pandemonium, I'd managed to explain to my lawyer about the shooting.

"Well, Your Honor, I don't see how it's relevant, but four years ago, my client did shoot and kill her husband in self-defense after he physically attacked her, causing injuries severe enough to end her career in the New Mexico State Police, including a broken neck," he said. "As there were no charges filed and the shooting was ruled self-defense, I don't see how Mrs. Shannaker's inappropriate outburst has any bearing on this hearing."

"So noted. Mr. Mecklenburg, do you have anything further to add?"

"No, sir," he said.

"Due to the nature of this case, and not because of the demands for explanation or the subsequent information provided by Mr. Vance, I hereby set bail at $250,000. This case is held over for preliminary examination in no greater than fourteen days."

With a last bang of his gavel, I was free to make bail and leave, an offer that sounded very appealing. It was a hell of a way to tie up $25,000, but worth it to sleep somewhere else, even if the process took several hours to arrange.

Although a nice dinner and a night in my own bed would have been my choice, the publicity, unfinished shopping and empty cupboards made going home impossible.

Mr. Vance insisted my home or a hotel would invite a media circus. Instead, he took Zach and me to a private gated residence on the western edge of the county.

I tried to argue and received a lecture that some things in this case were non-negotiable.

He gave us a brief tour of the condominium. "Staying put would be a good idea for a day or so," he said. "The guard at the gate will report any attempts to reach you as trespassing. Regardless, do not speak to anyone from the media."

Mom joined us after Mr. Vance's associate had driven her to a nearby grocery store to buy fresh food for a couple of meals. She set about making beef stew while I took my second shower of the day.

I'd finished rinsing shampoo from my hair when I heard the bathroom door open and shut. Peeking out, I saw Zach peeling off his shirt. I let the curtain close again, smiling.

Without explanation, he stepped into the spray with me and wrapped his arms around me from behind.

"Sneaking up on me again?" I teased.

"I might have had to break in if they hadn't let you out on bail," he whispered in my ear. "Damn, Julie, I've needed to hold you like this for a long time."

I leaned my head against his chest and sighed, feeling totally protected in those arms. "Me, too." I turned around to face him, and he leaned down to kiss me, water splashing our faces.

"I want you, Julie. I . . ." He hesitated.

"This time," I said between kisses, "tell me you love me."

CHAPTER

5

Dinner was supposed to be relaxing – home-cooked food, no intruders. But Mom had thought of questions about everything, and she started with how Zach and I had become so close without telling her or Vera Samualson – her best friend, Zach's mother.

"When I was still in New Mexico, I told you I ran into a couple of cops at the bar and stayed out all night. It was Zach, Pauly and Domino," I said.

"Domino sounds like something you'd name an Appaloosa, not that I'd ever own one," she commented editorial-style then took another bite before she continued. "So you've been seeing each other all this time and didn't think you'd tell your mothers?"

"Well, ma'am," Zach said, trying to relieve me of further explanation, "the whole thing was tenuous for us as far apart as we were and what little time we spent together. I'm not sure either of us believed it would become anything serious."

She wouldn't understand without all the facts about us, and I was not willing to reveal the whole story to her about what had happened over the last few years.

"And what about Jeremy? How did you get involved with him again?" she asked, changing subjects as easily as she buttered her freshly baked bread.

"Mother, I really don't want to talk about –"

"Julie, it's okay," Zach said quietly, maybe thinking I didn't want to talk about Jeremy in front of him.

I meant I didn't want to talk about Jeremy at all.

I sighed. "He showed up from the CDC for a consultation. I tried to be distant, to remain professional. I wanted to be angry at him for dumping me years ago, until in the middle of everything else, being around him started to feel like it had before. Then came the lies about his wife and their daughter."

Where's Daddy? A little girl's voice echoed in my head.

The room suddenly felt like a jet decompressing at 36,000 feet, suffocating me. I bolted from the dining room out onto the deck, where I stood, gulping in cool air.

I could hear Zach's voice but not his words. A chair scooted on the hardwood floor, and I expected him to join me.

My mother came out instead. "I'm sorry, honey. I didn't mean to upset you."

"He's dead because of me," I said, looking out into what was left of a pale sunset, trying to calm the rapid beating of my heart.

"You can't blame yourself –"

"Jeremy's dead. Matthew is dead. Kim could have been killed. You and Zach..." I trailed off the list of casualties and victims. "Who *is* to blame, Mom? Do we blame Dad for having sex with a teenage girl before he met you? Why not blame me for leaving Dad to die? None of this would have happened if Anthony had killed me that day, too."

"Julie, don't talk like that," she said reaching for my arm. "You shouldn't feel guilty for the choices anyone else makes."

"What about *my* choices?" I bellowed, jerking away.

"Why are you so upset?"

"Upset?" I echoed. Upset didn't seem to come close to covering what I felt.

She didn't understand, or maybe she couldn't.

Realizing the scream on the verge of my control would echo past other townhouse balconies, I stomped inside, and she followed me.

"I'm *upset* because I might be convicted of a murder my bastard half-brother didn't technically commit himself. I'm *upset* that I killed a man whom I considered to be a friend, yet I didn't hesitate to yank a knife across his throat in a way he would not survive like I did when David cut mine. What kind of *choice* is that? You're telling me I'm not *supposed* to feel upset?"

I left her standing with her jaw slack and went to find alcohol.

Surely a man like Crockett Vance drank. . .

Searching cabinets in the kitchen until I found a collection of liquor, I picked out a bottle of Crown Royal in its purple flannel bag and broke the seal. Finding a tumbler on the shelf above, I dumped in a couple of shots' worth and slammed it back, wincing as my eyes watered. I was pouring another when a large hand tipped the bottle down to the counter.

"Thanks," Zach said, "I think I will." He picked up the glass and drank its contents in a single gulp, then slid the bottle out of my reach when I reached for it again.

"This won't help, Julie."

I glared at him.

He shrugged and poured another shot and pushed it toward me.

We stared each other down over the glass.

Drowning in anger and guilt, all I could see were Zach's green eyes, full of love. Someone offering a hand to save me, if I'd reach out and take it.

I turned and slid down the wall, curling up into a ball, trying to keep the tears from becoming sobs I feared might never stop.

Zach came around the bar and sat down in front of me, putting one leg on each side of me and scooting me closer, lifting my feet over his thighs.

"I don't know how you feel, Julie, but I know you hurt. I told you a long time ago that when you think no one else understands, I will, or I'll at least try if you let me. I won't judge you, and nothing will ever change the way I feel about you. Nothing."

I let him wrap his arms around me.

"In my heart, I know you did the right thing, and I'd like to think that even if it was me in Matt's situation, you'd do the same thing to save someone like Kim."

"I'm so tired of feeling my guts being ripped out," I whimpered, feeling irreparably broken, shattered like crystal.

"I know." He stroked my hair. "I wish I could snap my fingers and make it better. But I'm here, baby. I'll do what I can."

We sat in silence as I cried, until sobs turned back to tears and finally exhausted themselves.

"What can I do?" he asked.

"Talk to me. Tell me about the shooting on the beach. I need to know what happened to you." I looked up at him, touching the wound on his neck.

He wiped away the tears on my cheeks with his thumbs. "Okay, but maybe we can find somewhere more comfortable than this." He helped me up, poured us each a drink, and led me downstairs. Turning on the stereo, he pulled me to him to dance first. "I'll tell you, but there are parts of it I don't want you to hear because one of us hurting over it is enough."

"And if I'd said that about anything I've been through, you'd tell me it's a bullshit excuse, right?" I asked him.

He smiled. "Probably. Before all this happened to you, I'd have told you and not hesitated. I needed to tell you. But you don't need to shoulder my emotional disasters right now, too."

"I'm a little unglued, but you've never treated me like I'm damaged," I said. "There's so much information missing in my head, like that night on the beach. I heard the bullets hit you. Maybe it won't help, but I feel I deserve to know what happened. What happened to the kids only matters because I know how badly it tore you up."

With a kiss at the end of the song, he led me over to a buttery-soft leather sofa. Propping himself up in the sectional corner, he turned me across his lap onto a pillow that seemed to have been made of clouds.

"If I have to tell you, I want to hold you when I do," he said. "You're the only reason I'm here now."

And so Zach's story about the shooting on the beach began with the assignment that moved his team from New Mexico to the Tampa Bay area, on the heels of a cocaine smuggler and a biker meth lab.

"Cocaine and marijuana were being dropped by airplanes in the Gulf," he explained, knowing this was fairly common knowledge in law enforcement. "As a new twist, although sometimes recovered by high speed boats, the packages were being handed off and brought to docks by other less suspicious vessels, such as sailboats or fishing boats. Some of it was even being towed in by jet skis to houses along the intercostal waterways."

"Sure, that makes sense, I guess," I said, sipping my drink.

"Several arrests went down, going higher and higher in this organization, but infiltrating the coke operation by someone local hadn't worked," Zach explained. "The DEA figured it would take new faces, new money, so we moved in and became players – Dom as lead, Oz as his driver and main hand. Pauly and I posed as bodyguards."

I'd never been around Oz, but Pauly was also a big man.

He continued, "We picked up this boat from a seizure in Miami, a cabin cruiser named *Wind Dancer*, and we floated into Boca Cielo right up to the dock at a house worth about three million, got off and settled in like Dom owned it. Fast cars, loud music, expensive restaurants and nightclubs – Dom flashed lots of cash. So when Pauly or Oz discreetly began to ask about drug connections here and there for the boss, the money talked. We had parties and for them, we bought dope – a grand of cocaine a night several times a week, and a couple hundred for crystal meth here and there, until the money got the attention we wanted."

The day came when the seller wanted proof Dom was legit, so he asked about taking a cruise on *Wind Dancer*, offering Dom a bonus of another two grand in coke. The bust was set into motion. While Oz took Dom and his guests out on the boat to make this pickup, DEA was also set to track the plane back to its base, and Pauly and Zach went with the Pinellas deputies to the meth lab.

"Dom and his party picked up the drop and were cruising offshore, killing a little time. As planned, the Coast Guard helo made a pass then circled, called for a boat to board in regard to suspicious packages being towed. That all went off as planned, except a Coastie took a cheap shot and broke Oz's nose in a scuffle," Zach said with a chuckle. "He was hot about that."

I smiled, waiting for him to go on about his part.

"On land, our bust was flawless except we were missing two players. Then the woman told us about the kids, so we went to find them."

Zach had been speechless two days later when he called me to talk about it, and I could feel the tension in his body as he paused, searching again for the least painful words.

"In the warehouse, the two men had separated the boy of about three from the younger girl who was maybe two." Again, Zach fell silent as the scene replayed in his mind. His chest heaved beneath me.

A tear slid down his face, and I wiped it away.

"You don't have to tell me what happened to the children," I whispered. "Sometimes there are no words. I know they died horribly. That's not what is missing in my head about this."

He kissed my hair and ran his fingers through it. "When Internal Affairs got through with us the first evening, I was so screwed up I could barely drive away from the office," he said.

"I wish you'd have called me."

"A dozen times that night, I picked up the phone, but I just couldn't do it."

"Why not?" I asked.

"Because as bad as I already hurt, I couldn't stand the thought of not hearing you say you love me. I sat in the hotel, holding my gun, waiting for that moment when I'd given up. But every time I went to put it to my head, all I could see was your face. No matter how much I hurt, I couldn't do that to you." His voice was sad, but not accusing.

"Zach, I'm sorry I haven't been there for you all this time. I've been such an idiot."

We hugged in silence for a while, enjoying the warmth, the relief.

"Would you really have pulled the trigger?" I finally asked.

"I always believed in you, Julie, but that night, I hurt so much, I was really close."

"Did you get any help?" I asked.

What a hypocritical thing to ask. We both know I refused counseling after David nearly killed me.

"No, but I need to," he said, knowing what was on my mind. "You realize the only reason I told you this is because I know you understand."

I nodded.

I know a lot about not wanting to live anymore. And about having to keep it secret.

"The whole time I was in the hospital in Albuquerque, I felt hopeless," I explained, "but while I was at the very bottom, I had no way out – trapped and immobile in ICU. The feeling got worse when I was in a regular room when I really had to make a choice. Initially even rehab was a hole. Each time I tried to come up out of the darkness, I sank again."

Zach nodded.

"After I could drive, I'd get in the Jeep and pick a highway. When I got somewhere – Denver, El Paso, Phoenix – I'd turn around and drive until I was exhausted, sleeping in the car."

"Where did you go two days after I saw you in the bar on Central?"

A blur, empty highway miles. I shrugged. "No idea. Why?"

"Just curious. I couldn't follow you. We had something going down that night."

"Could have been Colorado," I said. "I don't know. One trip around that time, I ended up in Lubbock, Texas, after midnight on a Saturday. First I got lost, and then I had a flat tire west of town on my way home. Freezing my ass off, I struggled to change the tire by myself. When I was finally finished and thought I'd put everything away, I found the lug wrench on the ground. I exploded. On the side of the highway, I threw a raging irrational temper tantrum, waving around the lug wrench, kicking and stomping. Then a state trooper pulled up to see if I was okay."

"Oh great. Poor guy."

I felt Zach chuckle.

"I was already pissed off, then he spotlighted me. He screamed at me three times to drop the crowbar, but I didn't understand what he was meant. I didn't *have* a crowbar, I had a lug wrench. So I started screaming back," I said. "I'm surprised he didn't shoot me. When I finally got what he was saying, I tossed the tool into the Jeep and walked to the passenger side, spreading my hands and feet without being told. After I showed him my ID and badge, which I still had at that time, the flat tire, and I blew zero on the Breathalyzer, he let me go. I got in my Jeep and drove away."

"Bet he doesn't stop for damsels in distress anymore."

I shrugged. "Later, I realized why I was so mad. The whole day, I'd been thinking about dying – as you said, that last moment. On the side of the highway, I'd been waiting for the opportunity to step out in front of a semi rolling past, but there wasn't a single vehicle except the trooper the whole time I was changing the flat."

"That's fate. Why something so potentially painful?"

"Why a gun?" I countered.

"It's what I had."

"I don't think I could shoot myself. I'll always wonder if, in the microflash of time between when the bullet leaves the barrel and the shockwaves liquefy your brain, whether there is time to think, 'Damn that hurts.'"

"How morbid," he kidded. "So what kept you from finding some other way to die later that night after you drove away?"

"Part of it was what you said to me on the phone about leaving me in an alley – maybe there was just enough fear. But that's why it was so devastating later when you showed me I still wanted to die but I didn't have the guts to do it myself," I said. "That's what this feels like, killing Matthew and being charged with murder – an overwhelming depression of choice and circumstance that I cannot escape. Not really wanting to die but being at the mercy of others."

Zach kissed my forehead. "Think we'll be okay?"

"Together, I think so."

"Me, too."

I considered the conversation and where it had turned from what I'd really wanted to know about the shooting on the beach in Florida. "You still didn't explain why you left your gun at the station the night you called me. It was a setup, wasn't it?"

Zach looked away before he answered. Finally, he nodded. "We were running really tight till four hours before the bust when we called in the county deputies. Our meth bust was compromised, which is why the two men had taken the kids. We needed to know who'd narc'ed."

"So you were the bait," I said, my voice squeaking at the end, making it a question I didn't intend. "Do you find out who arranged the shoot?"

"I can't prove anything," he said, still not meeting my eyes, which flat unnerved me.

"Who, Zach?"

He shrugged, but he didn't look at me. "I can't tell you."

His refusal hit me square in the stomach – Zach thought it was one of his own team.

CHAPTER

6

I found my mother in the kitchen and went to talk to her before going to bed.

"You're different than before you left Albuquerque," she said, finishing up dishes she'd washed by hand instead of putting them in the dishwasher. "You were so isolated and angry before."

"Yes, I was. Bitter and depressed and miserable."

"What changed?"

"I did," I said, hoping not to have this conversation, but I could see I was not getting off the hook. "Part of me changed when I met Zach."

"You two have been seeing each other that long," she said in amazement. "I still don't understand why you never told me."

"'Seeing each other' is a stretch. We were friends, but I didn't want a relationship. He showed up once in a while," I said, not wanting to explain how Zach broke into my house to scare me before we screwed our brains out. "After the assault, I was trying very hard to not feel anything remotely emotional about Zach. Then I moved to Michigan, and he kept showing up. He never asked for anything more than I gave when he was with me. In for an evening and maybe breakfast. Sometimes he'd stay a few days. I'd have turned away from him, had he pushed for any sort of emotional response, I think. But he said he never gave up hope."

"And Jeremy? What made you want him back when he showed up?"

I wanted to laugh. Or cry. "Wouldn't you still love Dad if he walked through the door tonight? No matter what's come since, your feelings didn't die with him, did they?"

"No, I guess they didn't." She shook her head. "So all this time you'd talked about the deputy," she paused, searching for his name. "What about him?"

"Matthew," I supplied. "Matt was a friend. We enjoyed each other's company. We hung out now and then. What I let you believe about him was to convince you I was not being a hermit."

"But why tell me about him and not Zach?" she asked, genuinely confused.

"Because it was safe to not get involved with Matt. I could tell you about him without feeling anything. He wasn't interested in a wife and two-point-three kids in a house with a thirty-year mortgage. He didn't pry into my past – he hadn't even known I'd been with the New Mexico State Police until I was in the hospital," I said.

She nodded, but I could tell she didn't get it.

Struggling to find a way to explain, I continued. "In this investigation, secrets I'd tried to hide were being exposed. Innocent people were being killed because of some irrational connection to me we couldn't find. When Jeremy showed up like a white knight, there came a point it was easier to remember how good it had been than to remember how badly he'd hurt me. He made me believe it was safe to feel again, that he wanted me again."

"I see."

"When Jeremy said his marriage was over, I believed him. Or maybe I chose to believe that meant he was divorced," I said. "But to him, he was getting a new chance at an old fantasy, the greener side of the fence in his memories. When he finally climbed over, he ended up knee-deep in the same tough grass he couldn't stomach before."

I got a glass of water and came back to where she sat.

"Zach was different. He wasn't afraid of my past or the scars, which scared me at first because I didn't understand why or how. As long I didn't acknowledge I felt something, I could pretend it didn't exist. It took hearing him get shot on the beach to realize I really love him."

She shook her head. "I've never understood you, Julie. You are so like your father."

"What about you, Mom? This whole incident with Anthony has to affect you, too." I didn't want to talk about it, but better to discuss how she felt than my own feelings.

"It's like dating Jekyll and Hyde, meeting the evil person at the end. I still have trouble reconciling it was the same man. And what's worse is now I realize how much he looked like Stony."

"That really stunned me, too," I said, remembering his face in the light of the fire.

Mom shared how she'd gotten to know the man she knew as Everett Lawson, whom she'd met in the tram on her way up to Sandia Peak. "We bumped into each other again at lunch, and he asked me to have dinner at the top that evening to enjoy a beautiful sunset. At the bottom, I figured he'd be pushy or something. He gave me a business card with his number and said he would like to see me again, if I might be interested." She shook her head. "I was a little surprised."

"I can't imagine you met him by accident, no matter how he made it seem," I said. "Did he look his real age or did he make himself look older?"

"I knew he was younger than me, but I didn't ask. I guessed he was in his late forties, maybe fifty. How old was he really, do you know?"

"He was forty-one," I said.

"I'm old enough to be his mother." She sighed. "I can't believe Stoney actually did what you said."

"Me, either. No one knows anymore what really happened, but I never believed it was malicious like Bock thought. Dad would have just graduated high school or maybe in his first year in the military."

"Lawson was malicious – the whole thing. I'm appalled I ever spoke to him, much less that I spent time getting to know him."

I shook my head. "The man he wanted you to get to know wasn't who he really was, and he was deliberate in making you think you had a choice. Everett was a Navy guy whose last post was as a recruiter up in Chicago, which probably made it easy to hide in plain sight."

"But his photography," she said, still trying to put it all together. "Do you think that was fake, too?"

I did, but I didn't say so. "Mom, he would have told you anything to interest you – photography, horses, medicine. I'm sorry you were involved in any of this, but it's over."

She looked away, as if I might say the words but they couldn't erase what he'd done, especially to her.

"How did you escape from the barn?" I asked.

A moment passed, almost as if she hadn't heard my question, before she said, "Friction. I just kept rubbing the knot against the beam I was tied to over the last day or so until it loosened." She held out her arms. "Hard to believe I don't have blisters or rope burns."

The phone rang, and I heard Zach answer and asked the caller to wait.

"Julie," he said, peeking around the corner, acting like he couldn't have been listening. "It's Mr. Vance."

I looked at Mom in dread, then went to the phone in the kitchen.

"Sorry to bother you so late, Ms. Madigan. I was reading through your summary – it's quite detailed, thank you. How well do you think you'd survive on the stand, talking about what you had to do in that cabin and why?"

"You can imagine it's a bunch of raw nerves a prosecutor could short-circuit pretty easily."

"That's no problem," he said. "Being emotional makes it real. Do you think you could keep the facts straight?"

"Truth is a lot easier to keep straight than a pack of lies," I said. "Yes."

We chatted about the presentation points he'd chosen. I voiced concern about the graphic nature of the facts, but Mr. Vance insisted that gruesome or not, the facts would support the premise that I'd had no other choice to try to save Kimberly Katz.

"If I were prosecuting you, my big question would be, 'What other options did you have besides killing Deputy Shannaker?'"

"None, sir."

♦

"Zach," I whispered as we cuddled in bed later, "When you were shot, you can't imagine how much I wish I'd said –"

He squeezed me. "I heard it. Even though you didn't say the words, I knew, Julie. I've always known."

"You really thought you were going to die, didn't you?" There was a little bit of bruising around the wound under his ear.

I was still amazed how a bullet had passed through his neck, almost exiting, and hadn't caused any critical damage inside. The odds of that were astronomically small.

"On the beach, yeah," he said. "Later, before Bock came in, I asked McNeeley why he'd come to tell me I was in danger – what an illogical thing for a man to do. He said, 'Because she loves you. The way she screamed your name when you got shot, I knew. I think she used to love me like that.'" Zach touched my hair. "I'm truly sorry for what happened to him, Julie. But for me, if getting shot was the price I had to pay for being here with you now, it was worth the bullet."

As I snuggled up to his overly warm body, I wondered what else I thought of when I saw the bomb in the barn. I didn't remember thinking of anyone – only of getting out. Then the explosion.

Well, two explosions.

Although I didn't have any memory of being trapped under the debris toward the rock wall, I'd been told that small pocket of space had protected me from both the weight of what fell around me and the flames. Had I not been in the chief's turnout gear – helmet, coat and pants, gloves and boots, and especially the SCBA – I'd probably have died, too.

I felt my heart rate pick up, and my mind replayed pictures from the details I'd been told.

Same old rush of adrenaline, fueled on a memory.

I focused the energy on the warm body next to me – he didn't seem to mind a bit.

CHAPTER

7

Zach and I stayed at Crockett Vance's summer home until the preliminary exam started a week later.

Mom had flown home to Albuquerque on Saturday morning, as I'd suggested, though I worried whether she thought I sent her away for intruding in my life. There was so little we could do for one another to make this whole crisis better, and perhaps being together only made her experience with Bock unavoidable.

After she left, I spent the weekend in wild mood swings – the man I wanted in my arms every time I thought about it, yet the possibility of prison taking me away. New emotions were born along with new physical and emotional scars.

With yet another rollercoaster climb and panic-inducing drop into the dark unknown. My period was late.

I couldn't even go home and check my calendar to see how late.

Finally, unable to stand the suspense any longer, I asked Sharron to bring a pregnancy test the next time she came out to the house with papers from Mr. Vance.

She arrived the next day and excused herself to the bathroom with her purse, and tucked it into the cabinet beneath the sink. When I found the box, it had a little scribbled note that said, "Good luck, either way."

After she left, Zach wanted to go walk, so we bundled up, walking hand in hand toward the beach, listening to the breeze whisper in the trees and grass.

"Okay, Cowboy," I said as we strolled along the trail. "What's on your mind?"

"Me?" he said absently, his focus on the horizon.

I made an overture of looking for other people, certain no one was in sight. "Yeah, you."

"Pauly called yesterday from Florida. I need to go back," he finally said.

"Okay," I said. "I understand."

"I bet," he said, pulling his attention back to me. "Running out on you in the middle of this hearing?"

I stopped and tugged on his arm to turn him around to face me. "You have a job, Zach. I never questioned that you'd have to return to work. Just come back to me."

"You couldn't keep me away." He pulled me against his chest and wrapped his arms around me.

I laughed. "Never could before."

We turned and walked in silence to a spot where we could sit.

"Did you know I've had a crush on you since you were sixteen?" he asked.

"When you were still shorter than I was. And I thought you said you fell in love with me after the first kiss."

"I did. You don't remember? You kissed me on the cheek after your father's funeral. I was smitten." He took my hands in his and held them up. "There was still dirt under your nails. I thought that was so cool when my mother told me about what you'd done at the cemetery. I told her I wanted to take you back so you could finish, promising I'd help you if you wanted. She said we were both crazy."

"Oh, I was crazy all right. I don't recall much after Uncle Jeff took me home to change clothes," I said. "I wish I remembered that kiss, though."

Zach snuggled me into the crook of his arm around my shoulders.

"When do you have to leave?" I asked.

"I'd like to go tomorrow. I don't know how well Pauly's able to take care of things, with his foot, you know?" he said.

"Is there anything I can do for you?"

He shook his head. "I talked to Domino about it. They pulled him to DC for a class. Education is the government's way of getting you off the street for a while." He looked at me and smiled.

"What's so amusing?"

"I was thinking. By the time you'd gone to the state police in 1984, I was deep in puberty and dreaming about you." He closed his eyes. "You're why I decided to be a cop."

"Oh, that's an outstanding reason to choose a profession," I teased.

"As good as any. You?"

"It's hard to say, now that it's so far away. I think I did because of my dad."

"You wouldn't have chosen law enforcement if he hadn't been killed?" he asked.

"No, I'd be working for Microsoft or Intel. I loved working on the computers with him."

"All the time I've known you, you've never talked about him."

"When did we ever talk, Zach?" I asked, laughing. "You never said anything about your dad, either."

"Isn't much to tell."

"Oh, come on."

"My folks met in Albuquerque and moved down to the Permian Basin, moving around a lot until Zoe and I were born. Dad was killed in a drilling rig accident when we were six. Mom moved back to New Mexico, where her parents lived. When Zoe and I left for college, she moved out to the ranch."

I nodded. Maybe I knew that from something Mom had told me, but I couldn't quite remember.

"Was your dad tall like you?"

"To me, he was huge, but Mom said he was only about six-foot-two and heavier."

"What did he do?"

"In the oil boom, he started as a roughneck and finally made driller. The bosses were really pushing them hard, double shifts and crap. Five or six men died with him," he said. "Mom told the company she didn't want to know what happened to him, but I suspect it was hydrogen sulfide gas."

"I'm sorry," I said softly.

He shrugged, then looked at me. "I miss him, sort of. Mostly I miss what we didn't get to do together."

"Yes, I know that feeling." I reached over and ran my fingers through his wavy hair, blowing wild in the breeze. "All too well."

"How'd we end up talking about my dad?" he said. "I asked about yours. Thomas?"

"Thomas Jackson. You know, Stonewall. Kids called him Stoney after their first U.S. History class," I said, trying to forget that Anthony Bock's mother had named him after his father, wrongly thinking his name was Tony.

♦

When we got back to the condo, Zach called to make airline reservations before he fixed a light supper. Afterward, we cuddled up to watch a movie, but Zach fell asleep in the first thirty minutes.

I wiggled out from under his arm, envying his ability to sleep through most anything. Wandering the house, I found Crockett Vance's library and went to the Michigan Civil Law books behind his desk.

Might as well see what I'm in for.

In two hours of flipping pages and making notes, I figured out the majority of the crimes and maximum sentences Anthony might have been charged with in our investigation, whether they were in Michigan or not. The list included life sentences for murder, poisoning, explosives, assault to commit murder, and kidnapping. From there, maximum sentences ranged from two years for photographing a body to twenty-five years for intent to cause serious injury with explosives.

Without adding any time for the first-degree homicide for multiple victims who were killed previous to the barn bomb explosion, I calculated Anthony Bock could have received fourteen life sentences and more than three hundred years in prison in Michigan.

I also added up possible charges against me, which could have included everything from interfering with a police investigation all the way through assaulting an officer and first-degree homicide. Along with murder, I had been charged with mutilating a dead body, for what I did to Matt to get out of the cabin, which carried a maximum sentence of ten years.

However, I was also miffed to learn that a person can be sentenced to life if convicted of compelling a woman to marry, according to Michigan law.

Though I suspected that the statute was an antique, if a man could actually *compel* a woman to marry, did it stand to reason one could *compel* a woman to take a life in defense of an innocent child? That would certainly be worth a life sentence, too, if the logic could be applied.

Obviously I had been facing a man with a long and extremely violent criminal history. How could anyone think I could resist him compelling or manipulating me to do anything?

I finished my notes and closed the book, looking up to find Zach leaning on the doorjamb, watching me.

I was startled because I hadn't heard him.

I swear he's part cat to move such a large body around so quietly.

"I got cold," he said.

"That's not possible. You've never *been* cold," I said, turning off the banker's light on the desk.

We went to bed, and I put my head on his shoulder.

"Can I tell you something?" he asked.

"Of course."

"I was a little mad today when you didn't ask me not to go to Florida," he said in the darkness. "I guess because you didn't say you need me to stay."

I tried to lean up on my elbow so I could see him, but he rolled me back and on top of me.

"Zach, you know I –"

"No," he said, putting his fingers on my lips. "You once told me that you didn't want to hear the words. I know you'll let me go, Julie. Show me that you don't want to."

CHAPTER

8

The next morning, Zach dropped me off at Crockett Vance's office for a 7:30 meeting. I'd convinced him to leave my vehicle at the airport, that I'd retrieve it later.

"I'll be back as soon as I can," he promised, standing with me at the building door. "I don't know how well I'll keep in touch, but I'll try."

"Any time you can."

Zach watched me enter and disappear before driving away.

Inside, Mr. Vance welcomed me to his conference room with a cup of coffee. His discussion agenda included the previous two days of testimony.

I showed him the list of sentencing maximums I'd calculated for Bock as well as the "compel to marry" crime and its life sentence.

"Interesting concept," he said. "We can't make a comparison of your actions to this list, but it certainly shows the staggering violence against which you were defending Kimberly Katz."

He asked Sharron to verify the charges against the case file and then to make enlargement of the information to poster size.

Mr. Vance told me. "They've heard enough bunk. What is it you wrote – the truth isn't always the same as the sum of its facts? That's a beautiful way to approach this."

Each witness who testified so far had offered a vague but incorrect interpretation or assumption about my actions or motives, as if I had something to gain by killing Matthew Shannaker. The morning session would be no different.

During the lunch recess, Mr. Vance and I reviewed key phrases for my testimony in the office over deli sandwiches brought by Sharron.

"It's unusual to put a defendant on the stand in a preliminary hearing, mostly because it's detrimental to defense," he explained. "However, you are not a criminal with something to hide. We're not trying to dispute that you did what you are charged with, only to demonstrate that the court hasn't got enough evidence to send you to trial."

I nodded.

"Don't be afraid to be emotional," he said, "but do not get angry or sarcastic, under any circumstance. Our goal is to show you were defending the helpless, facing unimaginable evil with absolutely no other choice."

I nodded, wishing I'd asked Zach to stay one more day.

"Take a breath after every question is asked and count to at least five before you say a word. Think about each question completely; if it takes longer, that's fine," he said. "Answer the prosecutor's questions with the fewest words possible and make him restate any question that may lead you to use more than one sentence."

I nodded.

"He doesn't want you to give any answer requiring a lengthy explanation, so that usually works; however, very few answers are as simple as yes or no, so try not to say them. 'I believe so' and 'I don't believe so,' are good responses," he continued. "There are few absolute facts in the courtroom that cannot be argued."

"Mr. Vance, when it comes to answering hostile attorneys, I've had some painful lessons. I learned that 'No, sir,' is the correct answer to 'Do you know what time it is?' and 'Can you tell me what color my tie is?'"

He chuckled. "Very good. Don't overwhelm the judge with technical terms or analyze the situation. Make him feel your pain. Put him in your shoes to make the same decision."

I nodded.

"Where's Zach?" he asked, taking a bite of his sandwich.

"He had to go back to work," I said without details. "He left me in your capable hands."

♦

Mr. Vance put me on the stand in the crowded courtroom at two o'clock, and he guided my story through his questions, weaving together the connections between the man who had kidnapped Matthew, Kim and me.

"Miss Madigan, what was Anthony Bock's demand of you the night you were held hostage at the cabin in Leelanau County?" he asked, pacing back and forth in front of me.

I paused as I'd been told. "Bock demanded I take the life of a man he'd already beaten, raped, mutilated, blinded, and permanently disabled."

The prosecutor objected that I was speculating about the consequences.

I wasn't sure which consequences he meant – those of Matthew's injuries or those of Bock's intentions. The judge sustained the objection, so Vance reworded the question.

"Specifically, what did Anthony Bock tell you he would do if you did not comply?"

Thankful none of the Katzes were in the courtroom, I took more than five seconds to gather my thoughts, then I said, "Bock told me he would torture Matthew Shannaker to death and make Kimberly Katz watch, even if he had to cut off her eyelids. He said he would then make me watch as he raped and tortured her, and he would cut her up and mail the pieces to her parents long before he let her die. He said he would leave me alive and unharmed, tied to a chair in a building rigged with explosives to kill those who came to rescue me."

"You believed his threat?" my attorney asked.

"Yes, sir." I said without hesitation, which earned me a raised eyebrow.

"Did you believe Anthony Bock would keep his word and let you and Miss Katz go if you complied?"

"I didn't care whether he let me go," I said. "I didn't count on him keeping his word, but he hadn't hurt her at that point."

"Why do you think Anthony Bock had not harmed you?"

Again, my pause was longer than five seconds. "Anthony Bock

was my illegitimate half-brother. He told me he believed that I enjoyed killing as much as he did, because it was a genetic trait. He said that even if he had to force me to kill, he would do it over and over until he proved I was a killer, too."

Despite being in front of an audience, answering these questions, I felt my skin prickle and my heart rate kick up.

"Let's go back. Anthony Bock was determined to be your half-brother during the investigation of the bombing of the barn. Was this the first time Bock had crossed paths with you?"

"I don't believe so , sir."

Mr. Vance smiled at my answer.

"Can you briefly explain?"

I took a deep breath. "Anthony Bock murdered my father when I was sixteen. I was in the office building when the attack began. When I tried to help, my father insisted I escape. After I ran from the building, Bock cut my father's throat." Unable to prevent it, a shiver ran through me.

There was an objection to this as well, but Mr. Vance explained that he had evidence to support this at trial, if need be. Objection was overruled.

"Is that the only incident?"

"No, sir," I said. "After Matthew Shannaker was kidnapped, investigators received a number of photos, including two taken moments after I shot my husband, David Wesley, in self-defense. Photos support the theory that Bock was present during the assault that ended my career with the New Mexico State Police," I pulled down the scarf to reveal the scar around my neck, "and nearly ended my life."

Someone gasped, but I didn't look away from Crockett Vance's face as he marched left and right. I continued to watch him as he'd told me – answering his questions deliberately, concisely, and after an intentional pause.

"Any other times?" he asked.

"Yes. After I moved to Traverse City in 1992, I bought a new SUV in December. I'd only had it a short time when I was rear-ended. When I finally saw Bock in the cabin, I realized he had been the driver of the other vehicle."

"Are you aware of any incidents involving your family or close friends?"

I paused. "Anthony Bock had introduced himself to my mother and had been seeing her socially for a time. Before kidnapping me, he had also kidnapped her, as leverage to manipulate me, to coerce me to choose which person he killed. He left her to die in a barn in New Mexico, rigged with explosives, while he went to Florida to kill a drug enforcement agent with whom I have a relationship."

The prosecutor objected that Bock's crimes and supposed motives were irrelevant to the issue of whether I should stand trial.

"Your Honor," Vance said, "I simply wish to establish a broader picture of the situation facing my client. Her actions were responses to this man who had considerable destructive influence in her life long before he gave her an ultimatum."

"Overruled."

"Ms. Madigan, that night when he held you hostage, what did you think about as you weighed the decision to do as Anthony Bock demanded of you?"

"My only consideration was whether Kimberly Katz would walk out of that cabin alive."

"Not revenge, not to save your mother?"

"No, sir."

"Not to save yourself?"

"No, sir."

"You thought of no other alternatives?"

"None, sir."

"What sort of weapon did Bock provide you to complete this task he demanded?" Vance asked, almost as if this were a sudden revelation to him.

"A kitchen knife."

"Can you elaborate on this?"

"He told me this was the knife he'd stolen from the scene of his mother's murder, which he had witnessed as a young child. The same knife he used –"

Another objection was voiced, cutting me off.

"Your Honor," Mr. Vance said with exaggerated patience. "I believe my client obtained knowledge from Bock as to where the knife came from, though its actual relevance to her actions is negligible."

After further debate, I was asked to explain whether or not I had other information about the history of the knife.

"During the investigation, Detective Brandan Callaghan and I interviewed one of first officers on scene of the murder of Bock's mother. The officer told us the knife used to cut her throat was never located," I said. "At the cabin, Anthony told me he witnessed this event, that he hid the knife from police and took it with him when he went to live with his mother's sister and her family in Traverse City. He told me how he'd used it over and over in the following decades to kill. It was symbolic to his mother's death."

Again, the prosecutor stood and objected that the dead man was not being charged in this courtroom, nor could his psychological motives be discussed.

"Your honor, I again offer that this dead man had a staggering criminal past. Ms. Madigan had professional knowledge of Bock's history of killing and had no reason to doubt his specific threats," Mr. Vance said, standing up a little taller. "And having spent time with him, my client, who has a degree in psychology, has sufficient education to offer an opinion about him that no one else alive can."

"Overruled," the judge said, putting the prosecutor into his chair again.

"Ms. Madigan, you stated you felt no choice but to obey Bock's order?" Vance asked.

"I believed that no matter what I did, Matthew Shannaker was going to die." I turned to the judge. "This isn't about whether I cut Matt's throat. The question is, given those exact circumstances, would you want me to do the same thing to save your child?"

The courtroom went wild, but all I could think is how I'd just committed myself to prison for life. Or worse.

Crockett Vance turned his back to me and stood at his table, which made blurting out what was on my mind feel even worse.

When the judge regained order of the courtroom, he adjourned for the weekend, leaving my question as the last thing on everyone's mind.

"That was an excellent statement, and the timing was

impeccable," Mr. Vance told me on the way to the airport to get my truck, "even if I wish you hadn't said it. We'll let Edward do his cross-examination Monday, then close."

When I got to Mr. Vance's summer home, I called my mother and brought her up to the minute on the proceedings. She had questions and many concerns, which I tried to answer, spending almost an hour on the phone with her. But I really wanted to talk to Zach.

Instead, I had the weekend alone to think about the words I'd chosen on the stand. Alone to worry, to wander around someone else's house without any of the comforts of my own home – not that there were any left after my house had been cleaned out.

Later in the evening, I called MaryAnne Katz to see how she was doing.

Medical procedures blazed at light speed for her — the biopsy had shown an aggressive malignant tumor, and MaryAnne had undergone a radical mastectomy within a few days of the return of her daughter, but the cancer had already spread to her lymph nodes.

"That's not good news, of course, but it hasn't spread elsewhere." Her normally chipper voice was strained. She'd finished her first course of chemo with minimum side effects.

I asked about Kim.

"She's had some down days, but I guess she's okay overall," MaryAnne confided. "She's devastated you'll go to jail if she doesn't testify."

"I appreciate how much she wants to help," I said. "But even as well-behaved as the lawyers have been so far, I'll do anything to keep her from taking the stand."

"You're trying to protect her, Julie, and I understand," she said. "But it would be good if she heard that from you."

I promised to call Kim over the weekend.

With that settled, we said goodbye and hung up, leaving me again in the heavy silence of the strange house. Solitude itched like a poison ivy rash, making it impossible to sit still. And my late period still hung as a question mark.

At least I could answer that, I decided. Then I began to consider all the implications of answers.

Sharron's little note – good luck, either way.

I tried counting backward in my head, went in search of a calendar. After the barn explosion, so many days blurred together. Maybe if I had my date book, I could remember. I was almost positive my last period had been a week before the bomb.

Almost positive?

That made it six weeks.

Problem was, I had missed several birth control pills – while I was in ICU and the second day Jeremy and I had been in the Upper Peninsula.

Lots of expletives came to mind. *How could I have been so stupid?*

I could still hear Jeremy's words about that first kiss. "Do you believe in accidents?"

Getting pregnant when we dated before had been an accident. I'd been taking the pill religiously. The doctor guessed the failure stemmed from antibiotics I'd been prescribed for a sinus infection. Ninety-nine percent effective. . .

Great odds. Unless you're that one pregnant woman in a hundred.

"So what do you think, Jeremy?" I said out loud to a ghost. "Think I forgot my pills this time intentionally?"

And what would I do if I am pregnant?

Never mind that. What would Zach do?

After a while, I realized I was needlessly torturing myself over the whole issue – I could go to the bathroom and take the test, know for sure in the time it takes to boil water.

Yet I didn't get up. I didn't want to know. Not for a while.

Not knowing, I had the luxury of pretending for the rest of the night.

Either way.

Because I had not gone to funeral services for so many people – Jeremy, Matthew, Penny Daniels, even David Wesley years ago, my goodbyes and grief for each had stacked inside me like dominoes. No way to knock down one without making them all fall, and I'd tried to keep them from crashing around me until I had no room to move, but I still had other emotions to deal with as well.

Though it had been easy to find those old feelings for Jeremy, I resented the half-truths and whole lies he gave. The last time I saw him, he had looked down at the blood on my hands and shirt, and nothing could ever erase that image. I was bitter he couldn't let go of my past as easily as he let go of me and the future. That aside, I was sorry he hadn't made it home to his daughter.

I regretted I hadn't been closer to Matt. In our friendship, there had been no room between us for the secrets we protected. Until he offered me his life in exchange for Kim's, until his last words, I didn't understand how he could have shot his father and seen it for the gift it was, even if he had to keep it secret.

Looking back, it was likely that David Wesley had invited Anthony Bock into our home. Though I'd never know how they met, surely it was intentional. I still could not find a way to forgive David for his part in the events that ended my career and almost took my life. I don't know which of them cut my throat, but I knew for certain my husband had initiated the attack.

As for my half-brother, I hated Anthony most for what he'd done to Kimberly Katz, and the many other families he robbed of loved ones. Worse, we might never find or identify them all if other causes of death were as unusual as the methods we uncovered.

My mother once told me I should pray for the strength to forgive David. I wondered if she would forgive Anthony.

I couldn't wrap my head around that – how do you forgive evil?

CHAPTER
9

By sunrise Saturday, I had imagined all the possible endings to my circumstances. I'd sobbed my way through the darkness alone, pacing, talking to the victims, apologizing for not being able to stop the insanity wrought by Anthony Bock. Putting all that hatred into words and tears, I blamed him for choosing the evil and leaving me the pieces. But Bock's goal was to make me hate enough to enjoy killing.

I said aloud to Jeremy all the things I'd kept inside more than a decade and a half, letting go and gathering the pieces of my heart he'd broken again. I grieved both the death of the man and the idea of motherhood when the pregnancy test I'd done at midnight was negative, leaving me with both relief and disappointment.

I said goodbye to Penny Tucker-Daniels, Bock's last cousin, who had brought us pieces of the investigation about the death of her brother that we might never have seen. I hated Anthony for the scars he left on her husband and other two children, another family suffering the grief of losing loved ones.

Thinking of Matthew, I pondered the cabin where I'd spent a night and a thousand years contemplating the fates of the two people with me. I said a last goodbye to him with gratitude that I finally understood.

Katzes faced recovery in several facts as well, and it hurt that I could not be with them to offer support. I resented not being close enough to help them during MaryAnn's cancer treatment. Still, regardless what happened to me, the fact they had Kimberly was all that really mattered to me.

Grief was beginning to blossom as I made peace with each of these people who'd touched my life, but eventually I let go of the dead and faced the living.

Now there was Zach, and I wanted to talk to him, needed to let him comfort me, and he was gone. That would have to wait.

I had no idea how long.

Sunday afternoon, I called and talked to Kim Katz for a long time.

She told me she was being sent to a counselor, as if that were punishment. "I'm not crazy," she insisted.

"Kimmie, no one thinks you're crazy," I offered, "but what you and I went through was something awful, wasn't it?"

"Yeah."

"Do you think you can tell your friends about this without them getting all weird? Is it something you really want to talk about with them?"

"No," she sighed. "I tried telling Ashley about some of it, but she kept asking questions like it was a horror movie."

"Exactly. That's the closest frame of reference most people will have to your experience. I think you'll see that a counselor is someone who can let you tell your story," I said, feeling a little hypocritical, "and ask questions to help you understand how you feel about it."

Oh, those dreaded words – "How does it make you feel?"

"How do you feel about it?" she asked.

"I'm angry. I feel guilty about what I did in front of you. I am ashamed that one human being could manipulate me to do something so horrible, but I did it to protect you."

"How can you say that? You killed the deputy!"

That was the reaction I was waiting for – not exactly an accusation or abhorrence, but sheer incomprehension.

"Yes, Kim, I did. I'm not telling you it was right, but it was the only chance I had to save you. Matthew was going to die, whether I did it or not. Anthony had blinded him, crippled him," I said. "Did you hear Matt when he told me to remember his father?"

"Yeah."

"When Matt was sixteen, his father developed a brain tumor. He asked Matt to shoot him and make it look like a hunting accident, so that his family wouldn't have to watch him suffer."

"Oh my God!"

"Matt had to live with his choice to do something wrong to protect someone else, so I know he would have wanted me to take his life rather than let you suffer."

"How do people get so f. . ." she hesitated at the profane word she wanted to use.

"You can't shock me, Kim. Anthony Bock had been screwed up since he was a little kid. He made choices and then went out of his way to hurt people for his own enjoyment. That's evil. That's fucked up."

She giggled when I said it. "If I go to the counselor, will you come with me?" she asked. "Just once."

"Ask the counselor when you make the appointment. I'll go with you if it's okay."

If I'm not in prison. . .

CHAPTER

10

Monday, I returned to the witness stand to complete my testimony for Mr. Vance, and then Mr. Mecklenburg began cross-examination. Despite the coaching, my confidence wavered. How do you tell two lawyers, a judge, and all those gathered to listen how it felt to hold a knife that killed a man? Does it justify saving a girl's life?

When Edward Mecklenburg started, I steeled myself for the fight.

"You admitted you did, in fact, kill Deputy Matthew Shannaker," the prosecuting attorney stated, so I did not respond.

My silence earned my attorney a look from Mecklenburg that I could not decipher – appreciation or determination, I wasn't sure.

The prosecutor continued. "And you explained to this court why you committed such a heinous act."

Again, I did not answer because he did not ask me a question.

"You expect this court, this state, to believe that you made your choice in order to save a teenage girl, and not for your own benefit."

I looked over Crockett Vance, who finally stood up. "Perhaps the prosecution can do something besides repeat my client's statements so far. Does he have a question?"

"Agreed. Mr. Mecklenburg?" the judge prompted.

"I am only trying to make sure we have a complete understanding of what happened in that cabin, Your Honor," he said, returning to his table. "Ms. Madigan, did you cut Deputy Shannaker's throat?"

Staring him straight on, I replied, "Yes, sir. I did."

"And did he die from this knife wound?"

"Yes, sir."

"I'm still confused, Ms. Madigan. Can you explain why you did this?"

"Anthony Bock demanded I cut Matthew Shannaker's throat in order to save Kimberly Katz," I said. "I did that. Just like I'll go to prison before I'll let you bring her in here to testify on my behalf."

"You'd go to prison?" he asked, half hiding his astonishment. He might not have even wanted to say the words out loud.

"If that's what it takes to keep her away from the attorneys who would make her feel responsible for my actions or the outcome of this hearing, yes, sir."

Unsure how to respond, Ed Mecklenburg looked at Crockett Vance for a sign. Crockett's eyebrows gave a shrug his shoulders could not.

"Your honor, the prosecution rests." Without dismissing me from the stand, he returned to his chair and sat down.

The hush in the courtroom strained while the judge gave final instructions to the attorneys, "This Court will reconvene tomorrow for a decision," he said, then stood to leave. Then the silence broke like a dam, flooding the room with noise.

After we made our way to the hall, I heard Carolyn Shannaker's voice to someone behind us, like nails on a chalkboard. She was not happy with what had just happened.

Smiling, I wondered if she thought she'd paid Mecklenburg's office better than that.

"A very fine performance you gave," Crockett Vance said, clapping me on both arms when we got to the parking lot. "We'll be done tomorrow."

"Done?" I echoed.

"Judge Hiatt can't hold the case over for murder one on what was presented, Julie. We all knew this from the beginning, but you had to undergo due process," he said. "I'll meet you here tomorrow, then we can give the media a quick statement before you go home."

I spent the evening, wondering why I got to stand outside the law for a crime I technically did commit, and then chided myself for questioning the decisions that would let me walk away from the charges of killing Matt Shannaker.

Nothing the court said would erase the memory of that morning. I doubted I could ever close my eyes and not remember how the knife had felt when I closed my fingers around it or when I pulled the blade across Matt's throat and blood ran hot and sticky over my hands. The thought caused a shiver to run down my spine.

The night seemed to last forever because I could not sleep.

The next morning, waving off the reporters, I met my attorney in a private room before we went into the courtroom.

"Are you certain of this?" I asked, still unsure I could walk away.

"Julie," he said, taking off his reading glasses. "In the same circumstances, I would want you to do what you did to save my child. That's really all that had to be said."

"But jurisprudence doesn't –"

"The law defines crime," he stated. "Jurisprudence is the philosophy that allows law to make decisions based on individual circumstance."

Inside, Judge Hiatt sat in front of lawyers and their teams. "This court determines that Julie Ann Madigan will not be held over for Circuit Court trial for any of the charges brought against her by the State of Michigan with regard to the death of Matthew Shannaker." With a bang of the gavel, he stood and disappeared behind a door.

Spectators erupted into loud conversation.

"See?" Crockett Vance asked as he hugged me.

Outside the courthouse, the media swarmed like bees, stinging here and there, mostly being a nuisance. Mr. Vance gave a short statement. I said nothing but tried to look moderately happy.

Regardless what he said, I knew the decision didn't mean I was innocent, or that I didn't deserve to pay for killing Matt Shannaker. It only meant that the lawyers and judge had decided to let me walk away from this crime without facing a trial. Without a legal background, I doubted most people would know the difference.

The decision of the court seemed anticlimactic compared to the pressure I'd felt in that cabin, trying to protect Kim. Had anyone who heard the story really understood?

I felt relief, of course, walking out of the courtroom a free woman. Having taken Vance at his word, I'd packed my stuff before leaving his place that morning, and after our last appearance in the courtroom, I drove home.

A few reporters sat outside my house after I got there, hoping I'd give in to persistence. I really had nothing more to say than what they'd already covered, quoted or not, so I ignored them.

My life was returning to normal, whatever that was, but Zach wasn't around to share the good news.

CHAPTER

11

With the charges against me cleared, I returned to work but asked Dr. Katz for two afternoons off to put my house back into shape for the living. From the missing pieces of furniture to the empty shelves throughout my house, I took inventory and made a list, determined not to replace items I seldom used. Did I need four bottles of shampoo or cake mixes I'd never make?

Shopping has never been my favorite activity, but even this far from the Thanksgiving and Christmas holidays, it had become a contact sport in the stores. It took all week to get my house back to where I could live without missing something I absolutely needed.

Returning to the medical examiner's office the following Monday morning, I slogged through a mountain of paperwork Connie had stacked on my desk, accompanied by a steaming cup of coffee with a sticky note that said, "Glad to see you!"

Time crawled by as I struggled to stay focused on reports and cases, which seemed so dreary compared to the last few weeks of my life.

I jumped when my cell phone rang, shattering the silence in my office.

"Madigan," I answered.

"Hey, Sweetheart," Zach said softly. "I heard the good news about the hearing. I told you everything would work out. I'm sorry I wasn't there with you to dance."

"I'm glad it's over. This could have dragged out for months."

Or longer. Maybe for life.

"Can't talk but a second," he said. "I wanted you to know I love you. You've moved back to the house now?"

"Yeah, slowly buying new stuff."

"Don't get a lot of perishables. We still need to take off on our little escape," he said with a smile I could hear.

"I'll keep a suitcase packed," I replied. "Somewhere warm, remember?"

"Anywhere but Florida," he concurred. "I gotta go, babe. Be careful, okay? I love you."

"I love you," I said, and the connection dropped.

Only a second to talk, indeed, but hearing his voice lifted my spirits.

A half-hour later, my office phone rang.

"Julie? Hi, it's Kim Katz."

"Hey there. How are you today?"

"Okay, I guess. Dad said you were back to work," she said. "I called the shrink, and it's okay for you to come with me. The appointment is tomorrow afternoon at three."

"You still want me to go?" I asked.

"Please?" she asked as if she'd have to beg.

"Of course I'll be there. I thought you might have changed your mind, that's all."

She gave me the particulars, which I noted in my planner.

I told her I'd meet her there and offered to take her home afterward, if she needed a ride, to save her mother a trip.

"So long as we don't go for ice cream again," she said with a little laugh. "Just in case."

"Deal."

♦

I met Kim at Dr. Shane Dillard's office, and together for the first time since being kidnapped, she and I openly discussed the experience we shared, starting with when I picked her up after swimming lessons, ending with her pleading with me not to go back into the cabin to get Matt's body.

Dr. Dillard agreed that being able to fill in the missing pieces would be helpful to Kim, such as my conversations with Matthew in the cabin before she was brought in. On the other hand, I learned what Bock had done with Kim during those hours we were apart as well. We stayed well past the two-hour appointment, telling the story, with the doctor taking notes.

When we got ready to leave, Dr. Dillard handed me his business card, without necessary explanation he would be available to continue conversations with me, should I wish to return.

Happy to help Kim. Not happy to let you pick my brain further.

I drove her home, and MaryAnne asked me to stay for dinner, which I had to decline in order to review a year-old case for which I'd been subpoenaed to testify, regarding an elderly couple whose car was broadsided while crossing a highway.

This hearing would delineate survivorship. Both the 76-year-old man and his 73-year-old wife were declared dead at the scene by EMS during triage. Bystanders reported both the man and woman had been breathing immediately after the crash but gave conflicting details as to who was alive longest.

The issue was crucial because the couple's marriage was the second for them both. Without a will or definition of "survivorship," their combined estates would pass from the first one to die to the "survivor," and then to that spouse's family exclusively. Apparently the families weren't going to make nice about this, so the court had to decide who died first.

All morning, the attorneys for each side took turns quizzing the poor souls who had been kind enough to stop to offer assistance, trying to discredit them. I knew I'd face worse treatment when I was called to the stand – I was just a bigger piece of meat for the sharks.

Finally the list of bystanders was exhausted, and it was my turn.

I was sworn in, took my seat, stated my name and job title for the record, then waited for the attack.

"Ms. Madigan," one claimant's attorney began. "Could you explain your response to this accident?"

Crockett Vance had taught me terrific tips for dealing with adversarial lawyers, starting with making them ask exactly what you are willing to answer.

"Response" could be interpreted in a variety of ways, so I asked him to restate his question.

I got a nasty squinted look for this, but I was perfectly within my rights to make the request. I had considered answering something totally off the wall, such as my *emotional* response, but there was enough blood in the water already.

Don't pester the sharks too often with irrelevance.

"Were you dispatched to the scene of this accident, and if so, how were you notified and what route did you travel to get there?"

"Yes. Grand Traverse County Central Dispatch notified me by telephone at the medical examiner's office. I drove to the scene of this *collision*," I said sharply, "via an alternative route from Traverse City as the highway traffic had already backed up," I said, describing my drive road by road.

"What was your response time on this alternative route?" he asked.

"Approximately 22 minutes." There is no such thing as exact time in a courtroom.

"And upon your arrival, what did you do?"

I explained that I confirmed both occupants were dead, followed by a short debate with him over the definition of "dead." Then I examined the vehicles for mechanism of injury, I said, which he asked me to define.

"Mechanism of injury evaluates structural damage and estimated energy forces involved in a collision of two objects to correlate certain types and subsequent severity of injuries a victim might receive," I said.

"You made predictions regarding the injuries?" he asked.

"No," I smiled, "sir."

My father had taught me that you address as sir or ma'am those people you respect, and more importantly, those you do not. The difference was definitely sarcastic when spoken.

"You just said that the damage predicts the type and severity of injuries of a passenger," he countered.

"No, sir. I did not. I said damage and energy forces can be correlated to certain types and severities of –"

He interrupted me, which I found irritating. "And what such predictions did you make, Ms. Madigan?" he asked again with a tone that was more sarcastic with each question.

"I made no predictions," I said one more time.

He inhaled forcefully through a bulbous congested nose, making his face turn a deeper purple, if that were possible. "Did you draw any *conclusions* from your investigation?"

I smiled again and reworded the question to suit myself. "From inspection of the vehicles, I *estimated* the impact had been roughly perpendicular to the driver's side of the Bartlesby's car, causing approximately sixteen inches of intrusion of the car structure inward toward the driver, *suggesting* the structure made contact with the driver's body. Potential common injuries from this type of structural damage could involve head, chest, abdominal, and pelvic areas."

"Did the passenger's side of the car have any 'intrusion,' as you put it?"

"No, sir."

"So the passenger would not sustain injuries to these areas?"

"The passenger's mechanism of injury would differ, thus the cause of any injury sustained would be different," I said.

At this torturous pace, he often offered interpretations of my previous statements, followed by a question of my agreement, to which I simply stated, "No, sir," when necessary, leaving him to rephrase until he either asked a question I would answer or reworded my testimony in manner I agreed I'd said. We played this game of silly questions and answers that led nowhere for over an hour, but I refused to let him corner me.

"So, Ms. Madigan, are you an *expert* in crash investigation?" he asked in a haughty voice, as if he'd just thought of the idea, which he probably had.

"Could you *define* 'expert'?" I asked.

After sparring about his definition, I stated that I believed I met his criteria, much to his surprise.

The judge asked me to elaborate on my qualifications, despite loud objections from both attorneys. Neither of them wanted a crash expert on the stand.

I smiled and waited till the judge had parked them both in their chairs before I explained I had been trained in crash investigation and reconstruction when I worked for the New Mexico State Police. I also had experience with evaluating the more subjective mechanism of injury dynamics working as a paramedic and medical examiner investigator.

Obviously, someone failed to do the necessary homework to find out I wasn't simply a morgue tech sent to pick up the bodies.

It's nice to bite the sharks back once in a while.

By five o'clock, both attorneys had given up on getting their most-wanted answer from me. The best professional opinion I would offer was that while it appeared that the injuries of the driver *could* be potentially more severe, this would not necessarily indicate sequence of death. Neither the sheriff's department crash investigation nor the autopsies had conclusively determined the order in which the occupants had died, and I refused to offer an opinion based on the testimony of the previous witnesses, despite being asked and finally ordered to do so by the other attorney.

"Excuse me, Mr. Lipinski," the judge interrupted the lawyer. "I believe I'm the only one in this courtroom who gets to make those kinds of demands of witnesses."

A few jurors laughed out loud this time.

I knew I'd left Dr. Katz a beehive for his testimony Monday morning, but in the end, the answers would all be the same – we did not know who died first.

CHAPTER

12

The phone ringing stirred me in my sleep.

Let the answering machine get it, I thought, flipping over the pillow to find a cool spot to put my face.

Another ring.

Except I don't have an answering machine. It's still at the sheriff's department as evidence.

I reached for the phone, checking the clock.

"It's 3:37. This better be damned important," I said as a grumpy greeting instead of my last name.

"Julie, it's Domino. Come let me in."

"Huh?"

"I'm almost to your front door. I need to see you."

"Just a minute," I said, almost awake as a cold shiver radiated through me.

"No, Julie, right now," he demanded and disconnected.

I hung up. Grabbing Zach's denim shirt from the lounge chair next to the bed, I managed to bump through the house in the dark, fumbling with a couple of buttons to hold the fabric together over my camisole. I got to the door at the same time Dom knocked. I opened it and let him in without a word, without turning on the lights, closing the door right behind him.

"You're kinda pissy in the middle of the night," he kidded, shivering.

"And you're pretty demanding for an obscene phone caller, too." I rolled my eyes and hugged him. His coat was cold against my skin.

He hadn't come to tell me Zach was dead.

My heart began to slow down.

Then again, why *was* he here in the middle of the night?

I reached for the switch, but he caught my hand.

"No lights."

"Okay. Coat tree to the left. Boots on the rug. Head down the hall, last room on the right," I said, directing him. "I've gotta pee." I ducked into the bathroom, did my business, then splashed some cold water on my face to help my bleary eyes focus. Baggy sweatpants went on below the shirt.

Before I returned to my bedroom, I circled through the kitchen, closed the shades and grabbed a couple of bottles of beer.

Domino Hurley slouched in the lounger when I came in and closed the bedroom door.

I turned on the reading light by my bed.

He frowned up at the windows, looking like he wished I hadn't done that.

"They're blacked out. I can't stand light in the morning," I said, tossing him a bottle. "I don't think you're at my door in the middle of the night just to cheat on your wife for the very first time in twenty years."

"I swear you'd be my first choice, Julie, but I'll have to pass. I hope you understand," he grinned and raised his bottle to me before taking a drink.

"I'm afraid I'll understand something I'm not going to like when you're done telling me what the hell you're doing sneaking into my house this time of night," I said, feeling the first inkling of doubt.

He took a deep breath and then nodded. "Yeah, you're right." He emptied the bottle and studied me. "Before I start, I need to know if you trust me. Do you believe Zach still trusts me?"

"I have no reason not to, Dom. Yes, I'd say he trusts you." I hoped it was true.

"What did he tell you about Florida?"

I squinted and waited out an explanation in silence.

"I'm here because I don't know who else to trust, Julie. Something is very wrong wherever Zach is. Gimme a place to start."

"You need to start at the beginning, but I'll make this easy. Zach told me the bust at the meth lab was compromised. You wouldn't tell me why he got shot," I said, "and he didn't, but I know he was bait on that beach for whoever it is, wasn't he? Only you guys didn't find the badge who paid for the hit, only the gunner for hire."

Domino nodded.

"He wouldn't tell me who he suspected," I continued, "but from the way he acted, I'm sure it was an agent."

He set the bottle on the floor and rubbed his face in exhaustion. "That's pretty good for no one telling you anything. Here's what I know, but the bottom line is I need your help."

We traded facts.

Zach left Michigan after he got a call from one of the DEA guys in Florida, saying something else was going down. He'd mentioned being concerned about Pauly physically, but I didn't ask who called. He said he had to go and flew out the next day.

"I've only heard from him once, but that's not unusual," I said. "He called after the judge let me walk."

"Maybe that wasn't unusual before," Domino said, "but things are different between you two now. I don't know what, but something's not right, Julie, or he'd be calling you every night."

My stomach churned, seeing where this conversation was going. "Another beer?" I asked, needing to get up and digest a little of this information.

"I hate to ask, but I haven't eaten anything all day. You have chips or something?"

"Give me a few minutes to close the rest of the blinds, then I'll find you something." I said, intending to leave him sitting in the bedroom until I returned.

"You make that damned shirt of his look good, Julie," he said, almost bumping into me when I stopped abruptly. He'd followed me into the hallway.

I turned and stuck a hand to his chest. "Stay here," I said, going on into the kitchen.

"That's a good idea, closing the curtains. I don't think I was followed, but. . ."

Please don't finish that sentence, Dom.

"You want chips or something more substantial?" I interrupted him on purpose as I closed the last of my blinds and curtains. "I can fix you something."

"You don't mind?"

"Of course not. What would you like?" I said, opening the fridge. "Toast and eggs? Ham sandwich? I have leftover pizza."

"Pizza's great." He peeked first, then came on around the corner into the kitchen and sat down at the breakfast counter.

I pulled out a bag with four huge pieces from the night before, put two on a paper plate and stuck it in the microwave. While the pizza warmed, I got him another beer.

"Okay, just because Zach's not in contact from Florida doesn't mean anything," I continued, tearing off paper towels as napkins. "Aren't you over-reacting?"

"I don't think so. We started a code about a year ago to swap simple pager messages, something to check in every so often. It's only between Zach and me," he said. "Two days ago, I got a page from him. Usually it looks like a phone number, but it's a sequence of numerals."

He picked up a pen from my counter and wrote on the paper towel.

5/6/1967

"Zach's date of birth," he said, showing me.

I nodded.

Then Dom wrote out several other numbers, inserting them between the month, day and year as a demonstration until I got how it worked.

"So he dialed a code like this on your pager?" I asked.

He nodded and wrote down a string of numbers and spun the paper towel toward to me. "This is what he sent me. In the first part, the month and day are stars, meaning unknowns," he said, rewriting it separately as ?/?/95. "The sequence around the date is 911," he pointed. "After the pound sign for a break, the numbers 22323 meaning ABD2D."

My look of bewilderment must have been enough for more explanation.

"You may not have ever seen this, but Zach has ABDTD written on the inside of his body armor," he said, pointing to the letters again.

"It stands for 'A bad day to die.'"

Domino let this sink in – the date, the abbreviation.

The room spun around me. "He means they intend to kill him."

When Domino nodded, I had to sit down.

He looked at his watch. "Not quite twenty-four hours ago, I got another page," he said and scribbled it for me to read.

My date of birth mixed with the 911.

"And the letters. 143 meaning ADC?" I asked.

"No, I think in this case, it's the number of letters in a word. I use this when I want to let Roni know I'm thinking about her – 'I love you.' When I got this message, I knew I had to come here, but I don't know why. For you to tell me something, to protect you, maybe. I don't know what he meant, but I'm here."

My head reeled from the beer and growing panic.

"What do you expect me to do, Domino? I don't know where he is," I said, flinching when the microwave buzzed.

I removed the pizza and handed him a piece, but I had no appetite for the other.

"You're not going to like this idea, but it's all I've come up with in the last day. Have you ever worked undercover?"

I took another hit off my bottle, staring at him as I thought this through.

Dom may be the one person I can least afford to trust, with either of our lives. What if the whole idea is to find out what I know, then use us against each other? What if Zach is already dead and I'm a loose end? Domino could walk out of here before sunrise, having taken care of that end.

I had to consider whether I'd be having this conversation with Pauly or Oz, but I didn't think so.

"No, I've never been undercover, and I've never worked narcotics," I finally said, emptying my own beer. My balance rolled slightly off vertical.

"Actually, not having any history is an advantage. You still think like a cop, but you don't smell like DEA. Plus you're not bound by a badge now."

"Unsanctioned," I asked, shaking my head. "You're suggesting I break the law?"

"Maybe you could bend it a little here and there if necessary," he conceded with a half-shrug. "Money isn't going to talk to the people involved. Word's out after the boat deal."

"Great," I moaned. "Drug trafficking in cocaine."

"No, I'm thinking the meth crowd is the one we need to get into. I bet if you show up, looking a little strung out, spend some bucks on a little meth in this bunch, you'll be accepted. These guys are looking for a few new faces with a dozen of their old ones in jail. And to get you in, I can teach you a skill that is extraordinarily valuable to people like this."

I don't want to learn a new skill.

"It's dangerous, but if you can cook good meth, you'll be everyone's friend."

"Gee, Dom, thanks. I needed a new career. Apparently murder doesn't suit me," I said, bending to bang my head on the counter.

"They dropped the charges, I heard," he said, ignoring my sarcasm. "No one could blame you for doing what you did."

I certainly blame me.

"What kind of crowd are you talking about?" I asked, taking a deep breath.

"Unfortunately, it's bikers. I'm not certain how to make you fit in."

I laughed. "Open that door."

He got up and looked into the garage, where light from the kitchen sparkled on the chrome of my 1987 Harley-Davidson Heritage Softail.

"Oh damn. . ." he said, chuckling, then closing it again. "So you could ride anything?"

I nodded. Bikes get smaller or a little bigger, but not any more difficult to ride.

"How drastically could you change your appearance?" he asked, sitting down.

I pondered a moment. "Cut my hair, go dark. Couple of sessions in a tanning booth. The scars are the problem," I said, pointing to my neck.

"Not really, and you've got with a solid story – your old man did it, so you shot him. Dues paid, you know?" He paused with a devious smile. "Any tattoos?"

"Uh, no and no thanks," I countered. "Someone might still recognize me up close."

"If you hang with the bikers, you shouldn't see anyone who knows you," he explained.

"You think someone in that crowd will lead me to Zach and then we can walk away?"

"No, it won't be that easy, but you'll get close enough to the operations to find him," Dom said. "Can you get the time off?"

I nodded.

Do I have a choice?

♦

Dom ate the other slice of pizza I'd warmed but hadn't touched while I went to put clean sheets on the spare bed, despite his objections to staying at the house.

"You walked here from the airport, right? I can't have you running through the neighborhood in the middle of the night, Dom," I said. "How did you find my address?"

He sighed. "Zach made me memorize it. In case I ever needed to. . ."

I put up my hand to stop him. I didn't want to hear Dom say he would show up one day at my doorstep with the news Zach was dead. I'd been much too close to that. Twice.

When he finished eating, neither of us was sleepy, so I turned off the lights and we retired into my bedroom to talk.

"I love this chair," he said, relaxing into the feather-soft fabric.

That's why I chose it when I was replacing furniture, I thought.

"Tell me about Zach," I asked, changing the subject. "What's he like to work with?"

"He's a great partner and a damned good cop. I can always depend on him," Dom explained. "He's easy in a crowd. Attract lots of attention or melt into the walls and vanish. But most of all, he always does exactly what I expect him to do, every time."

"How does he blend in?"

Dom sighed. "I wish I knew. It's natural for him." He paused.

"No matter what shit he's in down there, I know he's not corrupt. But whoever it is also knows Zach wouldn't turn, which is why I'm worried about you."

More things I didn't want to discuss, so I twisted the subject again.

"Is it hard to turn it off and on, this identity thing?"

He nodded. "Most of the time, the undercover bit is very short. But after we run a longer operation, I have to go be in a neutral zone for a few days before I can go home to Roni. To remember who I am."

"I'm sure your wife appreciates that. Can I ask what you do?"

"Usually I spend a few days in Vegas. Mindless reintegration into a world where I'm still invisible and where normal is a little more liberal."

I'd never thought of anything being less normal than Las Vegas. "Does Zach go somewhere?"

"Sometimes. I know he's come up here a few times, but he's also got somewhere else to go. We try not to discuss our real lives. It's confusing enough to swap fake identities without a real one interfering. As close as we are, there are things we don't share about the outside."

I was surprised anyone knew Zach had visited me in Michigan until I'd been arrested.

"So, Julie, if I asked what was really going on that night in Albuquerque at the bar, would you tell me?" he asked, stretching out more.

He wasn't mocking me like I thought he might, but I knew he'd go along whether my answer was serious or flippant.

"Sure, if you want," I said with a shrug, "but you won't like it."

He nodded, eyebrow raised.

"Zach dragged me out the emergency exit of the nightclub to the back parking lot and threatened to slice me into roadkill-sized pieces unless I got in the car. You guys came out and drove us west of town and left me in handcuffs overnight with a huge maniac who pinned me down, held a knife to my throat, and threatened to finish what David Wesley hadn't."

"Wha-?" He sat up, shocked. "Wait, no. . . You're kidding! I mean, Zach wouldn't. . ."

"Yes, he did."

Domino stammered a few more incomplete sentences interspersed with some rather colorful profanity before I let him off the hook.

"Zach knew who I was, but I didn't recognize him. I'm pretty good at spotting cops, but I didn't have a clue, if you care to take it as a compliment," I said. "That night, his intention was to scare me into thinking I'd walked into the end of my life."

Dom had become speechless.

"I showed you what David did to me." I pointed to my neck. "With or without the help of Anthony Bock. I was having trouble coping with the whole thing – surviving, losing my career. I was chasing trouble, and ultimately we agreed to call my behavior 'attempting suicide by tempting fate.' Basically, Zach said I had the same look as his sister the last months before she was murdered."

He nodded that he knew about Zoe.

"Zach's demonstration was to prove I really did not want to die."

"But he didn't hurt you, right? It was just a game. . ." Dom couldn't quite reconcile his partner's outrageous conduct after having extolled his virtues.

"He did exactly what I said, Domino. Even nicked my jaw with the knife before I broke." I tilted my head up to point at a tiny little scar – no more than a paper cut really. "As he assured me, he could have done anything to me he wanted. How could someone like me resist a man his size, even at my best physical condition and before you handed him your handcuffs?"

Domino wilted back in the chair. "Oh geez. I'm sorry, Julie. I had no idea. . ."

"What did you think was going on?" I asked, trying to hide a smile.

"Neither of us knew anything except Z' told us he was looking for you, to cut you out of the crowd, and to be careful because you were ex-state. I thought maybe it had to do with the case we were on," Dom shook his head. "He really did all that?"

"Yup. In fact, one of his favorite pastimes between assignments has been to show up here unannounced and break into my house or car, to scare the crap out of me."

"Wow, too kinky for me." Dom emptied the last beer. "All I know is he loves you more than I could find words to explain. He's like a brother to me, and I'd do anything for him." He paused. "Well, I might not do *that* again without explanation."

I laughed.

"Julie, I'm sorry to drag you into this, and I know Zach'll be pissed about it, but you're the only person I know I can trust."

"Why, Dom? Why can't DEA do this?"

"I don't know who's involved, and I have no proof. One wrong contact and we're all screwed."

"Not a very encouraging invitation," I said.

Domino stood up, taking his time before answering. "Better than anyone I've ever met, you know how one person's life can be used as leverage against another's. If someone wanted to get to Zach, you'd be the perfect target."

CHAPTER

13

"Mom, I don't think I'll be able to get there for Thanksgiving," I said a week before I should have been in Albuquerque. "I'm sorry, but something's happened, and I can't be sure when I'll get away."

"I don't understand, Julie." She whined like a four-year-old, and I couldn't blame her. "You promised."

"It's something I have no control over, and I can't discuss it."

Spending Thanksgiving with her was a huge vow to break, but I was packing for Florida as I tried to break the news.

"When *can* you come?" she asked, upset enough for tears that made me feel guilty because I hadn't been there to help her with what Anthony Bock had done to her life. She'd invested a lot of herself into their budding relationship, only to discover who he really was when he made her a victim, too.

I suspected my mother had finally reached a point where she wanted, or maybe needed to talk about what happened with Bock, but I didn't know how to make that better for her, any more than she could fix the aftermath of Bock's rampage for me.

She'd returned to Albuquerque before my preliminary hearing, rather than staying with nothing to do in Michigan. I didn't ask her to come back to be with me when Zach left, even though the hearing was still going on, mostly because I didn't want her to know – or Vera Samualson to find out – that he'd gone back to Florida. Or why.

Now I didn't want either of our mothers to know Zach was possibly in trouble or that I was going to find him.

"I'll come as soon as I can get loose of this case, I promise. Trust me that a mother needs us to make this right with her child, okay?" I said.

Domino's head popped up.

Mother relented finally, and we said our goodbyes.

"That went pretty smooth," he commented, rolling his eyes. "A mother needs us to make this right?"

"It's the truth, isn't it?" I asked. "You said you wouldn't want to come tell me about Zach. If this goes to hell, you'll be the one to explain to his mother about what really happened."

And to mine. Because if I don't bring Zach back alive, I won't be coming back, either.

"Julie, stop. This is going to work," he said, putting a hand on my shoulder.

"I don't have a clue how," I said, "but it's got to, Dom."

♦

We spent a couple of days prepping me for the role, staying up late into the night to help me build a new personality and break old habits. I sat through lessons in the chemistry and making of methamphetamines, LSD, and MDMA – ecstasy.

Dom got quite a kick out of my description of the hallucinogenic experience I had when I was in the hospital after the bomb, thanks to Anthony Bock.

That all seems like years ago. . .

"What if I get into a situation I'm expected to use something, Dom? I don't know how to do any of this."

"Follow your guts," he said. "That's the only thing I can say. If you're on a bike, it's easy to blow off that you don't ride stoned. You can't afford cocaine. Tell them you won't take shit you don't cook yourself, which takes care of the meth. You're skinny enough to pass for a speed freak."

"Thanks, I think."

"If you get busted, we can take care of charges later, but you'll have to make those decisions about what you'd in the moment." He gave me an eye drop bottle. "Scopolamine. It's a rapid-acting sedative and hypnotic. Carry it in your boot or socks. Three or four drops in a drink should get rid of anyone seriously hassling you. It's absorbed through the skin, so be careful about getting it on you." He winked. "Don't forget and put it in your eyes."

"I'm terrified I'll screw something up, Dom. How will I know what to do?" I sounded more like my mother than I intended.

"Let me ask you something. When you worked with the state police, did you ever have civilian riders?" he asked

"Sure. We had a chaplain ride along with us occasionally from the post, reporters, that sort of thing."

"Could you tell them what to do in every situation possible?"

I shook my head.

"So basically you said that if something bad happened, they should duck behind the firewall, and use the radio or unlock the shotgun only as a last resort? They always asked how they'd know when to do that? What was your answer?"

"You'll *know*," we said together and laughed.

"Okay," I said. "But it bothers me to leave those at home." I pointed to my body armor and holster, hanging where they always did.

"Yeah, and I don't blame you, but the vest is a dead giveaway. Your best defense is your brain. You'll do fine."

"Does Roni really know what you're doing here?" I asked.

He pulled me to him and hugged me. "No, and I can only pray she thinks I'm having an affair with you, or she'd shoot me dead."

♦

With money from my bail that I'd left in a savings account, I bought $25,000 in traveler's checks. When we were ready to go, I rented a car one-way to Lansing, where I bought a 1989 conversion van from a small lot.

Along the way, I searched several pawnshops until I spent $250 for a Lorcin .380 from an older guy who let me walk out without any paperwork for another $200 and a little wiggle.

Money does talk. *So does cleavage, what little I have.*

I shopped secondhand stores until I found a leather jacket and other well-used clothing, the likes of which wouldn't be in my closet if I didn't replace my wardrobe for the next decade. Denim with ragged edges, holes. Skimpy shirts.

From there, we stopped in Macon, Georgia, where I shelled out cash for a bike in much worse shape than my own. The bike looked like shit, but better than its owner, who certainly could have used a good scrub and some bodywork.

In St. Petersburg, I checked into the Western Bay Star Hotel on Burlington Avenue North, a dive where they didn't care if you paid by the hour or by the month, so long as it was in advance. Amenities included local phone service and clean linen once a week, which was probably the rule for every bed, no matter how many different people occupied the room every seven days. I sprayed disinfectant on everything. Twice.

After sleeping in the van the first night, Dom checked in the next day. We lucked out getting rooms on the same floor, but almost three-quarters of the length of the building apart.

I arrived in Florida with short muddy brown hair, brown eyes thanks to the colored contacts, riding an ugly grumpy-sounding bike, and sporting a nasty attitude that was becoming more genuine every day. In fact, the more I practiced the new persona, the more I marveled at how guys like Zach and Dom could turn it off at the end of the case. I only hoped I could do the same.

Once we were settled, Dom's task was to pick a couple of bars for me to cruise each day, and then I would ride around, go in and hang out for a while, scoping out the crowd for Zach and for this certain group of bikers Dom had described. Sometimes I played pool or video games, but usually I ordered a couple of beers I didn't drink, then moved on.

"Go in. Don't try too hard to disappear into the woodwork. Blend in, but you don't want to be singled out," he told me after I described my first day's events.

"Fine line, this being invisible and getting noticed," I shrugged. "The come-on lines are amazing – I've never heard of some of the things I'm being asked to do."

Dom laughed. "See? You'll find Zach and get an education at the same time."

Odds of meeting the right people in the right bar in a county with over two million residents this time of year were less than slim. I'm not a gambler, but Dom kept telling me my chances of finding Zach were simply 50/50. Either I would or I wouldn't. I wasn't sure if he meant to be encouraging, but using the same theory, I bought a lottery ticket each time I got gas for the bike.

November, even in Florida, isn't the best riding climate. The weather held for the most part, but I rode back to the dingy hotel drenched once.

"So how'd it go tonight?" Dom asked when he came to the room, trying not to grin as I toweled off.

"At the second bar, I ran into a group of bikers that might be a possibility. One guy made a remark as I left about taking me for a ride," I said, pulling off my boots and pouring out a cupful of rain.

"What'd ya say?"

"Told him I already had a bike, I didn't need a man."

He laughed. "Universal appeal. Now he thinks you're a lesbian."

"Wait, that's not what –" I shook my head and gave up.

Tuesday night, after a couple of beers at the first place, I was sure there was nothing happening except a revolving door of men – and two women – hitting on me for various favors, so I moved on.

The next bar was very much like the inside of the place in Albuquerque where I'd first bumped into Zach – loud, stinky and sleazy. I got the feeling Dom had been breaking me in slowly, but this place hadn't had fresh air in years.

At the bar, I reached over to help myself to a bottle of beer from the cooler and tossed the bartender a five for my trouble, flashing more cleavage than I've ever shown in public.

The scars didn't bother him, if I read the leer down my chest correctly. It's not like I have much there to stare at, but whatever crossed his mind left a grin on his face. I winked and turned around to scan faces in the crowd.

Not five minutes passed before a squirrelly kid in his late twenties came up and asked if that was my ride at the corner of the building.

I nodded.

"Ain't seen you 'round before," he hollered over the music in a Texas twang that was as bad as his breath.

"Just got here a week ago. I thought the weather here was s'posed to be nice," I yelled back. "This is shit."

It *was* November, after all.

"Could be worse," he said. "You missed the hurricanes. Buy ya 'nother?"

"Maybe something stronger," I suggested.

He eyed me briefly, and then asked if tequila was okay.

I shrugged slightly, nodded.

He ordered from the bartender and seemed to ignore me until two shots and beer chasers appeared on the counter.

"Come on over," he said, pointing to a table across the bar, taking one of each glass.

Giving the bartender a screw-you-I-ain't-paying-for-this look, I grabbed my drinks and followed the kid to a table where five men and two speed-freaked, skanky women sat.

"I didn't get your name," the kid yelled, kicking a chair out for me as if that were good manners.

"Call me JJ." I sat down and emptied the shot in one swallow before leaning back with the bottle of beer, not interested if anyone else spoke or not.

The music was so loud it could be heard two blocks away, making conversation a yelling event, even when negotiating the price of a night and extra benefits, which was being discussed somewhere behind me.

"I'm Donny," he said, leaning toward me so I could hear.

"Yeah, thanks," I said, lifting the bottle. I shot a bored look over my shoulder toward a pair of pool tables toward the far wall.

"You ride with anyone?" the poorly and not recently bleached blonde across the table screeched at me.

Taking a second before looking over my shoulder, I glanced at her as if she'd interrupted an important thought. The disdain I felt was genuine. Seeing rotten teeth and a scrawny frame under faded black leather, I dismissed her with a simple, "No," and turned away.

Not siding up with the females caught the attention of two of the men at the other end of the table. I also ignored them until I sensed one of them staring at me. I turned to find one of the ugliest men I've ever seen.

Nasty pitted, uneven skin, blobbed like Play-Doh over a Neanderthal skull, crowned by hair styled with used motor oil. Domino's description had been perfect – practically any common power tool applied to his face would effect an improvement. Belt sander, chain saw. . .

I waited until he blinked, took a swallow from my beer bottle, in obvious indifference to the scrutiny, and then turned away from his gaze again.

Dallas Bowers, gang leader, drug dealer. Just the man I'd been searching bars to find.

CHAPTER

14

Hiding the excitement, I knew this was who Domino had me looking for.

"Boog!" the repulsive biker yelled at the kid who'd introduced himself as Donny and nodded toward me.

"Red Springer," the kid shouted, thumbing over his shoulder to the corner of the building where I'd parked.

"With the crappy paint job," I added, tipping my bottle to Dallas.

Now the focus of his attention, I answered a few questions over the thundering music, not offering much, not asking anything. In a lull, I left an empty bottle and strolled to the restroom, stopping for another beer on my way back by the bar.

When I returned to the table, the women and two of the men were gone, leaving Dallas, Boog and another amped-up idiot someone called Fred, whose attention span was about four seconds unless he was looking at boobs. Even mine.

Someone had replaced my empty with a full bottle of beer I would not drink.

"You ain't got much to say, Darlin'," Dallas said, closer to me after the latest musical chairs arrangement.

I shrugged.

"What brings you to Florida?" he asked, trying again.

"Change of scenery," I said. "Better weather. Looking for new work."

"Whaddaya do?" he yelled when the jukebox started up again with *Bad to the Bone*.

"Whadda you care?"

"I got connections. Jus' thought I could help." He grinned like a 13-year-old peeping through a hole into the girls' showers. "I like to keep the ladies busy."

"Zip up. I ain't interested in a job interview."

"What do you want, then?"

I looked over at Fred, who could barely stay in his chair, like a human version of Wile E. Coyote being electrocuted.

"How about a little of what he's been having," I said.

Dallas turned his head and looked at the other man, then back to me and nodded. "I could see about that."

"I don't want any crap, either. Any idiot can cook shit, and I know the difference."

He introduced himself, then looked me in the eye and asked if I was a cop.

"No, I'm not a cop. Are you?" I flipped back to him in perfect truth.

He actually laughed, showing poor but not rotted teeth. "Nope. Hang on, I'll be right back." He excused himself and dragged Fred outside behind him.

Boog leaned closer to me and made a disgustingly sexual offer.

I rolled my eyes. "I wouldn't do *that* with you until long after hell freezes over and the Devil has frostbite on his dick."

He laughed, as if what I said was funny, even if it was a rejection.

A few minutes later, only Dallas returned, slipping something into my leather vest pocket as he scooted into the chair next to me.

"Try that," he said, leaning to my ear. "If you like it, we can talk."

"Sweet," I said, finishing the beer I'd bought. "I'll find you here?"

He looked around, trying to be casual. "Enough."

I set the bottle on the table. "Then I hope it's worth coming back for more." I got up and threw down a twenty. "For my drink."

Outside, the air was cool and salty, but even the dead-fish odor was an improvement over the smell of the bikers and the smoke-filled bar.

Although those who had left the table huddled outside, I ignored them as I pulled on the leather jacket and donned a pair of pink glasses from the pocket. Then I climbed on the bike and rode off into the night, likely above the legal limit for blood alcohol and in possession of something I was pretty sure was a federal offense with at least five years attached.

No one followed me.

No one pulled me over.

At the hotel, I knocked on Domino's door, then hurried down the hall to my own room, knowing he'd come down after a few minutes.

I left my door ajar and went to the bathroom, picking a washcloth that might have been white at some point before I was born. Wetting it in hot water smelling more like chlorinated pond scum, I was washing my face when I heard him come in.

"How'd you do tonight?" he asked, stretching out in a threadbare chair in the corner next to the television set that didn't work.

"I don't know much about narcs," I said, coming out of the bathroom. "You know anything about hockey, Dom?"

He tilted his head in confusion.

"Score!" Using a tissue, I pulled the baggy I'd yet to touch from my pocket and tossed it on the table. "Guess who's giving away samples?"

I related the evening to him.

"You did great, kiddo!" he finally said with a big hug.

"Think so? Not too aloof?"

He shook his head. "Make him work for it. Tell him you didn't like it. You warned him you didn't want crap. Imply you could do better."

"Okay."

"How'd it feel," he asked, "making your first working contact?"

"Like I was in a dream," I said. "They bought a beer for me while I was in the restroom, but I didn't drink it."

"Good choice. Remember, until you show your worth, you're a stray dog they'll kick just to see if you run away. You don't want to bite anyone needlessly, but stand your ground."

Returning to the same bar the next evening, it was more crowded than before.

I didn't see the bikers, so I went to play pool. If they saw the bike, that's all they'd need to find me.

Didn't take long.

The lanky guy playing my table was taking his next shot when four of them strolled in and commandeered a corner table, and Dallas came toward the back.

I nodded in recognition as he came within ten feet, then bent to take my next shot. After I walked to the other end of the table, I looked up to see Dallas had taken my opponent's place.

"Same wager as his," I said, nonplused. "I'm solid."

The next shot I missed on purpose.

"So," Dallas said, coming around the table toward me, "was it worth coming back for?"

"No, not really." I stepped away from the table so he could shoot.

He made a nice two-ball shot.

"It was cut, which is why I hate buying," I said. "I got no interest in snorting powdered sugar or any other trash."

He scratched. Looked as intentional as my miss.

"I guess you'd do better?"

"Yeah," I took a gutsy shot and slammed the red solid into a corner pocket. "Much better than what you gave me."

"Who taught you?" he said.

"Ain't rocket science." I took another risky shot, but missed. "I did a little cooking in Seattle till the house got busted."

"Springer's got Georgia tags."

"You a detective or something?" I shot back. "I lost mine in the raid. I took a bus to Atlanta, bought that red piece of shit so I'd have a ride and came south where it's *supposed* to be warm. You wanna see the title or you gonna play?"

"You're a damned mouthy bitch," he said with amusement, trailing a hand over my jeans pocket as he strolled behind me and kept going around the table.

"I ain't one of those dumbass bimbos you guys find to decorate your rides as long as they put out and follow orders, so let's not pretend I'm gonna be."

He lined up a shot. "Not every man'd take that sorta shit from you," he said, putting his last stripe into the pocket.

I marched around the table right up to him and yanked down the bandana around my neck, revealing the scar. "Last man who thought I ought to be his bitch and follow orders took this last liberty before I shot him twice in the chest. Not taking shit isn't solely a male trait."

He took a step backward and tried to save face. "Still looking for a job?"

"Maybe."

He called a pocket for the eight, lined up and missed.

I shot, but he put a dirty hand down to stop the cue ball before it made contact with its target.

"What do you say we gamble?" he asked, though it was not a question. "New game. You win, I'll try you at what you say you're good at. I win, you spend the night with me first, then we talk."

"Yeah, right," I said.

"We play or we're done."

I looked him in the eye and saw this was not about the game. "I guess we play."

Shit. . . Okay, Domino, that scopolamine had better work.

CHAPTER

15

Domino shook his head as we discussed the night's events. "Agree to make a batch once a week, haggle a little over the money. Hang with 'em a couple of nights."

"Zach's not where they go," I argued. "This just feels wrong, Dom."

"If Zach's doing his job, he'll find this pack to see where the money's going," he said. "You have to trust me, Julie."

My shoulders sagged. "Yeah, 'cause I don't know what else to do."

Thus far, Domino had eliminated from suspicion the entire DEA team except Pauly Brodenshot and Caleb Osborne. In fact, he'd seen Pauly from a distance, but not Oz.

Or Zach.

The next afternoon, I met Dallas Bowers at the meth house and negotiated a test batch.

Someone musta liked what I cooked. Two days later when I saw Dallas, we agreed to two batches a week. They couldn't guarantee the necessary chemicals and ephedrine to make meth each time, so I'd cook something else if that were the case.

Dallas told me he wanted a full batch later in the week. That settled, he said he wanted to go cruising.

Riding with half a dozen of Dallas' guys around town was not how I wanted to spend the afternoon. I needed to focus on why I was here in the first place – Zach. After an hour of putzing aimlessly, Dallas led the group to a little white house with no visible neighbors.

There aren't many places in Pinellas County, Florida, where someone lives without another residence within an arm's reach, much less within visual range. Not on a peninsula twenty-four miles long and only eight miles wide at the widest point, with an additional 1.8 million retirees who arrive during the winter months.

Snowbirds, they're called, those transient travelers from up north. Permanent-resident Michiganders celebrated their southbound departures in the fall, so I had to wonder whether the year-round Floridians cheered every spring when the migration north began.

By late-November, the snowbirds were here en masse.

There are other unbecoming names for the elderly, but I hadn't heard "frogheads" till Dallas cursed one who pulled out from a side street and slowed our pace.

"Frogs, 'cause, like, all you can see of 'em when they drive is the tops of th'ur heads and their eyes peeping up behind the steerin' wheel," Dallas declared and then roared like it was the most hilarious thing ever said.

Certain that Dallas lacked the intellectual capacity to have thought this up on his own, I laughed, too.

In front of this little house, the group pulled to the curb and parked.

"So JJ," Dallas told me as several of them dismounted, "we got a little business in here. You wait with the bikes."

I might be a mouthy bitch, but I knew better than to disobey an order like that from Dallas. Throwing down the kickstand on my Springer, I leaned back onto my pack to soak up the weak sunshine.

The bike looked as ragged and barely held together as I'd felt since I snatched the title from the guy's hand and counted out $5500 for it – far more than it was really worth. The "custom" paint it previously sported looked like enamel house paint, so I hadn't felt bad buying a can of glossy red to cover an ugly attempt at flames that trussed the tank before. But after a new set of plugs, the bike ran okay and sounded like a screaming banshee at full throttle.

The seller had apparently entertained thoughts about an alternative plan where he kept the money and the bike and got a little something extra on the side, until I'd flashed enough of the butt of my pistol and a few scars I sported for him to see it wouldn't be wise to change the deal.

I'd never considered that having a couple of nasty scars might be intimidating, but added to a body rebuilt by three years of lifting weights and a new posture and attitude coached by Domino, the people I was running with had left me alone.

So far.

But I didn't question being told to stay with the bikes when five guys walked away. I figured a "few minutes" would turn out to be half an hour or more.

An elderly lady had gone scuttling into the house when we turned onto the street. I didn't figure I'd like what was going on inside, because this didn't seem like milk and cookies at Grandma's, but I could accomplish nothing by getting involved at that moment.

The first to reappear was Dallas' younger brother, Donny. Everyone called him Boog. I didn't want to know what the nickname meant or why it stuck.

He came out and sat sideways on his Lowrider, trying to look sexy. Younger than Dallas by as much as ten years maybe, he could be doing more with his life, but "Do you want fries with that?" wasn't much of an improvement from where he was now. Boog wasn't going to be signing on at NASA anytime soon.

Despite a cocky attitude with everyone else, he acted and looked like Dallas had busted his face more than once, but it could have been a multitude of other people he'd pissed off.

I'd considered the idea several times already.

"Collecting a debt," he said, nodding toward the house.

I shrugged and looked away, running my fingers through my wind-blown mud-brown hair, now a cropped mess about two inches long. It still felt strange, except when I was riding.

"How come you ride alone, JJ?" He pulled out a knife from a Velcro sheath on his hip, pretending to clean his fingernails with a blade he'd used a grinder to turn into a double edge. "Ain't none of our bitches rides."

I turned to him with a look of annoyance. "I ain't one of your bitches."

He laughed. "You oughta be my bitch, honey." He holstered the knife and slid off the bike to take a couple of swaggering steps toward me. "I could take real good care of –"

Reaching under the leather vest into my waistband, I rolled off my bike and produced the pistol in a smooth motion, leveling it at his chest when he was about six steps away. "Do I *look* like I need a man to take care of something, *honey*? Go sit your horny ass back on your bike and shut up."

I'd stopped him in his tracks, but as he turned tail, I caught sight of Dallas coming out the front door, adjusting the crotch of his jeans.

There was no question he caught me drawn down on his baby brother.

"Wha-the-fuck's this all about," he bellowed across the lawn, shortcutting through the grass toward me.

I slid the gun into my jeans. "Just explaining to Junior here why I don't ride bitch to none of you."

Dallas stomped close enough to backhand me across the face then grabbed me by the shirt. "If I ever see you with that gun out again, I'll cram it so far up your –"

He stopped dead when he felt me jab the barrel into his overhanging gut.

"And if you ever hit me again, I'll fill your chest full of lead like I did the last fat bastard who laid a hand on me," I whispered. "Now back off or find yourself a new cook. I guess all your bitches can *cook*, right?"

I'd left him room to save face, but not much. I put the pistol away before he stepped back.

"I've had enough testosterone for today," I said, swinging my leg over my bike. I left the two men standing in front of the old lady's house.

Riding far enough I was sure no one was following me, I stopped at another of the many bars I'd scoped out recently, this one had a pay phone inside the ladies' restroom. I called Domino.

"Hey," he said at the end of the first ring. "How's it goin'?"

I explained what had happened.

"Be careful," he warned.

"Yeah." I touched my cheek where Dallas had hit me. "Hope to be in before dinner."

I hung up, checked the mirror. The bruising had begun, but the

97

swelling wasn't bad yet. I pulled my pink sunglasses down before I went out and ordered a beer at the bar, then took it to a booth in the corner.

Three o'clock was early for a bar like this – maybe a dozen patrons hanging around, a few watching television in the far corner, a couple playing pool. The big draw here was the burgers, but I didn't have much of an appetite.

Over the next half hour, I cooled my fingers on glass, transferring the sensation to my stinging cheek. When the bottle was nearly empty, I'd decided it was time to leave.

Then he walked in, and I almost wet my pants.

Zach.

Sort of limping, favoring one side. Although he seemed to be alone, I couldn't tell for sure. He sat on a stool away from the only other patron at the bar.

A bartender poured him something straight up then slid what looked like a five into her pocket and left him alone.

He sat there with his back to the room.

I wasn't done with the beer but thought better of the idea of chugging down the last swallows, so I poured the rest on the floor under the table.

Like anyone will notice.

The waitress brought me another bottle when I motioned to her.

I laid down a couple of extra bucks when she set the beer on the table. "They sure grow 'em big where he's from, huh?" I said, hoping for more information from her.

"Like a damned bull moose," she agreed in a voice as Wisconsin as cheese, looking over her shoulder. "Ya gotta wonder if he's that big all over."

I grinned, thinking how I didn't have to wonder at all. "Seen him before?"

"He's been around a couple nights here and there. Always alone. Ya get some of that, honey, ya let me know what it was like, eh?" She waddled over to the bar, poured a shot of something I couldn't see, placed it in front of him, nodding toward me in the corner.

He said something to her, then lifted the shot glass and glanced over his shoulder in thanks. I raised the bottle of beer as we locked eyes for about ten seconds before he thought to drink, his face turned to stone.

Crap, I thought, maybe he isn't alone. Still, I would be simple enough to ignore if that were the case.

He turned back to the waitress and indicated two more. When she poured his order, he tossed down more cash, and then carried the shot glasses to my booth and slid in across from me.

I nodded and lifted the shotglass to smell what was in it.

Tequila.

I licked a spot on the back of my hand, then sprinkled salt on it, mostly to kill time and figure out why he'd come to my table at all if he didn't acknowledge who I was.

Worse, Zach didn't look good. In fact, he looked like shit, pale and unshaven, though I couldn't put my finger on what else was wrong other than the limp I'd seen.

He picked up his glass, and we clinked them together. He watched as I licked off the salt and then slammed the shot of what turned out to be Cuervo Gold. No lime. I licked my lips and the remaining grains of salt off my hand, staring at him.

In response, he tossed down his shot and chased it with a couple of swallows of my beer.

When he set the bottle back on the table between us, I picked it up and took another drink, eyes locked with his like we were having a blinking contest.

"Your place or mine, baby?" he said, but he didn't smile.

In fact, he looked threatening.

"Mine. Follow me," I said, glad to get him away so we could talk. "Park on the street. Room 314."

"Sure."

"I should go powder my nose first," I said and slid out of the booth.

He grabbed my arm and stood up beside me. "Later. Let's go."

Whatever the hell it meant, I didn't like it.

I tossed down a twenty-dollar bill for a drink I'd already paid for, a way of making an impression with the waitress, and gave her a sly smile as he followed me to the door.

She winked.

I walked out into the late afternoon sun, straight to the bike, and he followed part of the way then turned to get into a red Mustang convertible.

I shoulda known. I probably could have just scouted bars and motels for the damned car to find him.

Twenty minutes later, I pulled into the parking lot of the old hotel. In those minutes, a hundred thoughts plowed through my head.

Lots of questions, but not a single answer.

I pulled up next to the building, messing with my pack to make sure he saw where I went when he parked half a block away on the street.

He walked toward me, still limping but moving quickly, so I headed inside to the stairs.

The dirty glass door creaked closed when he followed me inside, his footsteps echoing up two flights.

I'd wanted to call Dom – my reason to go "powder my nose" – so he could get into my room before I arrived, but that didn't happen. Nor did I get a chance to go down the hallway and knock on his door because Zach had almost caught up to me on the second floor landing.

Zach must have taken the stairs three at a time behind me.

At my room, I wiggled my hand into the front pocket of my tight jeans for the key. By the time I stuck it in the lock, Zach stood behind me, breathing hard.

He wrapped his left arm around me and lifted the pistol out of my waistband with his right hand, then shoved me into the room when the door opened.

I stumbled, whipping around to see him pointing the gun at me.

He slammed the door behind him and leaned against it. In the dingy light from the window, he was ashen and sweaty. "Who sent you?" he demanded.

I blinked in disbelief, speechless.

"Someone paid you to finish the job?" he asked again.

What job?

The gun looked tiny in his hand. His knuckles were bone white.

"Zach, it's me, Julie." I started to move, and he waved the gun at me in warning. But with the sound of my name, his head cocked slightly. I raised the pink glasses.

100

Maybe from across the bar, he could have mistaken me for someone else, but he sat in my booth. Now, from this distance, I couldn't imagine how he didn't recognize me.

Except how much different could I make myself look?

"Your mother and mine are both nurses at UNMH," I tried.

I'd touched a nerve, but the gun didn't drop.

"You came to my father's funeral, Zach. That was the first time I kissed you."

"No . . . ," he said, shaking his head as if to clear his thoughts.

I took a step forward and pulled down the scarf around my neck, revealing the scar. The pieces fell into place in his head.

"What the hell are you doing here?" he asked.

His extended arm wavered like the pistol suddenly weighed forty pounds.

"Dom came to me after you paged him that you were in trouble. He's in a room down the hall. We've been trying to find you."

"It's really you, Julie?" he said, more like a child.

"Yeah, Zach, it's really me." I took two steps and took the pistol from his hand.

He reached out to touch my short windblown dark hair and the spreading bruise on my cheek, and whispered, "Help me, J'."

Then he passed out cold.

CHAPTER
16

No way could I catch Zach as he crumpled to the floor, but I managed to keep him from hitting his head.

"Zach," I pleaded. No response.

He was breathing, but I had no idea what was wrong, so I yanked up his shirt to check for injuries. I didn't find anything on his left side, but when I leaned over to see his right flank, I found a gaping inch-long entry and a large collection of blood under the skin beneath his ribcage. The bruise looked more than a day old though the stab wound still oozed. A bandage he'd had taped over it had slipped away.

Knife injuries are hard to assess for direction and depth, and this one had distinct bruising around the edges where the hilt had struck skin, so by sheer force, it was possibly deeper than the length of the knife – could have hit his liver or gallbladder, lung, intestines, maybe even kidney. He was hot to touch, so I worried the knife might have nicked his bowels. If it was as old as it looked, he must not be bleeding fast, but it could be just as fatal.

But what to do with him now on the floor?

Call EMS, send him to the hospital, maybe even fly him to Tampa? I wasn't sure he'd be safe anywhere in Florida. I couldn't focus on anything but keeping him alive. There was nothing I could do for him myself, but we had a bigger picture to consider.

When I picked up the phone, the line was dead, which was no surprise.

I left Zach on the floor and ran down the hall to Dom's room.

"You're not going to believe this," I panted, grabbing his arm and dragging him with me down the hall.

"Julie, what the. . ." Dom said, pulling up short to avoid stepping on the hulk lying on the floor of my little room.

I slammed the door shut and started talking in what I knew was overdrive speed. "I was in the bar when I called you, and I was getting ready to leave and then he walked in. He was acting weird, but after a drink, he followed me here. At the door, he took my gun, like he didn't recognize me. Then he said 'help me' and hit the floor. He's been stabbed."

"He needs a hospital," Dom said, stating the obvious. "I'll call an ambulance. We need to go. Get your stuff."

"No, he's not safe till this is over. I'll go back to the bar like he ditched me. That covers all my bases."

"You can't stay –" Dom started to argue.

"The only way to bring this all down is for me to stay. I don't have a choice, Dom, or we'll all be running."

"Ju. . . lie?" Zach said, stirring.

"Zach, when did this happen?" I said.

"Oz. . . He's. . ." His eyes rolled back again.

"Zach!" Domino said, slapping him several times. "What about Oz? Who did this?"

His eyes fluttered open again, "Oz's dead. It's Pauly, man. We're all gonna die. . ."

Dom and I exchanged looks.

I heard a loud motorcycle pull up down below and shut off.

"Shit, we've got to get him out of my room," I said. "If that's Dallas or one of them, they can't find either of you here. Take him to the hospital."

It took both of us to haul Zach to his feet so Dom could steer him down the hall.

I was almost at my door when Boog turned the corner from the stairway, coming at me like a train.

"What the fuck you want?" I said, stopping at the open door.

"That's egg-zackly what I want," he said, knocking me into the room with an outstretched arm. "Dal' wudn't happy you pulled that piece on me, and he said I could take it out on you any way I wanted." He reached for his belt buckle.

"Even if you find it in your pants, you won't know what to do with it," I said.

A fist to my face sent me sprawling onto the floor, and Donny dropped down on top of me to deliver another punch that made my jaw crack. Before I could recover, he flipped me face down on the dirty carpet and jacked my right wrist up as far up my back as he could, ripping apart the rebuilt shoulder, causing excruciating pain that took my breath.

Velcro zipped – Boog's knife sheath.

No doubt Dallas told him he could do anything but kill me, but there's a long way between being dead and wanting to die.

From where I lay, I could see my pistol under the bed to my right, where I'd dropped it when Zach hit the floor, but I couldn't reach it. I raised my head up but Boog slammed it down again, making me see stars.

The blade tugged on my leather belt as he cut through it with little effort, then the point dug into the small of my back as he jammed the blade into the waistband of my jeans and sliced them open.

When he leaned to yank down my jeans, I kicked him with my heavy boot, connecting the heel solidly with his lower back or maybe his kidney.

He retaliated with a burst of nonsensical profanity punctuated by whipping the knife across my lower back several times.

Fearing I was about to die, I was about to make a last-ditch effort to roll to my right onto my immobilized arm to throw him off balance and –

But as I began to twist, the weight was suddenly gone, and my effort launched me completely onto my back and right arm. My agonizing scream was lost in the three or four seconds of chaos that followed.

All I could see was Boog being lifted up by his jacket, a fist smashing his face, and his body flying toward the only window in the room.

Glass shattered, then I heard the gurgling sounds of a man, dying badly.

I looked up to see Zach standing over me, filled with rage unlike anything I'd ever seen on his face before.

He dropped to his knees beside me and helped me roll off my dislocated shoulder, onto my stomach, then edged my right arm to my side.

I tried not to scream again or vomit.

"Are you okay?" It felt like he touched the bloody fabric on my back.

Hell no, I'm not okay!

"Zach," I panted, "you can't be here when the cops show up. Go with Dom. Go to the hospital. I'll get there when I can."

Dom was standing in the door behind him.

"Please, Dom, get him out of here," I groaned, unable to move from my stomach. "Get my pistol under the foot of the bed and go."

"Yeah, come on, buddy," Dom coaxed with a hand on Zach's shoulder after getting the gun.

"We can't leave her," Zach said, looking down at his bloody hands.

Knowing it was my blood, I felt dizzy. "I'll be all right, I promise. I love you." I heard sirens. "Go," I pleaded.

And so they left me on the floor.

I intended to feign unconsciousness, but it wasn't much of an act.

Cops found me on the floor, dazed.

In fifteen minutes, the room was full of police and medics. I could hear the manager out in the hall, ranting.

No one mentioned the big man who'd followed me into the hotel, only the biker trash – a description that included me as well as the dead guy hanging halfway out the window.

The EMT taped a trauma dressing over my lower back and suggested I go get it sewn up, as if I wouldn't think that was a good idea. Based on the blood on the floor around me, it looked like a splendid notion. Every movement felt like I'd been mauled by a bear.

The medics helped me from the floor to the edge of the bed, and my shoulder clunked partially into the socket when I bent my elbow and tucked my forearm against my stomach. The pain made my head swim.

The EMT mentioned getting a gurney for me, but there was no elevator in the building, and I wasn't interested in being strapped to a stretcher and carried down two flights of stairs, having toted a few folks down myself. I didn't take the offer lightly, considering my condition, but I refused nonetheless.

"I'll walk," I said, "if maybe you could help me stand?"

No argument.

Before the cops let me go, I got one more round of questions about what happened.

"Could you identify the dead man?" was a new one.

"Yeah, they call him Boog Bowers - Donny. He came for a little revenge over an insult earlier today. You'll be looking for his brother Dallas, who'll be looking for me, I expect."

They let me take clean clothes and my pack after a quick search. The medic helped me down the stairs to the ambulance, wrapped in the sheet from the bed to cover my blood-soaked wide-open jeans.

No sense changing, I'd get clean ones bloody and have to take them off at the hospital when I got there anyway.

The medic gave me a hand up into the side door of the ambulance.

"Have a seat there," he said, pointing to the gurney.

I practically fell on it, on the brink of passing out from the walk. The ride was a blur, and I didn't notice when he placed an oxygen mask on my face or started an IV line.

At BayFront Hospital, they rolled me into a room where several people were waiting, listening to the medic's version of my story, which included a possible rape.

I wanted to tell them Boog hadn't gotten that far, but the words wouldn't come, and the room drifted out of focus.

CHAPTER

17

Pretty soon, the easiest answer to the redundant questions was, "I don't remember," which fit almost everything and was easy to say.

They had given me pain medication before making an attempt to reduce the shoulder dislocation. So much for riding the motorcycle again this summer, I thought, but at least my shoulder was not fractured this time. Having failed in their first try, I got more drugs and don't remember the next attempt, thankfully.

A while later, I awoke on my stomach, jerking in panic before I realized where I was. The motion was painful. Everything hurt.

"Whoa, hang on there," someone said. "I'm almost done with your back."

I panted, fighting a wave of nausea.

"Can you tell me what happened, Ms. Wesley?" the man with the needle and sutures asked.

Wesley?

Oh, yeah. . . I'd brought my old New Mexico driver's license instead of a current one.

I explained the run-in with Bowers earlier in the day, that I pissed him and his brother off, and apparently the kid had followed me to the room and hacked away, though come to think of it, I wasn't sure how he'd ended up at the hotel.

"Yeah, he did that. I've done 57 stitches so far, I think, but I lost count twice," a resident said. "We'll get this done, then have one of the rape nurses come do an exam."

"That's not necessary," I said. "He didn't get that far."

"You're sure?"

"Not for lack of intention, but he died with his pants on," I murmured.

Whoever was suturing became silent for a while as he continued to sew me up, only responding when a nurse peeked in and asked if he needed anything. Before he was done, a couple of St. Petersburg police officers showed up to finish questioning me. They stood where I couldn't see them, which I thought was rude.

Again with the same open-ended statement to get me talking: Tell us what happened.

So I explained again. "I knew he'd kill me if I didn't do something, but I don't remember what happened after I pushed him. I woke up on the floor," I said, which wasn't really a lie because I didn't see Zach throw him.

"You know both the Bowers?" one asked, still out of my view.

"Yes, and most of the rest of them."

"Excuse me," the doctor said to me. "I'm done, but the nurse needs to come clean this up and dress it, then put on a shoulder immobilizer. Don't try to get up before then." He snapped off his sterile gloves.

I agreed, then tried to turn my head, more aware of the pain in my jaw and everywhere else. "Yeah, I've been riding with them a little since I got here." With one eye swollen, I still couldn't see the policemen well.

Two uniforms, one a ranking officer.

"A rough crowd for a woman," the younger man said. "You're aware these guys are manufacturing and selling meth?"

"I sorta figured," I replied. "But I'm clean."

I still couldn't make out a rank on the older officer's badge, but it was gold. He dismissed the younger man.

"So you know about the Bowers Brothers?" I asked, feeling the stinging sensation on my back when I moved a bit to see better.

"Yeah, which makes me wonder more what you're doing with them, because you don't talk like a brain-damaged biker bitch," he said, arms crossed.

"I'm not, and I made that plain to Donny Bowers this afternoon."

"Well, he's dead biker trash tonight, and you sound smart enough to know they'll be hunting you down to even the score. I don't know what your real story is, but I'm prepared to offer you protection and make this whole dead body thing go away if you cooperate," he said quietly. "Otherwise, you hit the streets and take your chances."

A nurse came in to clean up and bandage my back, and the officer fell silent as she worked.

"While she finishes, I'll give you a phone number." I said, hoping to speed things up a little. "Talk to Agent Forrester. He can tell you about me – only my last name is Madigan."

Without speaking, he wrote it down and left.

Putting a large dressing over the cuts first, the nurse then helped me sit up and get dressed before she fitted the shoulder immobilizer strap around my torso and right arm. She was competent, but I could tell she thought she was treating biker scum – no smile, no conversation.

An evolving black eye and a sore jaw went along with the shoulder and the stitches on my back, which included a couple in the muscle tissue. The nurse told me I was lucky I'd been wearing the heavy leather vest.

I feel pretty lucky I'm not dead, considering.

Maybe it was the leftover drugs in my system, but even with the IV fluids, I felt light-headed when I stood. But I knew better than to say so and risk being admitted.

With my discharge instructions, I received a prescription for antibiotics, a couple of extra dressings, and a thoughtful six-pack of Tylenol with Codeine. The nurse also gave me a stern warning not to bend or twist, to watch for signs of infection, and to have the sutures removed in ten to fourteen days.

I nodded to each item, signing several sheets of paper as she indicated. All her tasks took half an hour.

The officer came in as I tucked the handouts into my pack, introducing himself in a much different manner. "I'm Captain Garrett Carlson," he said, shaking my left hand. "I'll give you a ride to the station for more paperwork." He offered up a bag from McDonald's, which he swapped me for my pack, and we headed out to his car. Outside, he continued, "Odd friends you keep, Ms. Madigan. And interesting stories they tell about you."

"Yeah, I bet," I said, trying to dig into the fries on top of the bag as we walked, but not having much luck with one arm immobilized.

He took the bag and held it while I grabbed a handful.

I realized how agonizing chewing really was. The pain wasn't going to get any better later, so I kept eating.

"You have somewhere else to stay tonight?" he asked.

"My room at the Ritz isn't ready?" I retorted.

He laughed. "You've been evicted. We collected what was yours."

Opening the passenger-side door of an unmarked patrol car, Garrett helped me sit down carefully, then gave me the bag again before closing it. He dumped my pack in the backseat before going around to get in.

Unmarked on the outside, the patrol car was still rigged out completely inside – radio, computer-aided dispatch screen, shotgun.

I managed another handful of fries.

"The soda's yours, too," Garrett said, starting the car and backing out of the reserved space. "The best place for you tonight is at the station, like you're being held for questioning or even booked. Whatever we need to do to protect you." He stopped at a red light and looked at me. "You're lucky Bowers didn't finish the job," he said.

"He wouldn't be the first man who's taken a knife to me and didn't survive. I shot the last one, and I was married to him." I took a long drink through the straw before getting down to the Quarter Pounder with Cheese, which wouldn't have been my first choice for a meal, but I hadn't eaten since breakfast, had drunk too much beer earlier, and it was long after dark already. I ignored the pain in my jaw and took a bite. "Thanks for dinner," I said after chewing enough to talk again.

"Cheap date," he said with a smile. "You know, this drug war isn't the sort of game you walk in and walk out of." His voice changed to a more serious tone. "Did the DEA help you out this afternoon?"

"What help?" I said, evading the question. "You don't think I could shove a scrawny crackhead like Boog through a window?" I took another drink.

Carlson shrugged. "Gotta hand it to you... you've got a lot of moxie coming down here alone."

I wasn't by myself. He thought I'd tell him if I was.

My guts tightened with suspicions that I'd screwed up. I'd wanted someone from a neutral agency to be involved, to ensure I walked away from this. But I hadn't arranged it – I left it to a stranger to make that phone call for me.

After only a few bites of the burger, a wave of vertigo and nausea hit me.

"Stop the car," I said. My voice sounded odd. "I think I'm gonna be sick."

Garrett Carlson pulled to the curb and stopped, but he did nothing to help me.

I intended to open the door but was too weak to reach the handle with my left hand. My heart raced out of control, and my vision swam lazily. I managed to turn and look at him as my head rolled onto the rest into near blackness.

He chuckled as he signaled his return into traffic. "That's better. The conversation was getting boring."

CHAPTER
18

Garrett Carlson drove until I was thoroughly lost, which didn't take much in the dark, given my scant knowledge of the area and no way to tell which direction we were going or where I'd just been. Things I saw dissolved from memory before I could figure out what they meant. One thought melted into the next.

My brain fired flares, however, warning me I was in deep shit and ought to play dead before I got that way permanently, so I stayed slumped as Carlson drove, peeking out when I could.

The Skyway Bridge sign whizzed over our heads.

I'm not going to a police station tonight. If I'm lucky, I might make it to the morgue after he throws me off the bridge.

Panic jacked up my heart rate even more. City lights zipped by when I was able to open my eyes at all. But in time, the dizziness faded, and my thought processes began to clear. Trying out muscles to see if I had regained any control, everything seemed to improve with the same speed it had failed. With my body and brain starting to work again, I sorted through options to get out the mess.

There was the shotgun, but with one arm useless in a sling, it would be impossible to maneuver it in the car, even if I could get it unlocked. Worse, I was likely to get hurt trying it with Carlson driving.

A panic button was built into the radio console, which brought up more questions. Had he radioed central dispatch when we left the hospital? I couldn't remember. Was his vehicle part of a computer-aided dispatch system that showed his location at all times? What would happen if I pushed the alarm? Would dispatch make radio contact to confirm he was okay?

Better to save any attempts for something more likely to succeed, whatever that might be, but the panic button kept creeping into my thoughts.

I had explained everything to Nolan Forrester before leaving Michigan because he was the only outside help I could trust if I were arrested. At some point, if I had to go to the local cops, he agreed to send an FBI agent as a neutral party to make sure what was happening right now wouldn't – being snared by another rogue officer.

How stupid I'd been to leave the hospital with anyone.

No way to tell if Garrett Carlson really had called Forrester after I gave him the number and my name – there was no clue about the conversation I could remember. Someone would have to miss me before anyone thought to look. My only hope was that maybe Domino contacted Nolan to get help with Zach.

If Carlson intended to do anything to me, it would have to be something he could explain away if there were any tracks. But I couldn't remember what sort of tracks there were.

I couldn't be sure how long the drug would last – something he'd slipped into the drink, most likely. But I'd only had a few swallows and a couple of bites of the burger and fries before the effects took hold.

Enough to incapacitate me; not enough to keep me that way for long. Good.

He parked the car, and when I peeked out of my right eye, I knew in my gut this was the warehouse where Zach's team found the men who'd slaughtered those two children.

I continued to play possum when Carlson nudged me, so he left me there when another vehicle pulled up next to the entrance to the building. I couldn't see the driver through the reflections of tungsten lights on the windows.

The car looked civilian, but it might have been unmarked or undercover.

Panic burned in my stomach.

Do I push the alarm or not?

I decided I needed to unlock the shotgun when I got a chance.

After a look over his shoulder satisfied him that I was still unconscious, Carlson moved, and the other man got out of the car with a cane. They walked together toward the warehouse.

Pauly Brodenshot.

Zach's words echoed in my ears – *We're all gonna die.*

Unconcerned with me, they went inside.

Not locked in the rack, I slid the shotgun to where I could maneuver it with my left arm. Making as little noise as possible, I unlatched the door and left it slightly open.

Then I noticed something. The radio was not set to scan frequencies, just to monitor channel C, whatever that was. There was little traffic on it. Was that normal? Was he listening for trouble? Did he have a portable set the same way?

My last best chance became offense.

I peeled a piece of tape from my arm where the IV had been and put it where I could get to it. Then I changed the radio to channel A where there was more traffic and listened. Satisfied this was the frequency I needed, I hit the red panic alarm, heard a double beep. When this cleared, I picked up the microphone and said what would bring the absolute biggest response – *officer down, shots fired, unable to declare my location.*

I switched back to frequency C and taped the button down to transmit everything else that happened, stretching the spiral cord far enough to hang the microphone out the door.

With nearly exhaustive effort, I swung my legs out and stood, propping the shotgun over the door.

In less than 60 seconds, I heard the first sirens in the distance, but then a low rumble echoed through the metal buildings as Dallas Bowers rolled up on his motorcycle. By the look on his face, he expected something very different than me standing with the car door open. Whatever had brought him here took backseat to the rage directed at me. He dismounted and started toward the patrol car, reaching behind his back for something.

I leveled the shotgun at him.

"Don't pull a gun on me, Dallas. I'll shoot you where you stand," I warned him, prepared to defend myself.

In frame-by-frame slow motion, he brought his arm forward, and

I tucked the shotgun to my left shoulder, hoping to incapacitate him in one shot. But in those slowed seconds, before either of us could turn to see the next roar coming toward us, a red streak blurred through my field of vision.

With a howling engine and screaming tires, Zach's red Mustang slid to a 180-degree stop in the gravel, throwing up a cloud of dirt behind it.

Dallas was gone.

I blinked, unsure what had just happened.

Domino stood up in the driver's doorway and yelled to see if I was okay.

I pointed to the door of the building.

Garrett Carlson came running out of the building with his sidearm drawn, looking for a target. Pauly stuck his head out then ducked back in.

I leveled the shotgun at Carlson. After seeing Domino and Zach both drawn down on him, he dropped his gun and hit the ground, arguing that he was a police officer.

"Pauly's inside," I called to them.

Leaving me to cover Carlson, Domino glanced down at Bowers' broken body on the far side of the car, then took off running. Zach looked to make sure I was really okay, and hobbled in behind Dom.

Seeing two-thirds of the threat was gone, Carlson got brave and got to his hands and knees to move toward his gun.

I knew I couldn't shoot him until he got to it, so I aimed at the shotgun at his weapon on the ground and pulled the trigger.

Nothing happened.

He laughed.

There was no way I could pump the shotgun and fire before he got to his pistol and shot me from twenty feet away.

Carlson laughed at me and stood up. In two steps, he was close enough to pick up his gun. "You stupid bitch," he said, aiming at me. "How did you think you could stop an operation like this by yourself if the DEA couldn't?"

"By taking down bastards like Pauly Brodenshot, and you, Carlson."

"It'll be a pleasure to kill you all."

"You liked being the hitman. Did you kill Caleb Osborne, too?" I asked.

He laughed. "Yeah, Pauly didn't want to get his hands dirty."

Live or die, I played my last ace.

"Nice confession, Garrett Carlson. You broadcast it all over the county," I said, nodding toward the mike. "Everything you and Pauly Brodenshot did is over."

Only because he hesitated long enough to look at the mike did I have a chance.

In those seconds, more cars careened toward us, sliding on the gravel. Men deployed to cover and starting yelling for us to throw down the weapons.

I shrugged and tossed the useless shotgun over the door sideways at Carlson, letting it bounce at his feet.

Maybe seeing his future on the other side of prison bars, Garrett Carlson took the cheap way out. The gunshot echoed against the metal buildings as even more patrol cars approached and occupants scattered. Some of them entered the warehouse, and the rest surrounded the perimeter.

Nolan Forrester galloped toward me from one of the last cars to arrive.

I hung on to the door. "See?" I told him, thankful he was there. "I told you this would be a piece of cake."

I passed out in his arms.

CHAPTER

19

Pauly hadn't been alone in the warehouse, but with the backup FBI agents and deputies who followed Dom and Zach in, rounding up the trio inside was easy.

Dallas Bowers wasn't dead, I learned later, but he'd probably wish he were if he could wish at all. Impact of his head on the Mustang's hood left him only vegetative brain function.

Not much of a step down, in my opinion.

Zach and Domino came to the ambulance where I lay on the cot, conscious again, another IV hanging to help boost my blood pressure.

I'd convinced the same medics who'd transported me earlier that I had only passed out from the pain, and I refused to leave the scene without Zach, so they waited.

"I wonder if the hospital patched up the bullet holes in my room from the last time I was a patient." Zach said, stepping into the side door and slumping onto the bench seat.

"Let's go find out," I said.

With a somewhat different attitude now that I wasn't biker trash as previously presumed, the ambulance crew transported us back to BayFront, where the night crew of ER nurses and doctors went through the new story. The same resident who'd sutured up my back came to fix a couple of places I'd torn open. An orthopedic surgeon looked at my shoulder and decided surgery was in order but should wait a few days for the swelling to go down.

Zach went to surgery to explore his abdominal wound because he was running a fever.

They admitted us to share a room on the surgical floor, and the same charge nurse who'd thrown everyone out of Zach's room weeks ago came to explain the new security procedures. "A lot of things have changed since your friend was here last time."

"You remember us," I said, floating away on Demerol. "Nice to see you, too."

♦

I heard voices, but they didn't sound important enough to escape the narcotics that lulled me away. It wasn't good sleep, but I wasn't ready to join the world.

Scenes played out in my nightmares, sometimes with different outcomes with gory details that shook me. I dreamed that Carlson had shot Zach – and I knelt beside Zach, holding him as he bled out onto the gravel, sobbing.

"Julie, honey," I heard him saying somewhere far away. "I'm okay. Shhh . . . Go back to sleep, baby. Everything is all right."

I woke enough to realize Zach was actually holding me, and that my face was really wet. I clung to his arms, but I couldn't stay awake even when he kept talking.

"Julie?" a voice called sweetly from far away.

Had to be later, I was in pain.

"Julie? Wake up." Not so sweet this time.

When I opened my eyes, the colored contacts I wore felt like shards of shattered steel.

In a hospital again. This has got to stop.

I had to blink to remember which hospital. Which state.

"Julie?"

Turning to my left toward the voice, I saw Zach stretched out on the other bed.

"Hey." He smiled.

I opened my mouth to speak, but the motion made my jaw zing. "This isn't my idea of sleeping together," I said.

"Mine either, baby." He tilted his head. "Do you know you actually look worse than I feel this morning?"

"Terrific. I don't feel so great either, Z', but I'm alive."

"Not for lack of trying, I hear. Remind me to yell at you about that later," he said, squinting at me. "You look so different with short hair and brown eyes."

"I'd like to have blue eyes again if someone can help me with these," I said, knowing I'd never get the lenses out with my left hand.

Zach pushed the call button and explained when a voice answered. Then he crawled out of bed and came to hug me, dragging an IV pole and probably exposing his entire backside.

"I can't believe you're here, Julie. That you came for me. I could kick Domino's ass for getting you involved in this," he whispered in my ear. "But thanks."

He held me a long time, until the nurse came in with saline solution.

She brought a lens case, too, but I told her to throw the contacts away. "I'm not wearing them again, ever."

Zach laughed, but I didn't think it was funny – there was nothing funny about anything we'd been through.

With nimble assistance, the contacts were gone, and I thanked the nurse, who left me saline drops if I needed them.

"I can't wait to explain this adventure to a dozen local, state and federal agencies," I grumbled. "Especially about the dead guy in my hotel room."

"No need. FBI and the Department of Justice know enough," Nolan said, coming in the door. "As far as everyone else is concerned, there are still details and people to bring in, but you're both clear."

"Nolan wants to get us out of here," Zach said. "Do you have a surgeon in Michigan?"

"For my shoulder?" I asked. "No, the orthopedist who fixed it is in Albuquerque."

"Even better. Let's get you there and fixed, then off the continent," Zach concluded.

"We can't just go –"

"Sure you can," Nolan interrupted me. "It's simple. You find your passport. You buy tickets. You go to the airport, and you leave the country. New Zealand's nice this time of year. Maybe Rome."

"I've been gone weeks from work already," I argued.

"You'd be on medical leave anyway," Nolan said. "The doctor

says you'll both be cleared to leave today. Neither of you made any friends down here. Go get your shoulder fixed and then disappear for a while, Julie. That's not a suggestion."

I convinced them both I had things to settle in Michigan first. Truth was I needed to be in my own space for a few days.

True to his word, turning off an alternate personality isn't instant, so I understood why Dom went to Las Vegas after an undercover operation to find himself. I'd altered my appearance so much, I was stunned again every time I saw myself in a mirror, new bruises aside.

I actually looked about as bad as I felt, and I couldn't even see my back.

We were discharged by noon. Domino said he'd take care of the vehicles and anything else, and Nolan drove us to the airport for an afternoon flight.

Waiting at the airport, my back throbbed though the pain was dulled by a couple of pills that almost made sitting tolerable.

When we changed planes in Detroit, a woman approached me in the restroom and whispered, "Honey, you shouldn't stay with a man who'd do that to you," nodding to my reflection in the mirror.

Great. She thinks Zach did this.

CHAPTER

20

We arrived in Traverse City at sundown, and Zach rented a car. He dropped me at the house and got me settled before making a quick trip to the grocery store. When he returned, he cooked a dinner we ate by candlelight, complete with a dozen roses. Then we sat together on the sofa, listening to music, and holding on to one another in lovely peace.

When it came time to go to bed, he told me he'd take the other room.

"No," I argued. "Why?"

"I don't want to bump you."

"I'm all sewn together, Zach, just like you are," I said, getting a glass of water. "In fact, I could use help changing the bandage so you can see for yourself."

"What about your shoulder? How are you going to sleep if I'm taking up half the bed?"

"Only half?" I kidded. "We'll manage, I promise. Please, Zach? I didn't go through all that just to sleep in separate rooms."

We went to the bathroom. I released the Velcro holding the shoulder immobilizer around my arm and waist, then I supported my elbow as he lifted the tail of my shirt and began to peel the tape up around the edges. But when he tried to pull the dressing away from the sutures, it was stuck.

"Julie, I can't do this," he said, sitting down on the side of the tub. "I'm terrified I'll hurt you."

I turned around to find his eyes squeezed shut, moving his fingers as if they were wet and sticky.

"I'm sorry," he said. "I just keep remembering your blood on my hands."

When I wrapped my left arm around his neck, he leaned his head against my belly. "So turn on the water, help me get out of my clothes, and we can shower till it soaks loose."

He helped me slip the shirt off, then he pulled my jeans and underwear down so I could step out.

"You know, I don't know what's worse, thinking I'll hurt you peeling this stuff off or seeing you naked and not being able to do anything."

"That'll be the day. . ." I watched him pull his long-sleeved t-shirt over his head. "I get to peel your tape off, too, right?" I said, pointing at the dressing over his right abdomen.

Zach had a fair amount of fine dark hair on his chest and belly.

"Sure, I got a waterproof thingy underneath this. Help yourself," he said, smiling.

I pulled away a small dressing held in place by paper tape. "Apparently your nurse wasn't a sadist like mine."

His stab wound was greenish purple now, with two sutures, and a matching surgical entry about an inch away, with another pair of stitches.

"Very tidy," I observed.

Zach turned on the water and finished undressing while it warmed up.

"After you," he said, offering a hand and holding open the shower curtain when the steam billowed over the top.

In the hot water, it only took a few minutes for the dressing to peel away, and I reached around with my good arm to catch it before it fell. He wrung it out and tossed it out into the trash.

I turned around under the water so he could see my back.

"Oh, Christ . . ." He gasped.

I glanced over my shoulder in time to see him cross himself, then put his hand over his mouth, pale in the steam like a ghost.

"Baby, I'm so sorry," he whispered. "I had no idea it was that bad."

I turned around so he couldn't see it any more, afraid he'd pass out. If he went down in the tub, we'd both crash. Hard.

"Sorry? You kept me from getting a lot worse than this, which was my fault for starting with the kid earlier in the day."

"You wouldn't have been there if I —"

I put my fingertips against his lips. "Remember the times I wouldn't let you turn on the lights when we made love because I didn't want you to see the scars? You told me one night that they're just marks," I said, running my fingers across a scar on my chest. "They're just marks, Zach. I went to Florida prepared for much worse."

I went to Florida prepared to die to save you.

He kissed my forehead and turned me around. He took a deep breath, then touched my back.

"You know, people might think I did this," he said, tracing the lines for me. "It sorta looks like a big Z."

"I'd have settled for a tattoo of your name on my butt, really," I kidded.

"An interesting idea," he laughed and pointed to a spot. "Right here?"

He used my favorite scrubby sponge and washed me nose to toes, avoiding the sutures on my back. We stayed under the spray until the hot water ran out.

After helping me dry off, Zach taped another dressing on my back, then put the shoulder immobilizer on over a silk tanktop.

"I guess I need a haircut," he said, running his fingers through his wavy hair and shaking out droplets before tousling mine, which was at least six inches shorter than his. "I liked yours long, but this is kinda fun."

"I could use a trim. It's pretty ragged," I said. "I was thinking of going red next, just for sport. Whaddaya think?"

We looked at each other in the foggy mirror and shook our heads in unison, laughing.

"How long was it when you cut it?" he asked, lifting it again.

"He whacked off a twenty-two-inch braided ponytail at my collar and kept cutting."

"Him?"

"Yeah, Domino did it," I said. "I had him leave you enough to run your fingers through."

"Thanks," he said, running one hand up through my hair at the side of my neck, pulling me close for a kiss. "It's perfect."

Several diversions later, including digging through luggage for the antibiotics we were both supposed to be taking, we finally made it into my king-size bed. After a bit of trial and error, we snuggled into a comfortable position, curled like spoons on our left sides, bodies not quite touching.

The whole Florida experience was something we'd chosen not to try to discuss in the hospital, airports or planes, but I could tell parts of it bothered Zach. Once or twice, I'd seen him staring out the window of the jet, lost in painful thought. Like so many of our other shadowy secrets, we needed a quiet place, cool crisp sheets and darkness to talk about them.

Alone together where we could touch, we could finally discuss why Zach went to Florida to meet up with Pauly, only to find out his partner had turned to the business of dealing drugs and was in so deep that murder was reasonable operations. We talked about how Zach sent the coded numbers to Domino when he realized he was in trouble, hoping his vague message would be interpreted correctly, and then worrying it had.

I told him how I'd taken on an undercover identity as a drug maker in order to find him.

"Dom taught you to cook meth?" His voice broke. "Do you have any idea how dangerous it is?"

"Oh, I got that lesson twice. As if taking on a whole new identity and charging into the land of drugs and criminals wasn't dangerous enough, I didn't do well in chemistry."

Zach shuddered. "He did fail to mention several details, but he said you did a hell of a job, though. I'm proud of you. And I'm grateful that you came for me."

"I didn't have a choice."

"Sure you did. You could have said no."

"No, I couldn't. I had to find you," I said. It wasn't pride or defiance. It was a revelation of love that hung in the darkness – but I didn't say aloud that I'd have done anything to save him.

Finally, he whispered, "Thank you."

"You're welcome."

"I gotta know, J'," he said, carefully moving closer to my back. "You've had a taste of my world. Did you like working undercover?"

"No," I said. "I might have, except the stakes were personal. I had nothing to go on – no plans, no training, no backup. All I knew was that you thought it was someone in the DEA."

He hesitated. "I didn't tell you that."

"Yes, you did, Zach," I said softly. "You just didn't say the words."

"Then I'm glad you were listening," he said, brushing his fingers through my hair, then he leaned closer to kiss my bare neck. "Saying thank you doesn't seem to be adequate."

"That fact that you're here to say it, it is."

His warmth radiated into the sore muscles of my back, and we lay in silence for a while.

"You didn't recognize me at the bar, did you?" I finally asked.

I heard him swallow.

"What I saw was a woman who looked like you," he said. "Someone I wanted to be you, and then again, I didn't. At first I thought it was, but the brown eyes really killed me. Then I brought over the tequila and you licked your hand and shot it. I was sure you wouldn't drink the stuff, so then I was more confused."

"I like good tequila, which does not have a worm in it, by the way. I don't like the next mornings." I didn't explain all the things that tequila could make happen in the middle.

"I'll try to remember that," he said with a quiet chuckle.

"What about in the hotel room?" I asked, my voice breaking into a whisper.

"By the time I'd followed you halfway across the county, I figured I was imagining the resemblance. That Pauly'd sent someone who looked enough like you to finish the job," he said, then sighed.

"You thought I was someone hired to kill you?" I asked, feeling him nod in reply. "I knew something was wrong in the bar, but I didn't realize until you passed out that you'd been stabbed."

I felt the muscles tighten in his body.

"I don't know how you can ever forgive me pointing that gun at you."

125

"Zach, it's over. I forgive you. You were hurt and trying to stay alive."

"I wasn't just hurt, Julie." He rolled away from me and dropped a forearm over his face, then made a confession that had to hurt as bad as anything else he'd ever done. "I was high. I mean *flying*."

"I don't understand," I said. I honestly didn't believe that he'd taken anything.

"Pauly spiked something I drank at his place the first night I got there, when I still trusted him. A week later, he put Oz and me in a situation where the only way to walk out alive was to use. It was a test – demonstrate loyalty or die."

I didn't know what to say.

"Oz refused, and Pauly had Carlson shoot him with my gun. I didn't have a choice, and Pauly knew it. He could have dumped me so far out in the Gulf I'd never be found, but instead he hung a murder rap on me, something that would screw up my career and my life." He paused. "And if that didn't work, he said, then he could always get to you, too."

CHAPTER

21

Although I had checked in that evening with Gerald Katz to let him know I was home, I hadn't expected a phone call from him a few hours later.

Zach handed me the handset on the fifth ring.

The clock said 4:39.

I'm getting rid of the phone.

"Julie," the familiar voice of my boss said. "I know I shouldn't bother you, but I could really use a hand. It's okay if you need to say no, though."

"Doc, I look like bloody hell and one hand is all I can offer, but it's all yours. What's up?"

"I'm at an accident scene south of Blair Township, and I'll be here several hours, but there's a call in Torch Lake I think someone needs to see now."

"Let me get something to... Hell, I can't even write. Hang on," I said.

"Everything okay?" Zach asked.

I said yes and padded down the hall to my office where I could use a speakerphone and scribble left-handed the address and directions Dr. Katz gave.

"It's not trauma, and there's only one family member to interview, the grandson."

"What am I looking for?" I asked.

"Well, I really don't know. EMS was called for a man down that became a cardiac arrest, but what little I got from the medics doesn't add up. History for three or four weeks. I'm thinking something environmental."

Nothing unusual for Dr. Katz not to share his hunches. Objectivity was important to him.

"Is it okay if I have Zach drive for me?" I asked.

"Absolutely," he said. "It shouldn't take long, and again, I'm really sorry to impose."

"I'll check in when I'm done." We said our goodbyes.

I looked up to see Zach standing in the doorway, naked and yawning.

"You're going to work?" he asked.

"No, we are going to work. I need you to drive," I said.

We went through the complicated task of getting me dressed. Though in November, I'd normally wear bulky sweaters with cowls, turtlenecks, or scarves around my neck, regardless of the temperature, I picked out something different.

In the middle of the night, I made a decision about the rest of my life. I chose a plain maroon sweatshirt, which left the dark mark across my neck partially exposed. And I left the body armor on the chair, along with the shoulder holster, since I couldn't draw the Glock from it anyway.

It was time I stopped reacting, stopped being afraid.

If Zach noticed I'd skipped the vest and gun, he didn't say anything.

I did put concealer on my bruised face out of courtesy to the family.

It's poor decorum to show up at a scene looking worse than the deceased.

Zach drove my Suburban while I gave him directions to the east side of Grand Traverse Bay and north into Antrim County.

We passed the intersection where the elderly couple had died, and I'd had to testify about their order of death. Barry and Cecelia Bartlesby.

Remembering names and faces and stories was one of the overwhelming issues of my career. I simply did not forget. Like the first patient I'd transported alone in an ambulance in Albuquerque, a stroke patient named Oscar Germany. He couldn't speak, so he drew letters with his finger on his chest, and we communicated that way.

"So what is this call?" Zach asked, followed by another yawn.

"I don't know. Dr. Katz likes to let me make my conclusions without his interpretations. I know it's not a trauma-related death, but that's about it." I checked my map again and told him to turn right at the next intersection.

Ten minutes later, we arrived at a lakeshore cabin where the lights were on. Two sheriff's department cars and the advanced life support ambulance from Traverse City were in the driveway, as well as what were probably the resident vehicles.

"I'll stay here," Zach concluded. "Looks crowded."

I nodded and took a microcassette tape recorder out of the center console and checked the battery, and grabbed an extra tape. "Unless you know shorthand?" I grinned. "You could be my secretary, and later you could..."

He rolled his eyes and reclined the seat slightly, dismissing me into the darkness with a smile he couldn't quite hide.

I slung my MEI jacket around my shoulders, fighting to keep it there as I approached the house. Sure enough, ten feet away, one of the deputies came to intercept me.

I actually had to dig out my ID for him, then I pointed to my vehicle, which was more recognizable than I was.

He looked me up and down once more, still questioning my identity and then my abilities to function, I suppose. Or maybe I still didn't look much better than the dead.

"I had a little scuffle in Florida," I said, trying to dismiss the subject as we walked on toward the house together.

"Gee, I'd hate to see the other guy, then," he quipped.

"Yeah, he didn't look much better," I mumbled. "So what's the story?"

CHAPTER

22

"No idea. Just here waiting for you," he sighed.

"Do you have names for the victim and family?"

He identified the deceased as Marvin Scott, his grandson as Chris Brandt.

When he held the screen door open for me, I entered a small rustic cabin with sparse furnishings.

Smelled like cooked fish.

Two paramedics stood to the right, talking to the other deputy. Nodding a silent greeting, I continued over to the young man who sat alone on a sofa staring down at the body on the floor.

"I'm Julie Madigan from the medical examiner's office in Traverse City," I said, thinking how odd it felt to say those words after the last few weeks away. "You're Chris?"

His head barely bobbed without looking up at me.

"My job is to help find out the cause of your grandfather's death. I have a few questions, and maybe you have some as well. Do you have any other family or friends we can call for you?"

"No, I called my mom already and told her. She's in Ohio." He raised his head. "I don't know what I can tell you. I don't know anything about medicine."

"I understand, Chris. But if I come up with the right questions, answering won't be hard. It's mostly memory. I'll talk to the paramedics about the medical part. You think about what your grandfather had been doing recently, and something you can answer might be helpful. Things like whether he'd mentioned not feeling well, changes in how he was getting around, that sort of thing."

He nodded again.

I went to the huddle, got a myriad of surprised looks about my appearance, and made another vague excuse.

One of the medics, Todd Holden, explained they'd been called for what sounded like a stroke – poor coordination, difficulty speaking. When the Torch Lake volunteers arrived, the patient was in respiratory arrest with the grandson doing mouth-to-mouth. As they began manually ventilating the patient, he went into cardiac arrest. When the paramedics got to the scene ten minutes later, the patient had a cardiac rhythm but no pulse, all of which presented a mixed picture.

I scanned Todd's not-yet-complete run report for the particulars he had written already.

"I'm not trying to second guess," I said, "but why not transport if he had a witnessed arrest?"

He frowned at the second-guessing that it sounded like.

"Really, just curious."

"He was in pulseless electrical activity, a junctional rate of about 45 when we started, then he went straight into asystole," he said, showing me the EKG strip that suddenly to an electrical flatline. "We paced him without capture; we gave him fluid and drugs for almost half an hour with absolutely no response. Medical Control called it."

"Works for me." I looked at his report again.

Skin – Hot and pale.

"You think he was running a fever?" I asked.

"Felt like it to me when I intubated him," Mitch Seaver concurred. "I definitely expected cool and clammy after looking at him."

"Ugh, this makes me think meningitis, guys. Give the ME's office a call in the morning before you go home, noon at the latest. Dr. Katz will let you know if you need antibiotics."

I excused myself to return to Chris.

For the next 15 minutes, I quizzed him about his grandfather's health history, recent travels, hobbies and so on. What I came away with was that Mr. Scott had been a pretty healthy 68-year-old who lived in Charlevoix but spent a good deal of his time at this cabin fishing since he retired.

Chris graduated from Michigan State University in June. He had come here three weeks ago to spend time with his grandfather before leaving for boot camp. They hadn't been anywhere but the boat since they'd arrived seventeen days previous, with their food and bait with them.

While the meningitis incubation period can range from three to ten days, there are hundreds of bacterial and viral sources that do not require other humans to be communicable.

My recent lesson about *Naegleria fowleri* was an example of how a common single cell amoeba could fatally wreck the central nervous system in short order. The microbes that cause meningitis could be as damaging.

However, chances were high that both men would have been infected if the meningitis had come from a common source such as contaminated food or water.

"Had he injured himself in any way, even slightly since you arrived? Bumped his head on a cabinet, cut himself while cleaning fish?"

"No, I don't think so," he said, thinking. "No, he complained about nicking himself shaving the first few days after we got to the cabin, during the first week," Chris told me. "It bothered him for a couple of days."

"On his face or neck?" I asked.

"Kinda below his earlobe," he said, pointing to his own jaw. "It was tiny, but he said it hurt. It bled a couple of mornings after he shaved, I remember."

"Did he complain about not feeling well after that?"

"He had a sore throat this last week. I hoped it wasn't anything I'd catch. I hate being sick. I noticed he took aspirin a couple of times, but not the last few days. Today, he was energetic until about dinnertime, then he looked exhausted," Chris explained. "He went to bed early tonight, about nine, after I'd beat him playing dominoes three straight games, which has never happened before." His eyes left me and focused again on the body under the sheet a few feet away.

"Then what happened?" I asked quietly.

"I didn't go to bed for another hour or so. Later, I was still reading when I heard him get up to go to the bathroom, which was normal for him, but then I heard him fall."

"And how was he when you got to him? Did he recognize you? Could he say words that made sense?"

"He said my name, but the rest sounded like gibberish. My cell phone was dead, so I had to stay connected to the car charger to call 911. When they finally let me hang up, he wasn't breathing. I took CPR training, so I knew what to do, but..." he trailed off.

I touched his arm. "Chris, in many cases, mouth-to-mouth and chest compressions don't fix the problem. They teach it because it does work once in a while in the right circumstances."

He nodded, but he continued to stare at the white sheet in front of him.

"I know that what paramedics do can look brutal. I'd be happy to explain any of the things they did, if you have questions, as well as to the procedure for an autopsy."

He looked up in horror. "You can't cut him up!"

"Chris, people do not want an autopsy performed on their loved ones – I hear that a lot. But your grandfather died suddenly of something that follows no clear medical logic. He had no known heart problems, you said, but his heart rhythm was disrupted. He had neurological symptoms of a stroke, yet other symptoms suggesting internal bleeding or shock. The slight illness in the last few weeks could suggest an infection, which needs to be identified so you and the others who took care of him tonight can be treated, if necessary."

"I don't know," he said.

"Actually, it's a legal requirement, Chris, but I want you to understand its importance." I managed to suppress a yawn triggered by one of the deputies. "I'd like to take a look at your grandfather. You're welcome to stay or not. I'm not going to do anything but a brief external exam."

He nodded again.

The medics had covered the body with a sheet, including his face, so I revealed the head with an endotracheal tube protruding from the mouth. His eyes were slightly open, and the surfaces were already drying.

"Do you remember which side of his face he cut, Chris?" I asked.

133

"His left."

I knew I wouldn't be able to lean close enough to get a good look at the area, and the lighting was terrible. I pulled the sheet on down to his waist so I could look at his chest. Large reddish-purple bruises were visible on the mid-sternum from chest compressions. There were large adhesive pads on his upper right chest and lateral left chest – combination defibrillator and external cardiac pacemaker electrodes – as well as small EKG connections. He had an IV in his right arm near the elbow with significant bruising around the insertion site. I dictated all these findings on my tiny recorder, then paused it.

"Hey, Todd, did you guys draw bloods when you started the IV?" I asked as they were getting ready to leave.

"Sure – a red top and purple top."

Red top vacuum tubes do not have an anticoagulant so the blood cells will clot in the tube to be separated from the plasma for chemistry testing. Lavender-stopper tubes use an anticoagulant to prevent clotting so cells can be analyzed in a complete blood count.

"Can I see them?"

"You can have them." Todd opened his kit and pulled out a sealed biohazard specimen bag with the two tubes inside and handed it to me. "I'd just drop them in the sharps box."

I held them up to the light and tilted them several times. The blood in the red tube had not begun to congeal. It should have been sluggish by now at least.

Looking more closely at the body, I saw other dark splotches on his arms where the tourniquet had been and on the lateral ribs from where he'd fallen, I surmised.

"Could you go on and tag it for me, estimate time of the draw?"

"You bet," Todd said, taking the bag and getting a pen from his shirt pocket to write down the specifics of the blood for identification. He sat down on the edge of a chair and scooted his boots up to use his thigh for a writing platform.

Something squeaked.

"What the…" he said, moving his feet away.

Under the chair, I saw what I'd once heard described as a mouse with wings – a bat flopped and squealed again.

"Close the door!" I yelled to the deputy who had intended to leave. "We can't let it out."

"Oh, there's bats in here pretty often," Chris said. "We leave a window open so they'll fly out."

"We need to catch this one," I said. "Bats are probably the most common carriers of rabies, which could explain everything, unfortunately."

CHAPTER

23

"Rabies?" a groan went around the room.

"It's the second of December, for crying out loud. What's a bat doing out now anyway?" Todd pondered aloud for us all.

With heavy leather gloves, Mitch used a large pickle jaw to catch it. "It was probably still in the house because it was too sick to fly," he explained for my benefit, mostly.

"Okay, gentlemen. Everyone goes to the emergency room now," I said, struggling to get to my feet. "That includes you, too, Chris. Most especially you. It's possible that what your grandfather thought was a shaving cut was a bite."

"No, really," he tried to argue. "There've always been bats in and out of the cabin. He left them alone because they eat tons of mosquitoes and stuff. When I was a kid, we used to catch them –"

I shook my head. "I understand, but this is not negotiable," I said. "We all go. We'll let the doctors figure out who gets immunized. Mitch, get him a mask. We need to call the volunteers from Torch Lake, too."

Chris' mouth-to-mouth would be enough to infect him. If he'd been exposed several days ago, he might now be contagious.

Rabies, once the symptoms progress to a certain point of neurological symptoms, is always fatal. It's only survivable with early treatment, and as such, any sort of exposure needs to be evaluated and treated without delay.

I walked out to my Suburban, where Zach reclined behind the steering wheel with the window cracked. I knocked on it, stepping back to more than an arm's length away.

"Hey, Gorgeous," he said, sitting the seat up and rolling down the window. "Can I take you home?"

That's an improvement over, "Your place or mine, baby."

"Sorry, as inviting as it sounds, I have to go to the hospital with this crew." I didn't come any closer.

"Why?" He frowned.

"Well, everyone who's been to this house tonight gets to go to the emergency room for evaluation," I said, "including me. You might as well go home and get some sleep. We'll be there for a while, I'm afraid."

"You're not riding with me?" he said.

I shook my head. "Not unless you'd like to be evaluated for rabies vaccine shots with the rest of us."

With a smile, he rolled the electric window shut and waved through the glass.

"Chicken."

He nodded.

◆

I finally called Zach to come get me at a quarter to nine. The emergency room had been chaotic. I was exhausted and my back hurt, but Zach sounded disgustingly awake and cheerful.

I'd made my argument about the bat and suspected rabies with Dr. Channing, who was on duty in the emergency department. Sometime after 4 a.m., Dr. Katz stopped by on his way home after being at a three-car multiple-fatality collision. I'd spent close to an hour on the phone with the CDC specialist at the rabies lab. Putting the patient's history in context with a possible bat exposure was significant enough to start Chris on the immune globulin plus the vaccine, which would be repeated on days 3, 7, 14 and 28, if the tests for his grandfather and/or the bat were positive for rabies.

Dr. Channing agreed with the CDC that Mitch, who had managed the patient's airway and would have been near airborne particles during the endotracheal intubation and ventilation, should get both injections immediately as well. The rest of us would be best served by an injection of the immune globulin and awaiting the test results. The group numbered ten. Part of the issue was the availability of the vaccine. There wasn't enough for all of us.

I stopped by the room where Mitch and Todd were awaiting clearance to leave, their shift over by a couple of hours now.

"Do you really think he died of rabies, Julie?" Todd asked.

"If I'd mentioned any other disease, would you go along with my hunch and take the shots?" I asked.

They both nodded.

"Then cross your fingers and hope I'm wrong. I'm okay with that."

I was almost out the door when I bumped into Rory Stewart, one of the deputies from the day shift.

"You think they ought to let you out of here in your condition?" he asked, and maybe even meant it sincerely.

Yeah, right.

"I think I'll survive, Rory, but thanks." I didn't offer him any explanation.

I walked out into a drizzle and found Zach in the ED patient parking lot with the stereo up, playing Meatloaf, drumming his fingers on the steering wheel and singing "You Took the Words Right Out of My Mouth."

He looked a little sheepish when he realized I'd seen and heard what he was doing through the rainy windows. He turned the music down before he got out to help me in and close my door.

"Let's see 'em," he said, climbing into the driver's seat.

"See what?" I said, confused.

"Yer' dog tags. You always get a tag when your pet gets its rabies shots."

CHAPTER

24

When we got home, I called the airlines and scouted tickets for a flight to Albuquerque and booked two first class open-ended tickets for Wednesday. Then I called Dr. Charles Caldwell's office for an appointment, and the receptionist put me down the following Monday. I tried to convince her to schedule me for an arthroscopy as well, but she argued, "The doctor will want to see you first."

I rolled my eyes and hung up without arguing. I knew Dr. Caldwell would want to look inside for damage he could fix. Half an hour later, he called back.

"So what have you done to my magnificent work, Julie? Donna says you wanted me to schedule a 'scope?"

"I had it forcefully dislocated by a drug dealer several days ago in Florida,"

"Crap," he said, sounding like he took it personally that I got hurt. "You're back into law enforcement?"

"Not exactly. It's really a long story." I'd have to tell him, but I knew he wouldn't like it. "I'm home in Michigan, but I wouldn't dream of letting anyone else fix me. When can you work me in?"

"Can you make the nine o'clock appointment on Friday? I'll 'scope you then here in the office."

"Perfect. See you then."

I hung up and went to the backyard to find Zach rocking in the hammock in a cold drizzle.

"We're all set. Tickets, appointment, surgery."

"Already?" He offered to make room for me, but there wasn't

really enough left.

"No sense in having to wait. I knew he'd want to do an arthroscopy and fix it." I looked up at gray skies. "You're getting wet."

"I don't think I'll shrink."

I laughed.

"Someone's at the front door," he said, though I hadn't heard the doorbell.

I hurried through the house to the door and opened it to find Sheriff Lomas and Laser, Matthew's police dog.

"Frank," I said, hugging him. "How nice to see you two. Come in, please." I bent down and rubbed Laser's ears. "Hey, Buddy. Are you working hard these days? I bet I have a chewy for you somewhere." I scratched the spot under his chin that would have made him purr if he were feline.

Zach came into sight from the kitchen, and Laser's attention turned to him.

"Frank, this is Zach Samualson," I said, introducing the humans. "Sheriff Frank Lomas."

They stepped toward each other and shook hands.

"Zach, this is Laser, Matt's partner," I said. "Sit."

Zach squatted down to meet the dog, who also sat. Laser sniffed Zach's hand but seemed otherwise unimpressed.

"They both follow commands pretty well," Frank observed with a chuckle. "Which is sorta why we're here today."

"Come on to the den," I said. "Can I get you something to drink?"

"No thanks. I'm fine, really. Thanks."

In the kitchen, I dug under the sink for a plastic bag of rawhide chews while Laser sat patiently behind me, tail thumping on the refrigerator almost hard enough to leave dents.

When I found the bag, I hesitated. No one had thrown them away during the clean-outs of my house. Could Bock have been contaminated these? None of the food and sundries removed by the crime scene techs had been poisoned.

I refused to give in to more fear, handing the dog his treat.

We joined the men in the den.

"I know you've been through hell with this whole thing," the sheriff started, scrutinizing the shoulder immobilizer and the bruises, but not asking. "You'll never know how much it meant to me what you did to help."

"Frank, it was nothing any of your guys wouldn't have –"

He held up his hand to stop me. "You were special to Matt, and as much as it hurt you, I'm glad you were with him those last hours. I know in my heart he was, too. I'm at peace with that, and I hope you will be some day. But I'm here about Laser," he paused.

The dog raised his head when he heard his name, checked around the room for someone to speak to him, then went back to his chewy.

"We've put him with several deputies, but nothing's worked out. The guys took a vote and wanted me to ask you to adopt Laser in retirement."

I looked at Frank, then at the dog, who seemed to offer his sad expression to the plea.

"Sheriff, I don't . . . I mean, I just . . ." I stammered. I was flattered. Flipped out, but flattered. "He's a good dog. Can't you find someone who can work him?"

"He's six. The trainers tell me he wouldn't make a good transition to someone else at this age. We'd retire him in a year anyway."

"Well, I don't know, I . . . uh, oh wow . . ." I looked at Zach, who only offered a smile of support.

Without cue, the dog got up from his corner and came to put his head on my lap.

"Poor Laser, I bet you miss Matt a lot, don't you? Me, too." My eyes filled with tears as I cradled the dog's head. I turned to the sheriff and nodded. "How can I say no?"

"That's terrific, Julie. He'll be happier with you than with anyone else. He has a retirement fund, and coverage for vet bills and stuff. I'll put you in contact with the trainer so you can get all the details."

Frank asked Zach to help him get Laser's gear from the car. When they finished, Frank gave me a large envelope of paperwork for the dog, and another note.

"I told you once this was over, I was going to retire. Here's my address and number in Galveston. I'll be there a couple of weeks after

New Year's, but I'm going to California to see my brother for a bit first," Frank said. "I'd be tickled if you'd drop me a note once in a while to say hello and let me know how you are."

"Things won't be the same here without you," I said, hugging him again. "I'll miss you."

The whole county would miss him.

I waved as he drove away, then went inside.

"I guess it's a good thing you didn't bite Zach when I introduced you," I said to the dog.

"Yeah, that coulda been awkward," Zach said. "We'd have to have a big alpha male challenge. Growling and fur flying. But I bet we can share her without any biting or snarling if you remember one rule – three's a crowd in bed. Fair enough?"

Laser came over to where I sat in the kitchen chair and turned to Zach. The look was pretty clearly one of possession.

"You just take care of her," Zach told the dog. "We're cool."

CHAPTER
25

Rabies testing gets high priority with any lab, and I got a call from Dr. Katz about Mr. Scott and the rabies results later that afternoon. Unfortunately, the bat and Mr. Scott both tested positive for rabies, but it wasn't the same genetic strain – different bat or other source of exposure, one possibility was his recent corneal transplant, which his grandson had not mentioned.

The health department had recommended the first responders to the scene – deputies, firefighters, EMTs and paramedics – all take the full series of vaccine. The consensus was that I could make a choice based on my own exposure possibilities, since the patient was dead when I arrived.

I declined.

"Why don't you and Zach come over to the house tonight for pizza?" Dr. Katz asked. "I promise to warn MaryAnne about your current state of black and blue."

Pizza sounded like a good family invitation, so I accepted.

Although it was not necessary, we took Laser to the pet store. By six o'clock, we'd bought all remaining big dog toys not already in his collection with time to spare before dinner, so Zach drove us to a beach park on the Old Mission Peninsula.

"It's time we took that walk on the beach together for real," he said, putting my Suburban in park. "I'll try not to get shot this time."

I couldn't help rolling my eyes. "How very thoughtful of you. I wouldn't want to be late for dinner."

We strolled down the shore, hand in hand, dog on a leash.

"Let's go to Hawaii instead of New Zealand," he suggested. "I don't want to mess with my passport. We can get a hotel with room service, find a quiet beach. You know, a *warm* beach."

"Pffft! It's nearly 40 degrees out here," I said in defense of our current location. There'd already been spits of snow, but nothing that stuck. "Still, I think I could relax and drink Mai' Tai's all day."

"You could work on your tan, too," Zach teased. "Not much call for one here."

After our walk, we went to the truck and drove northward on the peninsula.

Zach pulled into the Katz's driveway just as the delivery car was leaving.

"Perfect timing," we said together, laughing.

I went to the door behind Zach and Laser. Zach rang the bell, and I could hear Kim bounding through the house, yelling she'd get it.

She yanked the front door open to find Zach standing there, dog leash in hand.

I recognized the terror in her eyes as she slammed the door and screamed.

"Oh, crap," I said, realizing what had just happened. "Would you put the dog back in the truck?"

Clueless about the reception, Zach did that while I knocked quietly. Behind the wooden door, the household had gone to complete panic.

Gerald let me in, and I asked if I could go talk with Kim. He gave me a helpless nod.

"Zach will be back in a minute," I said. I walked down the hallway to Kim's bedroom, but I found her in Kayleigh's room instead, hunkered down behind the twin bed.

"Kim, it's Julie. I'm alone. Can I sit with you?" I asked from the hall.

She was crying, but she wiped her face on her sleeve and said yes.

"Hey," I said, sitting down beside her on the floor and waited for her to regain her composure. "That pretty much took you by surprise, huh?"

"It's like, I knew it was your truck, but when I opened the door and saw that man and the dog, I freaked out and I couldn't help it."

"That's my fault. You haven't met Zach. I'm so sorry."

"I guess I was expecting to see the other guy," she explained. "I mean, I know Jeremy was, you know, killed. I'm so embarrassed. I don't know why I did that."

"No need to be embarrassed, Kim. That was a perfectly normal reaction for someone who has been through such a bizarre situation."

"That was normal?" she asked in a more normal teenage response, sniffling.

I handed her a tissue from a box nearby. "Absolutely. Your mind saw details – a strange face, a large dog – things connected to a real threat in your recent memory. The warning system works much like the muscle contractions when your knee jerks are tested. You have no conscious control over it."

"You mean I'll always be like this?"

"No, your brain will learn new associations, like that not all dogs are dangerous, for example. The reactions will calm down," I explained.

"Thanks," she said, leaning on my left shoulder. "That's good to know."

"Finding out that what you feel is normal – regardless how bizarre it might seem – is sometimes enough to get you through," I said. "How are things with you and your mom?"

"We've had our days, but we're better."

I put my arm around her. "Sometimes the best you can hope for out of something bad is to be closer to those you love."

"So what's with the hair and black eye and sling?" she asked.

"It's all a very long story, but," I said, leaning closer to whisper an almost-truth. "I got my ass whipped in a fight in Florida when I went down to see Zach."

"The Incredible Hulk at the door, right? Did he come rescue you?"

"Yes, he did. He's an excellent knight in shining armor. You ready to meet him now?"

Nodding, she blew her nose. "Is he really as big as I thought, or did I imagine it?"

"Oh, he's a big guy, all right," I said, thinking how he towered almost nine inches over me. "But he has the tenderest heart."

"What about the dog?" she asked.

I explained that Laser had been Deputy Shannaker's K-9 partner, and the sheriff had asked if I'd retire him.

"You mean they let you have him after what you did to –" She slapped her hand over her mouth, as if she had almost said something wrong.

"Yes, even after what I did to Matthew," I finished her sentence. "It's okay to talk about what happened. I did what you saw me do."

Her eyes squinted in an anger she tried to hide.

Having gone with her to the first session with her therapist, I suspected she wasn't mad at me for killing Matthew, or even at Bock for making her watch me do it. She hated the fact that I picked up the knife to take Matt's life in hopes of saving her.

I remained silent, waiting for her to work through the feelings, understanding completely how they rocketed from one extreme to the other.

Maybe she gave up trying to reconcile how she felt about what I'd done with me sitting there with her, but I couldn't blame her, no matter how she felt.

"Kim, it's okay to be mad. Even at me."

She nodded, but didn't move for a moment. "We can't hide in here all evening," she finally said, getting up and offering me a hand to help me to my feet. "Thanks."

One word from her seemed to be enough, no matter what it covered.

Joining the family, I made introductions.

"Kim, I'd like you to meet Zach Samualson. Z', this is Miss Kimberly Katz," I said, letting them shake hands, "and Miss Kayleigh Katz."

Being small for her age, Kayleigh giggled when Zach had to bend down to take her hand.

"Looks like you've met MaryAnne," I finished.

MaryAnne was pale but chipper as always. Gerald hustled glasses and bottles of pop around for us as we found places at the table, and the pizza was served.

Kayleigh started and then Kim join in with all sorts of questions for Zach about the places he'd been with the Drug Enforcement Agency and what it was like to work undercover. He gave his best public education answers instead of his worst-case-scenario stories.

Pride filled my heart as he talked to them.

I downplayed the whole injury thing as having crossed paths with one of the suspects in Zach's case.

When MaryAnne got up to go into the kitchen, I followed her.

"What was that about?" she asked, referring to Kim. "I thought she was doing so well with the psychologist."

"That was her first interaction with both a stranger and dog, so her body reacted to the danger whether it was real in a particular context or not," I tried to explain.

"She's had several episodes I thought were over the top, but nothing like that," MaryAnne said. "I don't know what I'm supposed to do."

"It's normal, and like I told her, it will get better. What about you?"

"I'll get better, too." She smiled a genuine MaryAnne smile.

I hugged her. "I wish I'd been here for you more," I apologized. "You were never too far away, Julie. I appreciate the phone calls," she said, her voice dropping. "When you two were held captive was the longest night of my life, but the best thing you could ever have done is giving us back our daughter."

CHAPTER
26

After our breakfast Wednesday, Zach loaded the suitcases for our trip to New Mexico. The dog's goodies took up a case of their own. I had two bags, Zach just one.

Laser's documents were in order, but we decided if anyone questioned us, Zach would deal with it. Having a DEA badge could be useful, and the dog was a police dog.

The connection in Chicago and flights were uneventful despite the bruises, and before five o'clock, we were in Albuquerque.

When Zach went to rent a vehicle, I worried all the stuff wouldn't fit into a Mustang, but he returned with a Jeep Grand Cherokee. Somehow though, he still managed fire-engine red.

Once he got everything loaded and I had a quick walk with Laser, he called his mother at work so she could meet us at my mother's house, then we could all go to dinner.

Half an hour later, we pulled into Mom's driveway.

She opened her front door to find three wayward-looking souls, one her only child who looked like she'd been hit by a truck. Again. The woman let loose several phrases in German that would have made Zach cringe if I'd translated.

You'd think she'd be used to this by now.

I took the evasive way out, promising to explain later.

Mom accepted that without the further inquisition I expected. She was delighted to see us, even the dog, and she hurried us into the house to freshen up before Vera arrived. "Flying takes so much out of you," she said, hugging me again. "I'll fix Thanksgiving dinner on

Sunday if your mother can make it," she called to Zach.

"That would be very nice, Dagmar," Zach replied, dragging my bags down the hallway to my old room without direction.

I smiled, knowing he'd been there before.

"Sunday would be fine. Dr. Caldwell is going to 'scope my shoulder on Friday," I said, breaking more bad news.

"For what? He hasn't even seen you!" she exclaimed. "What on earth happened, Julie? You canceled Thanksgiving plans because of a case, and now you show up looking like this?"

"Mom, please. You have to understand that I can't talk about some things I do."

Zach passed by us, headed to the kitchen.

She put her hands on her hips, unsatisfied with my answer. "You said it was about getting a child back to a mother. At least tell me whether you did that."

I looked over her shoulder at Zach, running water into Laser's dish.

"Yeah, Mom. We brought a boy safely home to his mother. That's what matters."

Zach's head turned when he realized I was talking about him, and he blushed.

Mom hurried off again, putting out towels and clean sheets, as if what was in use throughout the house wasn't pristine.

He finally came over to me and kissed my cheek. "Is that what you told her you were doing when you went to Florida?"

I nodded. "I couldn't have her telling *your* mother the truth, could I?"

"Very wise. Have I told you today how much I love you?" He wrapped his arms around me carefully.

Vera Samualson arrived a few minutes later, but the mother-and-son reunion was different. She had no immediate questions, didn't chastise him for not coming home more often. She just hugged him for a very long time.

Greetings accomplished all around, we left for dinner.

Over the sort of Mexican food I desperately missed in Michigan, we tried to catch up our mothers without sending either into a panic over the risks we'd taken or the dangers we'd faced.

Zach explained in truthful but incomplete details that he left Michigan to go back to Florida to finish the case, eventually discovering Pauly was the one working with a couple of St. Pete police officers to produce and control the methamphetamine distribution.

"I ended up in a mess and then I got hurt," he said, turning to my mother. "What Julie told you about bringing a mother's child home is true, Dagmar, but that boy was me. She came to Florida and saved my life."

My mother opened her mouth to ask more questions, but I stopped her with a look.

He'd left out the parts about Caleb Osborne being killed, and about me getting hacked up by one of the bikers, who died when Zach threw him halfway out a window. Topics we'd likely never share with anyone else.

Vera simply wanted to know if we were both okay, despite the obvious.

"I think we'll be fine," he said, sliding his arm around my shoulders. "We're together."

◆

The next day after my mother left for work, Zach and I drove out to the ranch west of Albuquerque so I could see Mom's new horse.

"At least you're not driving me out here against my will this time," I commented as he turned off the freeway.

Zach cleared his throat for effect. "First of all, I didn't drive last time, Dom did. Second, I don't recall you voicing an objection."

"Semantics. What option did I have when opposed by three men?"

He pulled onto his mother's property, past the house down to the barn, the SUV easily clearing center of the two-track road. When he parked, he came around and offered me a hand.

I hopped out, taking a deep breath, and looked at the landscape as we walked. "I sorta miss this wide-open horizon."

"Maybe, but I don't ever miss the heat or the damned wind," Zach mumbled pulling open the barn door. "God-forsaken desert."

His grouching made me smile.

I felt the same way about the New Mexico climate, but I liked the landscape. Even around Lake Michigan in the winter, I enjoyed the trees and hills, though the snow tended to make me cranky after six nonstop months or more. Sometimes the summer influx of people made me claustrophobic. Here though, I had to agree, I hated the hot, dry wind.

I followed Zach inside the barn where dust floated in beams of sunlight, and the smell of alfalfa was sweet.

He scooped up half a bucket of oats and dumped a handful into three side-by-side stalls, then stuck his head out the back door and whistled so loudly the birds in the hayloft screeched in alarm and fluttered.

Three horses came trotting into the corral from the pasture, stopped for a drink at the side of the barn, then meandered into their respective stalls.

"That's Shalisha," Zach said, pointing to a black and white paint mare who led the way, "and the bay gelding is Kalomar Tango. He's Dagmar's."

"And she made fun of Domino's name," I miffed.

Zach ignored me, watching the last one with a dainty walk. "And this is the Friesian mare I bought. She's in foal."

"Wow. She's magnificent."

Glossy black, delicate looking but not small. Long flowing mane and tail.

"Isn't she?" he said with a lopsided smile, leaning on the gate, watching her. "Her name is Julaquinte."

"What's it mean?" I asked.

"According to the breeder, it's an archaic musical term regarding a flute tone that apparently doesn't exist in modern music. His wife is a musician, so she named one bloodline in odd musical terms."

"This is all?" I asked, indicating the horses.

"No, Purgatory's in the south pasture."

"Purgatory?"

"As in Not-Quite-Hell. He's a champion cutting horse, but he doesn't play well with others anymore. He's mine, too."

"Now why wouldn't I know you ride?" I asked out loud.

151

"Same reason I don't know if you do, I guess," he said, turning to me and teasing his fingers through my hair. "We're still practically strangers out of bed. I know how to turn you on six ways to Sunday, but after chasing you across the country the last four years, I've never even heard your middle name."

I smiled. "Ann." I extended my left hand to him to shake. "Julie Ann Madigan, nice to meet you."

He took my hand and bowed. "Zachary Namakaeha Samualson. My pleasure."

"Nama. . . ka. . .?" My tongue got stuck. Too many vowels. Too much German in my blood.

"What? You think I get this complexion from south of the border?" he laughed. "My father was half-Hawaiian."

"I'd never given it much thought, but it's no wonder Zoe called you Cubby." I shook my head. "What a horrible thing to teach a kid to spell."

"Trust me, once the teachers saw it, my middle name disappeared."

"What does it mean?"

"You won't believe me."

"Probably not," I granted.

"It means 'all-knowing eyes.' It was my grandmother's maternal family name."

"Yeah? Why wouldn't I believe that? You always seemed to see into my soul," I said, thinking it was probably truer than he realized.

"I'm looking forward to getting to know you. The regular daylight, everyday Julie. I want to know everything."

"That goes both ways, but all you have to do is ask."

"Okay. What's your favorite album?" he began.

"Fleetwood Mac – *Rumours.* Who was your first best friend when you were a kid?"

"Zoe," he said, which only slightly surprised me. "What was the first song you ever danced to?"

"'Come Sail Away' by Styx. How old were you when you learned to ride a bicycle?"

"I was five when I found a wrench and took off my training wheels. Why did you buy a motorcycle?"

"Because I didn't need training wheels when I was 27."

He raised an eyebrow over my answer but kept going. "What was your final GPA in high school?"

"High school? I think it was something like 3.4," I said. "I wasn't trying very hard. What was your last range qualification score?"

"You first."

"No, you don't get away with blatant evasion."

"Okay, 234 on a 240-shot course. I'm rescinding the question. My ego couldn't take being bested," he grinned.

"If you don't ask, you'll never know," I kidded.

"I'll take you to the range someday, and we'll see."

"That's fair. Where were you when the Murrah Building was bombed in April?" I asked. I'd been worried about him.

Zach hung his head. "Here in Albuquerque. We were devastated, not knowing how many agents DEA lost in the building at first. There were five, among so many others. Images of that building still nauseate me."

I nodded. Like most other Americans, eight months later, the names McVeigh and Nichols still evoked a feeling something like evisceration, but I was sure astounding stories of quiet heroism would trickle from Oklahoma City for years to come.

Dismissing the subject, he opened the Dutch door to Julaquinte's stall.

The black mare came to nuzzle his arm, still chomping a mouthful of grain. "The first time I saw her, she came and sniffed me like this, reared up and whinnied, then made two galloping laps around the paddock. The trainer looked at me and said, 'She likes you.' I knew as soon as they told me her name, I had to buy her."

"Why?" I asked, not understanding.

"Because she reminds me of you. Free-spirited, wind blowing in your hair." He rubbed her neck. "I bought her *for* you."

"For me?" I said, stunned.

He only nodded.

I held out my hand. The mare turned to sniff it, and then swung her head back to Zach.

"Yeah, I'd rather cuddle with him, too, I guess."

We watched a little while, then walked hand in hand to the Jeep.

153

He opened the door.

"Zach, why would you buy a horse for a woman who lives 1800 miles away when you didn't know if she rides, and when she's never previously made any sort of commitment to you? I don't get it." I slid into the SUV.

He closed the door for me and went around. Inside, he hesitated, then looked at me. "Julie, I don't think I can make you understand what knowing you has done to me. Sometimes you talk about me like I saved your soul, like you need me. Don't you ever think maybe I need you just as much?"

Surprised, I shook my head.

"You said the night I brought you here that you didn't want anyone to love you," he continued, "but you needed someone to want you. You didn't want to feel it, but you let me love you anyway. I think maybe I loved you because you were the first person in a long time who didn't try to conquer me."

"I don't understand."

"Look at me. I passed six feet in junior high, was almost this big by the time I was a sophomore in high school, and you know what? I realized people were lining up to either fight or fuck." He said this with apology in his voice but continued. "My junior English teacher propositioned me. No one gave me a choice whether or not to play football, and when I did, opponents tried to take me out of the game every Friday night. I was hounded by military recruiters and college coaches, and when I took it, the scholarship was only a financial means to an education. When I got a badge, I realized nothing had changed. Everyone still wanted a piece of me, one way or another. Being a cop made it easy – too easy. I hated it."

"You must have broken a lot of hearts," I kidded.

He shook his head. "If you ever woke up in a strange bed with someone whose name or face you didn't remember, you'd understand I wasn't breaking hearts – I was just getting laid," he said. "After the first time I saw you, all grown up, in the hospital, I decided I was tired of waking up lonely, even when I wasn't alone. I knew in my soul that you were the one person I wanted to love. I didn't ask why, and I didn't know how, but I always believed that someday we'd be together."

Stunned, I turned and looked to the east toward the Sandia Mountains to the east of Albuquerque, already turning pinkish in the late afternoon winter sun.

"You could have anyone, Zach. Why would you want someone who's so –" My question ended abruptly with his hand over my mouth.

"If you describe yourself as 'broken' or 'damaged' or 'fucked up' one more time, Madigan, I swear –" He tried to sound tough but failed. Instead, he sighed, caressed my cheek, then dropped his hand to my lap where he wrapped it around mine. "Stop evaluating your life by its catastrophes, Julie. You're still alive, and you're everything in the world to me. I don't want anyone else."

I shook my head. "Sometimes I'm overwhelmed by your faith in me. You talk about us like it's fate and you're the luckiest man alive."

"I am. One of the most perfect things about you," he said, "is that you've walked through the fire. Not just law enforcement, but real life. You know how thin the line is between living and dying. Regardless of the tragedies, you keep making the choice to live, no matter how much it hurts. You understand who I am because of where you've been."

I swallowed, thinking I didn't want to continue the conversation. This wasn't supposed to be about me, and I didn't want to talk about my past, but he continued.

"When I called you from the station in Florida that night, I didn't have to say a single word for you to know – not just to think maybe I'd had a bad day, but to *know* – everything had gone to hell. And you understood how to let me talk about it. Even when I couldn't say a word, you listened."

"But I –"

He leaned over and stopped me with a kiss.

"Why did you choose me?" he asked.

"I don't think I had a choice," I said with a grin. "You just kept showing up."

CHAPTER

27

Dr. Caldwell performed an arthroscopy on my shoulder and did a bit of tweaking, as Zach put it. And as I requested, the doctor also taught Zach how to remove sutures by practicing on my back while I was sedated, though the explanation of how I came to have so many was a trifle much for the doctor.

At four o'clock, the nurse poured me into a wheelchair and discharged me, though I was barely awake enough to get in the Jeep with help. Zach drove me to my mother's place to sleep off overnight what would be an hour's worth of sedatives for most people.

"He says you're due for an oil change in 3000 miles," Zach told me the next morning, presenting oatmeal for my breakfast in bed. He also explained the drugs and instructions. "And by the way, the exercise in suture removal wasn't in my itinerary yesterday. I suppose that was your idea?" he asked with a scowl.

I shrugged. "Well, we could wait here ten days for his nurse to take out the stitches in my shoulder," I said, "or you could learn how to do it so we could be on our way. It's not nuclear engineering, is it?"

Zach's grumbles faded in the hall as he went back to the kitchen for more butter, but he babied me all day, making me feel like a cross between a patient and a queen.

The next afternoon, we had our late but traditional Thanksgiving meal, complete with turkey and dressing, candied yams, green bean casserole – which was not my idea, but everyone else said it was good – and pumpkin pie. Zach and my mom cooked together all morning, leaving everyone happily miserable by sunset.

Our flight to Hawaii wasn't until Wednesday, so Zach and I went to the ranch Tuesday, not telling my mother we intended to ride.

Getting into the saddle without using my right arm was anything but elegant, but Zach more or less lifted me. I tucked my hand into my jacket to reduce jostling.

We rode to the northwest corner of the Samualson ranch, which was much larger than I imagined. Zach explained how it went from the Robertson family name to Vera's married name when she inherited the land from her parents. "Mom really didn't want the ranch, but she moved here after Zoe and I left for college. It always amazes me that she doesn't like the horses or tending cattle but stays, and your mother loves them but won't budge from the city."

"That is odd," I agreed. "No idea why. Maybe in town, she's not as impacted by the weather. Moving here from Seattle, I didn't like the dry winds. I'd much rather be damp and hot than blasted in a convection oven."

"I don't remember much about living in Texas when I was little, but I never liked this," Zach agreed. "The weather in Michigan isn't bad most of the time, except when I had to shovel out my car to leave."

"Maybe you should have stayed those nights," I suggested. I knew sometimes he couldn't stay longer, but I was never sure why he snuck out during the night other times. "I don't really mind the snow, and the summers are great. I just wish there weren't so many people."

As we rode, he pointed to where Purgatory had bucked him off after seeing a rattlesnake.

"Walking home wasn't so bad, but he didn't run off," Zach said. "He stayed just far enough away I couldn't catch him. He has some big fancy show name, but Purgatory's probably the nicest thing I called him that day."

I laughed because Zach so seldom used profanity, I couldn't imagine what his horse heard all the way to the barn.

"Mom wasn't into horses when I was young," I said. "I only rode because several of my friends had horses. A couple of them did dressage, which I thought was boring. Lisa barrel-raced, well enough to go pro after high school."

"Lisa Chamberlain?" he asked in surprise. "You hung around

with her? And I thought you were a goody-two-shoes."

"I was, though I'm not sure what makes you think so."

"Lisa sure wasn't," he replied.

"No, not even in high school," I agreed. "How'd you know her?"

"She hung around bars, roping cowboys," he said. "Or cops. I heard she preferred bronc riders."

"Ha! She meant any man who could go more than eight, though I was never sure if that was eight seconds or eight inches."

He laughed like that meant something to him, but when he began telling me about the last time he'd seen her, I suddenly didn't want to know if Zach had taken her to bed.

"Lisa hung around this one bar – flirting, dancing, drinking a lot. Dom and I both warned him, but she managed to get her spurs into Pauly one night. The next day, he looked like he'd caught a bobcat and didn't know enough to let go."

"Son of a bitch deserved it," I said under my breath.

Zach turned to me, his voice cold. "I won't defend what Pauly became, but when I believed he was straight, I trusted him with my back. I've known him since junior high. He helped get me into the DEA when I worked in Houston."

No matter how far back his roots stretched with Pauly, my stomach churned every time I thought about how he called Zach back to Florida to either prove his loyalty or die.

"Why did Nolan want us out of Florida?" I asked, trying to defuse my own feelings.

"This didn't start or end with Pauly," Zach said. "Going away while they clean house isn't a bad idea."

"Like no one would look for us at my house," I asked, "or here in Albuquerque?"

"Here, sure. Although I spent time with you in Michigan, I tried not to leave any trails."

"After I was arrested, Pauly would have known," I argued. "You are a federal agent with plenty of ways to find someone. So was he."

"All I can do now is my best to protect us both. If that means we have to leave the country for a while, we'll do it."

"I won't spend my life running," I said, then wished I could take the words back. They were an accusation I didn't mean. I wasn't angry at Zach, but what Brodenshot had done made me furious.

Zach spurred Kalomar ahead of me then turned to face me so we stopped side by side.

"You won't spend your life running, Julie. I promise. From what Dom told me, this ring involved a dozen cops. Ugly as it sounds, most of them won't live to see New Year's. Carlson took the bullet for a reason. But I don't think Pauly will do that."

"I'm sorry, Zach, that really wasn't what I wanted to say. What he did infuriates me."

"Understood. Do you believe I love you?" he asked, leaning over to grab my saddle horn.

I nodded.

"Then believe that whatever I have to do for us to be together and happy and safe, I'll do it, okay?"

♦

Finally on the way to Hawaii the next morning, we sat outside a coffee shop at the Albuquerque Sunport terminal, waiting for our connection to LAX.

A woman in a too-short leather skirt and slinky top sauntered by on clunky heels, an ugly fur thing draped over her shoulder.

I was disgusted, but there was no doubt Zach watched her sashay away.

"Hey, Cowboy, you're taken," I said.

"Umhmmm." He pretended to ignore me until I elbowed him in the ribs. "Ouch! I happen to know he's a drug mule, so I was curious where he's been."

"He?" *Ugly as a mule.*

"Rumor has it he was born that way. He's certainly not my type in either gender or wherever in between he might be these days. Strictly professional, I assure you."

"I see. Out of curiosity, if you were emotionally unattached, who is your type?" I asked. "Pick out someone here you might go talk to."

"This curiosity of yours could get me in trouble," he said, raising an eyebrow. He scanned the crowd and finally picked out a woman who looked about my age or maybe a little older. "Her. Healthy looking. No jewelry, no kids, no fuss. A sensible bag and shoes. She's casual and comfortable, but not dumpy or over-dressed. Very little makeup. Small hands."

"Small hands?" I repeated, knowing my own did not meet such criteria. Thumb to little fingertip, my hand spanned over nine inches.

"My dad's father once told me to find a woman with small hands so they don't make your –" He made a fake polite cough. "Make everything they touch look small."

"Could be you didn't inherit your 'everything' from his side of the family," I suggested, clearing my throat in the same way he had.

We boarded, to LAX, then on to Honolulu, and a third time before getting to Hawaii.

"Mahala," each of the flight attendants said as we stepped off the jet, "aloha!"

We were finally in Hilo, where the air was warm, the sun felt like a hug from a friend, and everyone smiled.

Rules for the rental car included not driving it on the roadway crossing the main portion of the island, and a warning that one should not drive on flowing lava.

Just in case one is an idiot.

Zach again surprised me by passing up his typical Mustang choice for a Jeep Wrangler with a soft top, which he had peeled back in no time. I didn't know if I'd like it, but the wind felt delightful in my short hair.

Driving in the sun made my muscles relax, enough so I could have closed my eyes and taken a nap. But from the muted browns of the Southwest to the vivid colors all around us on the island, I didn't want to miss a thing.

Zach's reservations had included a beachside hotel. We registered then walked to a nearby restaurant for dinner. Afterward, we detoured for a stroll on the beach.

A warm beach, Zach pointed out for me. "In case you missed that detail."

"Oh come on, there's not but thirty degrees' difference," I countered. "Maybe forty. You'll be sweating in no time with this heat."

We kicked off our shoes to feel the sand, and holding hands, we enjoyed the sunset from the water's edge before going to our room.

Considering the time change, we were ready for bed early. We cuddled together into a comfortable position.

"Are you glad to be here?" I asked.

"I am." He snuggled up a little closer as we listened to the waves crash outside our lanai door. "This is nice."

The silence went on a while until he spoke. "So who was the first guy you slept with?"

An answer that should have been as easy as one name came to mind, but I found it difficult to say aloud.

The need to reply was negated by a slow nod from behind me. "I didn't mean to pry."

"No, it was Jeremy, but I'd never thought about it like that," I said. "So who was your first?"

"Her name was Amy Donlon. She was Zoe's best friend through junior high and high school. We were juniors – I was almost seventeen," he paused. "Wasn't love or even attraction. Amy was angry and getting even with her boyfriend, the football team captain."

"Wow," I said. "That's pretty angry."

"It was the first time for both of us, but I can't say it went well."

I nodded.

"If you could change one event in your life, what would it be?" he asked.

"Oh, the what if's," I said, then yawned. "I'd find a way to keep Anthony from killing my father. I used to wish I'd stayed, even if I'd been killed, too, because living hurt so much. Seeing how it ended, I was lucky compared to the others whose lives Bock destroyed."

"That's the way I feel about Pauly," he said. "I still can't believe he killed Oz."

"Altering one event would change so much. Is that what you'd choose to change?"

"No, I'd undo what happened to Zoe, for my mom's sake," Zach said. "You watched your mom grieve for your father. I was a lot younger, but my mother probably went through the same things when my dad died. But there is something unique about losing a child. Different than losing a spouse or a parent. What my mother went though after Zoe was killed was totally different than when my dad died." He stopped speaking, but I could tell his mind still played memories of his sister and her death.

"Losing a child must be like drowning forever and never dying," I said. "But it couldn't have been much easier for you when your twin died."

He shrugged in the darkness.

"You weren't responsible for her murder, Zach."

I was almost asleep when I thought I heard him whisper, "Actually, I was."

CHAPTER
28

Hawaii makes its money when tourists do touristy things. We could have contributed to the economy by snorkeling or riding horseback, but we didn't. Still, we found something different to do each day. Although I liked the air tour by helicopter, Zach was more at home on the sunset dinner cruise. I was too self-conscious of the bruising still coloring my face to enjoy being around a crowd of people.

Thanks to a suggestion from a couple standing in line with us at the luau in Kona, we discovered a secluded beach. After we snorkeled a bit, Zach stretched out in the sun, but I kept walking, letting the water splash up to my knees. Occasionally a bigger wave tugged at the bottom of the gauzy red wrap I wore over my one-piece swimsuit.

I still couldn't peel away the clothes without thinking it over, even though I'd tanned enough in a few days to not look like I had spent years hiding in a cave or in snow-locked northern Michigan. But the beach was nearly empty, and I did consider removing the wrap.

I looked back and saw Zach, propped on his elbows on a mat, watching me.

He smiled.

The night before, with his arms around me like a child holding a teddy bear, we'd talked.

"Tell me what you dream," he'd asked softly, running his fingers through my hair. "You don't dream about monsters now, do you?"

I thought about it and squeezed his hand. "Not so much, no. I think I finally just sleep. I'm sure I dream, but I don't remember. The nightmares are fewer than before."

"I can tell." He kissed me. "I'm glad. I love to watch you sleep."

I still found it hard to believe he made me feel so completely safe when I hadn't felt that way in years.

"What made you fall in love with me so long ago?" I whispered.

"Tight blue jeans and long legs," he said, running his hand down my side to my hip.

I nudged him.

"How about your beautiful blue eyes? The way you laugh. The way you cry. The way you kissed me that first time," he said. "Tell me about your day."

"You've been with me. What's to tell?" I asked.

"I sent you off to the day spa today, didn't I? Tell me everything."

I could hear the sincerity of his words, but when he reached to caress my face, I felt his hand tremble. I kissed his fingers, wanting everything to be all right.

"Since I left for Florida, I've been waiting for you to tell me about the pregnancy test you got in Michigan," he said. "Nothing changes, I swear, but I didn't ask because I wasn't ready to find out."

One little box had stirred up all that turmoil over being pregnant, when it had only been the stress – the test was negative. Still, Zach had hidden his worry for weeks before finally asking.

"No, Zach, I wasn't pregnant."

♦

"What would you think about leaving Hawaii before Christmas?" Zach asked the next evening over dinner.

I looked up from grilled mahi-mahi in surprise. Although we'd had a wonderful time in Hawaii, wandering around the island, playing in the water and sun, eating and drinking, I wasn't built for the sheer volume of choices of *which touristy thing* to do next. Doing nothing was even more difficult than deciding, though I'd hoped it wouldn't show.

"Okay, where should we go?" I asked, hoping I didn't sound too eager.

"Let's go back to Michigan. If it's not safe, we can drive

somewhere else from there. Getting to Canada is pretty easy."

"You think safety is still an issue?" I asked.

He shrugged. "Hawaii is an island with nowhere to go if someone finds us."

Perhaps something had happened that made him want to leave – he was far more adept at identifying threats than I was, and something might have caught his attention. His mood could seesaw from his normal easygoing nature to quiet and observant to even distant at times. I wasn't sure what to make of the swings, but I'd begun to notice little things, like when he checked his voice mail daily. I wondered if I'd missed some danger around us – and I didn't think he'd tell me if I asked.

Leaving made sense for all sorts of reasons, but mostly because I was tired of the stress of not knowing being disguised as leisure.

With Zach making arrangements, we flew from Hawaii on Thursday, December 21, on a packed jet back to the mainland with a connection through Portland, Oregon. After we got off the plane at PDX, though, Zach started toward the main part of the terminal, without explanation.

When he turned to leave the gate areas, I pressed him and got a nonchalant answer that ratcheted my nerves a notch tighter.

"What do you *mean* we don't have tickets from here?" I snapped, having endured a seven-hour flight cooped up with several screaming children.

"We have a layover," Zach said, leading me through the terminal with an arm around my shoulders. "Let's go find a hotel and have dinner."

"But what about our luggage and work and –" My voice climbed to screechy and loud, I realized when Zach put a finger on my lips.

"Shhh. We came home early, remember?" he said. "Trust me."

I wanted to stomp my feet and have an ear-splitting tantrum like the four-year-old sitting just in front of us on the plane, but I followed him in silence.

He left me waiting for our suitcases at the carousel, returning in time to heft the larger of the two onto the carpet, with keys to a rental car.

"Zach, what is going on?" My patience was past dead and well into decomposition before this latest travel complication.

"It's a surprise."

I don't do surprises well, I thought. He should know that.

As irritated as I was about his covert change of plans, I swore I'd keep my mouth shut while he loaded our luggage into the first Ford Mustang he'd rented during our travels.

He'd managed red but not a convertible. It was the rainy season, so it hardly mattered.

"Which way is north?" he asked, as he opened the car door for me, looking around.

"North to where?" I asked, totally exasperated, pointing over the trunk of the car. "There's nothing north of here but a river and Washington. What are you looking for?"

"I'll find it," he said, shrugging as I slumped down into the seat.

He climbed in, and I sighed and leaned onto the headrest, letting let him drive out Airport Way toward the interstate. Then before I could argue, he shifted the manual transmission without a bump, passing the right-hand onramp to go south and turned onto I-205 northbound toward Washington, accelerating.

CHAPTER

29

I hadn't been in Portland in years, but I knew from where we'd accessed the freeway, there was no choice but to cross the Glenn Jackson Bridge over the Columbia River. I resolved not to say another word as he drove into Vancouver, Washington.

Without further input, he drove straight to a hotel and parked. He came around and opened my door, offered his hand to me and held it as we walked to the check-in desk inside.

I avoided looking at him as he registered, scanning the tourist brochures in the rack behind him – a wide variety of places and activities from the recovering lands around Mount St. Helens to snow skiing on Mount Hood, Pacific Coast resorts, and so on. None of which was I interested in reading or visiting. I was so tired of touristy places, I wanted to scream.

He left me there while he went to get our bags, and fortunately, the young clerk who had oogled Zach practically out of his clothes while he signed in didn't want to chat with me.

I followed Zach down the hall behind two rolling suitcases.

We'd flown to Hawaii with the pair practically empty, one packed inside the other. I'd been wise enough to listen to the Katzes about taking a couple of pairs of shorts and half a dozen T-shirts, bathing suit, sandals and beach shoes, and to buy film and sunscreen before we left, but to get everything else there. After more than a week, we'd accumulated enough new stuff to fill both suitcases, plus we'd shipped home several boxes to New Mexico and Michigan.

Another night in a hotel meant digging through the suitcases to find stuff I wouldn't have needed again till I was home, even stopping in Albuquerque to pick up Laser.

Inside room 121 at the end of the hallway, Zach tucked our bags into a nook and looked around. The room included a whirlpool tub in the corner.

"This will do nicely," he announced with a satisfied smile. He sat on the foot of the bed, pulling me onto his lap. "What's wrong? Have I pissed you off?"

"Yes!" I exclaimed, frustrated at his nonchalance. I sighed, reining in the frustration. "I'm sorry. I was looking forward to getting home after so many nights in strange places the last few months. It's been a long trip, and I'm cranky."

He leaned back and pulled me with him, but I scooted off his legs to lie beside him.

"I have a confession, Julie," he said, looking at the ceiling.

"Damn, you can't imagine how I hate hearing those five words from a man," I murmured.

He rolled so he could look at me and smiled a little. "I can't live in the desert, not even in the mountains of New Mexico. I don't know what it is, but I . . . just can't. Because you lived out here as a child, I came out here a couple of years ago and began scouting around a little. I didn't like Seattle, but this part of the country appeals to me. There's a piece of land I found, and I wanted to see if you like it."

I was stunned.

A guy who didn't even rent an apartment because he was never there wanted to buy land?

"It's not much, but I'd like your opinion. I was hoping maybe you'd come live with me someday."

I tried to speak, but there was no sound.

"If you don't like it, I understand. We can live in Michigan if you want to stay there or –"

The only way I knew to make him shut was to kiss him.

He didn't need to keep talking. It wouldn't matter to me whether it was forest or desert, mountain or valley. Only that he would be there.

♦

The next morning, Zach let me sleep late, though we'd both been awake at unspeakably early hours in Hawaii because of the time difference. I woke to the smell of coffee and toast.

"Morning, Blue Eyes," he said, setting down the tray. "Hungry?"

"Ravenous."

I rolled over, stretching like a cat. I'd had weeks of sleep like I hadn't experienced in years. Sleeping and waking up feeling good was terrific. Even the aches and pains and itching of the injuries was getting better.

He set the table while I went to the bathroom.

I came out to find him silhouetted against the light in the window. Hawaiian sun and surf had bronzed him like a Greek god, weaving streaks of gold in his dark wavy hair.

I couldn't keep from running my fingers through it and stealing a kiss.

"So where is this property," I asked, sitting down and buttering my toast.

"Northeast of here." No further details.

Impatient, I said, "Are you going to describe it for me?" I took another bite.

"Nope. But I'm serious, if you don't like it –"

I swallowed. "I'll be brutally honest, I promise."

We finished breakfast, shared a shower, repacked our bags, and checked out of the hotel by nine.

He stopped at the mall and insisted we each buy a jacket and a change of warmer clothes, citing recent cold weather. Our luggage was full of shorts and tanktops.

"I have a dozen coats at home, Zach. I don't need another."

"Please. We're going out to wander around a piece of property, and you're making me cold standing here in the store dressed like that."

"You, cold?" I laughed. That wasn't physiologically possible. The man was a 50,000 BTU human furnace.

"Humor me. Get jeans, a long-sleeved shirt and a jacket."

So I did.

From my childhood, I remembered winters in the Northwest being rainy and gray, usually cool but not cold. Facing blue skies and bright morning sun, I needed both my sunglasses and the sweatshirt Zach had insisted I get.

He drove eastward along the Columbia River Gorge, then north. Almost two hours into the excursion, he turned left off the highway onto a gravel road and drove to a heavy metal gate that was chained shut. The view beyond the fence was all but obscured – the age-old problem in the Northwest – you can't see the forest, or anything else, for the trees.

He parked, shut off the ignition and came to open my door to help me out.

We walked to the steel gate where he took out a ring of keys and opened the lock, pushing the gate open a little. Then he turned to face me and took my hands, locking our fingers together.

"Julie, I love you with all my heart. Your past doesn't scare me, and I won't run." He kissed me and let go of my hands and then pulled from his pocket a long satin ribbon, folded it onto itself, and placed it in my palm, closing my fingers with his, then dropped to one knee. "Will you be with me tomorrow? And will you marry me, some day, when you're ready?"

I looked down into his anxious green eyes and ran my fingers through his unruly hair.

My vision wavered in tears.

"You not only saved my life, but you made it worth living, Zach," I said. "I'm not sure about getting married yet, but yes, I'll share tomorrow with you."

He spread his hands so I could open mine, revealing a heavy gold ring with a large emerald set between two diamonds.

The emerald matched his eyes.

"The diamonds, one for yesterday, one for tomorrow. All the color is for today."

I didn't know what to say.

Standing up, Zach untied the ribbon, removed the ring and placed it on my finger. He scooped me up in his arms and whirled around in circles, letting out a laugh that echoed around us, and then he carried me through the gate.

"Close your eyes," he told me, setting me back on my feet. And he tied the wide satin ribbon like a blindfold so he could lead me down the gravel road about a hundred steps, keeping me from tripping here and there. He stopped, turned me one direction, then moved behind me and wrapped his arms around my waist.

"Okay, you can look."

I pulled down the ribbon and gasped.

We stood, gazing across a meadow sloping down into a deep valley over a distant river, with Mount Hood in the distance.

"Property starts at the road," he said, pointing left from where we came, "and goes down to that fence," pointing toward the river. Then he swung me around to face a log cabin-style house. "This's the part I didn't know about."

CHAPTER

30

I tilted my head up at Zach.

"When Nolan showed me old pictures of the cabin where you and Kim were held, I was sick," he said. "I wasn't sure I could ever bring you here. I didn't decide till the day before I asked you if we could leave Hawaii."

I took a breath. "What you said to me about not being afraid, not running?" I felt him nod, his arms still wrapped around me from behind. "This isn't Michigan. Those aren't the same logs, and a building's not to blame for what happens within its walls. I'm okay with that." I turned to look at him. "This is incredible. Can we see inside?"

"Sure," he said. "It's ours."

"What? You said you'd looked at it!"

"Oh, yeah, I did that. A lot." He smiled. "Even after it was finished, I came here between assignments to chill sometimes. I'd pitch a tent, watch the stars, and dream about the day I could bring you here. I never slept inside, though, and I never told the guys. If I couldn't share it with you, I didn't want to share it with anyone."

"This has to be a chunk of change, Zach," I said, walking toward the house, stopping to take it all in again. "How can you afford it?"

"I had a bit tucked away," he shrugged. "And my grandmother died two years ago, so her estate, which would have gone to my father, then to Zoe and me, all came to me. I paid off the rest of Mom's second mortgage in Albuquerque, and I bought the land last February. The house was finished in July."

"Wait, are you saying you've *paid* for all this?"

Digging out his keys out again, he stepped onto the wrap-around deck, ignoring my question. He unlocked the door and let it swing open.

"Zach?" I prodded, pulling his sleeve.

"Yes'm," he said, turning to look out over the valley with an expression of satisfaction. "I did." Then he scooped me up into his arms, kissed me, and carried me over the threshold.

From what he'd said about sleeping in a tent, I didn't expect furniture, but there were a few basics – a sofa and recliner, end tables, a bookcase and an entertainment center, a dining room table the size of my truck.

One more kiss, and he set me on my feet, though I was a little dizzy.

"Lots of stuff to buy. I had the realtor bring enough furniture that we could spend a comfy weekend." He grinned like a kid at Christmas. "Come on, you should see it all." He took me by the hand.

To our left, the living area faced Mount Hood through a huge bay window. Between the living room and a dining room was a walk-around fireplace. The mantle in the living room was a quarter trunk of a twisted juniper tree. Above this hung a pale charcoal drawing of a face I hardly recognized after seeing it with bruises, swelling, and short hair over the last few weeks.

"Where did you get that?" I was astonished.

He didn't answer.

"Zach?" I repeated, annoyed he chose to ignore my questions at his discretion.

"I drew it."

I was speechless, but I couldn't look away.

"This drawing's not my favorite, but I didn't think you'd want the other one hanging on the living room wall," he said.

I couldn't think of anything to say, but I finally managed to close my mouth.

A staircase went up from the middle of the house, but I turned left into a dining room with an oak table large enough to seat eight. The kitchen had a wrap-around counter and a breakfast bar with stools. French doors opened onto a deck across the back of the house, and I stepped outside to find a covered hot tub to the garage side.

"How could you keep this all a secret?" I marveled, going inside again.

"It wasn't easy, trust me."

Through the right of the kitchen was a hallway, including a bathroom and empty bedroom. A laundry room occupied the passage to the garage.

I climbed the stairs to find two more nearly empty bedrooms and another bathroom along the banister.

"Empty rooms can be offices," he explained. "I chose this one to dump my stuff." He swung the door further open, revealing another large framed image, the one I presumed he meant I didn't want hanging over the mantle.

I guess he was right.

It was a nude drawing of me, stretched out on my stomach with long hair draped over my shoulders, something pulled across most of my hips. Like the other, it was pale, very low contrast, almost misty.

"I spent a lot of nights alone thinking about you the last few years. I hope you don't mind."

"Uh. . . no." I swallowed. "Why would I mind?" I finally managed.

He led me on to the master bedroom that also faced Mount Hood.

The king-size bed had been made with a beautiful red and gold satin comforter and matching pillows.

The downstairs fireplace extended up into the bedroom as well.

"I didn't order furniture for the other rooms," he explained. "None of this stuff is permanent, so we can send it back and buy whatever you'd like, and bring everything from Michigan when you're ready to move. Except the dining room table and the bed – I bought them special."

Following him around the fireplace into the master bathroom, I saw an enormous jetted tub set in the corner, surrounded by stained glass windows. A walk-in shower with double heads was glassed-bricked into the other corner. Countertops made of pale marble sat between. Behind the shower wall was a walk-in closet as big as my first apartment.

On the far side of the bedroom, he opened the balcony doors

facing the mountain. A cool breeze brushed by us.

"Z', I'm blown away."

He pulled me into his arms. "Your face is worth every minute I've had to keep it secret."

I nudged him. "You know, for a tough guy, you're pretty soft."

"Only when it comes to you, but don't tell anyone."

Then a horrible realization struck me. "If you'd been killed on the beach," I said, hands to my face, "or at the hospital –"

"As much a pain in the ass as it was, your name is on the deed, too. It's all as legally yours today as it will be the day we're married."

"But what if I didn't –" I started to stay, only to be interrupted by a kiss.

"I always knew."

We leaned on the balcony railing, taking in the view.

I finally worked up the courage to ask a question slogging through my mind for weeks. "Are you mad I slept with Jeremy?"

"No," he said with only a heartbeat's hesitation. "That night I called from Florida, I heard you get out of bed to talk. I figured you were with the deputy, until you said he'd been kidnapped." He shrugged. "Afterward, I had other priorities, under the circumstances."

Yeah, like not dying, I thought.

"Matthew and I were friends," I said, "but never more. We both had secrets to hide from the world, and neither of us crossed that bridge to the other side. When we did, it was a disaster."

He nodded. "But Jeremy was different, I know."

"When he showed up, everything was already so upside-down, and I was scared. Then all those old feelings surfaced and it felt good to . . ." I paused.

"Good to not be afraid to love someone?" Zach offered.

"I guess." I walked inside and sat on the chest at the foot of the bed, "I'm sorry."

Zach came in and knelt down in front of me, taking both my hands. "Julie, I know you were afraid to feel that sort of emotion again after what David did to you. Things might be different today if not for Jeremy McNeeley. If feeling something for him is what it took to tear down the walls around your heart, I'm happy he went to

Michigan. He took a bullet for me in the hospital room, so I certainly have him to thank for caring so much for you."

"You can just dismiss what I did?"

"If you think I've ever been disappointed, much less angry, about how you've lived your life, you're completely wrong. You are who you are, and I told you, I'm not afraid of anything in your past. I won't run."

"This isn't about running; it's about trust," I argued.

"You went to Florida to find me, Julie. To save my life. That's all the trust I could ask, and more devotion than any man deserves."

"That's not the same as sleeping with –"

Zach interrupted me on purpose. "I can't blame Jeremy for wanting you, even if he was an idiot for letting you go. Twice. And I don't blame you for loving him. Love like that doesn't die, or else you wouldn't have felt anything when he showed up. God forbid, if I ever hurt you so badly, I'd hope you could still love me like that."

"I never slept with anyone else –" I blurted, but he put his fingers to my lips.

"Julie, would you feel any differently about me if I had?"

Without hesitation, I shook my head and pulled his hand down. "I'm not asking."

"I didn't think you did, but for the record, the answer is no," he said. "Not since I saw you in the hospital in Albuquerque."

Words failed me again.

"I am curious, though – regardless of what had happened to me, if McNeeley'd lived and you'd been pregnant, would you have wanted him to stay?"

I shook my head. "I don't think so, not the way he left his family in limbo in Atlanta," I said. "But the possibility I was pregnant must have been on your mind when you went to Florida. Why didn't you ask?"

Zach was silent a moment but never looked away. "Didn't think it was my place to ask, but I was upset because you didn't tell me. After McNeeley got shot, I decided it didn't matter whether it was mine or not – if you had a baby, I'd be the best father I could, if you'd let me. Even if it was his, I'd take care of you both because he saved my life."

"You know, it wasn't until I saw you cross yourself that I realized you're Catholic," I said. "There is so much about you I don't know."

"A rather stray Catholic, actually," he confessed. "I still find it comforting. Maybe one day you'll find something to believe in again."

I shook my head.

He kissed my forehead. "For the record, though, what would you think about having a baby with me?"

CHAPTER

31

We spent the first night cuddled up in a new bed, warmed by a fire we really didn't need, with the doors open out to the balcony, wasting heat and listening to the wind in the trees.

Zach'd had the good sense to install gas fireplaces with remote controls, so the luxury didn't even require setting foot on the floor. Being able to turn the heat off was more important than turning it on.

"Now that you've seen the cabin, can you live with it?" he asked in the darkness.

"Definitely," I said, kissing the fingers of the arm wrapped around me. "I could live almost anywhere so long as you were there."

"Can you live with what I do?"

"Of course."

"I'm asking you to leave your job," he offered.

"Actually, you said if I didn't like this, you'd consider Michigan. I think that was more than fair."

"I sorta stacked the deck, don't you think?"

I laughed. "Yeah, you ended up with five aces with this place."

"That's what we'll call it. Five Aces."

Finally, he got up and closed the balcony doors, and sleep came peacefully.

Somehow, I slept through Zach rolling out of bed the next morning. Sleeping was quickly leading to sleeping in. It was nearly eight o'clock, but then we had gained a couple of hours leaving Hawaii.

I padded into the bathroom and splashed water on my face and brushed out my short hair, which tended to be all mussed by morning, much like Zach's.

"So what do you want to do today?" he said, standing at the door, watching me brush my teeth.

I jumped. Spitting a mouthful of toothpaste into the sink, I shook my head in amazement I hadn't inhaled it.

"Sorry, babe, I didn't mean to startle you."

I shrugged and dried my face and hands. "Any ideas?"

"We should pick out plans for the barn," he said, leaning against the doorframe. "Or we could go buy more furniture."

"You've got to be kidding, a barn?"

"We've got to have a place to put the horses. Winters aren't that rough here, but still we should get it ready."

"A storm out of British Columbia can strand you in ice or what is aptly called Cascade concrete," I said. "Nothing like the snow in Michigan or New Mexico. We could be stuck out here without power for weeks with no way to get out."

"Sounds divine," he said with a grin. "But there's a generator, so I think we'll manage."

No doubt he'd thought of everything.

"Let's go to Whidbey Island. I'll show you where I grew up," I suggested.

"Really?"

"It's time you learned something good about me, don't you think?"

"Julie," he said, taking me into his arms. "I've haven't learned anything bad about you in all these years of following you around. I doubt you could surprise me now, no matter what you showed me."

I raised an eyebrow. "You might be wrong."

Watching him make his way around the kitchen, the sweet smell of blueberry pancakes and smoky crisp bacon made my stomach rumble long before they were ready. After we ate and cleaned up, I went to change and met him in the garage, where he'd parked the Mustang.

"Wait a minute," I said. "This isn't a rental car. It's got Washington license plates!"

Zach shook his head. "No, it's mine. Didn't make sense to rent a car every time I came here. I picked it up from a kid who couldn't afford the payments."

We crawled in and headed to Highway 14 west to I-205 into Vancouver, then north to I-5.

I spent our drive telling him about places my family had gone in the Northwest, like when Mom and I went skiing for a weekend at White Pass and she broke her leg on the steps of the lodge, or when Dad took me to Vancouver, B.C., to watch the Canucks play.

"She likes hockey," Zach said to himself. "That *is* a new one."

"See? You don't know everything," I teased. "You've never seen the Cam Neely Canucks and Bruins sweaters in my closet?"

"Julie," he said, the serious sound offset by a smile, "I don't forage through your closets. That was the other guy who broke into your house."

"Oh yeah, my other monster." My fake sarcasm poorly camouflaged the anger I felt flaring up again at Anthony Bock. "There's no telling how much of my stuff Anthony rifled through, and it still burns me. He got into my house as easily as you ever did."

"You never did really make many security improvements after my visits, or else maybe he wouldn't have," Zach said. "Most of the time, I picked the lock on the front door and walked right in."

"Oh, now there's a skill I need to learn," I said.

"I think you learned enough criminal activities when Domino taught you to cook meth," he said. "What makes you maddest about Bock being inside your house?"

"My journals. Bock probably read through them all," I said, hoping explaining would help calm my irritation. "They're in a box in my closet. He called Jeremy and told him to read marked sections. Some of them were about when you and I met."

Zach's head tilted, then he nodded. "Now I understand. In the hospital room, McNeeley mentioned reading about me. I didn't have a clue what he was talking about and didn't get the chance to ask."

"Bock put markers in practically every book. It's nauseating to know anyone read them, much less a maniac." I shook my head and looked out the side window, thinking about the journals. I never wrote for other people. The journals were where I processed and stored memories, passages of black, ugly self-pity and hatred.

"Julie, you don't have to apologize for being upset about such an invasion in your privacy. And for what it's worth, if it'd been me he'd called, I wouldn't have looked for the box, much less read your journals."

I smiled. "Thanks. You've spent an awful lot of time in my house alone though. Even without opening a single door, box or drawer, you can't tell me you didn't learn things from what's in plain sight."

"Sure, I know a lot about you from your house," he said. "You're obsessively neat. You overfed your fish, under-watered the plants, and spoiled Laser when he visited. Books and music are the only things you collect. There's no craftsy stuff. And though you spend billions of hours at the computer, I don't know what you do."

That caught me off guard – I never used my computer when he was around, so I didn't see how he could have known how much I used it. My surprise must have shown.

He laughed. "You've worn half the letters off a keyboard you bought two years ago. It would take me a decade to do that."

"You should use more than two fingers," I suggested.

Zach arched an eyebrow at me.

"I'm extremely left-brained," I said. "Not creative at all. I don't paint or play an instrument, nothing like that."

"Did you as a kid?"

I thought about it. "I took piano lessons for a couple of years, not long after we moved to New Mexico, but I had a teacher who was obsessed with classical music. I hated it because I didn't know how it was supposed to sound. Why?"

"Curious if you became more logical and less creative after your father was killed."

Damn, he didn't bother pulling that punch.

I shrugged instead of answering.

"Have you been to Seattle since you came here in '92?" he asked.

"How'd you know I was here then?" I asked, wondering where the change of subject came from.

"I followed you. Same flight, same hotel."

Zach had followed me around Albuquerque a lot, I knew. At the end of my official recovery from injuries suffered at David's hand, effectively ending my career with the New Mexico State Police, I drove around at night. The first time I bumped into him, Zach had guessed I was prowling, looking for trouble, and he was right. After that, I knew he followed me on occasion, but I didn't know he'd shadowed me to Washington.

I sighed. "You must really be good at what you do."

He tried to suppress the smile but failed. I pretended not to notice.

"Any part of that trip you missed out on?" I asked hopefully.

"No, I even saw you in the bar. I wasn't twenty feet away from where you sat."

I cursed under my breath.

"I'm glad you had one last fleeting thought that throwing the bottle at the waitress was a bad idea. It would have blown my cover to have to bail you out of jail."

"Um, yeah," I said, feeling my face flush as I thought.

I'd gone to the hotel bar and sat down at a table, but despite the place being almost empty, the server walked right by me several times and didn't even acknowledge me. I finally went to the bar and bought a beer in a bottle, took a napkin and went to my table to drink it. When she still ignored me rather than ask if maybe I'd like another, I finally got up and took my empty and the napkin and placed them neatly on the bar.

"Here," I'd said. "I wouldn't want to impose on anyone to have to clean my table, either."

I would have left it at that, except the waitress hissed "Bitch!" as I turned to leave.

Enraged, I whipped around and grabbed the bottle by the neck and reared back to throw it at her, but somewhere in the next fraction of a second, as Zach had said, I changed my mind. Instead, I busted the bottle against the black marble bar. "Okay, clean *this* up, then."

"I was surprised," he said, reeling my thoughts back to the present. "I hadn't seen you react with such uncontrolled anger. I began to think that maybe what you say when you answer your phone is really Mad-Again, rather than Madigan."

No doubt I blushed.

The incident had stunned me, too. I'd really wanted to hit this woman for little more than unnecessary rudeness. The anger scared me. I took it as a sign I needed to leave New Mexico and move on with my life from what David had done. Once in Traverse City, there'd been no more physical outbursts, but mostly because there had been no provocation.

Until I'd slapped Jeremy. But he had provoked me, hadn't he?

"I heard you crying in your hotel room that night," Zach said quietly, knowing he was interrupting the memory. "I wanted so much to hold you."

"Why'd you follow me up here?" I asked.

He hesitated for just a moment before he answered. "Because in all the weeks I'd tailed you in Albuquerque, I kept wondering when you'd turn around and nail me, but you never looked."

Throughout the drive, I hadn't paid attention to where we were going until he turned off I-5 in Tacoma.

"Whidbey Island is still . . ." I said, confused.

"I've been to Whidbey. Driven by your old house. I don't need to see the suburbs," he said. "Unless you have some particular reason you want to go there?"

I shook my head. "Where are we going then?"

"The Point Defiance Zoo," he explained. "It's only open till four in the winter."

"A zoo?"

"It's one of my favorites. I love the beluga whales and the polar bear tanks."

"He likes zoos," I echoed his observation about hockey. "Who'da thought?"

Zach smiled. "You like them, too, or I wouldn't have brought you here."

"And how do you know this?"

"You have a framed photo from the Denver Zoo hanging in your den."

He was right, though I couldn't believe he could identify the place from a photo I'd taken.

Inside, we strolled through the zoo and aquarium, holding hands, watching children's faces as polar bears played ball and sea otters danced in the water.

"If I had to be reincarnated as an animal, I'd like to be an otter," he mused. "They're small and agile and always seem to have so much fun. What would you want to be?"

I pondered the idea. "I'd want to be a butterfly."

Zach stopped and pulled me against him as he backed up to the wall of the exhibit. Cradling my face in both hands, he looked at me for a moment. "Butterflies are beautiful. They start out life as one thing, and then they magically change into something delicate and fragile. You'd be a lovely butterfly, but why?"

I thought about the anger I felt and sometimes had trouble controlling. "Because butterflies never hurt anyone," I whispered.

CHAPTER
32

"Did you do any hiking while you were out here?" I asked Zach the next day on the drive home from Vancouver. We'd shopped for food and supplies to extend our stay, including clothes as our Hawaiian wardrobe wasn't suited for the cold damp weather.

Neither of us admitted the fact that shopping on Christmas Eve morning had been an insane idea.

"No, nothing off the property."

"Off the property?" I asked, confused.

"It's a hundred acres. There's a bit of wandering to do where it's not cleared."

"Holy cow, I didn't realize it was so big." I was surprised, but I didn't know where the fence was behind a wall of trees north of the house. "I've always wanted to climb Mount St. Helens. We had already moved to Albuquerque when it erupted in 1980, but it used to be as beautiful as Mount Hood or Mount Adams."

Today though, none of the peaks were visible. While in the rainy season, the clouds often concealed them, the air in the Northwest could also hide the mountains on a clear day when you'd swear you could see forever.

"Mountain climbing, huh?" Zach said.

"Not technical climbing like on Denali or Everest, or even Mount Hood. No ropes or that sort of thing. Call it mountain hiking. There are also lots of horse trails in the state and national forests, too."

"If you say so. I'm game if we —"

Watching his face as he spoke, I saw his expression change

between words, and I turned to see what he saw.

Not a hundred yards in front of us, an oncoming van plowed down two bicyclists from behind and barreled on toward us.

Zach swerved to the shoulder to miss the van straddling the double yellow line as it passed us without slowing. Then he hit the brakes.

I picked up my cell phone and dialed.

"911, what is your emergency?"

"We just witnessed a gray or silver van hit two bicyclists on Highway 14 westbound at around mile marker 46, Washington plates," I said. "My name is Julie Madigan. I'm a paramedic and am getting out to assist two victims. These are priority one traumas. I'm requesting medevac to respond. My partner will turn around and pursue the van."

The dispatcher started talking, but I tossed the phone to Zach. I bailed out and crossed the highway, waving to stop the few cars going west. I found a man and a young teenage boy on the shoulder of the road about twenty feet apart.

I looked at Zach, made a circle in the air indicating I definitely wanted a chopper.

Nodding, he whipped the Mustang in a U-turn and sped away as more vehicles screeched to a standstill behind me.

The occupants of the first few cars that stopped got out to help.

I made a quick exam of the boy first. He was conscious but not making sense. He had what looked like a femur fracture and both wrists broken in multiple places.

I asked an older couple to stay with the boy, showed them how to hold his head still and to open his airway if necessary, and instructed them to keep him from moving. I sent a handful of bystanders to find blankets and a cell phone. I directed another two bystanders to stop traffic in both directions.

Making my way to the other victim, he was unconscious with gurgling respirations. Opening his airway with a jaw lift did not help, so I waved to another group of bystanders to help me roll him onto his side while I stabilized his neck.

Blood poured from his mouth, but the next few breaths cleared slightly.

A woman brought a blanket for him, too.

Someone else came to where I was kneeling on the gravel and dropped an orange pack with "EMT" on the side. Then he just stood there.

"I'm a paramedic," I said when he didn't offer to help, trying not to sound aggravated. "You wouldn't happen to have any oropharyngeal airways in there, would you?"

He hesitated a moment, blinking at me as if I'd appeared by magic. "Yeah, sure."

"I think he could use one," I said. "And if you have a precip pack," – a kit for delivering a baby – "we could use that, too." A bulb syringe wasn't the best way to remove blood from an adult airway, but probably the closest thing he had.

The EMT knelt down beside the patient, opening his kit and pulling out a set of curved oral airways. After a deep breath and an owlish blink that said in a thousand silent words he'd never seen what lay before him, he measured one against the patient's cheek, and easily inserted it to hold the tongue out of the back of the mouth. He then found the suction from his delivery kit and began to remove more blood.

"Terrific," I said, still a bit perplexed I had to make the suggestion. "Can you do a quick exam? I didn't get past his airway."

He nodded and raised the blanket to do a quick assessment.

"Flail chest left," he said as he felt down the man's thorax, meaning that several ribs were broken in at least two places, so the chest wall was unstable and compromising his breathing. "Femur left, maybe right also."

"Good, maybe you have a roll of wide tape in there, too?" I described how I wanted him to put strips over the ribs to keep them from moving so much. Then I asked him to place one of the bystander's hands over the flailed segment to stabilize it further. "I think we're okay for a minute. Can you take over holding his head while I go check on the boy?"

He nodded, and we carefully traded places.

"Any ideas on how long for an ambulance?" I asked as I stood up.

"Ground had an ETA of about eight. Dispatch said someone had requested the helo – I guess that was you?"

I nodded and went to the boy, still conscious but becoming lethargic. His belly was rigid, indicating internal bleeding – nothing I could do to fix that. Like I was taught years ago, trauma was a surgical disease.

In the distance, I could hear the welcome sound of sirens, ambulances making their way through the stopped cars.

Within fifteen minutes, two paramedics had taken over care of the man and packaged him for transport to meet Life Flight out of Portland several miles away at a landing zone. Another pair transported the boy by ground.

Patients both gone, I became aware of how fast my heart was beating. With several deep breaths, it began to slow down.

A Washington State Police lieutenant arrived to investigate. Probably a bystander pointed me out, at the rescue truck, trying to wash the blood off my hands with a liter of sterile water and paper towels.

"I'm an ex-New Mexico State Police sergeant, a paramedic, and a medical examiner investigator from Michigan," I said when he asked. "We witnessed the crash. I got out to help. Zach Samualson turned and followed the van."

"The big guy in the red Mustang?"

I smiled. "Yes. He's DEA."

"So I was told."

He didn't sound impressed, but he should have been – otherwise there would be two dead cyclists and a van that was long gone.

I walked with him down the highway to where we saw the van hit the bikes, and I described what I'd seen.

"The driver didn't try to miss them, from what I saw. He didn't veer at all until the one bike hung up underneath," I said, looking for skid marks and scrapes in the pavement. "Maybe about there. This is where we swerved to miss him."

I detailed the critical nature of the victims' injuries, then gave him my home address in Michigan and my cell phone number.

He suggested I catch a ride to meet up with Zach in Camas with the EMT who'd helped me with the one patient. "We'll get him on his way; otherwise, there won't be much other traffic moving either direction for a while," he said.

I accepted the offer without further explanation and went to the young man's pickup. He introduced himself as Doug Logan.

"The paramedic who transported him to the helo says you probably kept Darrell from dying," he said as we got buckled in.

"All I did was roll him to clear his airway," I shrugged. "No big deal."

"Yeah, it's a big deal," he said as he put the truck in gear and started past deadlocked cars. "Until you prompted me, I froze. Couldn't think. That was my brother and nephew."

"Oh, Doug. Why didn't you say something?"

"Losing my head wasn't going to help. But if you hadn't gotten those bystanders organized, hadn't said whatever you did to 911 to get the chopper in the air," he drifted off.

"I'm sorry, I don't understand."

"You have to be a paramedic to request Life Flight. Even I couldn't have done that, but they lifted off for you, even though they didn't know who you were. And 911 kept talking to your friend while he followed the van, until deputies caught it. Thanks to the two of you, things are a lot better than they could have been." He was fighting tears. "I felt so helpless."

"So did I. We do what we can with what we have," I said. "All I had were my hands. At least you had a response kit."

Doug turned onto a side street on the outskirts of Camas, Washington, and drove to a chaotic scene of police cruisers in a parking lot.

"God bless you, Julie. Merry Christmas," he said, extending a hand. "Thanks for everything."

"Merry Christmas to you, too." I shook his. I'd forgotten all about the holiday.

I climbed out and went to Zach, who was leaning against a Clark County patrol car, talking to a couple of deputies from there and Skamania County as well.

He hugged me when I got there. "How are they?" he asked.

They all wanted to know.

"Bad, but hopefully they'll both survive. Thanks for getting the helo," I said.

"Sheriff said to tell you both thank you. You did a hell of a job," a Skamania deputy told us, handing Zach a business card. "Drop by after Christmas; he'd like to meet you."

Zach shook his hand and thanked everyone for their quick responses. We walked to the Mustang together.

"Well, I think we earned our supper tonight," he said, taking my hand. "I wish I could have watched you work."

"That's funny – I was wishing I could have ridden with you instead."

We laughed.

"Do you know you called me your partner when you called 911?" he asked.

I stopped at the door and thought. "Did I?"

He kissed my forehead. "Yeah. I liked it. We make a good team."

He stopped at a convenience store so I could wash my hands again with real soap and running water.

Days of being bloody from an EMS call are long gone, I said to myself in the mirror. Used to be a badge of honor, proof you'd gone all out for a patient, to go home with blood on your uniform. Now there were nasty incurable diseases spread by blood and other body fluids. Gloves and goggles were the basics of standard protection.

I'd had neither, but my only exposure was blood on intact skin.

When I returned to the car, Zach had bought us each a bottle of water and a doughnut to share. "I'd have bought two, but that's all they had," he said. "It looked lonely."

I took a bite and blushed when he leaned over to thumb away a crumb of icing from my chin.

"Shall we go home now?" he asked.

"If we go that direction, we'll get stuck in traffic," I said. "Let's go have dinner in Vancouver. Then we can take I-84 down to Cascade Locks if we need to detour later."

While Highway 14 was a two-lane highway along the north side of the Columbia River in Washington, the Oregon side sported four-lane Interstate 84.

We found a seafood restaurant in Vancouver, but it was packed. After waiting 45 minutes in the bar, we finally got a table. I had lobster and Zach had steak.

"I can see why you'd want to be a cop. You'd be good at it," Zach said, sliding his knife through a rare T-bone.

"You know, with a defibrillator, I might actually be able to save its life," I said, motioning with my fork to his steak. "I like my meat pink, but it shouldn't kick when I stab it."

Zach rolled his eyes at me. "Why the paramedic part?" he finished saying then stuffed a bite into his mouth.

"I don't know. It all fell together," I shrugged. "Losing Dad the way I did, I didn't think I could watch someone die again without trying to help. Once I got into the state police, staying at the Albuquerque post would have been a poor career decision, I think."

"Even though you were fast-tracked on a case in Albuquerque?"

"How do you know about that?" I asked, irritated he remembered a kidnapping and murder of a mother for her unborn baby.

"Gossip, I suppose." He shrugged. "I probably know a lot of things about you I take for granted."

"So make it up to me. Tell me more about you."

"Okay, the nickname. My sister couldn't say Zach, so she called me Cubby, which was also her stuffed bear's name."

We made another round of cutting and chewing before he continued.

Occasionally in the lapses, I heard Christmas carols from the speakers above our heads

"Did you know I wet the bed until I was almost six?" he said, not the least embarrassed.

"No," I said. "Tell me about when you got shot the first time."

"Houston. Dealer with a 20 gauge," he said, pointing with his fork to the shoulder where he carried the scars. "He'da blown my head off if I'd been his height, the little runt."

"Something to be said for being built for the NBA," I agreed.

"Shotgun is a perfect defense weapon that criminals don't think about more often, fortunately." He swirled a bite of steak into its mushrooms. "You?"

"My life has run to sharp objects instead of bullets and shot. Does your vest really say ABDTD?" I said, dipping a chunk of Maine lobster tail and trying not to drip butter on my shirt.

"Domino told you that, I suppose?" he said, raising an eyebrow.

"No, actually since I fell in love with you, I stuck a V in it – a *very* bad day to die."

I kicked him under the table.

"What? It's true! It's a reminder why I want to go home at the end of the day," he said, reaching to dip a piece of his steak into my butter. "Do you want me to quit?"

CHAPTER

33

"Quit the DEA?" I repeated, astounded at the very idea. "You wouldn't be happy doing anything else. And like today, it wouldn't matter – you'd still end up doing something dangerous."

"If I recall, I was following a drunk driver. You were the one who ended up –" He looked around the crowded room and lowered his voice, "the one who ended up all bloody on the side of the road. You saved two people's lives."

"What I did today wasn't rocket science," I said. "And it wasn't dangerous."

"Wasn't it? I saw the gears change in your brain as you dialed the phone," he challenged. "You found that zone, whatever it is for a medic. And you miss it, just like you miss the badge."

I opened my mouth to argue. We both knew he was right, but I suspected what I liked about it wasn't so much what I'd done as much as how I liked the feeling of adrenaline surging into my bloodstream. The sort of release that gives a mother the power to lift a car off her child.

He waited.

I sighed and nodded in agreement. "Yes, I miss it. I can't physically do either for a living anymore though. But this discussion isn't about me. It's about whether I have the right to ask you to quit your job, and I don't."

"Because McNeeley asked you to quit?" he ventured.

"No," I said, then paused. "Jeremy dumped me *without* asking me to quit, or without explaining why. He wasn't afraid I'd be killed doing the job – he didn't want to live in the shadow of the fast-track career he anticipated. He threw away everything we had because of jealousy over a career choice. That's why I didn't tell him I was pregnant a few weeks later. He made his decision, and I didn't want him coming back to me out of senseless obligation."

"I see," he said, stirring in more brown sugar before scooping up a forkful of sweet potato.

"I accept your job as part of who you are. I can't imagine asking you to quit."

So low I barely heard over the background cacophony of holiday cheer, without raising his head, he said, "Maybe you should."

"Zach, you can't put this decision on me. It's a –"

"It's a job, Julie. It's dangerous. I've been shot three times this year. Hell, twice in one week. Is it worth the paycheck? Do you want to go to bed alone, wondering where I am and what I'm doing the next time I leave?"

"No, I don't," I said much too loud, so I collected myself and lowered my voice, "but I want you to do what makes you happy. From what I can tell, you like it and you're damned good."

He stared at me but said nothing.

"Okay, Cowboy. So you don't do anything dangerous from now on. I want you all for my own for the rest of my life in a safe nine-to-five job, home in my bed every night so we can have a perfect safe relationship, a perfect white picket fence, and a house full of perfect kids."

"Don't patronize me, Julie."

"You don't think that sounds pretty odd?"

"A job where no one shoots at me? A great relationship and a family? In your bed every night? I think it's more than perfect."

"If that's what you want, that's terrific. But when was the last time you had a permanent address and didn't sleep with a gun on the bedside table, Zach? And what the hell is a safe job, anyway? You could have the world's safest work, whatever it might be, and still get plowed down by a drunk driver on your way home, like those bicyclists."

I saw something I didn't understand flash in his green eyes.

"If you don't want to work DEA, then quit. I don't have an issue with you wanting to do that," I said. "But I don't want you to quit because of me."

After a manager in reindeer antlers came by our table to make sure our meal was suitable, offering a special holiday dessert, discussion of Zach's career in the DEA ended.

"Tell me about what happened to you in the hospital," he said as we escaped the crowds and walked to the car hand in hand.

Which hospital? Which time?

"You told me you got candy that was laced," he prompted.

"Presumed to be from Anthony," I said. "I never learned why, except maybe to make me feel I couldn't trust anything. A terrorist's power play. You saw how well it worked."

He nodded, opening my door for me. "How did it feel?"

"Feel? It didn't feel good. Why would people *want* to do hallucinogens? No matter what was happening around me, I couldn't tell whether it was real or not. Like being trapped inside my worst nightmares – David not dying when I shot him; being hacked up by monsters that were really the hospital staff. I remember those visions vividly."

"Ugly," he agreed, starting the car and heading out of town. "I never heard anybody talk about those kinds of trips. Usually it's pretty colors and an enormous feeling of understanding of the cosmos."

"Nope, helpless and paranoid," I said. "So what did it feel like when you were high?"

We hadn't discussed Zach using drugs since his confession in Michigan.

"The first time, it was really good blow," he said, the slang second nature to his profession. "The cocaine Pauly gave me was from his personal stash, so it was pristine, likely pharmaceutical grade. I'm not sure I can explain the feeling."

In the pale light of the dash, I could see his expression grow tighter as he thought about what had happened.

After a moment, he continued. "High was a perfect word for it, both mental and physical. But by the time you saw me, being high or feeling good wasn't on my mind. The stuff was getting me by, nothing but energy to work through the pain."

"Did it affect your perception of me in the bar?" I asked.

"Sure. I didn't believe it was you because it made no sense at all for you to be there. Still, I wanted the woman I saw to be you with this crazy desperate physical desire. I'd have thrown you down on the hood of my car right there in the parking lot if you'd stopped long enough. I know you don't get it –"

"Oh, I get it, really," I grinned. "I'm almost sorry you passed out."

"No," he said softly, "trust me, you're not sorry. I wasn't me any more than I thought it was really you."

He pulled over into a scenic lookout and shut off the engine. We gazed out toward the Bonneville Dam, looking upriver at the green and red lighting that seemed festive, even when it was no different than any other night.

We didn't talk for a long time, just held hands.

"I don't want to keep playing at this relationship like it's a game," he finally said. "You need to know who I am."

"I agree. Let's move out here, get married. You can take a leave of absence. We need time to do this right. Like dating in reverse."

"Julie, you can't believe how happy that would make me, but I have to tell you –"

The conversation was interrupted by the sound of tires on the gravel as a sheriff's department patrol car circled and pulled up beside the driver's side of the Mustang.

Zach sighed. He rolled the window down and turned on the dome light.

"Is everything okay?" the deputy asked.

"Yeah, we were looking at the lights," Zach said, handing out his license and other identification without being asked.

The deputy leaned forward and looked at me to make sure this story was true and that I wasn't a minor.

I nodded and smiled.

"Didn't mean to disturb you, but we get kids parking out here a lot," the deputy said, using his flashlight to read the cards. "Hey, you're the DEA guy from Camas this afternoon, who chased down the van, right?"

Zach nodded his head and accepted his identification back.

"They told us at shift change. Doug called to say his brother regained consciousness before going to surgery. He's still critical but stable. The boy is listed as serious."

With several more minutes of updates, verbal back-patting and questions about what we were doing in Washington anyway, the deputy finally drove away after holiday greetings.

When he left, Zach started the Mustang and headed on for home. We discussed the afternoon's events and the good news from the deputy, not whatever we'd be talking about before. Eventually, the conversation fell to silence.

At the cabin, we unloaded the car – clothes, things for the house, a few groceries that fortunately hadn't spoiled despite the delay because of the cool temperatures. Afterward, I took a quick shower and found Zach in bed waiting for me.

Wrapped together safely, words that had been interrupted spilled out of us.

"You're sure you're ready to get married?" he asked.

"Spending this time together has been good for us. Yes, I'm ready," I said. "There really is more to us than adrenaline and darkness."

"Merry Christmas."

I realized this was the first Christmas Eve I'd spent with a man since the year I'd married David. For the subsequent holidays, one or the other of us had been on duty. Or dead.

CHAPTER

34

"Hey, Sleepyhead! Santa Claus finally caught up with you, if you decide to get out of bed any time today," Zach called up the stairs, stirring me from sleep.

I rolled over to look at the clock. A quarter after six, and it was still dark outside. A groan escaped me as I yanked the blanket over my head.

Santa Claus?

After the trip to Hawaii, we'd promised not to buy each other anything for Christmas.

Now that I'd seen the cabin here in Washington State, and everything in it, I understood why he'd made his promise so quickly.

"I'm not coming down," I said childishly.

"I'll just have to bring you breakfast in bed."

What kind of threat was that?

"All right, all right." I threw off the covers and grumbled, "Obviously a girl can't even enjoy being difficult around here. I'll show you," I said, pulling on a pair of jeans and slipping his favorite denim shirt over my tank top. It hung down mid-thigh on me, but it was flannel soft and smelled like him. I put it on for those reasons, but I liked it even more because every time he caught me wearing it, he gave me this *look*.

After I washed my face, I padded barefoot down the stairs and around into the kitchen where he was pouring what looked to be a dozen whipped eggs into a skillet already full of diced potatoes, onions, and fried bits of ham and mushrooms.

"You," I said with a kiss when he set the bowl into the sink, "are much too good to me."

"Probably," he said, making a sour face at what I was wearing. He pointed with the spatula toward the front door, where indeed there was a box measuring three feet in each direction. "Merry Christmas."

"Zach, we agreed not to buy –"

"Don't start with me. I did not purchase a single thing in that box since I promised you we wouldn't buy gifts. I merely had it shipped here for you to open."

I started toward the box, but he grabbed my arm.

"Oh no you don't. Since you slept late, you can wait till after breakfast to open it."

I stuck out my bottom lip and made it quiver.

"Geez, stop that!" he said, wincing as he turned away. "I can take just about anything but you pouting, even when you don't mean it. Go sit down." He went back to stirring the contents of the skillet. "And by the way, that's *my shirt*."

I smiled and pulled up a barstool.

As usual, his breakfast was far better than anything at a restaurant or that I could have fixed myself. I'd put on several much-needed pounds since we left Florida.

We finished eating, and while he was cleaning up the dishes from the breakfast bar, I went upstairs to get dressed, finding the last nearly clean shirt in my suitcase. Time to wash everything.

I looked around the bedroom and smiled at how much like home it felt for a place I'd only been a few days.

"That's a contented look," he said.

Again, I jumped.

How does he walk up those stairs without a sound?

"Very content," I said, trying to breathe again.

"Why?" He sat on the hearth.

"Belonging, I guess."

"I like seeing you like this. Now come downstairs and open this box. I think it will keep you busy while I run an errand."

Following him down to the living room, I sat on the floor in front of the sofa. "I still don't get it," I said as he nudged the box toward me with his foot.

"Just open it." He handed me his pocketknife, open, Boy Scout style for safety. "Carefully," he added.

The box had to weigh over forty pounds, and I slit the tape along the edges, struggling to turn the box as I went. Cutting the last strip, the top burst open. I folded the flaps back, revealing envelopes, small boxes, loose paper, CDs, and more.

I was speechless, working on some word greater than flabbergasted.

"When you moved to Michigan," Zach explained, "I wanted to send you stuff and write letters, but I knew I couldn't without risking you shutting me out completely. So I got a post office box at one of those shipping places there and mailed you the things I wanted to send."

"You sent all of this to Michigan?" I asked.

"Over the years, yes. I even hid a key at your house, in case you came to your senses between my visits." He shrugged. "When the space got full, they repacked it all and shipped everything to Albuquerque where it accumulated."

In a small box, I revealed a pale seashell.

"I guess we really don't need any more beach souvenirs from Florida, huh?" he smiled.

Next, I pulled out a red envelope and carefully slid my finger under the flap, revealing a Valentine that was almost two years old. I flipped it open and realized it was the first time I'd really seen Zach's handwriting – a medium-sized print used by someone who had to write a lot of reports. I was a little surprised how much it looked like my own.

That little tidbit was as revealing as the message he had written in the card, a short statement about being in El Paso for training, hoping he'd get to Michigan in a few weeks, missed me desperately, and signed "love, forever & always."

"You can't imagine what this means to me, Zach. It's incredible." I reached to squeeze his hand before digging into the box again.

I pulled out a folded sheet of white paper and opened it to reveal a pencil drawing of me, sitting on a rock next to a backpack, leaned backward on my hands, face turned to the sun. The detail was extraordinary but not harsh.

"How can you do this? It's not even from memory." I thought of the nude upstairs in the other bedroom.

"Not your memory, maybe. Can't you see things you imagine?"

"I suppose, but I can't draw them. Are there more?"

"Probably. I framed a few I really liked, mailed or stashed a few, but I destroyed most of them. Things hidden in my closet, I guess you'd say."

"Will you keep writing and drawing now?" I asked.

"It was what I did instead of what I wanted to do. Why would I choose to eat porridge when I can have steak and lobster? It's like your journals – a place to keep memories."

The drawing drew me into its details.

"I have to run an errand," he said.

"You don't want me to come with you?" I asked, looking up at him.

"Nope. Keep digging through the box. You can't read all the letters in one sitting. It's part of the amusement, I hope. I wouldn't have been around to offer immediate explanations for every tidbit, and I think it's only fair you get to experience them that way."

I shook my head again at the enormity of the gift. "This is great, Zach."

He ruffled my hair then kissed the top of my head. "I won't be too long." He gathered up some stuff, but I didn't pay attention as I became immersed in the box.

Picking objects at random, curiosity overwhelmed me. Digging down, I pulled out what had to be well over a hundred envelopes, mailed from all over the country. There were a dozen CDs, a cap, a pair of deerskin motorcycle gloves, strings of plastic beads, and a tiny bottle of my favorite perfume. Inside an oversized coffee cup from the Metropolitan Museum of Art was a baseball signed by Nolan Ryan, May 1, 1991. I had no idea of its significance or meaning.

The box also yielded four more loose drawings of me, a package of photographs, and one glassine envelope holding a single .44 Magnum round.

Before I became too involved, I got up for a drink and decided while I was moving around, it would be a good time to start laundry. Zach might not be out of clean underwear yet, but it was certainly time to deal with my dirty clothes.

Upstairs, I gathered what needed washing and tossed it down the chute, another thoughtful convenience built in the house. Next I started on Zach's pile and pulled his suitcase from the closet floor to grab several shirts and a pair of jeans to toss down, thinking I might as well do it all.

Downstairs, while sorting clothes into loads, my mind wandered again to the box. I wished I had a CD player to listen to the music he'd bought. Although I recognized several artists, more than half I did not.

My hunch was that Zach bought music with an underlying meaning. I could imagine what he was thinking when he bought The Eagles' *Hell Freezes Over.* We'd had a laugh about the name when he asked if there really was a Hell, Michigan. Yes, I'd explained, and it does freeze. We'd driven there for dinner one night at the Dam Site Inn.

I had all of Boston's CDs, but he'd included *Walk On*, the latest. Never heard of Mason Dixon, but the cover looked a bit more like what Zach might like than Jim Steinman's *Bad for Good.* I'd have to listen to the others to find out what made him think about me.

After I started a load of light colors and underwear, I returned to the living room to the box.

Three years of Zach Samualson's thoughts of me – I was astonished as I sat down again.

Stories. Everything in the box had a story, which would make this so special. Learning the meaning behind each item.

I picked up the gloves, purchased at Downtown Harley-Davidson in Seattle. What had he been doing there? When had he bought them?

Photos – I opened the package to find someone had taken pictures of the guys working on a boat. After six shots, I saw the name *Wind Dancer* – the cabin cruiser they'd used in Florida before Zach was shot. All four guys in were in one pose – Zach, Pauly, Domino and Oz – so I wondered who had snapped the picture.

Probably means more to Zach now than it ever would to me.

Coffee cup. What was Zach doing in the New York at the Met? I didn't seem like his sort of place at all. Did the coffee cup go together with the baseball? I knew Zach was a Ranger's fan, but my understanding of baseball ends at a bat and three hot dogs.

The single cartridge caught my eye, and I picked up the plastic pouch – clearly an evidence envelope – and looked more closely. Brass jacketed hollowpoint, starting to turn dull. The stamp of the manufacturer's name and caliber surrounded the primer.

Then I saw the indentation in the center – a clear firing pin strike. FTF.

Failed to fire. My heart fluttered. Zach didn't own a .44, leaving me to imagine a scenario where the gods Smith and Wesson had somehow intervened. My heart might not be able to take hearing this story – I'd really had enough guns and knives for a while.

I picked a letter from the pile, dated two springs ago, mailed from Albuquerque. Inside were pieces of paper torn from a yellow legal tablet. It looked like maybe it had taken several sittings to finish because the handwriting changed midway.

He'd been out at the ranch for several days alone when his mother had flown to Denver for a nursing conference.

Purgatory and I took a ride west toward the Navajo Reservation this afternoon. I couldn't get the song "Desperado" out of my head. I was out riding fences, and you're the one who won't let somebody love you. I believe we'll be together, some day. I hate to see the sun set without sharing a fraction of your life. Without holding you.

Hopefully I'll get up to see you soon.

Maybe this time I won't break the back gate. You never ask me how I get in. Maybe you think that's part of the challenge. I figure one day I'll get snagged in a professional alarm system or your deputy friend will catch me. I always wonder if I'll find you with someone else. I guess that would be hard to explain.

I wish you knew how much I want to tell you I love you. You're forever on my mind and always in my heart.

zach

My heart ached at the way he'd worried about "someone else."

Hadn't he been right? But it wasn't the deputy, it was Jeremy.

I opened another envelope, one that had not been mailed.

While he often wrote about missing sensual things, like the feel of my hair against his skin, or even flirty innuendo about dropping by to see me again soon, this was different. The scenario was similar to

Zach's stealing into my house during the last few years, and though raw and powerfully sexual, it was written from a woman's point of view.

He had an incredible artistic talent for capturing image, but his ability for capturing erotic sensation and emotion in words was almost as exact.

I was engrossed in the story about a woman snatched from a parking lot and blindfolded when I heard the Mustang pull into the garage.

There didn't appear to be any chance of finishing before I was interrupted, so I folded it up and waited, ready with a flurry of questions. When Zach didn't come in, I opened the door and looked into the garage. Still not seeing him, I slipped on my shoes and walked outside in the damp cold and found him behind the house, splitting wood.

In a fluid motion, he hefted the ax over his shoulder and swung. He didn't acknowledge my presence until I spoke.

"Wow, Zach. The stuff in the box is incredible. I have lots of questions."

The first one that occurred to me I didn't voice – why was he splitting wood when we had a gas fireplace?

He pulled the blade from the stump where he was setting logs and looked at me. "So ask."

"Well, the .44 round has me curious, but I don't want to hear that story on Christmas Day. It can't be cheery, regardless how it ended. Tell me about the baseball."

"Nolan Ryan pitched the seventh no-hitter of his career in 1991," he said, swinging the ax again. "I was at the game in Houston, and with a little leftover connection, I got a signed ball."

I think I was supposed to be impressed, but I really didn't know what he meant. "Why would you give it to me? Is it worth a lot?"

He shook his head before standing up another piece of wood and swinging the ax again. "I brought it to you in the hospital in Albuquerque, but you weren't up for an explanation. I wanted to give you an example of what could happen when you keep trying."

That was a little surprising.

"The story about the woman being dragged into a van in the

casino parking lot? In what dark corner of your imagination had it hidden?"

He swiped his nose with the back of his right hand and sniffed, then he shrugged. "And what did you think?"

"I only got to the part where the woman was led inside with the black bag over her head," I lied.

Just a little.

His gaze shifted out to the horizon, as if images played in his mind, but he said nothing.

Leaning against the hot tub, I waited for him to answer.

Splitting a half dozen more logs, he knocked the last piece of wood off the stump with the ax, and then walked to where I waited. He draped his arm over my shoulders. "Come on, I could use a beer."

We headed toward the garage, and it didn't immediately occur to me that it wasn't even nine in the morning.

Inside, he wiped off the blade with an oily rag and hung the ax on the wall then turned toward the door open into the house. He froze mid-stride. "What are you doing?" he asked in a toneless voice I almost didn't recognize.

"I needed to do laundry," I said, waving toward the utility room floor where clothes were sorted into piles. "I thought I'd throw in your stuff, too."

He stood motionless, except for his eyes darting back and forth.

"I'm sorry, if you don't want me to do your –"

"Forget about it," he interrupted and walked past me into the utility room. He dug through the dark clothes for a pair of jeans, searching the pockets until he located what he was looking for. Whatever it was, he stuffed it into the pocket of the pair he was wearing.

"I'd have emptied out your pockets before I washed them," I said defensively from the doorway into the small room, intending to follow him into the house.

Zach wheeled on me and took two strides that made me step backward into the garage. He matched me two steps down, and I kept backing up as collision avoidance.

"Just drop it," he said with each step. He towered over me, and I put my right hand up to try to maintain some space.

Zach snatched his hand around my wrist and simply held me where I stood. His grip was firm though not painful, but I had no doubt he could break my arm if he squeezed.

I tried to move around him to get into the house, but the hold remained.

Our eyes locked, and it felt like time stopped. I couldn't identify his expression, but I'd seen it one other time – when he pointed a pistol at me.

"Let. Go. Of. Me," I said one word at a time. There was no way I could overpower him, but I could make him hurt me by the look in his eyes. Adrenaline dumped into my bloodstream, making my heart rate soar. I could hear my pulse pounding in my ears.

"Remember last night," he said, reaching out for my other hand and pulling me closer, "when I said I'd have taken you on the hood of the car in Florida?"

CHAPTER

35

I left Zach face down on the bed in a tangle of sheets, snoring softly. Putting on one of his t-shirts, I tiptoed to the kitchen for a glass of water to take a couple of ibuprofen, rubbing my shoulder as the tap ran.

The washing machine had long since cycled through its first load, so I went to the utility room and tossed the wet stuff into the dryer. Then I went out into the garage to gather up the clothes I'd been wearing before being ravaged on the hood of the car and elsewhere.

I stood there, collecting my own jeans and shirt, looking at Zach's discarded clothes on the floor.

"Very interesting, Samualson. So what's the big secret?" I said out loud.

"What do you mean?" he said, scaring the hell out of me. He stood in the doorway naked.

He moves around like a damned ghost!

"I mean I was about to dump your pockets and throw all this into the wash," I said, holding up my own clothes as an example, but throwing down the challenge. I bent down and picked up the jeans he'd been wearing.

His pupils dilated. He opened his mouth to speak but made no sound.

"So do I stick my hand in this pocket and find out, or are you going to tell me what the hell is going on?" I asked.

"Julie, don't push me into a corner," he said, but there was no fight to it.

I stared at him for several seconds, then turned toward the still-open double garage door, pondering my options.

Tossing his jeans to him, I said, "Fine. Do your own laundry."

A woman's ultimate word – fine. Defiance or resignation – I wasn't sure which.

I yanked on my own jeans without panties since I couldn't find them, then grabbed the denim jacket he'd tossed on the roof of the car when he came back, and left him standing in the doorway when I walked out onto the back deck.

The water drops were so cold my bare feet ached.

I tried not to be mad.

Couldn't two adults with such separate lives keep things from each other? We'd shared so many secrets that I could see both sides of the coin.

But my mind jangled with warning lights and sirens I didn't understand. Something was wrong – I didn't have any idea what. I sat, leaning against the hot tub, rubbing the ache in my right shoulder.

Finally, Zach appeared around the corner, dressed, but he didn't come close.

"You know, this isn't about whatever is in your pocket," I said. "It's about your reaction to me. I don't understand."

"You're wrong."

"Then explain to me what's going on."

"I can't."

With his second two-word answer, I closed my eyes and let my head fall against the hot tub, unable to rein in the questions spinning around in my brain.

He walked away a short time later, without explaining anything.

Despite the jacket slung around my shoulders, the drizzle chilled me, so I retreated inside to the window seat in the living room where I curled up with a pillow to sulk.

The shower was running upstairs.

A while later, Zach came into the room and turned the rocking chair toward me, leaning his elbows on his knees. "Before I start, do you remember what I said a few days ago about praying you'd never have to, but that if I screwed up and hurt you, I hoped you'd still love me like you loved Jeremy?"

"I love you, Zach," I said. "Just be honest with me."

He nodded, then locked his fingers together and rested his forehead against them a moment before he raised his head to look at me again.

"First, I'm sorry if I hurt you. I didn't mean to be so rough, especially with your shoulder." He took a deep breath and held it several seconds. "At the bar in Florida, you know I didn't believe it was you, as much as I wanted it to be. But in that dingy hotel room, I don't think you understand how close I came to pulling the trigger."

"Yes, I do. Maybe even better than you do. I knew how white your knuckles were."

"I want you to know I'm sorry," he said. "For that. For today. For everything. When I grabbed your arm out there in the garage, I saw more fear in your eyes than when I pointed that gun at you. More than the night I picked you up in Albuquerque. All I can say is I'm sorry. It won't ever happen again."

My heart fluttered in my chest.

Zach stood and slid his hand into his jeans pocket, closed his fingers around something and pulled it out again.

"I swear I thought I could stop, Julie." He tossed two glassine envelopes onto the cushion in front of me.

One had about a teaspoon of cream-colored powder in it, the other was almost empty. I didn't know specifically what it was, but I knew it was some illicit drug or another.

He dropped hard to his knees.

"I'm gonna ask you one more time, J'. Please help me?"

CHAPTER 36

Despite being rocked back on my emotional heels, things that had not made sense before became painfully clear. I ran both hands over my forehead through my short hair, taking time to gather my racing thoughts, wanting my reaction to be more than an anger or fear reflex. Still, I had no idea what to say.

"You can't imagine how pathetic I feel, knowing I can't control this."

"Do you want to stop?" I asked.

Zach had been looking down in genuine shame, but he raised his head to face me. "Absolutely. I put you at incredible risk with this, in more ways than I ever want to think about. There's nothing to say except I'm sorry, but I'll make it right, Julie. I promise. I don't want to lose you. Whatever it takes, I'll do it."

"Why today? Is that what you left me here to do?"

"No," he said. "I went to take care of a neighbor's stock."

I shook my head in disbelief. "I'm not sure which would upset me more – knowing you had it with us all along or thinking you went out and bought it." I held up my hand to stop him from answering. "And I don't want to know."

He nodded. "I never understood what guys who use it really meant. It's like needing to breathe, this craving." He struggled to make me understand. "It's like wanting you – the feeling it's never enough when I touch you –"

"Don't you dare compare –"

He stopped me, holding up both arms in surrender. "You're right.

I don't mean to desecrate something so beautiful."

I took several deep breaths, trying to get my heart rate down. "I think I understand now what you were trying to say last night at dinner. I wish you'd have told me sooner." I swung my feet around to the floor and faced him. "I have a couple of rules. First, you don't go back to work until you're clean."

"Okay."

I took his hands, felt them tremble. "Next, we've got nothing left here but bare honesty, Zach. I can't afford anything else, so you have to understand I just need to say this: You've never so much as raised your voice to me before, but if there's any sort of physical threat, whether you hurt me or not, I'm gone."

"Understood. You have my word."

"Give me your pistol."

He stiffened.

"I've been there once, Zach." I stared into his green eyes. "Don't think that if I end up looking at you over the barrel of a gun again I won't kill you in self-defense."

"Ouch," he groaned.

I started to speak, but he interrupted me.

"No argument, Julie. You're right," he said. "Before I left this morning, I'd have sworn you were in no danger from me. Now, I don't blame you, and it's a risk you can't afford to take. My gun's in the car."

"Next, you gather it all up and get rid of it. Now. Everything you take that changes the way you feel. It's all off limits." I said it, unsure what all 'everything' might entail.

"Okay. I can do this. Really."

I stood up and pulled him to his feet beside me. "Yes, you can."

His arms wrapped around me, and suddenly I was the energy holding up the man who'd once rescued me.

"Come on," I said, leading him out into the garage where I collected his pistol. Out of habit, I dropped the 15-round magazine into my hand to check, then slapped it back in place.

"You should go shoot it," he suggested.

"A .40 caliber isn't my first choice."

I wondered if he'd feel naked without a weapon like I did without mine. Then I considered the risks in neither of us carrying it, given our circumstances. Did anyone who'd do us harm know where we were?

The question must have been on my face.

"I never told anyone about this place," Zach said as we went into the kitchen. "My mother doesn't even know yet. That doesn't mean no one could find us, but it's a good start."

I nodded.

"You can leave the gun on the dresser or wherever, Julie. I swear to you I won't touch it."

"The bags," I said, ignoring his promise. "Those two all you had?"

"No, I have one more here," he said with a sigh. "In my kit. The shaving cream can has a false bottom."

"Get it." I followed him upstairs and watched as he unscrewed the can and dropped another bag onto the bathroom countertop. "Three? This is all?"

"I figured it would be way more than... I mean I didn't think I'd use any..." He trailed off. "I had no idea what Pauly gave me wasn't just coke – it had to be part meth. They always told us about how easy it is to get hooked, but I swear I never used anything before what happened in Florida."

I believed what he said, but still, he'd used half of it, looking at the full bag, which wasn't much – maybe a couple of hits or more. I had no clue. However, given his behavior this morning, I couldn't imagine when he might have used it in the last few weeks we'd been together.

"I'd go until I couldn't stand it anymore," he continued. "Then I'd tell myself that was the last time."

Using my nails, I picked up the clear envelope, afraid to touch it and appalled at how it changed everything I believed in.

"There's more at Mom's in Albuquerque," he said, barely above a whisper. "I didn't leave any at your house. I knew better."

After I made him dump it outside away from the cabin, we settled into the living room to warm up.

"So where did you go this morning?" I asked, trying not to sound accusing.

"I promised a neighbor up the road about a mile I'd feed his animals so he and his family could go out of town for the day. He breeds Trakehners."

"Which are?" I asked.

"Horses," he said, which was all I needed to know. "We can go look if you'd like."

I shook my head. "That was a nice thing to offer to do."

"You're the most important thing in the world to me, Julie, and hurting you is not acceptable, no matter what."

"Please, don't give up."

"I won't if you won't," Zach said.

But then a week later, I ran away from everything we'd put together in Washington.

Zach might have thought it was the drugs, but my departure really had nothing at all to do with him – it was all about me.

CHAPTER
37

Confessing to his inability to stop using had led to a long discussion about our future. I didn't harbor any anger about his addiction, but I couldn't fix it, either. Christmas Day had become a pivot point, probably not the best conditions to start a life together, but our relationship thus far had been anything but normal, so that's the direction we chose.

The next afternoon, Zach took me to meet the neighbors and see the horses he'd told me about, and Delbert Clinton insisted we saddle up for a ride. The day was chilly and damp, but as we rode through the forest behind the Clinton's house, all the struggles in my life seemed to shake off and fall behind in our tracks.

"I don't think I've ever ridden a horse this big," I commented as we skirted trees on a trail. "You look good on him."

"Trakehners," he reminded me, because I had trouble remembering the name of the breed. "Shall we buy a pair?"

"A pair? No. I think we'll have plenty of horses to go around when we get Julaquinte, a colt, and Purgatory up here."

"Not Purgatory," he said. "No way we'd get that nasty son of a bitch halfway across the country in a trailer. He'd kick it apart before we hit blacktop."

"Surely he's not so bad," I suggested.

Zach looked at me. "Yes, he is. I helped rescue him at a wreck on the freeway near the house. We offered to board their stock while the couple was in the hospital. One of the four horses died the first night. Two more were okay," he said. "Purgatory is so trailer-shy, we can't leave him in the paddock when we load other horses or cattle. They couldn't take him, so I bought him. He used to be a champion cutting horse. They bring mares up for breeding once in a while."

"You're full of surprises."

"That surprises you?"

"I don't mean I'm shocked you'd do such a thing for the horse or for strangers, but there is so much about you I'm still learning, along with the letters and stuff. I have lots of questions."

The horses walked along, hooves clicking on occasional rocks, thumping on hard ground or rustling through dead leaves without any predictable rhythm.

"And yet you don't ask," he observed. "How could you put up with me breaking into your house, sleeping in your bed, then disappearing again for so long?"

"Put up with it?" I laughed. "You were the perfect man! I didn't have to dress up for a date or be on my best behavior to impress you. I never wondered if you liked me or whether you'd call the next day. The sex was always fantastic. You knew my ugly secrets and came back anyway. If there's a why to this, Zach, I'd have to ask you."

"Because I love you."

"Even though you had to pretend you didn't?"

He shrugged. "Faith is believing in something you can't prove."

"Well, it doesn't mean I didn't miss you after you snuck away in the middle of the night."

"Did you?" he asked. "Miss me, I mean?"

Did I ever. . .

"Always," I sighed, memories flashing of the times he'd been to my house. "Yeah, I missed you. I hated when you left and I woke up alone."

"Didn't want to overstay my welcome," he said with a smirk.

"How do you function on so little sleep?"

"I learned to do without in college," he explained. "Zoe had a full scholarship, but Mom was trying to pay for her other expenses at school. To keep her from trying to pay all my tuition, too, I took a football scholarship and moved to Houston with Zoe so we could share an apartment. I bounced bars at night to pay my share of the rent and utilities. Finished a year early and went to the police department there."

"You played football, even though you hated it?" I asked, astonished.

He shrugged. "The scholarship was a way to get an education."

"What's your degree in?"

"Criminal justice with a minor in art history."

"Really?" I said, stunned again. I mulled over that piece of trivia about his minor. "What else is in your figurative closet of skeletons? Tell me about the .44 round in the box."

He ducked to go under another branch before he spoke. "Several units responded to a domestic dispute in Houston. Both parties looked like they'd been using baseball bats on each other and throughout the house. We cuffed and separated them, and I was taking the woman out the side door when her teenage son stepped out of the garage and stuck a gun in my face," he said and hesitated. "The kid pulled the trigger, but despite all the yelling and chaos around me, in a split second of perfect silence, I heard the firing pin drop. Nothing happened. That moment seemed to last ten seconds as I waited for my heart to beat again, but I don't think I'd even blinked before two other officers shot him, not knowing the gun had misfired."

"Oh," I said, feeling my heart skip a beat. I've had a gun aimed at me enough to know I don't like it. I changed the subject again. "Tell me more about Zoe."

"Zoe was always my best friend. You don't have a sibling, so it might be hard to understand. Being twins made us close." He guided his horse around a rock, rather than over it. "We were always happier together, from the time we were born. Mom finally had to put us in the same crib because we cried if she tried to put us to sleep separately. That went on until we started walking, I guess. In school, we made separate friends, of course, but even in our teens, we still preferred each other's company," he said. "At least until I had sex with Zoe's best friend. That took her a while to get past."

"Was she stubborn and tough like you?"

He turned and frowned at me, then rolled his eyes. "No, she was a pleasant soul who could make people laugh even if she'd kicked them in the shins. You'd have liked her. Everyone liked her."

"Losing her must have been devastating."

"In some ways, she was dying long before the homicide." His baritone voice dropped even lower. "Like a hurricane, I could see it coming, but I didn't know what to do about it. What they did to her hurt me as much as it hurt her."

"I'm sure it broke your heart," I offered, recognizing a raw wound.

"That's not what I mean. Maybe you've heard people talk about twins feeling the same thing? After I shoved my way past the guys who didn't want me to see her body, I fell to my knees. Looking at her, I could feel every blow, every. . ." His voice broke, but he took a deep breath and kept talking. "She'd been raped again, by at least two men. Even when they beat her, but I knew she didn't fight. They hadn't killed her – they left her unconscious, choking on her own blood."

"Oh, Zach, I'm so sorry."

"It was hard enough telling my mother she was dead. I couldn't tell her how much Zoe had suffered," he said.

I reached to touch his arm as we rode abreast. "No, Vera didn't need to know, but I think I understand why you had to see Zoe, no matter what."

He nodded but said nothing again for a while.

"Did the men who attacked her pay for their crimes?" I finally asked.

"If you mean did they go to jail, no."

I was pondering what that meant when he turned to me and said, "Just so you know, I didn't mean to kill that kid in Florida or he wouldn't have died that fast."

Before I could think of anything to say, Zach dug his heels into the horse's ribs and galloped off ahead of me.

CHAPTER
38

Despite all our discussions and promises about drugs and jobs and trust necessary to make a new home together, January 2, Zach unloaded my suitcases from his car at Portland International Airport.

"Please, Julie. Don't go," he asked once more, reaching but not quite touching me. "I'll do whatever you ask. You could stay a few days in a hotel here, get a car and drive up to Seattle. Anything but this."

I'd spent the morning hyperventilating every time I looked at him, at the bandage around his arm, panic clenching my throat shut, my stomach full of acid and lead, thinking back to what had happened.

We'd bought a stereo system a few days after Christmas and a dozen more CDs. On New Year's Eve, we pushed the living room furniture against the walls and danced in the light of the fireplace and candles. We cooked and ate and snuggled and danced some more.

At midnight, we walked out onto the front deck to look up at the sky, and with his arms wrapped around me from behind, Zach whispered something I didn't quite understand, but I didn't ask. But in bed later, making love, there was no doubt in my mind he called me Mariah.

I was insulted, furious he'd called me by another woman's name after all his romantic words and promises. The rest of the night, I stewed about it, didn't drift off to sleep until after five o'clock, and I woke with a migraine headache after Zach'd bounded out of bed to start a brand new year.

It was a quick recipe for disaster.

Digging through my suitcase for the narcotic nasal spray I use for severe headaches, I couldn't find it. Then I smelled bacon frying.

I'd staggered downstairs as if I had a hangover, though likely our evening's champagne hadn't helped, shielding my eyes from the lights.

Zach stood at the counter, chopping walnuts for pancakes. Sounded more like he was using a sledgehammer on them to me, the sound was so distorted.

I came up behind him on his left and reached to take the knife from his right hand. "Please *stop*!" I'd groaned.

"It's early, but I was thinking after breakfast we could—" he'd begun.

"I don't *want* to eat. I want to find my pain medicine and go back to bed!" I held the knife at chest height, giving it no thought other than maintaining its current silence.

He'd wiped off his hands on a towel. "Okay, Julie, I'll help you look."

The sound of my name after I'd replayed him calling me Mariah all night long crashed inside my head, and I snapped.

"*Now* you call me Julie? Whose name did you whisper last night in bed, Zach?" I'd yelled, despite the pain it caused. "Who the hell is Mariah?"

I'd swung my arm to point up at the bedroom at the same time Zach reached to take the knife away – and I'd cut him. Very badly.

Now, standing outside the airport doors, I could barely maintain any control over my runaway emotions. "Zach, I'm sorry," I whispered, though it sounded like a mouse. "I can't. . ."

Can't explain why I have to leave.

He pulled me to him, but the embrace only made me sob harder.

"I know you have to go through Albuquerque and get the dog. Will you call when you get back to Michigan, so I'll know you got home okay?" he asked.

I nodded.

I needed to run away.

Zach kissed my head and let go. "If it's not the drugs, I still don't understand why you're leaving," he said, head hanging, "but please, be careful."

He thought this was about him, his addiction to the meth, or that he'd possibly hurt me, but it really had nothing to do with him at all. I'd tried, but I failed to find words to explain the emotions burning inside my chest.

Bolting with my luggage through the electric doors, I prayed I could make it far enough that when I gave in and looked, he wouldn't still be there, leaning against the Mustang.

He was.

Crying.

Seeing that almost brought me to my knees, knowing I was hurting him as much as when the knife blade had sliced through his arm. Still, I knew I had to go.

The airport was packed with holiday travelers, but other than conversation buzzing in my ears, it might as well have been deserted.

I made my way to the ticket agent and checked my bags, then I found an empty gate down the terminal in a corner and cried some more.

Finally aboard the aircraft, I sat next to a cheerful couple on their way home from a New Zealand honeymoon. Any other time, I would have been interested in their stories, but I only wanted to shut them out like all the other noises.

Physically exhausted, emotionally short-circuited, mentally unable to process what had happened the last few days, I felt like an alien. A mutant in a world of normalcy.

Maybe I should have checked into a hotel to clear my head for a few days, I thought as the jet taxied to the end of the runway.

Too late now.

I spent the flight to Albuquerque, thinking about the last week, how precious so many of the moments with Zach had been before everything spun so wildly out of control the day before.

The jet engines whined so loudly I thought my head would burst, but I couldn't stop thinking about him. Our time together in Washington broke my heart even more, and I sat with my jacket pulled up around my neck and let tears trail down my cheeks as the jet carried me southeast, leaving Zach and a close-to-perfect world with him behind.

When my plane landed in Albuquerque, I rented a car, not knowing whether my mother was working and not wanting to be quizzed about my sudden return alone if she wasn't.

Having no plan in particular, I wanted to get drunk, though having not eaten in almost two days, that wouldn't have taken much. I wanted to scream. I wanted to sleep. But for the first time in several years, I realized I had a gnawing urge to prowl through the streets.

I picked up my phone and hit a programmed number, waited.

"Hello?" a woman's voice answered, which surprised me.

"I, uh. . . My name is Julie Madigan. Is Eric home?"

"Sure. Just a minute."

"Hello?" said the familiar voice I'd hoped to hear.

"Eric, I hate to interrupt your holidays, but have you got a few minutes?"

"Julie? Sure, what's up?" he said.

I gulped. "I need a friend right now, Rader. I've done something bad."

Eric Rader had been the commanding officer when I worked at the Alamogordo post. He was now a deputy chief for the New Mexico State Police and lived in Santa Fe. His friendship had endured my career, even after he investigated the domestic shooting fatality by one of his officers – me. We'd kept in touch after I left for Michigan.

"Where are you?" he asked.

"I just flew into Albuquerque."

Although he offered to drive down, it made more sense for me to go to Santa Fe, and I hoped I could use the time to pull myself together. He gave me directions to their house, and I hit I-25 northbound in a rented Grand Am I had trouble keeping under the speed limit.

When I arrived, Eric made a quick introduction to Samantha, the woman he'd told me about several months before – now his very pregnant wife. I apologized for missing their wedding, and then he led me into the den where my composure and resolve melted into more tears.

"I'm sorry to just show up," I said. "It's a really lengthy, complicated story."

"The last update you gave me wasn't that long ago," he kidded gently. "I followed the rest of the investigation and the hearing. I'm sorry about what happened to your friends. You must have been devastated."

"Matt, then Jeremy," I said, trying not to close my eyes and cry more. It might have been old news, but I discovered it tore me apart to say their names. "Jeremy was going home to his wife and daughter. But apparently he identified Bock and followed him to Florida instead. There was a shooting in a St. Petersburg hospital room."

"Oh," Eric managed.

"Bock had gone to kill Zach. He's with DEA."

"Samualson?" he said, making a connection that stunned me. "I know Zach."

Great.

I confessed to Eric what had happened on New Year's Day, trying to explain why I'd left Washington, why I'd left a man I loved. "I've become the monster, like the one I was trying to catch."

"You're not a monster, Julie." Eric leaned forward in his chair and studied me. "I'm sorry. I don't think you want to hear what I have to say, but we've been friends too long for me to let this go on."

My tissue was damp and kneaded into a wad. I stared at it, silent, afraid to look up and ask what he meant.

"I knew you before, and although you were intense and wired for sound, you weren't strung out like this. Especially on the heels of what happened to your father, no one could've imagined how David trying to kill you or you shooting him would affect everything in your life," Eric said. "Now all this."

His words about my past felt like daggers, whizzing by, threatening to do more damage. Causing more fear.

"You deserve to know what really happened the day David attacked you." He paused until I looked up at him. "And maybe I was wrong, but I believed I needed to wait until you came looking for the answers."

"What answers?"

"I got my hands on a dub of the surveillance tape from the Air Force. It took every favor I had on base and then some. Never found out why they had your house bugged. They did censor the tape, so I only know what happened shortly before you came home and after."

"How long have you –" I started to ask, but I realized it didn't matter.

"It took me more than a year to get it. By then, you were packing to move to Michigan. I figured since you hadn't asked, you didn't want to know. Your mother said you were doing okay, so I waited." He hesitated again. "I also have a copy of the recording from your father's office. I think it's time you heard them both."

I held out my hand.

He shook his head. "There's a catch. The only way you get to hear them is by going to see the department psychologist."

"I'm not going –" I started to argue.

"Julie, I won't fight with you about this," he stated. "I would have insisted before, except you didn't come back to work. Whatever you think did or did not happen on those two days is destroying you, and I can't watch it any longer."

Looking up at the ceiling, I wrapped my arms tightly against my body, holding together all the pieces I felt I'd become. "Honestly, Eric, do you think that's the solution?"

"You trusted me enough to come here tonight. Trust me a little more. I think you'll find a lot of the answers you've been running from. Maybe you'll find a little peace."

"Peace." I repeated. A concept Zach had mentioned – it seemed meaningless, like faith and forgiveness or the infinity of the universe. "I'll stay until we can do this, but it's still under duress."

"No doubt, and duly noted," Eric said with a relieved smile. "If your mother isn't expecting you, you're welcome to stay."

"No, she doesn't know I'm here, but I think I need to be alone tonight. Thanks, though."

"I'll make arrangements for you to see someone tomorrow," he said. "Give me a call at the office first thing."

Samantha asked again as we stood at the front door if I wouldn't like to stay and insisting my apologies for interrupting their evening were not necessary. She seemed like a good match for Eric. They looked happy together, like I thought Zach and I had looked.

Before.

I went back to Albuquerque, where I drove around for an hour before I ended up in the parking lot where Zach had walked me to my

Jeep so long ago, the first time I remembered seeing him.

Drunks came and went while I watched from the shadows where I lurked for more than an hour before I started the car and went to find a hotel.

♦

Dr. Phillip Rothman had a very young face and no hair at all, making his age deceiving. Twenty or sixty, he could go either way. His voice sounded like a twelve-year-old's.

I didn't have the energy to figure it out.

He directed me into his study, asked me to sit wherever I thought I'd be comfortable while he picked up my file.

Sofa, chairs, desk. What a psychological test this is.

I chose the chair at his desk, and he sat down in the chair next to me.

"The state police put you on disabled status in 1991," he began, flipping pages in a folder resting on his crossed legs. "This was after a domestic assault that led to you shooting your husband, correct?"

Nodding, I couldn't think of anything to add.

My chest ached, and my temples throbbed. No doubt, I looked like crap, having gotten only snatches of sleep for the last two days.

"And reports say you refused to talk to the mental health staff during your lengthy hospitalization or afterward in rehab."

"Yeah."

"May I ask why?"

I turned away from him and stared at his expensive desk. Free of fluff or jumble, leaving lots of polished grain visible. *What is it they say – a clean desk is the sign of a cluttered mind.*

We played the silence game, which went on until I surrendered. I had come for help, so being obstinate made little sense.

"Those who tried to get me to talk wanted to find out how it *made me feel* to shoot my husband," I stated in a monotonous voice, "as if I were supposed to feel guilty."

"You didn't," he suggested.

I turned to look directly at him. "No, nor do I feel guilty that I don't feel guilty."

"You're an educated woman with a degree in psychology. Perhaps we can cut to the chase and you can tell me why you're here, then?"

What came to mind was *No, just play the frigging tape!* but I thought better of that response. "The murder of my father, the assault by David, and recently being kidnapped and forced to kill a deputy – a friend of mine – were the work of one man. We discovered he is my illegitimate half-brother. Was. There are portions of the first two events I don't remember, and what I do recall has reached critical mass."

"Interesting description. You don't have recall of all of these events, and so you want to hear the tapes to find out what you don't remember?"

I nodded.

"The mind stores stressful events differently than normal memories," he again stated, not questioning me. "Repression of emotionally difficult memories is not uncommon. Why would you want to remember now and not before?"

"I've had a lot of years to process these things, so I'm not even sure if what I think I remember is real."

He seemed to be satisfied with my answer, and he flipped through more pages before he continued. "Because we're doing this at the speed of light instead of taking months or years, I'd rather see what you do remember than just playing this information for you. Hearing the tapes might free all your memories, or it could further lock them down." He paused, awaiting my decision.

I nodded.

"Let's start with your father's murder. You were sixteen, right?" he didn't wait for an answer. "Tell me what you recall – only the basics."

Taking a deep breath, I explained I had been in a workroom when I heard the gunshot, had rushed to his office where I found him bleeding. "My father made me run for help before the killer came back, or I might have been able to save him."

"How did you feel about leaving?"

I glared at Rothman. "What do you think? I left my father on the floor, bleeding to death."

"Rationally, you understand that you could not have stopped the bleeding and fought off a killer, right?"

"You asked me how I felt about leaving. Rationalization about what I could or could not have done does not change the way it feels." I crossed my arms, getting angrier by the question.

"How did you cope with your father's death?"

"We were close. I was upset I'd been robbed of such a huge part of my life by someone who went unpunished."

"And how did you act out?" he asked.

"Isolation, depression, confrontation. It was hard when the police kept questioning me. Every time someone made me replay the details, my heart rate would soar, and I'd get all jacked up." I looked him straight in the eyes. "As much as I hated the story, I began to like the feeling."

"That's a good observation. So you came away from that experience liking the adrenaline. But over time, I'm guessing the response began to fade, right? What did you do then?"

Skipping through the years between, I said, "I grew up and went into law enforcement and EMS. Same feeling, different stimuli."

"Very good. Some people never see the connection." He nodded. "Tell me about you and your husband."

"David had a temper, but he controlled it while we were dating. After we got married, he'd get mad and go off for hours at a time, sometimes overnight," I said. "In a pre-Desert Storm exercise, he went overseas. When he came home, he became much more explosive and aggressive, breaking things, but not violent with me physically. That's when I recognized how I fed off his anger. The worse things got, the more I began pushing him, trying to see how far he would go."

"Were you physically aggressive to him?"

"No, I didn't have to be physical. I knew what buttons to push to set him off. Clothes he didn't approve of – low-cut or tight shirts. Smile at a stranger. He accused me of screwing around dozens of times, including with superior officers – his and mine – so it was easy to make him mad."

"Were you having an affair?" Rothman asked.

I shook my head.

"Did you get a rush when you shot him?"

I thought back to what I'd felt, but the only sensation I could identify was nausea. "I was nearly unconscious from the blood loss. If there was any rush, I was too sick to know it."

He nodded. "What about killing the deputy? That must have been a huge adrenaline kick for you."

"No, it was more like running blind into a wall full-speed." I took a deep breath. "Since then, there's been a side to my behavior I don't understand, a violent angry response. It's almost irrational. I have trouble controlling my anger at any level. Because of that, when I let my guard down, I seriously injured the man I'm involved with."

"Was he abusive to you?"

"Never, exactly the opposite."

But Zach fed the monster, too – providing me with the fear that supported my addiction, my need to survive. Had my uncontrollable anger surfaced when we no longer played the game because we'd been together so much?

"Did you harm him intentionally?"

I shook my head and explained what had happened on New Year's Day in details that made my guts burn.

"Let me see if I have this straight. You're here because you think something on these tapes can help you with this facet of violence you've seen in yourself recently?"

"Maybe, I don't know."

"Back to David then. Did you provoke his attack?"

"I remember being annoyed when I left for work about a project he'd scattered on the dining table. When I came home, I said something else about it, which probably fueled the argument. Upstairs, he blind-sided me."

I waited for the next question but realized Dr. Rothman was watching me. Right on cue, the adrenaline dump made my heart race. I didn't even try to disguise taking a deep breath and holding it, trying to relax. I hoped that if I kept talking, the rush would pass. "When David stuck the gun to my head, he wanted me to beg, but I wouldn't. Then he knocked me out and –"

No, no way to control it – the sensation finally took my breath away.

"You feel it again, talking about what happened," Rothman observed. "Do you like it?"

What I felt was no longer the excitement or thrill – only dread. The train wreck at the end of a runaway ride.

"Not this," I managed to say. "It's different than before, like something heavy on my chest. Instead of a rush, it's linked to every painful emotion I've ever felt. I can't separate them anymore. I can't ride the wave without fearing the crash."

We waited each other out in silence for a few minutes as the adrenaline wore down.

"I think I can help you moderate your body's stress response. Would you be willing to try something?"

I hesitated, then nodded.

Anything to gain some semblance of control. How desperate is that?

"Just like you learned to turn on and focus the adrenaline rollercoaster, I think I can teach you to turn it off when it doesn't feel good."

He moved me to a more comfortable chair across the room and sat down opposite me.

"Have you ever been hypnotized?"

"No." I'm sure my voice betrayed my skepticism.

"It's not voodoo, and you're not losing control. All I will ask you to do is relax your body, Julie. When you reach that level of relaxation, you'll continue your story about that day, no longer dominated by the fear and anxiety directly linked to the memory."

When I wasn't convinced yet, he continued.

"Without the physical stress responses overriding your memories, perhaps your mind can find all the pieces. You still have full control over the story and what you tell me."

I finally nodded.

Following his gentle voice through a series of steps, I began to feel warm and limber. My eyes closed, and we talked.

The next thing I realized, I was sitting in the chair, eyes opened, and feeling much less like a screaming zombie than I had for several days.

"Very informative. Bypassing the physical stress and emotional tags has allowed your brain to access real memories versus those you've created."

"What did I tell you?" I asked.

"You can listen to the tape. I'd like you to hear your own words."

"Really?" I asked.

"This is all inside your head, Julie. There's no reason why you can't hear it," he said and smiled.

"Wow. I wasn't expecting that, I guess."

He played it while we listened.

"Julie, tell me what happened on the day we were discussing, the day you shot David Wesley," he'd said. "Start at the beginning of your shift that morning. Remember, you're presenting this as history. There is no danger. You are perfectly safe."

I gave details about the day, even the parts of it I would not normally recall, such as the license plate of a vehicle I'd stopped during my shift as well as the cross-street location.

When I shook my head, Dr. Rothman stopped the tape. "Hearing this surprises you?"

"I guess it's amazing how much clutter one's mind really holds."

"Not clutter, all information gets filed away in archival folders. Every day, your brain processes billions of pieces of information you will never directly access again. I believe you never actually forget anything as long as the brain is intact and healthy, but your conscience may not know how to access data with no initial meaning."

"Like what I had for breakfast on any particular school day as a child?" I asked.

"Exactly. You might not remember, but it's not missing. Emotional tags make memories create cross-references. If you'd spilled oatmeal on your favorite dress and your mother made you cry that morning, the memory would be much easier to locate."

He started the tape again.

I listened as I described coming home, finding David working on an electronic gizmo on the kitchen table. This had irritated me, and I told him to move his junk so I could fix supper. Then I went to change out of my uniform.

Upstairs, when I began to unbutton my shirt, like a silent movie, I turned to see David saying something obscene to me, just before his fist smashed into the right side of my face.

"Crumbling to the floor, I thought I saw someone else standing behind David," I'd said.

Dr. Rothman had asked me if I recognized this man now, and I said yes, I believe it was Anthony Bock.

As the taped questions and answers continued, there were holes in my memory during several periods of unconsciousness. And while hearing these details disturbed me, panic did not overwhelm me as I'd always presumed.

Dr. Rothman had me end the story when the ambulance transported me to the hospital in Alamogordo.

"That's all," he said, turning off the tape. He rested his arms over his head casually. "How do you feel?"

"I knew that question was coming."

"No, I did not ask how it makes you feel, hearing the tape or talking about the events you described, Julie," he said firmly. "I've provided a vent for these memories and emotions, and hopefully as the pressure is released, you'll feel better. That's all I'm asking."

"I guess I feel a little more in control," I admitted. "Is this going to trigger any nightmares or flashbacks?"

"I don't think so. The nightmares were more likely your way of recreating the events to fill in the details, as you put it," he stated. "Whether and how you've been sleeping is a bigger indicator what your brain will do with this new information than anything."

"I've been fighting a migraine for days now. When I can't sleep, it gets worse."

"We need to get the pain under control and get you ten hours of good sleep." He wrote a prescription for me – a single pill. "Take this tonight when you get into bed, and do that before ten o'clock, please. Go to the bathroom, do all your nightlies first because this hits some people like a sledgehammer. Set an alarm for noon tomorrow, but get out of bed if you wake up before then. I'll see you at two o'clock."

He opened a credenza door and took out a bottle. "This is for the headache. I'm sure you've had plenty of stuff, but this is worth a try."

And he gave me other specific instructions – a particular meal for dinner, a music CD and a player if necessary, then a couple of mental exercises. And last, he told me to do something unusually nice for myself this afternoon.

He also applauded my choice to stay in the hotel rather than with my mother. "You can have lunch or dinner with her tomorrow."

"Should I call Zach tonight?"

"No," he said, "You need this time to work on you. Whatever the reason was you felt you had to leave is still buried. Give it a day or two."

CHAPTER

39

Bookworm that I've always been, the bookstore where I'd worked as a teenager remained one of my favorite places in Albuquerque. I picked out a new hardcover by John Sanford, one my favorite authors, the CD and a player that Dr. Rothman had asked me to get, and a small sampler of lotions and nail cream for something indulgent.

With time to spare before dinner, I went to the mall to browse and ended up with two pair of jeans to fit my new weight-loss hips. Then I spent almost three hours having the dark muddy color stripped from my hair, closer to my original shade of blonde.

Getting rid of the brown severed my last connection to Florida. This was my unusually nice thing to do for myself. With that, along with a variation of the cut, my hair looked better, and somehow I felt more like myself.

Add a blow dryer to style my hair, dark mulberry-colored polish for nails that had grown out since I wasn't working, and I felt like I'd had a productive day.

I was walking to my car when my cell phone rang.

"Madigan," I said, comfortable with the greeting again, though I didn't know why.

"Julie, it's Dom. What the hell is going on?"

So much for feeling good. . .

I slid behind the wheel of my rental car and sat, talking to Domino Hurley about why I left Washington.

"Zach called me, Julie, said he needs help."

"It's not my place to tell you what his problem is, Dom, but you have to trust me. Please don't let him go back to work right now."

"He told me about the drugs. I'm on a flight to Portland tomorrow if the weather holds – it's nasty out there. All I want to do is help, Julie. I don't think you'd walk away without a reason, but he wouldn't tell me."

I wanted to explain, though I was still struggling to make myself understand why. No matter how much I loved Zach, I had to leave.

". . . did he hurt you?" I heard Dom asking me.

"No!" I exclaimed and pushed the disconnect button, then threw the phone into the seat next to me. "No, Dom," I sobbed. "Doesn't anybody get it? It wasn't anything he did – I hurt Zach."

Waking the next morning at ten, I didn't feel groggy like I'd half expected with the sleeping pill. My headache had dissipated to a candle flame from its wildfire blaze before.

Looking at the bed, I don't think I'd turned over once, much less tossed and turned like I had the night before.

I took a shower and blow-dried my hair, still liking the cut. I'd grown it long before because whenever I'd have it styled at the salon, it never worked for me at home. Hard to screw up a ponytail, braid or bun, and it looks the same regardless of the weather.

The woman in the mirror looked a little less like she was spiraling into oblivion at the speed of insanity.

Whatever happened today, I vowed not to let it dominate me.

I called Mom at noon and found it was her day off. She was surprised I was in Albuquerque, and without Zach, but I told her he needed to stay in Portland for his job. I said I'd be over later in the afternoon, and we could go out to eat.

"Julie, is everything all right?" she finally asked.

"You know me, Mom. Is everything *ever* all right with me? I'll see you for dinner," I promised.

With a little bit of an appetite, I stopped on my way to Dr. Rothman's office and picked up a bagel and cream cheese, then sat in his parking lot to finish before I went in.

"You look more composed than yesterday. So, how did you sleep last night?" he asked when I settled into the chair next to his desk again.

"Like a rock," I said. "And my headache is better today, too."

"Great, so I think maybe pain and lack of sleep are components of a downward cycle we can give you more control over. Anything you'd like to discuss today before we start?"

"Well, I know you said to wait to call Zach, but his partner called me last night to find out what's going on, I guess. Why I left."

"Did you tell him?"

I shook my head. "I don't *know* why, except it was killing me every time Zach looked my direction, knowing what he was thinking."

"My guess is you did not know what he was thinking," Rothman said, "but you were concerned for everyone's welfare, and that was prudent."

He asked about having another session of hypnosis and talking about the day my father died. As I moved, he actually suggested I rest on the sofa instead.

I hesitated but did as he asked.

The next thing I was aware of, it was almost five o'clock.

"You mean I've been out for nearly three hours?" I demanded.

"Not 'out' at all. You've been talkative and quite introspective, too," he said. "I don't think you want to stay here to review the tape for another three hours, but I'd like to share a few things we can discuss tomorrow. I will preface this by saying I've listened to both tapes from Eric Rader, and I was able to direct some questions based on that, so I don't want you to feel I've gleaned all this from you blindly."

I nodded and sat up. Having to preface anything just seemed to make it bad news.

Dr. Rothman began. "The memory of the day's events is intact when you heard a gunshot and ran to your father's office. After you left him, however, you blocked at least one segment of the incident," he said, pausing for a moment. "I had a hard time getting you to acknowledge that you saw the killer's face before you left."

Stunned, the scene played out before my conscious mind for the first time in years as Rothman described it.

"He grabbed me." A shiver rippled through my body. "He grabbed me from behind and said something."

"There's nothing recorded on the evidence tape," Rothman offered.

"But I remembered it, didn't I?"

He nodded. "You tell me. Close your eyes and let it play in your mind. Don't think about how you felt, just remember the sounds, the words."

Very much not wanting to do so, I closed my eyes and remembered finding my father. He told me to leave even as I tried to stop the bleeding by putting my hands over his, blood spilling between all the fingers. He finally ordered me to get out of the building. Against all my better judgment, I scrambled to my feet and ran toward the east parking lot exit to get help. When I slowed to make the last corner toward the door, a man stepped from a dark office at the end of the hall. I screamed as the rough bear hug from behind jerked me off the floor, though my momentum spun him. When I kicked and twisted in his grip, he smashed his body against mine, pinning me to the wall. Then I heard him whisper in my right ear.

"I'll make them all pay. I'll kill them all but you. You're special. You'll be just like me some day," the voice said. "Maybe you'd like to kill your father. . ." Dark, evil laughter echoed in my memory.

My eyes popped open. "Oh," my voice squeaked.

"My question at that point was whether or not he said anything else to you." Dr. Rothman let the statement stand.

"Yes," I said, tears blurring my vision. "He told me he was my brother."

Rothman only nodded as everything whirled in my head.

Could I have given the police a description that would have made the case solvable? If I'd told them he said he was my brother, would they have located and convicted him?

I ran my hands through my hair, fighting tears I could not control.

The psychiatrist pushed the box of tissue toward me, and I took a handful and sobbed.

Seeing I'd finally calmed down, Rothman said, "You're upset, and rightly so. Since you haven't listened to today's session, it's possible the events may surface unexpectedly." He handed me a prescription for another sleeping pill. "Don't take it unless you're unable to get to sleep by midnight. I'll see you again tomorrow at two, and we'll listen to the tapes."

When I gathered my jacket and left, I felt raw, un-insulated, as if I'd grabbed an electric fence. My body tingled from the current, unpleasant but not unbearable as I'd feared. And I felt guilty because I hadn't provided police with a clue to solve my father's murder.

Worse, I wondered when I'd pushed that memory into the darkness where I could not find it – had it happened immediately after I left? Had I ever consciously remembered Bock's words?

But as I sat in the parking lot a few minutes, evaluating my sense of emotional balance, I finally decided I was okay.

♦

"Two days ago?" my mother repeated when I told her I'd flown in and was staying in a hotel. "Honey, you look awful!"

At least my black eye is almost gone.

The dog greeted me without disappointment or insult. I had to go play tug-of-war in the backyard before Laser would settle down.

I had to admit, burning off a little energy felt good.

"So what is this all about, Julie?" she started again when I came back in the house.

"I am not going to argue about this, Mom," I said, washing the dog slobber from my hands at the kitchen sink. "I have lots of reasons for what I'm doing, and I won't debate them with you. Eric Rader convinced me to go see the state police shrink, in trade for letting me hear the tapes from Dad's murder and from the townhouse when I shot David."

"Why on earth would you need to hear those –"

"Stop!" I put both wet hands in the air between us. Lowering the volume a bit, I tore off a paper towel and continued, "Just stop. Something is really wrong in my life – don't you have nightmares about Bock or something left over from all that?"

Stunned by the question, she nodded.

"I do, too," I said. "Lots of nightmares. I need answers – missing pieces to fit together. I'm driving myself crazy, avoiding these memories I never wanted to deal with, but I've got to do something. Please drop it."

She wanted to argue, but I refused to discuss it anymore, finally turning and walking away from her.

"You've always held on so tightly to what hurt you, Julie. I'm sorry I couldn't help you. I never knew what to do for you."

"Nor can I change what Bock did to you," I said a little too sharply. "I'm sorry, too. But you can't fix this. I have to do this myself."

Apologies accepted; subject changed.

We went to dinner at her favorite Mexican food place, and I ordered a taco salad instead of my normal fajitas.

After she tried to discuss how much weight I'd lost, the conversation somehow steered clear of irritating topics for the rest of dinner, and while she obviously wanted to argue about me returning to my hotel room for the night, I simply said I'd already paid for it.

Back at Mom's house, she was in the bathroom when her phone rang and the call went to her machine on the second ring.

"Dagmar, this is Zach. I was wondering if Julie had picked up the dog and gone back to Michigan yet. I was . . . I hadn't heard from her . . . please don't tell her I called."

I picked up the phone.

"I'm still in Albuquerque, Zach."

There was a silence.

"Zach?"

"I'm sorry, Julie, I was so worried. I know I said I wouldn't. . ."

"It's okay. Can I call you back when I get to my hotel room?" I asked. "Half an hour?"

"Sure," he said and hung up.

I hit the erase button.

"Who was that, honey?" Mom asked.

"Zach, just checking in," I said, evading the further questions I could see developing in her eyes. "I've got to go. Do you work tomorrow?"

She did, evening shift for the rest of the week.

I told her I'd be flying home to Michigan as soon as I could get cleared with the shrink, but I'd come stay at the house the following night. "We can have brunch the next morning before I leave," I said.

♦

At the hotel, I dialed Zach's cell phone number from my own as I collapsed into the chair and put my feet up.

"Yeah," he said. Not quite his usual answer.

I apologized for not checking in. He apologized again for calling. There was another awkward silence.

"I didn't know what else to do when I got here, so I went to see Eric Rader," I began. "I didn't know you two knew each other."

"In passing," he said absently.

"He blackmailed me into seeing the company shrink, the price for getting to listen to the tapes."

Zach knew what tapes I meant. We'd discussed them on more than one occasion.

"And you've heard them?"

"Actually, not yet. Dr. Rothman also uses hypnosis, which he's performed the last two afternoons to see what I remember rather than just playing the recordings."

"You must have wanted to hear those tapes pretty bad," he said with a little smile, "to let someone hypnotize you."

"Yeah, I guess so. Rader really didn't give me much choice. I'm not sure he wouldn't have had me committed on a 72-hour hold the other night to make his point. I guess I've looked better."

"Julie, you're not . . ." He hesitated, maybe searching for the right word.

"Not what?" I challenged.

"Did you go prowling?"

I wanted to say no, but my mind locked on sitting in my rental car at the bar two nights ago, leaving his question answered in silence.

"Christ, Julie," he groaned.

"I went driving, Z'," I said. "I never stopped the car."

Okay, so I lied. But I didn't get out.

"Please, Baby. I'd lose my mind if you got hurt."

"Zach, please don't," I said, struggling to get to my feet. "I can't argue about this."

"I'm sorry, but I'm so worried about you. Promise me you won't," he begged. "Talk to the shrink about it. Whatever you need to do. Please don't end up like Zoe."

The desperation in his voice was crystal clear, and I realized how afraid he really was. How much I was hurting him. Again.

"I promise."

Did I mean it?

Suddenly, my heart rate soared, and I felt like I couldn't breathe.

"I gotta go, Zach."

"Please don't hang up," I heard as I pushed the disconnect button.

CHAPTER
40

Hanging by frayed nerves, I couldn't bring myself to answer my phone when it rang again. I hurt, and as insane as it sounded, hurting was what I wanted to do. But I did not want to hurt Zach any more.

Finally ringing gave way to silence. The phone seemed to be daring me to call him back again, but I couldn't.

Motionless, incapacitated by a wall of emotions I couldn't climb, I didn't want to live, hurting those around me. That's what it all came down to – I didn't want to die, but I hated myself for hurting Zach so many times. He deserved better than a monster who'd turned on him like a rabid dog.

How'd I get this way?

A much younger face of Anthony Bock – one I barely recognized from the past – popped into my memory, fused with the voice in my ears, screaming in a whisper that made me shiver: *You'll be just like me some day.*

Had Anthony somehow branded his violence into my psyche, damning me for the rest of my life? He'd certainly driven me to the edge of suicide before. He'd forced me to let die or to kill men I cared about.

When I passed by it, I saw my reflection in the mirror, like something out of a zombie movie – pale skin, dark hollow eyes.

No, I didn't want to die.

I didn't know how to go on living at that very moment, but I could not let Anthony win my soul by giving up.

All I wanted to do was hear Zach's voice again. To talk to the one man who could reach out to save me from this demon.

Hitting redial, no one answered. After a dozen tries over the next hour, I gave up and took the medicine Dr. Rothman had prescribed. Still I called Zach's phone again and again. Each time it went unanswered, I sunk deeper into a black hole.

The sleeping pill didn't let my mind coast down like the night before, leaving me stuck in the zone just before sleep, where the mind begins to drift but muscles twitch, gasping for air.

Stretched out on the bed, I attempted to shut down my body, trying to recreate the relaxation I felt during hypnosis. It was a fight, at first, making the muscles in my back and neck relax and stay. I tried to concentrate on breathing.

Waves of memories washed in, slowly, like the incoming tide.

I could smell Dad's cologne.

I could see the two-day stubble on David's face when I shot him.

I could feel Anthony's breath against my cheek as he spoke to me.

Not at Dad's office, years later in my townhouse.

Anthony's words were masked by the ringing in my ears.

Was it ringing I heard?

The glint of light reflecting off a knife blade as it moved through my field of vision, disappearing beneath my chin.

I could feel the pressure of the blade, the motion as my head was yanked back, and the initial sting . . .

Screaming. . .

The sensation against my neck disappeared.

No, not screaming, ringing.

I sat up and grabbed for my phone.

"Zach?" I asked.

"Julie, it's Domino," he said sharply. "I need you to give me directions to the cabin."

Even had alarms not being going off in my head already, the sound of Dom's voice pushed me over into panic.

"What's wrong?"

"I told you I was coming out here. I can't find it," he said. "Zach's not answering his phone."

"Domino, there's no cellular service at the house."

"The landline was installed yesterday. He'd called me, and we'd talked for almost an hour, from the time I landed in Portland. He said he was coming down with something, felt like shit. The longer we talked, the less sense he was making."

"Did it occur to you to call EMS?" I asked, perplexed.

"And say what? I don't even know where the hell I'm going, Julie. Just tell me how to get to the fucking cabin!"

"Where are you?"

He told me he was in Carson.

I gave him instructions all at once, knowing I'd lose his signal, too.

Dom gave me the landline number to keep trying.

"I talked to him earlier, Dom. I hung up on him," I said, fearing the worst.

"He told me. Listen, Julie, whatever happened between you is none of my business except I see thousands of miles between two people who need to be together. Can you really work it out that far apart?" he said, beginning to break up. "He loves you, Ju. . ."

"I love him, too," I said, wondering if the connection had broken before I finished.

When I'd talked to Zach earlier, I'd called his cell phone, so he couldn't have been at the house.

I called the new house number Dom had given me.

I had to make sure Zach was okay, but hadn't I already caused him enough pain?

"Wha. . ." The groggy voice answered after a dozen rings.

"Zach?"

"Zoolie," he said, slurred.

"Zach? What's wrong?"

"I'm sick. . . My arm's bleedin' and it's hot. . ." He groaned. "I need you. . ." His voice drifted away.

"Zach, honey, I love you. Dom's almost there. He'll get you to the hospital."

"I want you to come home, Joolie," he said. "I won't ever hurt you again, I promise."

"You didn't hurt me, Zach," I said. "This is all my fault. I left because I didn't want to hurt you anymore."

What if he lost his arm because of this? What if . . .
"I'll do anything you want, J', please come home?"
He was breaking my heart.
"Zach, when did you get sick?"
"I was clearing brush yesterday and . . ." His voice faded again.
"Zach? Keep talking to me. When did your arm start to hurt?"
"Yeah, it hurts bad."
"Have you been taking your antibiotics?"
"My annie-whut?"
"The antibiotic pills for your arm?"
"Ain't touched no pills, Julie, I swear to you!"
Great. . .

I checked my watch. Only ten minutes had passed since I'd lost contact with Domino. Because he didn't know the area, it could be another ten or fifteen minutes before he got there.

Reaching for my handbag, I dug for the business card from the Skamania sheriff's deputy we'd met Christmas Eve. Maybe I could get through to someone and get an ambulance started anyway.

"Zach, don't hang up, okay? I'm still here."
"Yeah. . . 'kay."
I dialed the room phone and put the receiver to my ear.
"Sheriff's Department, Logan."
"My name is Julie Madigan. I need you to dispatch an ambulance to Zach Samualson's new house off Windy River."
"I can connect you to 911. Hey, did you say Madigan?"
"Yeah, Julie Madigan."
"From that bicycle crash Christmas Eve? It's Doug."

The connection to events of a few weeks ago seemed to take hours in my memory, then was inconsequential to my task. "Yeah, Doug. Listen, my fiancé is still there, and he's very sick. I'm in New Mexico. There's another DEA officer on his way to the house there, but he doesn't know his way around. Can you help me, please?"

"Please, Julie?" I heard Zach echo in the other ear.
"Stand by. . ." A series of clicks.
"911."
"Stacy, Doug at SO. I conferenced a caller who needs to give you directions to dispatch EMS. I'll put another deputy out to take the

call, too."

"You don't have an address?" she asked.

"I'm sure there is one, but I don't think I ever knew it. It's a new house, new road, new phone." I gave her directions, listening to the radio traffic in the background, the occasional question from Doug or Stacy, and the odd commentary from Zach in the other ear.

Finally in the background, I heard Domino banging at the front door. I'd told him where to find a key if he needed it.

God, I hope Zach doesn't shoot him by mistake.

"Zach, Domino is coming in. I told him where to get the key, so he can come help you."

"I want you, Julie."

"I can't be there, Zach. I'm in Albuquerque. Dom will take good care of you for me."

Domino's shouts got closer and closer until I heard them talking. He took the phone away from Zach and said he'd made it.

"I've got 911 on another line and EMS on the way," I told him.

Doug heard me say this and provided me an ETA of ten more minutes.

"What's he look like, Dom?" I asked.

"Kinda like the night he got shot on the beach, Julie," he said curtly. "There's a lot of blood. You *left* him like this? What the hell were you thinking?"

What the hell were you thinking?
What the hell were you thinking. . .

Beep, beep, beep. . . .

I rolled over and looked at the alarm clock, aware my body was cold and stiff.

I'd fallen asleep without covering up.

The alarm had been going off for ten minutes when I woke.

Zach, I thought. Did Domino get him to the hospital?

I looked around for my cell phone and the card I'd used to call the sheriff's department, for the number to the house Dom had given me.

My phone was where I'd left it on the dresser, next to my bag. Not on the nightstand.

I checked the last number dialed – Zach's cell phone.

No house number?

One incoming call, from Zach's cell at around midnight.

I searched frantically for the business card, a note pad, anything I'd used last night, but I found nothing. Looking at the bed, covers still turned down where I'd laid last night after taking the sleeping pill, I realized I'd dreamed it all.

I dialed Zach's cell again, but still I got no answer.

◆

Dr. Rothman probably decided his work and my recovery had crashed into the toilet with the desperate and ragged look I wore into his office.

"Are you ready to hear the tapes?" he asked, being polite instead of commenting on my appearance as I wilted into the chair.

"No, I'm not. I have a problem."

He tilted his head and waited.

"Last night, I ended up talking to Zach, but when he pushed me, I hung up. He knows about this adrenaline jazz thing I told you about. It began before I shot David but got really bad after I left the hospital."

"How perfectly vague," Dr. Rothman said with a gentle smile. "But I think I get it. Go on."

"After my father was murdered, I learned I liked the adrenaline rush. Then after I shot David, I realized the only time I really felt alive anymore was when I flirted with danger," I explained. "Zach said he saw the same behavior after his twin sister was attacked. He called it prowling – making risky choices, like going places a woman shouldn't go alone."

Rothman nodded.

"Zach showed me I was doing the same thing, committing suicide by tempting fate."

"Insightful phrase," he stated. "And when do you prowl?"

"When I hurt," I said, wondering if my response was a knee-jerk answer or truth. I sighed. "I don't know any more. Right now, I feel nothing at all."

"You didn't consider your actions suicidal?" he asked.

"At first I didn't because I clearly had suicide on my mind as I recovered." I explained how Zach'd stopped me from going inside a sleazy bar and given me a phone number I called later that night. "I asked him who he was, and he said something like, 'Someone who didn't rip you to pieces in the alley.' When I didn't say anything else, he asked if I was disappointed he hadn't." Sitting in the chair in the psychiatrist's office, I felt the panicky breathing again.

"Were you disappointed?"

"Yeah, in a way, I was," I said, feeling my heart sink in shame. "From that moment he grabbed my arm, I wasn't so much afraid as I was suddenly zinging on a bigger burst of adrenaline than I'd felt in a long time. Zach's big. If anyone could kill a woman barehanded, he could," I said, knowing he could wrap one hand far enough around my neck that he didn't need the other to drop me if he squeezed. "I remember thinking how badly he could hurt me, how little resistance I could offer." I looked away. "How much I'd deserve it."

"Deserve to be hurt? You mean like punishment?" he asked. "For what?"

I turned toward him, my mind overrun with possible bullshit answers. But only the truth came out when I spoke. "For letting my father die," I said. My voice cracked. "For not staying with him."

"For surviving?" Rothman offered, like throwing a life preserver to a drowning man.

I closed my eyes. "I ran away like a child."

"You *were* a child, Julie. Stop thinking about those memories as an adult, as a cop. You were not equipped in any capacity to change what happened when you were sixteen."

"I need to know what happened to my father," I said in desperation.

"And you will," he said calmly. "First, I'm curious about something. You could have accessed your father's case files, listened to this tape any time while you were with the state police. But you didn't."

I blinked at the realization he was right.

Why hadn't I?

"Deputy Chief Rader told me you had no idea your father's throat had been cut, even after he mentioned it when he did the database search. He said you didn't recognize the scene photos."

"No, I didn't." I swallowed hard. "Dad had been shot when I got to him, but the rest happened after I left." Fear churned acid in my stomach. "No one told me."

"You need to hear this tape," he stated, picking up a cassette. "Hear what really happened in that office."

I shook my head, closing my eyes to shut out the panic I felt rising in my throat. "I can't."

"Julie," Rothman said, as if addressing a small child. "What are you most afraid of hearing?"

Sweat chilled on my face as the potential force of the question's long hidden answer finally hit me. "I'm afraid that Bock made me do it," I panted, stunned at the words and the tears spilling down my cheeks. "That I killed my father, like he made me kill Matthew."

"No, Julie, you did not harm your father," he said gently. "That's all the more reason to hear the tapes."

And so I listened. No hypnosis to dampen the fear. When it was done, I cried at the relief I felt, finally knowing. Although I might have helped the police, had I remembered details about Bock, at least in my heart now, I knew I was not the monster I'd feared.

When I walked out of Dr. Rothman's office two hours later, the whole picture about my past was much clearer. I knew more about myself than I could ever have imagined.

I got into the rental car, dug my phone out of my bag, and dialed Zach's phone.

"What?" he answered on the fourth ring.

The greeting surprised me. "Z'?"

"Did you call to hang up on me again?"

"Zach, I'm sorry. I really need to talk to you."

"What about what I need, Julie? When do I get something in return? I'm sorry about what I did, but I can't take much more of this."

"No, it's not what you did, none of this. Look, I don't blame you for being angry with me, but –" I said.

"Julie, I'm not angry," he said, interrupting me, "but you need to decide what you want and whether I'm a part of it. But don't yank me around while you make up your mind. And don't rip my heart out, making me wonder every night whether you made it home to your bed or you're lying in a pool of blood in a dark alley somewhere. I can't take it."

"Zach, I . . ." I choked, "I'm sorry. I want you in my life–"

"Then you know what you need to do," he said, and the connection dropped.

The problem was, I really didn't.

CHAPTER

41

I'd flown home to Michigan and gone back to work.

Thursday afternoon, after a nasty day at the office, I came home to find a familiar box on my front porch.

Zach had sent me all the letters and stuff again.

Inside, I discovered two items not with the original contents. One was a new letter, brief but emotional, including a plea to call him. The other was his denim shirt, which made me smile.

I picked up the phone and dialed the number he'd included in the letter, but got no answer so I left another message. Foregoing dinner, I poured myself a tumbler of Crown Royal on ice. The hard lines of my day were beginning to blur as I refilled my glass a second time.

I pulled his shirt on over my own.

When I put on a CD from the box in my stereo, I heard Neil Young's *Harvest Moon*. The first track must have reminded Zach of me. "Somewhere on a desert highway, she rides a Harley-Davidson, her long blond hair flying in the wind."

Sitting on the floor, I sipped whiskey and read more unopened letters. I laughed some, and cried a little. I must have drifted off to sleep because I jerked upright with a stiff neck when the phone rang.

"Madigan."

"Hey."

I felt my heart pounding when I heard Zach's voice. "I got your present today. Thanks," I said.

"I wanted you to have it. I always have."

"It's still the most incredible gift you could've ever given me,

249

Zach." I lifted the denim to my face and inhaled. "You didn't have to send the shirt, though."

"Sure I did."

"Thanks for not washing it," I smiled. "It smells like you."

There was silence.

"How are you?" I asked. "Your arm?" Memories of cutting him sent a shiver through me again.

"Okay, I guess. I took out the rest of the sutures today. Thanks for the lesson," he said. "I've been waiting for you to call before I leave."

"Leave? Are you going back to work?" I asked, trying to disguise my alarm.

"No, I'm checking into a drug treatment program in Victoria, B.C. Dom helped me set it up," he said but his voice lacked any emotion.

"Oh," I said, feeling the numbness of the alcohol slipping and feeling even worse about running away from him.

"I have to do this right, Julie," he said. "I promised."

Glad he could see the value of getting help, I knew it was hard for him to admit it was a problem.

Oh, did I know.

"Julie, I don't want to get into another argument, but I need to know before I go. Why did you leave? What did I do wrong?"

I turned the tumbler up and emptied it, and ice cubes tinkled on the glass.

"Not you, Zach. It never was you. Wasn't the drugs or anything you did. It was me." I hesitated. "I was terrified of who I am and what I've become because of Anthony Bock. Finally something snapped and I hurt you, so I had to leave and find the answers."

"Getting cut was my fault, Julie. I knew you were upset, but I reached for the knife so you wouldn't hurt yourself. You didn't intentionally cut me, and I know it," he laughed, "because if you were really that mad, you'd have shot me."

Even though I knew he was joking, the comment struck a bloody raw nerve.

"I'm sorry," he said, "I just meant you already had my gun and –"

"Zach, stop." I could feel my face getting hot. "I know you were kidding, but it's true. How can you trust a woman who –"

"Julie," he interrupted. "I'd trust you to hold a knife to my throat or a gun to my heart, no matter how angry you might be."

"Maybe you shouldn't," I whispered. "The survival rate for men I care about isn't so good."

"I'm still standing," he said. "Can I ask you another question?"

"Umhmm." I sucked the last drops of liquor from an ice cube, dropping it into the glass, letting alcohol numb away my day. And somehow, it wasn't numb at all.

"In Florida, when I took your gun, you didn't flinch, even when I leveled it at your head. I could see in your eyes how much you loved me, which was the only reason I believed it was really you. You had the guts to believe I wouldn't shoot you. Why?"

"I don't have faith in much in this world, Zach, but I believe in you. If you'd shot me, if you were that far gone, I might as well have been dead, too. There wouldn't have been anything left of either of us."

It wasn't pretty, but it was the truth.

"So you believed," he said after considering my words. "And then you had enough confidence to try staying here with me after I told you about the drugs. I want you to know you're the only person I've trusted with everything, including my life."

"That's why I had to leave. You've always believed in something I didn't understand. When I cut you, it was as if my whole world shattered. I heard mental echoes of Anthony's voice." I realized my words had a slur. I got up and went to the kitchen. "He grabbed me at my father's office."

"You told me you didn't see anyone," Zach said, sounding intrigued. "You did? You figured that out in the hypnosis?"

"Yes, when my father made me run," I explained as I tossed a couple more ice cubes into the glass, not bothering to be quiet, and filled it again. "Bock asked me if I wanted to kill my father, told me I'd be just like him." Even when I said those words, they boomed in my head in Anthony's voice. I felt myself shudder. "I was terrified I didn't remember what happened to my father because I had, because Anthony *made me kill him*, just like he made me kill Matthew."

"You didn't kill your father," he said without question or hesitation.

251

"No, I didn't, but I didn't know that before. Then I hurt you," I continued. "Physically, seriously injured you. Cutting you felt the same to me as pulling the knife across Matt's throat. I had to leave."

"Julie, what happened here in the kitchen was an accident. I could tell by the way you were holding the knife, you'd forgotten it was even in your hand."

Maybe he was right, but it still rattled my nerves to have cut him so badly.

"Remember at the ranch, when you first showed me the horses?" I asked. "You said we're strangers everywhere but in bed. What if I'm not what you've dreamed me to be all these years? I'm not the golden princess in a fairy tale, Zach," I said. "I wasn't what Jeremy thought."

"My guess is you never were," he replied. "But I know who you are, and I haven't fantasized you into something you aren't. I've kept your dark secrets and I've touched your scars, but I can see your dreams, too. I'm telling you again, I'm not afraid of who you are." He paused. "Is that really why you left? You didn't leave because I hurt you?"

"No, Zach. You didn't hurt me. You've never hurt me." I went to take another sip, but the tumbler was empty. Again. I poured more warm liquor into the glass, amber liquid rippling over the smooth ice. "Until I heard the tape, until I remembered what Bock said to me, I had no idea how deeply he'd sabotaged my whole damned life." I took another drink and topped off the glass before going to my chair.

"Do you think seeing a psychiatrist helped?"

"Yeah. Dr. Rothman actually walked me through remembering before I heard the tapes, but that's what most of this came down to. I've been fighting those words Anthony said to me, that I'd be just like him someday. I hate who he's made me."

"You are not what he made you, Julie. You're shaped by those events, but not defined solely by those words."

"I told Rothman about the prowling, too. He's going to help find someone to see here."

"Thank you, Julie. I understand we both have to do what we're doing, or else we could lose everything."

"So, that's why I left Washington. I didn't know what I was looking for, but I had to find the answers. I don't like them, but I don't have to hide from the past anymore."

"Sounds like it's been a good thing for you." He hesitated, maybe weighing whether or not to ask. "Have you been drinking?"

"No, sir," I said. "I'm *still* drinking." I jingled the ice in the glass I didn't remember emptying again, meaning it was really time to quit.

"Julie?"

"Don't lecture me, Zach." I turned off the lights and felt my way down the hall to my bedroom. "Yes, I've had too much to drink, but I deserve this. I really did not want to come home and feel what's been spinning around my head all day at work."

"Why? What's going on?"

I turned down the covers and sprawled into the bed. "Because this afternoon, I started an investigation of a dead child. A five-year-old repeatedly stabbed in the abdomen with an ice pick."

"I'm sorry, Julie."

"No, you don't understand," I said, feeling I needed to explain everything. "No one questioned the SIDS diagnosis when his twin brother died at seven months, likely of shaken-baby syndrome or maybe plain suffocation, based on what I discovered today. The five-year-old and his half-sister, who is seven, both tested positive for heroin. She says her father was using them to deal drugs, and my guess is he was pimping her, as well."

"You and I have both seen what adults are capable of doing to children in the drug business. Killing a child is –"

"This five-year-old committed suicide, Zach," I interrupted him sharply. "These wounds were all self-inflicted. And it wasn't his first attempt. Last time, four months ago, he jumped out of a moving vehicle on the highway. So if I want to blot out today in a glass, I think I'm entitled."

"Damn," he said quietly. "Are you okay?"

"I'll be all right," I said.

"That wasn't what I asked you."

"No, I'm not okay or I wouldn't be through half a bottle of whisky."

"Then I'd say you're pretty sober at that," he observed. "Like you told me not too long ago, at least those children aren't going back to that hell again."

CHAPTER

42

Despite the child suicide case, one night of drinking was more than enough self-inflicted misery. I regretted my over-indulgence the following day with a dull headache.

The prosecuting attorney attacked the abuse cases like a mad dog, which thrilled me. I wanted someone to hang for putting those children through such hell. Seven altogether – five kids were in protective custody, the twins dead. The couple had two each from their previous marriages, and together their infant daughter and the twins. I had to wonder how long the baby would have lived, had the legal system not intervened.

In a meeting, trying to put as much evidence on the table as possible, we passed around photographs of all the members of the family. Something caught my eye. When everyone had gone but the attorney, I asked him to look at something with me and spread the photos out again.

"What do you see?"

"I'm sure what you see is much more revealing," he deflected. "Tell me."

"The five-year-old boy has a very cute chin dimple, right?"

"Cute, sure." He checked his watch impatiently. "Get to the point."

"Dimples like this are hereditary," I said. "And the man listed as the father doesn't have one. Neither does the paternal grandfather. While the genetics of this might not be perfect, I think it's worth your effort to determine whether the husband in this so-called family is really the father of these children. If the mother had an affair and –"

His eyes widened. "I get it – if they weren't his kids, then he had no investment in how they lived or died." He gathered up the photos. "Good catch! Thanks."

After the conference, I returned to my office to a job I'd begun to view as routine – filing reports, going to meetings, the occasional field case.

Save a couple of letters a week, I didn't hear from Zach. Being apart, though, I'd begun to feel I was making a little progress on getting my head straight. I spent evenings at home, reading old letters from the box and adding to my list of questions for Zach.

One Saturday morning, I drove to Grand Rapids to shop for Zach's birthday. Buying a Harley was tough these days. Few dealers had many bikes on their showroom floors, and orders were taking months to arrive. I put down a hefty deposit on a 1996 Road King.

Snow began falling about the time I headed home, and I almost reconsidered my plans to stop in Cadillac to visit K.C. Adams, the police officer we'd interviewed about Angela Bock's murder, which was the sentinel event that began the killer's spree spanning three decades. Given the horrible impact that single event had on his own family, Mr. Adams had asked if we'd let him know how it turned out.

What's a little snow, I thought, and turned off the highway in Cadillac to the retirement center.

No one was at the desk when I walked in, so I dusted the snow off my jacket and made my way to his suite and knocked on the door.

Bobbi, his assistant, answered.

"Oh, I remember you." She swung the door wide for me to come in. "Mr. Adams passed on just last weekend," she said, waving in a gracious sweep of her arm.

"I'm so sorry," I said, tears blurring my vision. "I should have come sooner."

She waved her hand. "No, no. He had another stroke a few weeks after you came. He didn't even know his family. While he would have enjoyed your company again when he was well, we're all thankful he didn't linger without his mind. He wouldn't have wanted that." Her Caribbean heritage was audible in her voice, and I found it comforting.

"We identified the killer, but not before he took more lives," I said. "I wanted to thank Mr. Adams for his valuable information."

"Did you, now?" She waved toward a chair. "I'd be pleased to hear about it, if you have the time. He did tell me more after you left."

"Sure, if you'd like."

Bobbi, still a hostess without her charge, offered me a glass of white wine, and I told her the story of Anthony Bock, who had been the little boy in K.C.'s story, and the devil in my own.

"Oh my gracious!" she whispered several times as I told her how Anthony had killed my own father, then had stalked me for years.

When I finished, she sat down her glass and leaned forward.

"Have you ever had your palms read?" she asked, the Jamaican lilt in her words even stronger.

"I don't think so," I said.

"May I?"

I held out both my hands, and she cradled them.

"You are right-handed, yes? The passive hand illustrates your inherited characteristics, more of your past. The dominant hand demonstrates changes to these traits. When they differ dramatically, it shows a person has worked very hard at becoming, as you have. You have a strong life line," she pointed with one long fingernail into my palm to show me, "and this line here on your right hand is called an effort line. The head line is long and deep. You absorb new things easily and have good common sense, but you are sometimes too independent for your own good."

She stopped and looked up at me for a moment, then continued.

"Your life line and head line touch. You're deeply emotional, easily scarred by others who love you. You want to be strong, but it is not always possible. You've had strong changes in your personality throughout your life. And last," she said, tracing in the palm of my hand, "your heart line. It ends here between your middle and index finger. You are determined to find the right man in your life. Maybe you have, but you are struggling with your emotions."

"That's a lot of truth in a teacup," I said with an uncomfortable laugh. "Perhaps you can tell me if he still loves me?"

"Say his name," she said, folding my palms together, holding them with her own.

"Zach Samualson."

She closed her eyes. "You would die for him, no? Then you should believe in him completely," she said. "Yes, he loves you in a very rare way."

"How can you tell all that?"

"It's a little practice, a lot of intuition. Like reading the Tarot, it's more how you interpret the questions than the meaning of each card."

I nodded.

"Shall I tell you about children?" she asked.

"Um, no," I said, pulling back my hands. "Thanks, but I don't think I want to know anything more."

I'd had enough soul-searching of my past with a bulldozer to last a while. I didn't need to look into my future.

CHAPTER

43

For some reason, my job had become a little crazy, trying to get the chain of command and all the paperwork into proper order. It had all been fine a few months previous, but my multiple absences had things out of kilter, I supposed. To catch up, I sorted and filed between cases, stayed late most days. And I kept a close eye on the child abuse case.

Dr. Katz called me at home on Friday morning before I'd left for work.

"I'm out in the west part of the county," he said, "so I was hoping you could take the call on Three Mile Road?"

That was my job, I was tempted to remind him, but neither of us seemed in the mood for a joke. I told him I'd get the details from Central Dispatch and be on my way.

As usual, he didn't bother to give me any other information about what I'd find, and I didn't expect him to tell me. From the dispatcher, I learned I was going to a crime scene with one fatality. EMS had come and gone.

I pulled into a business parking lot, unsure what sort of business it was by the name alone. Finding a place for my Suburban among the sheriff's department patrol cars, I parked and got out and zipped up my jacket to a brisk wind.

I turned to see one of the deputies coming toward me as I pulled out two evidence cases from the back of the truck.

"Kit Drdul," he said, introducing himself. "Anything I can help you with?"

We shook hands. "No, I think I have what I need, if you'll get the door for me?" I replied. When we got in the foyer, I stopped long enough to put on my surgical booties.

Inside, what had been an office – meaning desks and computers and copy machines and just office stuff – lay in what could best be described as a disaster.

While *stuff* at a scene isn't my primary concern when responding to calls regarding fatalities, the sheer magnitude of destruction astounded me.

Drdul interrupted my shock, pointing to the right to where three deputies stood, but he maintained his position by the door.

Blood.

I could see it, smeared over walls and furniture. I could smell it.

Looking down, the deputies standing down the hall wore booties.

Following my eyes, Brandan spoke up. "We put them on, but the EMS and fire crew did not," he said, reading my thoughts. "Victim's in the men's restroom."

The trio stepped apart to let me pass through the middle. Brandan, also wearing gloves, pushed the door open from about head height, hoping to spare any fingerprints.

On the bloody floor, I saw a middle-aged man on his side, also covered in blood caused by knife wounds.

A flash when I blinked was me, lying on the floor bleeding like that. I gulped air.

Beyond the body, on the blue tile wall, "two men" was scrawled in blood.

More bloody notes from dead guys.

"Hell of a fight," I heard someone outside say.

"I'll need my camera," I told Brandan, though I'm sure he already knew my routine and had snapped dozens of photos in the restroom himself before I arrived. "Any window for time of death?" I asked, opening my case.

"According to the alarm company, the building system was set at a quarter after five last night," he said, referring to a notepad. "Then it was unarmed about four this morning and never reset. Sales guys come and go, I'm told. Two secretaries came in together this morning a few minutes before eight and found that."

That referred to both the extreme catastrophe of office furniture

259

and desktop items outside the bathroom door and the dead man on the floor at my feet.

"That's our window. You?" he stated.

Estimating how much drying had occurred in smears but not puddles around me, I ventured, "About two hours." I stepped closer to the body and raised the camera, adjusting the focus slightly, index finger ready to expose the first frame. . .

When the victim took a snoring breath.

My eyes were every bit as wide as Brandan's when we looked at each other, but I think I refrained from simultaneously saying, "What the fuck?"

Maybe. Honestly, I'm not sure if I said it aloud because I absolutely thought it.

I stepped forward between pools of blood and put my fingers on the victim's neck, searching for a carotid pulse, and felt a slow but steady one.

"He's alive," I squeaked when my voice failed. Before me lay a man with dozens of wounds, including one across his throat much like my own. "Get an ambulance!"

Brandan blinked away the shock and keyed his radio to request an ambulance, which started a loud buzzing of conversation that led to hurried footsteps beyond the door.

Nothing in my cases to save a trauma victim who was apparently breathing.

Salvage of evidence would become a trade-off when EMS came busting in to grab the patient, working to save his life. Anything we could protect or photograph, we had to do quickly.

I lifted my camera partway up, then stopped, confused. "Wait," I said, squinting. "Wasn't EMS already here?"

Brandan pursed his lips together for a moment, as if he tried to hide a smile, then in a quiet voice said. "They were. Pronounced him dead. And we called you."

I began taking photos again, focusing on as much of the spatter patterns as I could in the few minutes before two paramedics rushed into the building, scattering the deputies. "We'll need fingerprints from the patient," I said, standing up as the pair knelt by the victim. "And blood, if he has any left."

Scene time for the ambulance was short – maybe due to the absolute embarrassment of declaring a patient dead without so much as touching him.

Granted, there was a lot of blood everywhere, enough to make one think a patient could not be alive. However, there was protocol, and crime scene or not, it was pretty clear the steps to declare someone dead had not been followed. Lots of stinky stuff was going to hit the fan when the medical director got his fingers around necks.

Oh, to be a fly on that wall...

They did draw me a vial of blood, then left with the patient whose name I still hadn't heard, leaving law enforcement to make sense out of the building.

"'Two men,'" I repeated the words from the wall as I followed them out of the restroom into the main part of the building. "I don't get the impression that it took two men to do all this."

"And to what end? Nothing appears to be missing," Brandan replied, shaking his head. "The timeline still stands for the attack, right?"

I nodded, with nothing else to dispute the two-hour period we'd discussed before finding out the victim was alive.

"What's the business?" I asked. "What they do here?"

"Communication, digital pagers and such. Not much here to steal," he said. He tilted his head as far left as it would go to look at something on the floor. "Other than what's upside-down and broken."

"Maybe something intangible, something you can't immediately see, like schematics or software," I offered.

Brandan shrugged. "It'll be noon before we get anyone in here to figure that out."

I began gathering samples from bloodstains at random spots throughout the building, trying not to think of the injuries suffered by either my father or me. Or Matthew Shannaker. Knowing the answers I'd found in Albuquerque just weeks ago, I felt better. But seeing someone else with a laceration across his neck still made me queasy.

"Not much else I can do," I finally said, stepping into a lull of conversation between the two deputies left on scene. A crime lab technician was working his way around the room and still had hours to go to collect photos, fingerprints and other evidence. We were not working this case as a homicide, though it went unspoken that this was still a crime and could become a fatality.

"Thanks for your help," Drdul said, as if he'd worked with me dozens of times, though he had not.

I hadn't even recognized the name.

Then it hit me – Kit Drdul was probably the deputy hired to replace Matthew Shannaker.

I wonder if he knows who I am.

CHAPTER

44

Winter brought patients with different injuries to the doctors and medical examiners in the Snowbelt. Hand mutilation causes changed from lawn mowers to snowblowers.

After four years, I'm still clueless what makes people stick their hands into the blades of running machines.

Living in a remote neighborhood but on a well-traveled road, Eli Horton was an independent man of 72, taking care of his invalid wife Georgia. She'd suffered a stroke years ago that left her unable to walk or use her right hand.

From what the first deputy on scene had put together, Mr. Horton had gone out in the dark morning storm to blow out the driveway, as he did every day snow fell. Not that they needed to go anywhere, but because it was a chore you couldn't let get ahead, his wife had explained.

Mrs. Horton heard the snowblower running, as usual. She was always afraid he would wake the neighbors at 5 a.m., though no one had ever complained, and often his wasn't the only machine running at the early hour. Then she must have dozed off in her living room chair where he'd left her, waiting for him to finish before he fixed their breakfast.

He had not returned.

Almost two hours later, she awoke and no longer heard the snowblower, but after Mr. Horton didn't return in a timely manner, she panicked and called 911.

A sheriff's deputy found the snowblower on one side of the

driveway near the road, the task only about two-thirds completed. Nearby, almost covered in the blowing snow, he discovered a mangled heavy work glove with two fingers inside.

When I heard the story, I secretly suspected the deputy had regurgitated his breakfast in the snowbank then covered it up, but when I arrived, it didn't seem worth mentioning.

A quick search around the driveway and house failed to produce the rest of Mr. Horton.

The deputy went to the house and, with instructions from Mrs. Horton via 911, located the hidden key to get inside, since she could not get up to unlock the door for him.

She explained Eli's morning routine, but from there, the story and brief search led nowhere – except the glove and fingers the deputy had been kind enough not to divulge to Mrs. Horton.

Fearing the man might have wandered away after being injured, the deputy called dispatch and requested search volunteers.

Grand Traverse County didn't have a search dog. The closest team was more than two hours away in good weather. And it wasn't good weather.

Brandan Callaghan, who was on the way to the scene to help, called me to see if I thought Laser could function as a tracking dog.

"Beats me," I said, almost out the door to the office when my phone rang. "Let me call the trainer and see. I'll get back with you."

I looked around for the business card Frank Lomas had left with all Laser's gear.

After a fifteen-minute conversation with the dog trainers as I drove to the scene, I was only remotely hopeful I could get the dog to search, but I was willing to try.

I called Connie at the office and let her know where I was going.

Slowly. The roads were a mess.

I arrived at the Horton house 45 minutes after I'd gotten Brandan's call, put a work harness and lead on Laser, who seemed excited by this new twist, and zipped up my sub-zero parka against a cutting wind before stepping out.

"Damn, Julie," Brandan said, meeting me at my truck. "Who ordered this freaking storm?"

"Wasn't me. I sure miss Hawaii," I moaned, slipping on a patch of ice and barely recovering.

"Hey, Laser," he said, thumping the dog's haunches. "I hope you're up to working today."

"No promises, but we'll give it a shot, huh, Boy?"

The dog wagged his tail like he was ready for someone to throw his favorite ball.

"Anything's a help. Thanks for coming."

The senior deputy on the scene, Rory Stewart, came over to brief us as we huddled out of the roaring wind behind my vehicle.

I'd worked maybe a dozen body calls with Rory over the last few years, and I considered his tact to be just shy of non-existent with the public in general and sorely lacking with grieving family members specifically. Seeing him here wasn't the brightest spot to the day.

"So we're looking for an elderly man who was physically able to do chores like this, and likely dressed for this weather, but obviously injured," I summed up. "Have you checked with the few closest neighbors, see if he walked to one of their houses for help? Maybe when he got hurt, he didn't want to upset his wife, or someone picked him up and took him to the emergency room."

Rory nodded with each point or question, scribbling notes in his pad, and I was surprised these things hadn't already been done.

I turned an evidence bag inside out over my hand and picked up Mr. Horton's glove, and gave Laser a series of commands I'd learned less than an hour ago from the trainer.

Laser turned and looked at me curiously when I repeated the command to trail.

"Find Mr. Horton," I told him. "Find."

There is a difference between dogs that track and those that trail. While all dogs have thousands more scent sensors than humans, some use the scent remaining on the ground to track, but others follow the scent drifting in the air.

Or in this case, blowing across the county at 40 miles per hour.

As high as the wind was, I wasn't holding my breath this would work, but Laser barked once and took off, jerking the lead and nearly yanking me off my feet on the packed snow.

The dog trotted along, eager to be doing something distantly related to work, it seemed.

Brandan walked along with me. "On that guy who really wasn't dead in the office the other day, did you find anything?" he asked.

"Nope. Lots of blood, but only the victim's."

"Okay, so let me share with you what the hospital determined," Brandan said, pulling his collar higher. "Unless you want to guess first?"

I thought for a moment of the most outrageous possibility. "An army of nanobots attacked him when he went to take a leak," I suggested.

He smiled. "No, but you might actually like that option better than the doctor's. The patient, Arthur Vanderveen, had almost thirty wounds, but," he said, drawing out the silence until I nailed him with a glare of impatience, "only two were severe, and none were life-threatening."

Trying to stay upright in the wind and being led by the dog, what attention I could spare was all his.

"So tell me," he continued. "If you were the assailant, how could you inflict two dozen non-lethal wounds on a man who was found unresponsive, breathing was so shallow as to convince onlookers he was dead, and still spread two pints of only the victim's blood all over everything in the building while wrecking it?"

I began what probably looked like math in my head. More or less, it was – adding and subtracting those facts and suppositions about the scene, until I reached a conclusion that left me almost as stunned as when the man had taken a breath that morning.

"There were no other attackers," I concluded. "He did it all himself."

I earned a big grin I couldn't return as the rest of the situation became clear to me.

"Somewhere in the building," I said, "you located the knife he used to cut himself, and a bottle of pills – likely benzos – that he took to knock himself out." Benzodiazepines, such as Valium, could produce a deep sedation without as high a risk of death as barbiturates or narcotics. Explained almost everything except . . . "So the question is, did he really *want* to kill himself but felt he needed to disguise his attempt for other reasons, or did he only want the attention?"

"Found the pill bottle in his car, so he probably took them before he entered the building," Brandan told me. "I don't know why he did it – he won't say."

I shook my head in disbelief.

"The real crime is that the manager wouldn't tell anyone the truth, so the two secretaries who walked in on this scenario went home, not knowing they wouldn't unlock the doors and find two intruders in the building the next morning," he said. "What Vanderveen did is no longer considered criminal because of mental illness."

"No, what's worse is that Worker's Compensation will likely have to pay for his medical bills, but the owners probably can't get their insurance to pay for the damages in the building because he was an employee," I said, "yet they can't terminate his employment for the very same reason you can't charge him. How would you like to be there when he shows up for work again?"

"Crap," Brandan nodded. "Leave it to you to find a silver lining that's really made of lead."

Coming back to why we were hiking through a snowstorm, I changed the subject. "At least this wasn't an abduction."

Laser did a circle around me to find the scent again.

"No, being abducted would have to be an improvement over this for Mr. Horton," he said.

"Do tell."

Laser started walking again, nose mostly in the air but sometimes returning to the snow, which I found interesting.

"It was dark. It's colder than a frog's butt in gale force winds out here. If someone snatched him, he'd have to be warmer than this." Brandan skated on a patch of ice, turned and looked back at the snowblower in the distance, a drift forming around it. "Think about it – you're squatting in front of the blower with your back to the street. Your glove is ripped off, and you're bleeding. What do you do?"

"I'm sure I'd curse like my father taught me, followed straightaway by fainting."

"Say you didn't fall down, what's your first physical reaction?"

"I'm not following, Brandan," I shrugged as we kept walking, heads tilted against the wind and whipping snow.

"I'd stand up and take a couple of steps backward, holding my hand like this," he said, demonstrating. "A few steps backward from the blades of that snowblower would have put him at the edge of the road."

Suddenly, I saw what he was thinking clearly in my head. Too clearly.

"Snowplow," we said together, turning to look behind us where traffic would approach.

Keeping roads clear for cars, plows sometimes run around the clock to keep up with the snowfall and the staggering number of miles of pavement. They have to run fast enough to bust through snowdrifts. With the blade dragging, any noise of impact would be diminished if heard at all.

"Can we find the last plow that went through here?" I asked.

Brandan pointed ahead. "I don't want to spoil Laser's fun, but I think we're done looking."

A black boot stuck partially out of an embankment created by the plow where it piled snow in a small park.

We were less than a half mile from the house.

To my surprise, Laser pulled us down the road and right to the snowbank and began barking, just as the trainer had said he would.

With lots of praise and a few treats, I congratulated the dog on his job.

We dug the body out of the snow using our gloved hands, and I determined the man was dead, though this was no surprise. I found multiple fractures and skin injuries that would be consistent with being pushed in front of a blade. There was significant blood pooled around him, however, which indicated that he was probably still alive when the plow shoved him into the snow pile, backed up, and continued on its way.

Brandan radioed dispatch to advise that the MEI was on scene but he'd still need a morgue vehicle.

Had the driver known when he hit Mr. Horton or when he made this dump? If he had, it's possible Mr. Horton might have survived, although the injuries would have been severe.

"You really think a plow did this?" Rory said, having jogged to join us.

"How else would he wind up here?" I asked, doing my best not to roll my eyes.

"Find out how many plows were through here this morning and get them off the road," Brandan told him.

"Could have been a private vehicle," Rory argued.

"Just do it," Brandan ordered, obviously frustrated at the deputy's laziness.

Stewart turned and left us at the snowbank, shoulders hunkered, probably grumbling as he went.

"You're not going to let him talk to the wife, are you?" I asked.

"No, but I'd appreciate it if you'd come with me when you're done," Brandan said.

I nodded.

"Speaking of Rory, I have a favor to ask of you," Brandan said, waving at the ME van coming down the road. "I'll drop by your office later so we can talk."

"That sounds obscure enough," I replied.

He glanced over his shoulder. "It's too complicated to discuss now."

It would have to be about sixty degrees warmer in my office, too, I thought. That's a plus.

The medical examiner's van parked nearby, and Jordan Scott climbed out, dressed like an Eskimo.

I helped him put the body on the stretcher, and then I met Brandan over at the driveway of the Horton house, stopping to put Laser in my truck and starting it up so the heater would run.

"This won't be easy," Brandan explained. "I know the Hortons from other calls here. They used to have problems with the neighbors' loud parties. Georgia can't live alone. I don't know if there is any other family near."

"How sad," I commented, wondering what I'd do if I ended up crippled and alone with no one to care for me. "We should get social services involved right away then."

He nodded and dug in his pocket for his cellular phone to call dispatch.

Call completed, he knocked on the front door and identified himself, then entered at Mrs. Horton's request.

She was a large woman gone slack, the weight of her pale skin pulling deep creases on her face and neck. Her eyes were clouded with cataracts, and one hand was curled up in a paralyzed contracture against her body.

I sat down in the chair next to her while Brandan knelt down beside her and took her other hand.

He took a moment to introduce me, and then began his bad news.

As he spoke, she began trembling, shaking her head to his words, willing him to stop.

"Mrs. Horton," I said when he had delivered his portion of the notification, "although we don't know yet exactly what happened, we will find out. But I am concerned about you right now. Is there family or friends I can call for you?"

She pointed me to an address book near the phone and asked me to look up her daughter. "I can't talk to her," she said, breaking down into tears. "How can I tell her this?"

Brandan offered her a tissue, and I placed a call to her daughter Melinda in Lansing.

Melinda took the news better than most. She said she would have to make arrangements for both her grandchildren before she could drive to Traverse City because she babysat, but she'd be on her way within a few hours.

"The weather is still horrible up here," I advised. "Do be careful. Is there anyone closer who could stay with your mother until you arrive?"

She gave me the names of a few people who were listed in the address book. I called until I found someone who lived only a few miles away but didn't have a car. I asked if it would be okay to send a deputy to pick her up and then sent Brandan on the errand.

I talked to Mrs. Horton about the investigation, autopsy, and subsequent arrangements she and her daughter could make for services.

While Brandan was gone, I made Mrs. Horton some toast and jelly. When he delivered her friend, I left my card with them. We let ourselves out the door.

"That never gets any easier," he said, maybe just to himself.

We shook hands.

Done at the scene, I went directly to the Annex rather than taking

Laser home. He made himself comfortable in my office with a bone that I really thought he'd earned.

Off in search of my boss, I found Dr. Katz in his office, eating a salad and leftover roasted chicken for lunch when it wasn't even ten o'clock, but his morning had begun long before mine had.

I explained my findings and the hunch that the plow had hit Mr. Horton before sunrise and carried him to the snowbank. And that I thought he had been alive at least that long.

"Damned snow," he grouched. "Some days, I wish I'd moved to San Diego."

CHAPTER
45

Thursday, a week later, while I made my rounds to the hospitals and law enforcement facilities, Connie called my cell phone.

"Central Dispatch specifically requested you for an EMS call. But this is kinda weird – the patient isn't dead," our office manager explained over a distorted connection.

"Okay," I said, writing down the address and hoping I could get out of the drive-through lunch rush at McDonald's sometime soon. "Any details?"

"Burns. That's all they told me. Said the crew on scene asked for you by name."

Finally I got my drink, fries and burger, resettled my sunglasses back to my nose, and turned onto the street to go south on US31 then west toward Long Lake. Maybe I'd have time to have a few bites, I thought. Then I wondered if I really wanted to eat before this kind of call.

The previous night's two inches of snow had been cleared from the main thoroughfares, and despite the fact I was plain sick of winter already, the new white stuff was no problem. All the time I'd lived here, I'd only put chains on my own vehicle once to get to a scene. Road crews were great at getting us around where we needed to be in an emergency. Still, working for the dead isn't as time-critical as working for the dying, so I hurried along.

I'd quit watching the weather because I kept looking at the Oregon and Washington area, wondering what those clouds were doing over a particular log cabin north of the Columbia Gorge. If I got socked in by another snowstorm like the one last week, weather avoidance would be the reason I wasn't prepared.

Turning off the road into a parking lot, I washed down the last bite of the usual rock that food had become since my return from Portland, then popped a breath mint.

I got out and grabbed a camera kit. Cold dry snow creaked under my boots as I walked, but I could feel the ice beneath. Watching where I put my feet so I wouldn't end up on my back, I made my way toward the quad apartment.

There was a fire truck and one ambulance from Blair Township on scene, as well as a county patrol car.

Deputy Rory Stewart headed my direction.

Oh, great.

"Julie, good to see you again," he said, turning to walk with me but not offering to carry my case. "I like the short hair, by the way."

I ignored the compliment. "What's the story?"

"Merle Arnette, age 76, found by his granddaughter this morning. She came to check on him when Meals-on-Wheels didn't get an answer at the door two days in a row. She's the only family he has."

I nodded for him to continue.

"The paramedic is trying to talk him into being transported. He's arguing the VA won't pay if he goes to the local hospital, and they're saying they have no choice."

"Okay, so what am I doing here?" I asked, stopping to look at him, shaking my head in deeper confusion than I'd started with.

"Medic thinks this may end up a fatality, and it's damned sure suspicious. You'll see," he said. "We're working on a psych certification to get him to the hospital."

Mr. Compassion, as usual.

I entered the tiny apartment, crowded with six people.

"Hey, Julie," Todd Holden said, extending a gloved hand to shake.

Last time I'd seen him, I'd left him and a partner to get rabies shots at the hospital after we all ended up at a cabin where a dying bat was found, presumed to be rabid. It had been.

"Good morning, Todd," I said. "You called?"

"This is Mr. Arnette," Todd said by way of introduction. "Mr.

Arnette? This is Julie Madigan. She's from the medical examiner's office."

"What the hell is she doing here? I'm as alive as I can be!" the patient bellowed.

Nothing wrong with his lungs or his brain.

The patient was lying on a sofa that looked a decade older than anyone standing around it. It had a deteriorating, stained eggcrate pad on it. A sickening sweet smell hung in the air.

"Can you sit up and let me show her the burn on your *arm*, sir?" Todd persisted, pointing to his own as an example.

"Don't know what for. I wish you people'd leave me alone," he grumbled, but he took Todd's partner's hand and groaned as he sat up on the sofa.

I moved around behind the patient to see his back, and I hoped I didn't gasp as loudly as the sound played in my head.

Todd nodded, eyes wide to express his predicament.

Through a lightweight cotton shirt with burned edges, the man had suffered a burn completely through the skin and fat, exposing muscle tissue, in an area fourteen inches across and maybe twenty inches high. There was a similar burn to the backside of his upper right arm about the size of my entire hand, which was what Todd had indicated.

The patient was lowered gently back down onto the sofa.

I blinked and took a deep breath before moving into the patient's view again.

"Mr. Arnette?" I knelt down next to him, hoping to gain his trust. "I understand you don't want to go to the hospital. We'd like to find out how you got hurt, though. I know you've probably explained to the paramedics already, but can you tell me what happened?"

"I told them, I don't remember. I knocked over the lamp yonder a day or so ago," he said, pointing to a table lamp on the floor nearby. "The shade caught fire, and I put it out with my hands." He held them up for me to see a couple of small blisters on the palms.

The lampshade had indeed caught fire, but other than missing maybe a quarter of its fabric, leaving burned edges, and a couple of dents, it was otherwise intact. Neither the lamp nor the light bulb looked broken, and nothing in the nearby area was black or melted. I was certain it was not the cause of the burns on his back.

Both Stewart and the granddaughter stood silent but appeared anxious for the medics to do something. I exchanged glances with the two EMS providers, then made another sweeping look around the room.

Heat for the apartment came from an old-fashioned floor furnace with a large metal grate, seeming to be doing its job well, but with six bodies in the small space, it was hard to tell.

"Mr. Arnette," I asked, changing tack, "what branch of the service were you in? My dad served in the Navy."

"I was just an Army grunt," he said. "End of the second war."

"No such thing as 'just.' Even the cooks did their part for our freedom," I said.

"Not our cook," he argued. "I swear sometimes he worked for the other side!"

We all laughed.

"Look, I understand how the Veterans' Administration system works. And honestly, I don't blame you for not wanting to go to the hospital," I said. "I really hated being a patient, too. However, you have a pretty nasty burn on your arm –"

"It don't even hurt!" he argued.

I nodded. "That's because it's burned all the way through your skin. There are no nerves left to make you feel pain." I pinched up the skin on the back of his hand to demonstrate. "Like cutting this away, the whole layer of skin is gone. And I have to be honest with you – it already looks badly infected."

He didn't reply.

"But that's not the biggest problem, Mr. Arnette. You also have a huge burn on your back, and you can't feel it, either." I held up my hands with space between to indicate how big.

His granddaughter gasped just like I had.

"I ain't got the money –" he started, so I interrupted him, but I took his hand in mine.

"This isn't about money, Mr. Arnette. You're granddaughter probably doesn't have the money to bury you, either. If you don't get treated, you're very likely going to die right there on this couch in a few days from a massive infection, and I don't want that to happen," I said with true sincerity.

He nodded, but I hadn't convinced him yet.

"Don't make them put you in police custody because you're a danger to yourself – they'll have to call a psychiatrist and all that crap. Let them admit you here and get started on treatment. Then you can argue about them sending you to the VA Hospital downstate, okay? I'm so certain the VA will cover you going to the hospital here first, if they don't, I'll pay for the ambulance bill myself." I turned to Todd. "Put a note on the billing sheet. I'll sign it."

The old man looked at me through dry red-rimmed eyes. "You ain't giving me much choice, are you, Missy?"

"Sure I am. I'll arm wrestle you. Winner gets on the gurney," I offered with a smile. "Please? Do it for your granddaughter."

He took a deep rattley breath, then nodded.

Todd and his partner, a younger man I didn't know by name, helped the patient onto the gurney and covered him up.

I stopped them and actually signed a spot on his billing form.

Todd hesitated, then mouthed a silent "thank you" as they went out the door. They rolled him out to the ambulance, and the granddaughter followed.

I nodded and turned my attention to the room when they were gone.

"What the hell happened here?" I said out loud.

"No kidding," Rory said, unaware I wasn't speaking to him.

"This was not a flame burn," I continued, walking around the kitchen and back to the lamp, a total of eleven steps apart.

I pulled on a pair of gloves before I picked up the lamp to check the bulb more closely. "It's not an electrical burn."

"I'm not much on electricity, Julie," he said. "I have trouble changing a light bulb."

"How many psychiatrists does it take to change a light bulb?" I asked one of the tired series of jokes, since it was only the deputy and me now.

"I don't know."

"Only one, but the light bulb really has to want to change."

"Cute. How many flies does it take to screw in a light bulb?"

I shrugged.

"Two," he said with a mischievous grin. "But the real question is, how did they get in there together?"

It figured his joke would be about sex, but I chuckled. Felt nice to smile. Maybe this indicated people I worked with were ready to go about normal business with me after the death of Matt Shannaker.

Those outside emergency services have trouble understanding professionals inside – cops and medics and firefighters and nurses – who often draw a different line between acceptable conversation and sexual harassment. A warped sense of humor goes along with that, and lets us wade through the darkest parts of the job with our sanity intact.

I roamed the bedroom and then the bathroom. "The burn is contact," I repeated, still talking to myself, eliminating the obvious, "and was not from the floor grate."

There were no obvious heat sources in the bathroom. The water heater was electric, but it sat in a corner closet so tiny I could barely reach over the toilet and around the folding closet door to touch it. If he'd fallen there in a way that left burns on his back, he wouldn't be able to get himself up.

By the time I circled through to the kitchen area again, I'd eliminated everything but the aged gas oven, which was diagonal in a corner, not against the wall or cabinet. As if it got too hot.

"The stove is the only likely thing it could be," I concluded. "I bet he fell with his back and arm against it."

"Surely it doesn't get hot enough to burn someone," Stewart countered.

"Let's find out," I said, turning the knob to 400 degrees. I pulled out my mobile phone to call Central Dispatch and requested a fire unit with an infrared thermometer gun to respond non-emergency.

I opened my camera case and took out a Nikon body and picked a wide-angle lens to attach.

"I thought you'd figured it out," Stewart said, hands on his hips.

I shook my head. "I eliminated all the other heat sources in the house. But I didn't say it wasn't a crime, and I didn't say he might not still die from this. Might as well get photos while I'm here, just in case." I set about taking pictures of the house.

"How's the dog getting along?" Rory asked after he'd watched me shoot two 24-exposure rolls of film.

He was thinking about the dog, but I was thinking how I wished digital images were admissible in court. The computer geek part of me wanted very much to replace the common film photography methods we used. I had to change mental gears to answer.

"I think we're doing okay," I said, looking up from my equipment. "He'd rather be working, like the other day in the snow, but maybe he's like the rest of us and doesn't know any better."

"We're all glad you decided to take him," Rory said. He sounded like there was something more he wanted to say, but the Blair Township fire chief walked past the window view.

I only nodded, glad for the escape from the conversation, wherever it was going.

Opening the door before he could knock, I shook hands with Chief Buck Zeiller, and then I explained my question.

After ten minutes to warm, the sides of the stove were already too hot to touch, but I was still unsure whether the surface could cause burns of the severity suffered by Mr. Arnette.

"Simple enough," the chief said, and turned on the handheld unit, pointed it at the front door of the oven. "Holy shit!" He showed me the display.

The outside surface was 284 degrees.

"That's hot enough," I concluded, a little stunned at the reading as I turned off the oven and stowed my camera. "Rory, you can decide if this was a crime or an accident." I picked up my case and followed the chief out into the cold fresh air without further discussion.

Zeiller was still shaking his head in disbelief when we got to the parking area. "The engine crew said the old man had a nasty burn, but I couldn't have imagined until I saw the stove."

"He didn't feel any pain, so he didn't want to go to the hospital," I elaborated. "There's already an infection, so he may still die of complications. Thanks for coming over."

"You betcha. Nice to see you," he said as we stopped in front of my truck. "I'd heard rumors you were leaving."

"It's still up in the air," I said.

Rumors are like farts. Whether you hear them or not, they pretty much all stink.

◆

At a quarter to six, I looked up to see Rory Stewart marching down the hall into my office.

"Julie. Got a minute?" he asked, coming inside and closing my door behind him.

Putting on my best manners, I replied, "Sure, what's up?" I gestured at the chair across from me, and he sat down but leaned forward onto my desk.

"Thought I'd let you know I don't think there's any foul play in the Arnette case, but they've already transferred him to the burn unit in Grand Rapids."

"I didn't think so either," I said, thinking a phone call would have sufficed for such news. "But I'm still curious what happened to make him fall and not remember. Do you want copies of the photos?"

"Yeah, that would be good."

I stood and unlocked a cabinet behind my desk, then unlocked a evidence box inside it, made to secure small items temporarily, like the duplicate prints from the film in a sealed plastic envelope. I took the extra set, locked the door back, and tossed the photos onto the desk in front of him.

He reached forward and picked it up, then hesitated.

"Is there something else?" I asked.

"I don't want you to get the wrong idea, but several of us are going out tonight to shoot pool, and I thought maybe you'd join us."

"What kind of wrong idea would I get about that?"

"Well, you know, with Shannaker, I wouldn't have asked. And Brandan mentioned you were seeing someone else, but when you came back to your job, he didn't know." He shrugged. "Anyway Parker, Micah, some of day shifters, you know, we've been talking about buying you a beer to say thanks for what you did for Matt."

The hair on my neck bristled. "Please don't take this wrong, Rory, but I don't really want to be thanked for that," I said softly, feeling my guts and teeth clench.

"God, no," he stammered, much more genuinely. "That's not what I meant. I mean, you put in as much effort to find him as any of us. You kept his dog for him. That would have meant a lot to Matt. You did it for him, not because it was your job."

The words actually sounded sincere, but I doubted Rory would have a clue what my keeping Laser would have meant to Matthew, and it irritated me to hear such baloney.

Shuffling reports into a pile then filing them in the cabinet beside my desk, taking time to regain my composure rather than ripping off his head, the words hung between us.

Stewart was smart enough to shut up rather than making the situation worse.

"Yes, I did take care of the dog for Matt. Thank you for the invitation, Rory, but I'm really not up for a tribute or a crowd." I said. "Maybe another time."

He nodded, knowing he'd approached the subject wrong. "Would you consider going out to dinner with me instead?"

I locked eyes with him.

"Just dinner, tomorrow night? Just dinner," he repeated.

"Okay."

He looked more than a little surprised.

"You get off duty at seven tomorrow?"

He nodded.

I scribbled out my new cell phone number on a message sheet and slid it across the desk. "Call when you're off. I'll probably be here late. There's a lot of work to catch up yet."

He picked the pink paper up off my desk and folded it once before putting it into his left shirt pocket. "I'm looking forward to it."

Rory closed the door behind him on his way out.

I picked up my cell phone and dialed.

Brandan Callaghan answered.

"He took the bait," I said, "Tomorrow night."

CHAPTER
46

Before lunch the next day, a soft knock interrupted routine paperwork I'd been reading.

Carl Rowe, the department janitor, stood in my doorway.

"Come on in," I said, closing the file and motioning for him to take a seat. "I hardly ever see you during the day."

"Miss Julie," he said, taking a few steps forward to lean on the chair as if he might crumple. "I hate to ask, but I was wondering if you could take a look at something for me."

"Sure, Carl. What's up?"

Probably old enough to be my grandfather, he still sported jet-black hair I vaguely suspected came from a bottle.

He held up one hand, wrapped in a white bandage. "I cut it last night at home."

I stood and walked around my desk. "Let's go to the supply room where the light is better," I suggested.

Appearing weaker than I'd first guessed, Carl followed me down the hall.

What we've always called a supply room was an overflow of instruments, tools and supplies, looking like a cross between a junk heap and a clinic exam room.

Inside, I flipped on the bright fluorescent lights and turned to him.

Standing with his head ducked, watching the toe of one shoe poke his other foot, Carl looked like a little boy in big trouble with the teacher rather than a man who pushed seventy around with his broom every day.

"Let's take a look, shall we?" I prompted, pulling a pair of gloves from a box on the shelf.

Carl only held his hand out for me, and I decided when I felt him tremble as I began unwinding the stretchy gauze wrap, finding him a place to sit down would be in order before he fainted. After he took a seat on a bare metal stool, I continued taking off the first twelve feet and finding another beneath with blood soaked into it. As I pulled each layer away from the one underneath, the red stain grew in size. But for a cut that happened yesterday, the gauze was alarmingly wet. The wound, when I lifted the single no-stick dressing, was still oozing.

"Carl," I said, trying to remain calm. "How'd you cut your hand?"

The laceration was about two inches long, all the way across his wide palm. Gaping about a quarter of an inch.

"On the edge of an aluminum ladder," he said, but I barely heard him. "I don't have insurance, so I didn't go get it sewed up."

I tried to hide my dismay at the whole situation – how could a county employee not have basic health insurance for himself? Worse, how did Carl think this would heal without being cleaned and explored to make sure he hadn't cut any tendons or ligaments in the palm of his hand? I didn't even ask him if he could make a fist for fear it would cause more bleeding.

"The first thing we need to do is get this clean," I said, considering options. Obviously anything I did to him would cause a lot of pain now that the nerves were inflamed and possibly even infected, and Carl didn't look too steady. Using a local anesthetic would help, but I didn't have the tools or the skills to administer it. We could wash the wound out in a suite, but I wasn't sure Carl would go into an autopsy room, even if we had one empty. I took out my phone and dialed Gerald Katz's number.

"Julie?" he asked, surprised.

"Can you come to the storage room? I have an issue we need to address."

"The storage room?" More surprise. "I'll be right there."

I'd have bought lunch to find out what he'd been thinking as he walked down the hall from his office, only to find me alone with the janitor.

"We'll get this fixed up for you," I told Carl, trying to sound positive.

Within twenty seconds, Gerald opened the door and peeked inside.

"Carl cut his hand last evening, but he didn't go to the emergency room," I explained, lifting the last bandage and dressing again so Gerald could see.

I heard him exhale with a similar exasperation to what I'd felt.

"Where can we get this cleaned up?" I prompted.

"At the hospital," Katz said, dismissing whatever idea I might have had for helping. "You can drive him. I'll call and let them know."

"I don't have insurance," Carl repeated.

"Doesn't matter. This is way past ignoring the need for a couple of stitches. You can make arrangements when it's done," the medical examiner said with ample authority to end further debate.

"Come on," I said, pulling off my gloves as Dr. Katz disappeared out the door, already punching numbers on his phone. "I've known him long enough to hear when the argument is finished."

I wrapped a blanket around Carl's shoulders, thinking it was senseless for him to struggle into a coat. On the way past my office, I grabbed my own jacket, then told Connie where I was headed.

Carl said nothing as he walked to my car, holding his hand carefully with the other as if it hurt him more than he let on. He got in when I opened my car door for him, remained silent on the short trip to the hospital. Only when the registrar asked him for information did he speak again.

When the paperwork was done, I expected we'd have to sit a while, based on the crowd in the waiting area, but a nurse stepped out and called his name, then escorted him into the emergency department without me. He turned to give me one last glance as the doors closed automatically behind him.

♦

When Rory Stewart called at 7:15, I was still at the office.

"Why don't you pick me up at my place in half an hour?" I gave him the address. My drive there would take no more than ten minutes.

He arrived in his take-home car a little early, still in uniform, so he wanted to go by his apartment to change and pick up his personal vehicle.

I was wearing black jeans and a gray blouse with a teal silk scarf tied loosely around my neck. Maybe he had wanted to see how I was dressed before he picked something to wear, I thought.

We rode to his apartment in his patrol car, where I went in with him. Rory offered me a beer, twisting off the top and getting one for himself. He gave the courteous make-yourself-at-home gesture and then disappeared down a hallway.

The starkness of his apartment made it seem abandoned. Nothing hanging on the walls. No personal items sitting around. No books, no magazines. Not spotless, but uncomfortably clueless about its occupant. Like a cheap hotel room – adequate to the functions, but anonymous. Basic inexpensive furniture. Large television and VCR. A computer that didn't look like it had been used lately, sitting on a corner desk.

I drank half the beer as I wandered around before I ended up looking out onto a balcony barely large enough for a couple of chairs. Snow piled up on the wooden railing, illuminated by the street light.

"I thought we'd go to Blizzard's," he called down the hallway. "Okay with you?"

"Yeah, sure." Emptying the beer bottle, I was surprised at the buzz in my head.

"So Julie, I've seen you wearing a holster. What do you carry?" he yelled again, which I found to be rude and annoying.

"Usually a Glock 9 mm. I had a Smith & Wesson stolen, but I didn't want it back."

Not after it had been used to kill Jeremy McNeeley.

"Shame," Rory said. "I've never handled a Glock. Do you always carry?"

Faucets screeched.

"Not always," I said. "Depends on where I'm going and why."

"You got it with you tonight?" he said, coming out with a towel in his hands, drying off his face.

"No, I don't," I said.

"Oh, what a shame," he said with a grin. "I wanted to see it."

CHAPTER

47

"Come in for a drink?" I asked when Rory walked me to my front porch. I wobbled, having had more than enough already, although drinking so much wasn't my plan.

"It's late and I really ought to be going, Julie," he said, sounding polite but stepping closer. "Unless you're sure. . ."

"Yeah, whatever," I said, taking a third stab at putting the key in the lock and finally getting the door open to step in out of the cold. "You can hang your coat here." I stripped mine off, put it on the tree and kicked off my boots.

Rory looked down at his, still packed with snow.

"Take 'em off or not. I don't care," I said, moving on toward the kitchen. "I've got vodka, tequila, Crown, or beer."

He took off his boots and joined me in the kitchen.

"Beer is fine," he said, looking around. "Nice place. Lot different than mine, I'm sure you noticed. I haven't lived there long."

I handed him a Labatt's from the refrigerator, then poured myself a generous glass of Crown Royal neat.

"Funny, I'd have thought a girl from the Southwest would drink Dos or Corona, not Canadian beer."

"'The girl' drinks beer to be sociable when nothing else is offered," I said, lifting my glass. "But never beer from Mexico."

Setting down the bottle, Rory reached to pull me face to face with him. "You know, I wanted to do this a long time ago, but I figured your relationship with Matt had settled into whatever it was going to be."

"I'm surprised," I said, turning for another sip. My voice had dropped in pitch after having drunk so much throughout the evening. "Why did you think Matt and I were more than friends?"

He tilted his head. "You weren't?"

"No, but we were good friends."

"And what about this guy Callaghan mentioned?" he asked, leaning against the counter and wrapping his arms around my waist.

"Tell me something, Rory, is there a point to these questions about other men?" I asked, feeling the liquor adding its effects to the previous drinks at dinner and hearing my words slur.

"I'm not above screwing someone's wife," he said, "but a cop has to be careful."

"Careful," I repeated. I'd been trying to dismiss the thoughts of Zach thundering through my head all evening. "I have to go to the bathroom." I took another swallow before leaving my glass about half-full on the counter to go down the hall.

When I came out, Rory was wandering in my den, checking out CDs in the large rack.

"Anything you want to hear?" I asked, turning on the stereo.

"Nothing particular. Checking out what music you like," he said, putting his arms around my waist again to dance.

The player was on random. The first CD was Stevie Nicks' *Street Angel,* the eleventh track started, "Just Like a Woman."

It was a little fast for slow dancing, but he pulled me firmly against him, and I could feel the bulge in his jeans.

We fell into a swaying rhythm to the music. Swaying was easy for me.

The lyrics dug into my guts. "She makes love just like a woman, but she breaks just like a little girl. . . ."

I could see him listening to the words, and I didn't think I could stand it if he made a comment.

"So if you'd screw someone else's wife, why not a cop's?" I asked, hoping to divert his attention.

"You never piss off a badge who might have to cover your ass some day. Matt was a good guy," he said.

"But someone else's husband might not be?" I asked. "Or do you ignore that and take what you want?"

"Only when I have to," he whispered in my ear, then turned my head. "Speaking of which, is your bedroom down there?" he asked.

"Rory," I said, "no."

He kissed my cheek before looping his hand into the scarf around my neck, twisting it around his fist. "Yes," he said in a low tone that was clearly threatening. He wasn't choking me, but the control was definite. He guided me down the hallway in a slow dance, kissing me as we went. Inside the dark bedroom, he backed me to the foot of the bed and reached to unbutton my blouse with his free hand.

"No, Rory, please," I said louder, pushing his hand away and trying to step to the side. "Stop it. Let go of me. I can't. . ."

He jerked the scarf tighter. "I think you can," he said through clenched teeth.

I tried to get my hands between us to push, an inebriated attempt to fight back, but then he yanked open my shirt, ripping off several buttons.

A chilling sound stopped him dead – the distinct sound of the slide being pulled and released – a round being chambered in a semi-auto pistol.

CHAPTER 48

"Take your hands off her," I heard a low voice demand, one word at a time.

Rory let go of me, and I almost fell to the floor, then I scrambled around the bed to the corner table and grabbed my own gun from the drawer.

"Put the gun down," another male voice commanded from the doorway behind Rory.

When the lights came on, what I saw damn near caused my heart to stop.

Rory Stewart stood at the foot of my bed, arms raised in surrender, with Zach holding a gun inches from his head. Brandan Callaghan stood at the doorway, his gun leveled at Zach's chest.

I wasn't sure who mine was aimed at, but then I'd have had trouble hitting one of the four walls of the room, much less any particular male body.

"Ah, shit," several of us said at once.

Zach withdrew his weapon and put it on my dresser, taking a step back.

I put mine down on the bedside table.

Brandan holstered his and stepped toward Rory, snapping one cuff around a raised wrist and twisting it down and behind his back.

"What the hell is going on here?" Rory asked.

"Shut up," Brandan ordered. "You're under arrest."

Without resistance, Rory dropped his other hand to be cuffed, still glaring at me.

Brandan turned him toward the door, looked at me and then Zach. "We'll be in the kitchen when you two are through."

He practically shoved Rory into the hall and closed the door behind him.

With an effort, I got to my feet and moved around the corner of the bed toward Zach, who looked down at my ripped blouse. I pulled it closed. "What are you doing here?" I asked, confused.

"I was about to ask you the same question." He was furious – I could hear it in his voice. Dressed in black with his Stetson pulled low on his head, he was flat intimidating. He took a step toward me.

"It's not what you think," I said with a slur not quite erased by the huge release of adrenaline that made me feel like I could run a six-minute mile if I could keep from falling. But I immediately regretted the choice of words and found myself backing up a step.

"Oh yeah? I didn't *think* you were about to crawl into bed with another man." He took another step forward. "So you like working *undercover*?" he asked.

We did that backward-forward dance until I was against the wall and Zach towered over me. Looking up at him made me dizzy.

My muscles trembled, but I could think of nothing to say.

Zach put his hands on the wall on either side of my head, leaning even closer. "You're plastered. So just how far should I have let him go, Julie? Past where he rips off your clothes?" His voice got louder with every word. "Till he chokes you unconscious? Or should I be polite and wait till he's done fucking you?" he bellowed, pounding one palm against the wall.

"No, Zach. Please listen," I said, lowering my voice to maintain control of it. "It was a setup. Brandan told me two other woman say he date-raped them, but because he's a deputy, they were afraid to press charges without more proof."

"So you volunteered to be the bait and make a case?"

"Brandan was here to cover me," I said defensively. Then rage took charge, and I smacked Zach's chest with both hands but failed to move him an inch. "And what's the difference between this and you sitting on a damned beach without a gun?"

"I only got shot that night."

"You almost died!" I yelled, then tried to regain some composure when my balance heaved.

We stood toe to toe, both of us fiery mad.

The door opened. "Would you two care to join me?" Brandan said, indicating it wasn't really a choice.

Always the gentleman, Zach took a step back and waved his hand to indicate I should go first. We followed Brandan into my kitchen.

"Zach, I was here two hours before you snuck in. When you came through from the garage and went into her bedroom, I didn't know what to do. They were only minutes away, and I wasn't sure I could explain in time, but I should have. I apologize," he explained.

Through the front window, I saw two uniformed officers place Rory in a patrol car, but not before he turned and scowled back at the house as if he knew I was watching him.

A shiver ran through me.

"Stewart was in possession of what we believe to be GHB. We set this up so Julie would only fix her own drink here to keep him from doping her," Brandan continued to Zach. "We have video in the kitchen, but he didn't put anything in her glass, which I told her when she went to the bathroom – we'd left a transceiver there for her." He turned to me. "I was going to tell you Zach was in the bedroom, but you didn't give me time." Back to Zach, "I promise you she was never in any danger. I was already at the door when you stood up."

Zach took a deep breath. "I'm sorry if I blew your case," he said to Brandan, not looking at me.

"No problem," Brandan said. "With the video and the physical evidence of Julie's torn shirt and her statement, I think we can get the other two women to press charges now."

I was still shaking when a female deputy accompanied me to collect my clothes, putting the torn blouse, jeans and scarf into separate evidence bags, followed by my bra and panties and socks. It irked me to have to give up my boots, but they were bagged, too. I put on warm-ups and a sweatshirt, and she took the evidence and left. When I came out of the bathroom, Brandan had gone, as well, leaving no opportunity to explain further.

"I'm sorry, Zach," I said, but when there was no response, I shuffled to the den and slumped to the sofa. All the emotions swirling around inside left me unable to explain any of them.

Zach grabbed a soft drink from the refrigerator and glugged about half of it before he slammed the can onto the countertop and came into the room with me. He tossed his hat into a chair, making him appear somewhat less threatening, then walked to the window facing the backyard and stared into the darkness.

"I'm sorry," I said again, watching his face in the reflection.

Anger bulged in his shoulders. He took a long time to answer but finally spoke without turning to face me. "I don't want you to feel like I own you, but watching him grab you –" He grimaced, squeezing his eyes shut as something painful played in his head. "All I could think of was finding Zoe and knowing what they had done . . ." He let his words trail off, without hiding the pain I heard in his voice.

"I understand."

"No, I don't think you do, Julie," he said, wheeling to face me. "I waited so long for you to be part of my life. The last three years, I had no choice but to accept that there might be other men in your bed besides me. I loved you anyway, and I waited. And then everything changed – I got my turn." His expression changed through a rainbow of emotions, but settled back to despair. "We were talking about getting married, you know? Then seeing him maul you, tearing your shirt. . ." He turned away, but not before I saw a tear spill over his cheek. His fists balled up, and I was afraid he might slam them into the glass.

"I'm sorry," I said again. I didn't know what else to say.

He wouldn't look at me.

The music had played through several more discs on random since I turned it on, and Fleetwood Mac's "The Chain" started.

. . . *Run in the shadows, Damn your love, damn your lies. And if you don't love me now, you will never love me again* . . .

I picked up the remote and turned the stereo off. There were a thousand more lyrics I didn't want to hear.

"I still don't understand why you are here," I said, not wanting to discuss the music.

He didn't turn around. "They gave me a weekend pass, so I flew over to see you. I thought maybe in person we could work everything out. I wanted to hear about the tapes, your hypnosis sessions in Albuquerque, everything. I needed to talk to you, to hold you."

All his hopes were stated in past tense.

"Yeah, we need to talk," I said, making a decision. I wobbled a little when I stood. "I'm going to shower. Why don't you call and get us a hotel? Neither of us needs to be in that bedroom tonight."

He nodded, but he didn't make any effort to touch me when I came near him.

Surely the chill radiated from the glass and not from him, but that's not how I felt.

"I'm sorry. Really, Zach," I said as I walked on past him to the bathroom, where I turned on the shower and let the water steam up the room. My pale face disappeared as the mirror fogged. Chilled at what had happened during the last few hours, my hands and feet felt ice cold. In my chest, my heart thumped wildly.

If Zach thought it was hard watching, he had no idea how I'd felt when Rory touched me.

A wave of nausea hit me, and I threw up, sick with disgust and alcohol and emotional havoc. When my stomach emptied, the retching turned to sobs.

Crawling to the tub, I finally turned off the shower, then I collapsed to the floor.

I woke up an hour or so later, cold and stiff, somewhere between drunk and hung over, but very much alone.

♦

I stood under a scalding shower and scrubbed my skin until the water ran cold. Twice. Afterward, I let the dog in from the garage and sat with the lights off in the den the next five hours, staring into the shadows.

My brain kept identifying the smell of Rory on my skin, but it might not have existed at all except in my imagination.

I called Zach but got no answer. If he left without an explanation, I figured he had nothing to say.

Finally, at daybreak, not knowing what else to do, I paged Brandan.

He called half an hour later, apologizing for the delay. "Are you okay?"

"No," I answered flatly. "I don't think so."

"I shouldn't have left, but I figured with Zach there, you two had things to work out."

"He walked out. I went to take a shower after you left," I closed my eyes and tried to breathe normally. "He was gone when I came out."

"Ah, damn it, Julie. I'm almost there."

"No, you don't have to come," I barely argued. "I'm a mess."

"Doesn't matter. Five minutes, okay?"

I sighed. "Okay." I got up and made a pot of coffee, a habit so simple and ingrained it took little thought.

When I heard the car in the driveway, I went to open the front door for Brandan. He stomped his boots on the porch and stepped inside, bundled in a green parka and gloves.

"Temperatures got downright bitter last night," he said, tossing off the hood. He tucked the gloves into his pockets, slid off the coat and hung it on the doorknob, and kicked off his boots before following me on to the kitchen.

"Really, I didn't want to bother you, Brandan," I said, somewhere between tears and feeling dead. "But I didn't know who else to call."

Truth was, I didn't want to try to tell anyone else about what happened.

"Julie, I shouldn't have left you here – I wouldn't have if I'd known you'd end up alone, I swear."

He sat down at the breakfast bar.

Even though my hands trembled, I poured us each a cup of coffee and sat down across from him. "You were doing your job," I said. "I didn't expect this. Any of this."

"My priority was to make sure you were okay," he argued.

"We set Stewart up. He did what you expected him to do. How ironic he came close to getting his head blown off by the very boyfriend he was laughing about earlier. He's lucky," I said. "The last man Zach caught tearing off my clothes went headfirst halfway out a window."

"Your mysterious trip to Florida?"

I nodded but provided no other details.

"I wouldn't want to cross Zach half as mad as he was last night.

But honestly, I was sure you two would be better off without an audience. I'm really sorry," he said.

"Everything's gone awry since New Year's, not just this. I don't know where it's going, especially now."

"Did you try to find him this morning?"

I shook my head. "I called, but he didn't answer. If he left, he's long gone." The abandonment I felt, the anger at him for walking away from me when I needed him was gone. I only felt numb.

Brandan's cell phone rang, and he excused himself to answer, talked for a few minutes, then disconnected.

"That was the lab, calling about your clothes, Julie," Brandan said. "Is there something else you need to tell me about last night?"

CHAPTER
49

Being home alone the rest of the weekend felt like being stuck in setting concrete – I was unable and mostly unwilling to get up and move. Nothing motivated me to rise from the recliner two days in a row. Not food, not alcohol, not even sleep.

Every time I closed my eyes, I either felt Rory's hands on me or Zach's absence. Hot hatred or cold loneliness.

I didn't feel suicidal but consumed by an overwhelming sense of nothingness. Grief, maybe. Something inside me had died and left an empty space in my heart.

Brandan called several times each day to check on me. I appreciated the effort, but I really had nothing else to say.

Monday morning, there was no reason I could think of to stay home from work without an explanation I couldn't bear to make, so I went to the Annex, hoping the distraction and necessity to complete tasks would help. Sitting in my office facing a stack of paperwork kept my mind occupied most of the time, but I still caught myself staring at the wall several times, lost in the emptiness I felt. When I did go to the scene of an investigation after lunch, I only noticed the details I'd been summoned to document. Fortunately, it wasn't a crime, just an unwitnessed death of an elderly woman.

No matter what the task, my body did its thing on autopilot, and mentally I went along for the ride. The best face I could present to the world was uninvolved, but for the most part, I didn't have to interact with anyone directly until Dr. Katz dropped by my office before five o'clock.

"Bad news," he said from the doorway when I looked up. "I got word this afternoon that Carl died."

I must have looked blank.

"Carl Rowe," he prompted. "The janitor?"

My thoughts jumbled. It was no easy effort to recall who or what Dr. Katz was talking about, but finally the connection snapped in my head like a dry twig. "No, it was just a cut," I argued, as if debate could change the outcome.

Katz shrugged. "He became septic, despite the aggressive antibiotics. After the onset of severe respiratory distress, he coded this morning."

I shook my head, unable to think of anything else to say.

Perhaps Gerald was going to elaborate, but his pager went off, and he excused himself to go down the hall.

Although I hadn't given it any thought since then, I remembered watching Carl disappear behind the emergency room doors three days ago. How he turned and looked at me, as if I'd done something horribly wrong taking him there and leaving him.

How had someone progressed from a hand laceration to death? Worrying about it just shifted my focus from one disaster to another for a little while.

♦

"Madigan," I said, answering the phone from a splintered sleep at 2 a.m. a week later.

"Julie, are you okay?"

It actually took a moment to identify the voice, I was so groggy and disoriented, finally in a sleep, but still barraged by nightmares.

"I guess," I managed to say.

"Sorry I woke you," Zach said. "I got your letter today. Can we talk?"

"Let me go to the bathroom first," I put the phone down and stumbled down the hall and back. "Sorry," I said, positioning the pillows to sit up in bed and throwing the covers over my legs.

"Julie, I'm sorry I left you. There's no excuse," Zach said.

I took a deep breath. "Is there a reason?"

"Besides all the anger? Mostly fear," he admitted. "It wasn't blame, I swear."

So much for not being afraid, I wanted to say, to throw his words back at him. But I had broken the same promise when I left Oregon.

"Guess we're even now on the walking-away scoreboard," I said.

"When you went to shower, you can't imagine all the things running through my mind as I sat there alone."

"Can you imagine me puking up my guts and passing out on the bathroom floor while you made your getaway?" I asked, my voice gravelly with sleep, sounding too harsh. "Can you imagine me waking up to find the one person I needed most had left without any explanation? At least I tried to tell you why I needed to leave Washington, Zach. I might have failed, but I didn't run away when you weren't looking."

"I know. It was a stupid thing to do."

We retreated to neutral corners in silence.

"Can I ask you a question?" I asked when I felt I could breathe again.

"Of course."

"If you hadn't been here, if I'd told you what happened over the phone after the fact, would it change how you feel about it?"

"I don't know. Coming on the heels of everything in Florida? I know it seems overly-protective or possessive," he began, then paused. "I really don't know."

"Okay, let me tell you something about Florida as an example. I ended up playing pool with Dallas Bowers, a bet I had no choice but to take. If I won, we talked about a job – the meth lab thing. If he won, I had to spend the night with him first."

"Damn it, Julie." He groaned. "Is there anything about your trip I'm ever gonna like hearing?"

"Sure, two things. One is I played the luckiest game of pool in my life, but Dom had given me a bottle of scopolamine, just in case. Two, there's an elderly lady who no longer has to worry about a bunch of bikers knocking down her door to assault her mentally-handicapped daughter every time they think about it."

"Really?" he said. "What's that about?"

"I was riding with them the last day, not long before I saw you in that bar. Dallas led the group to her house. He told me to stay outside with the bikes, so I knew something bad was going on. Something I couldn't fix right then," I said. "That was my concession to Nolan about leaving. I told him I wouldn't go until I knew the woman and her daughter were safe."

"I must have slept through that negotiation," Zach commented.

"You were in the shower."

"I see. You're right – I wouldn't be as upset if hadn't seen it. That really jerked my chain hard."

"Hard enough you'd loaded my new Glock, I noticed. Full of Glaser's."

Point-blank, it would have been an expensive waste of bullets. If he'd pulled the trigger once, I had no doubt Zach would have fired every round from the magazine.

"In the dark, I couldn't tell what they were. And yeah, I was feeling hostile, listening to what went on in the kitchen. Besides, what good is an unloaded gun?" he asked. His voice softened a little. "I was surprised it was a .40 caliber. Figured you'd stay with a 9 mm or .38 forever."

"Something different. I bought the .40 to try after I shot yours for practice. To replace the gun Bock stole – the one he used at the hospital in Florida. I didn't want it back."

"You mean he shot me with *your* gun?" Zach mused. "I didn't know that."

I hadn't realized it, either, even knowing Anthony Bock had shot Jeremy with it. "I haven't had a chance to go to the range with it, so I still carry the other one."

"The one you pointed at me," he stated.

My nostrils flared at the accusation. "First off, I wasn't carrying it that night. Second, you've managed to sneak into my car and my house at will for over three years, and I've yet to ever even draw down on you. I think the circumstances exceeded unusual."

"Yes, but you had been drinking."

"You really want to go there, Zach?" I demanded, willing to argue that while I was absolutely drunk, at least I hadn't been high on some drug likely to make me paranoid and psychotic.

"No, ma'am. Just saying I didn't like standing on the muzzle end of a gun in your hand, either."

"Well, that evens the score on another issue, doesn't it?"

"I guess it does."

More silence.

"I miss you, Julie," he blurted, as if the words slipped like a fish through his fingers.

My heart fluttered behind my ribs. "I miss you, too."

"Baby, please come back. We can work this out."

"Buy a ticket when you get out of the treatment center. Let's see where we stand face to face."

He laughed. "You know the only time we're ever face to face is when –"

"Yes, I know," I interrupted his blatantly sexual comment. It made me smile.

"Promise not to be groping another cop next time?"

From the smile to a stunned silence like he'd slapped me.

"I'm sorry. That was callous and stupid."

"Um, yeah. It was," I said. "You've had a few one-liners sharp enough to draw blood."

"I've had a tough time with this."

"So have I, Zach."

"I know. I was so blinded by my own emotions, I couldn't think about how you might have felt," he began. "I talked to Brandan tonight, just before I called you – he'd picked up his messages late. He told me you were distraught when he saw you the next morning. He said he tried to get you to see a counselor since then, but you wouldn't go."

"No."

"I'm not asking to criticize, but why not?"

"When have I ever wanted to talk to mental health people about this sort of crap in my life? And I'm already seeing someone, which is none of Brandan's business."

"Have you talked about this?"

I sighed. "No, I haven't."

"Brandan also said the video and evidence at the house aren't flying with the prosecutor. I know I screwed this up, Julie, but I don't understand how they can throw out what this guy did."

"The evidence doesn't fit the original charges, Zach," I said. "With all the video, they know Rory didn't rape me at my house."

"No, but he would have if –" he stopped as he processed exactly what I'd said. "Not at your house? Oh Christ, Julie. . ." His voice broke.

"Zach, please don't –"

"Damn it, Julie!"

I inhaled sharply. "Don't yell at me." My voice sounded strangely like my father's when he was angry – dead calm and slow.

"You . . . I can't . . . What did he . . ." He took a deep breath and groaned. "Julie, why didn't you tell me?"

I could hear he was crying.

"Tell you? Because you left, Zach. What he did was bad enough without you reacting like that, blaming me for it." I rubbed my left wrist, where a bruise in the shape of Rory's fingers was still visible in shades of purplish-green.

"I'm not trying to blame you," he countered.

"Isn't that why you left? It didn't matter what Rory had done, you were mad at me."

"I was angry, yes!"

Silence. Although I'd been angry as well that night, that emotion had been buried in so many others. Shame outweighed anger, knowing that I'd been the one to screw up the operation. Had I not been drunk, I might have found a way to salvage the setup.

"Did Callaghan know that night?" he finally asked.

"No, not until they processed my clothes," I confessed. "Someone in the lab called him while he was here the next morning."

"I don't understand."

"The prosecuting attorney said the defense would argue the evidence was only related to the arrest at the house and would suggest I had consented earlier; otherwise, why would I have invited him in? At the very best, it was entrapment." I explained. "I'm the one who messed this all up. If I'd told Brandan that night, they'd have charged Stewart differently, but honestly, I was too wasted to make sense of it by the time we got to my house."

"Will you tell me what happened?" he asked, his voice so low I barely heard him.

I could see it in my head, and sometimes I couldn't make it go away, but I couldn't speak the words. I'd tried to write out the details, to find a way to purge the memory, but somewhere between the safe clinical descriptions and the ugly truth was too much disgust and shame because I hadn't been able to stop what happened. "I can't, Zach."

Maybe what he heard was I wouldn't, not that I couldn't tell him.

A cold vacuum of silence filled the miles and seconds between us, stretching into black space.

"You have no idea how much I hate feeling this way. I hate what it's done to you," I whispered. "I'm so damned tired of the ugliest things in my life being made public, but I can't say the words."

Mostly, I can't stand the thought of reliving the mistakes.

He said nothing, so I kept talking.

"You know, Brandan insisted I go to the emergency room the next morning. By then, I wasn't even capable of arguing, so I went. The nurse came in and started asking me questions, whether or not I'd called the police. When I said no, before I could even explain, she stood up and lectured me on my 'social responsibility.' She actually threatened to contact the police and tell them everything I'd already told her." I wiped away the tears that wouldn't even fall – they puddled in my eyes and blurred my vision. "People wonder why women won't report sexual assault – because dealing with everyone afterward is almost as bad as being raped."

"Honey, I'm sorry." I could hear he meant it, but I couldn't tell what else was going through his mind, maybe about Zoe.

"I'm sorry, too, Zach. I should have told you. I think I would have that night, or I'd have tried. But I don't blame you for leaving. In fact, later I was sorta glad you were gone so I didn't have to tell you, to see what it did to you." I paused. "I thought maybe you'd seen it in my eyes so you left."

More silence.

Maybe I was right.

"Don't you have anything to say to me?" I asked.

In the dead air, I heard him breathing.

Something inside me broke, leaving an awful aching in my chest.

Finally, I said, "I'll take your silence as a 'no.' After all the promises, I guess we've finally found that part of Julie's life Zach can't live with."

When there was no reply, I hung up.

acConrad

CHAPTER

50

Zach had reacted like I thought he would, more or less, considering what had happened to his twin sister.

What sort of things had he said to her? I wondered. Maybe his words were kind and supportive, but then he didn't have to think about waking up next to her.

I walked to the kitchen to get a glass of water.

Headlights moved across the wall as a car pulled into the driveway. I opened the door moments after Brandan rang the bell.

"I came to see if you're okay," he said. "I talked to Zach a little while ago, and I thought he'd probably call you. I waited until I saw the lights, just to be sure."

I let him inside. "Yeah, he called," I said, feeling like it took all my energy for those three words and the next four. "I told him. Everything."

"You look like he didn't take it very well."

I shook my head.

"Julie, I am so sorry." He hugged me.

"Please, I can't stand to hear any more apologies. This is my fault," I said, backing away when he let go of me.

"No, it's not. I asked you to take the risk. Rory Stewart crossed a line and assaulted you. You are not responsible for how it turned out, I am. You'd never have gone out with him if I hadn't arranged this. I feel guilty because I encouraged him. I didn't see what had happened to you, but I should have."

"I'm a big girl, Brandan. I could've said no to going out with him," I said. "To either of you."

"I'm sorry Zach's not helping you get through this. That's gotta hurt."

"Yeah, well. . ."

Yeah. Like someone cut my heart out.

I turned and walked to the kitchen.

"Something else," he said as we sat down across from each other at the breakfast bar. "When I was circling the neighborhood, I saw Rory parked down the street."

I wiped both hands over my face and through my hair. "You don't think he would. . ." I let the thought trail to silence. I already knew what he was capable of doing.

"I have no idea what's on his mind, Julie, which is why you needed to know. I didn't want to interfere until I told you. Confronting him might make this worse. I recorded video as I drove by, so I have proof he was here. He drove away when I pulled into the drive."

His cell phone rang.

"Detective Callaghan," he said.

To offer a bit of privacy, I stepped to the sink to fill my water glass.

"No, I'm still up, Zach."

My heart fluttered.

"No, I didn't find out what really happened until the next morning when the lab called me." He paused and looked at me while Zach said something. "Not very well from what I can tell."

They talked about me, but I couldn't stand to listen. I walked down the hall to the bathroom and closed the door.

Zach couldn't even speak to me, but fifteen minutes later, he was interrogating Brandan about me. That hurt, too.

I wasted as much time as I could, pacing in the small room, avoiding the mirror. Finally opening the door, I hesitated, listening.

From the kitchen, I heard Brandan offering advice. "If you love her, she needs you to forgive her, Zach. You both have to find a way to forgive each other, whatever it takes."

The words made me want to clap both hands over my ears and scream.

I waited until the topic changed before I trudged into the kitchen.

Brandan looked up and pointed to the phone, silently asking if I wanted to talk.

I shook my head and went to the den to wait, staring out into the darkness.

Having heard enough gut-wrenching anger, blame, and disappointment in my own conversation with Zach, I didn't want to obligate him to express any more, verbally or in cold silence.

But Brandan's words echoed in my head – *You have to find a way to forgive each other, whatever it takes.*

Everything in my life seemed to boil down to forgiveness, but even if I could offer it, I had no right to ask for it.

Brandan disconnected so I walked into the kitchen. "Drop the charges," I said. "I can't do this."

Nothing but the assault charge would stand up in court, but I didn't see what good it would do.

"If you're sure," he said, waiting a moment for me to change my mind, maybe, "consider it done."

I nodded. "I lose, either way. The papers would blast me for wrongly accusing Stewart, or I'd be slaughtered in court for setting him up."

Juries don't like sting operations targeting law enforcement officers.

"After killing Matthew," I finished, "there's no more sympathy left for me around here."

"I'll stand behind you on this, whichever way you decide," he said. "What else can I do?"

"I don't know." Truth, plain and simple.

"Do you want to know what Zach said?"

"No," I said, shaking my head. "I don't think so."

"Okay. Tell me what happened between you two in Washington. Why'd you come back alone?"

CHAPTER

51

"It doesn't matter why I left, Brandan."

"Does to me." He leaned back and crossed his arms.

I wanted to argue with him, but he appeared unbending.

With a sigh of resignation, I explained why I left Washington.

"Being with Zach at the cabin for the holidays had been so wonderful," I said. Even after his confession about the drugs, I felt more alive than I had for many years – crazy in love. Everything felt so right. Until he called me Mariah. Until the incident with the kitchen knife.

"I cut him," I said to Brandan, blinking away the memory of the morning and afternoon we'd both spent as patients in the emergency room in White Salmon. "It was bad," indicating on my own arm where and how big the gash on his arm was. "After what I'd done to Matthew, I was so shaken by the violence of feeling a blade against skin, the smell of blood. . . I felt like I'd fallen off a cliff."

"Did you mean to cut him?" Brandan asked. "Even subconsciously when he tried to take the knife. Maybe you perceived it as aggression?"

"No, it was an accident – entirely my fault," I said, fighting tears. "But seeing the look in his eyes the moment he realized what I'd done, I lost it. I tried to bandage his arm, control the bleeding, but he insisted on digging through this huge box of letters and souvenirs he'd been saving for me, trying to find that drawing," I said, pointing to the framed picture now hanging on my dining room wall.

Despite my pleas, Zach had rifled through the box until he

located a mailing tube and extracted another of his exquisite pencil drawings, an image of me walking with Julaquinte though a rough trail in blowing snow. The tack looked medieval, from the scalloped reins and caparison-length saddle blanket and britchen, to what appeared to be a shield on the far side, opposing a broadsword and gauntlets hanging on the visible side of the saddle.

Zach had drawn me in a skirt to mid-calves, a thick loose shirt with long flowing sleeves and a hood cowled around my neck. Not elegant but functional. The shirt was light-colored, but seemed to have dark smudges. A long braid hung down one side, but a few wisps of hair blew loose in the wind.

Looking at the drawing, I couldn't help but feel the sadness portrayed by the figure on the paper, walking alone. In the bottom right corner, it was signed, "knight falls – i love you, sweet mariah, forever and always. january 1994."

"Zach told me he never called me Julie when he was working – he'd referred to me as Mariah since the first night we spent together. I didn't know that," I said. "He said he liked the name because of the Kingston Trio song, you know, 'The rain is Tess, the fire is Joe, and they call the wind Mariah.'"

"Mariah," Brandan echoed with a smile. "I could see why."

"There's blood on the paper. He wouldn't stop until he found the drawing, to show me what he meant. I wasn't sure one or both of us wouldn't pass out."

Zach had finally let me bandage his arm, but he obviously needed stitches. I'd driven to the hospital with what felt like a steel battering ram slamming against the insides of my skull.

"By the time we got back to the cabin, we were both exhausted, but I was determined to clean up the blood all over the kitchen. I gagged as I scrubbed the counters, table, tiles. He tried to help me, but I went to pieces every time I looked at him."

"Why?"

Tears stung my eyes. "Because I'd hurt him – really hurt him – in a blind rage. Because he kept saying it was okay." I swallowed. "Because I couldn't believe him."

"What about now?" he asked. "Why can't you guys talk this out?"

I shrugged. "Some of the things he said to me the evening you dragged Rory out of here or tonight on the phone were horrible."

"What can I do? You want me to talk to him again?"

Wiping my eyes with the palms of my hands, I said, "No. I'm going to be okay, Brandan."

"No, you aren't. Not by yourself."

His words were blunt and honest, like Zach. It made me want to curl up and cry.

"Maybe you can't tell him what Rory did, and I can understand only a tiny fraction of why," Brandan said, leaning onto his elbows, "but tell me. As much or as little detail as you want, but you need to say the words and let them go. There's no emotional tie between us except friendship. I'm not going to be mad at you, and I won't judge you. And maybe no one else ever hears you tell the story again, but you have to say it out loud just once. What happened with Rory?"

I shook my head.

"Julie, you can tell me now or you can get me a blanket and pillow, but I'm not leaving until I find out what Rory did."

"Couch or spare bedroom?" I asked.

CHAPTER 52

"I'll take the couch," he said, nodding over his shoulder toward the den.

I took a deep breath. "Brandan, I –"

His eyes said he was dead serious, regardless what argument I made. Telling him about leaving Washington had been awful enough, I thought. But still, if I had to explain to anyone all the details, perhaps Brandan would benefit. And maybe he was right, that I had to fight my way through saying it aloud just once before I could bury it.

"Not here," I said, filling my water glass again.

He followed me to the den. I turned the light off and sat down in my overstuffed leather chair after he took the sofa, maybe to make his point.

"I'm not here to judge you," he repeated, "just to hear what you say."

Remembering how much better I felt after talking through memories with Dr. Rothman, I nodded and closed my eyes. "Rory picked me up here after work. I'd stayed late at the office and needed to put the dog in the garage out of your way. We went to his apartment so he could change out of his uniform. I followed him up, and he got us each a beer then went to change. From down the hallway, in a seemingly casual conversation, he asked me about guns, what I carry, whether I had it with me. I said I didn't." I took a drink. "It was what he wanted to hear, that I was unarmed."

Brandan didn't say a word.

"I don't know if he'd put something in my beer. I felt buzzed and maybe a little weak, but not really impaired at first. Then Rory came down the hallway and grabbed me around the neck from behind, like a chokehold, and pushed me down to my knees, facing the couch. I struggled, trying to kick or hit him, but he pulled my scarf tight around my neck. When I was almost unconscious, he undid my jeans and pulled them down. He was still wearing his uniform pants and belt, including his gun."

The memories flooded through me, trying to all escape at once.

"He seemed confident, but I knew he'd cause the least physical injury possible. I kept trying to reach back, but every time I did, he choked me harder or jerked my neck," I explained. Up till that point, what Rory had done wasn't difficult to verbalize, but the story suddenly became awkward, uncomfortable. I kept going, one sentence at a time. "Once he unzipped his pants, I figured maybe he would let go of the scarf so I could breathe. He didn't, but the harder I struggled, the more he seemed to like it. He shoved my face into the sofa cushions to keep me from making noise. Kept saying he knew I'd enjoy it."

I stopped and took a breath. Still, the memory encompassed all my senses – visual, auditory, tactile, and even olfactory. Talking about Rory brought each sensation back from where I'd stuffed it, trying to forget. Using the relaxation techniques I'd been taught, I tried to calm myself. *They were just words now. I was safe. Words were powerless.*

I could repeat the mantra, but it didn't *feel* safe to remember.

Brandan waited for me to continue when I was ready.

"He hurt me just enough to control what I did. I couldn't reach his gunbelt because of my shoulder. When I finally got my arms under me and shoved backward against the couch to push him off, he dragged me backward with him, rolled and pinned me to the floor. I kicked and started to scream. He sat up, and I heard him unsnap his holster, so I quit fighting. I let him. . ." I couldn't say it, ". . . finish."

True to his promise, Brandan only listened to me, even when I struggled with words.

"When Rory was done, he stood up and zipped his pants, then he pulled me to my feet and shoved me into the bathroom to wash up. He finally pounded on the door for me to hurry, because he was hungry." I blew my nose and wiped away tears I didn't realize had slid down my cheeks. "At dinner, Rory sat across from me, trying to make conversation, as if nothing had happened. He asked about when I came back from Florida bruised and beat up, like it was completely different than what he'd done to me."

Looking at Brandan in the shadows, I saw something on his face. Not pity, not disconnection. Maybe it was understanding.

"Honestly, I didn't mean to get drunk. I just kept drinking." I squeezed my eyes closed, wishing I could say the same words to Zach. "Trying to make it go away. Then when he brought me here, I didn't know how else to make the setup work unless he came into the house with me. I should have let him walk away and filed a report, but I didn't think I could tell you. I'm sorry."

"You don't have to be sorry, Julie. I told you this is not your fault."

"Maybe if I'd told him I wanted to wait till after dinner, to get him here to the house. Or if I'd fought harder when he –"

"Stop, Julie. Say it, 'Not my fault.'"

The sound of the voice surprised me, and my eyes popped open, revealing Brandan across the dim room, not Zach.

A safe distance from reality, this far removed from the incident.

Nine feet wasn't far enough for Zach that night. Probably nine hundred miles hadn't been enough.

We sat in silence for a while as I put myself together.

I tried to act as though I felt better after having related the tale to Brandan, but I didn't. I still felt raw. When I walked him to the door, we both peered up and down the block to see if Rory was still out there, but I saw no strange cars.

Finally alone again, I made a decision and got dressed.

A half-hour after Brandan left, I eased my Suburban out of the garage. It was four o'clock in the morning when I drove to Rory's apartment complex and parked next to his car.

Dim yellow light was visible over the balcony.

He was on administrative leave, which made it easy to sit down the street from my house all night if he wanted.

Getting out, I crept up the steps to his door, knocked softly and moved out of direct sight of the peephole. I didn't care if he was awake or not – I'd have pounded on the door till he opened it anyway but I didn't want to wake the neighbors needlessly.

The deadbolt slid, and I saw light in the small crack when he turned the knob.

I bumped the door with my left shoulder and hip, pushing my way inside.

"Nice to see you again, Rory. Hope I'm not intruding." I smiled as he stepped backward. I nudged the door closed behind me. "I came to talk to you."

"I've got nothing to say," he said, regaining some confidence and turning his back to walk away.

"So you can listen. I came to tell you I dropped the charges," I said. "You win."

He stopped then looked over his shoulder with a predatory smile. "Win? Oh, Sweetheart, I'da beat it all anyway, thanks to your pitbull boyfriend screwing everything up."

"You have any idea how close you came to getting a head full of Glaser slugs, Rory?" I asked. "I watched Zach kill the last man who laid a hand on me. I'm surprised he hasn't come looking for you, now that he knows what you really did. But I figure, since he killed my demons, I could return the favor," I said quietly, pulling the Glock from my coat pocket.

"You haven't got the guts to shoot me," Rory said, facing me again, attempting a smirk that looked smarmy and fake behind genuine concern.

"Remember these scars?" I said, pulling down my collar. "Oh, yeah, that's right – you had me face down. I put two bullets through the heart of the man who did this to me. And I didn't hesitate to slit Matt Shannaker's throat. I had actually *cared* for both of them, so what makes you think I give a damn about killing you?"

"You'd go to prison."

"I've got nothing left to lose, Rory. The only thing that made my life worthwhile is a man who can't even talk to me because of what you did."

He forced a laugh to cover the anxiety.

"You must have thought what you did was worth the risks, right? Or do you think the guys at the station will be patting you on the back because you'll get away with it? I washed off the nasty spunk you left between my legs, and forgot the smell of your stinking breath. You can think of it however you want, but it was still rape."

"I don't recall you saying no." Rory sneered. "I remember you wiggling your ass against me. Begging for it, in fact."

"The only thing I begged you to do is to pull the trigger. You stuck your gun to my head, but you couldn't even fire it, you sleazy coward," I said, lowering my aim to his crotch. "Besides, I don't have to kill you to keep you from doing this to anyone else."

Rory took a step backward, and I got the feeling he thought about putting his hands in front of his crotch for a fleeting moment.

"Quite a few men have hurt me," I continued, making a sad face. "Maybe I could propagate a little sympathy with the jury. Or maybe I'll even get away with it on an insanity plea. What do you think?"

"I think you're crazy, all right." Sweat broke out on his forehead.

"So why don't you pick up the phone and call the police to come get me out of your apartment?" I asked, shrugging one shoulder. "I'm not stopping you."

"Gun or not, I don't need any help taking you down," he said, trying to sound casual. "Maybe I'll spread your legs and make you scream while I'm fucking you again. I liked it when you fought. Makes me hard just thinking about it."

"As much as I like it when a man talks dirty to me, Rory, it's really hot when he confesses," I said, returning his maniacal grin when I lifted up the wire to the microphone around my coat collar.

"That's not admissible in court," he stammered, taking another step backward and finding he'd run out of room. "You had me at gunpoint. You still do."

I smiled. "We'll see who believes who when we're all done. Won't make this any less painful."

"You won't shoot me," he said, sounding almost desperate.

"Wonderful firearm, the Glock," I continued. "But you never shot one, right? Have a quick lesson. No slide safety, no hammer. Chamber a round and pull the trigger. Maybe you think I'm bluffing, that it's not even loaded." I reached out and racked the slide back, ejecting a cartridge to the floor and chambering another.

The blue-tipped Glaser slug was easily identifiable on the beige carpet.

"Five-pound trigger pull. Can you tell whether I'm pulling hard enough to disengage the safety on the trigger? I bet it's tough to see from that angle, isn't it?" I laughed. "I love this gun."

Pushed beyond ego into fear, he squeaked, "What do you want?"

"I want you to pick up that phone and call Brandan Callaghan and confess to raping those other two women. I want you to lose your badge because you don't deserve to wear one," I said, on a roll. "I dream of hearing about your cellmates bending you over for a little of what you've dished out to women like me. Yeah, I want a lot of things, Rory."

The door opened behind me.

"Julie, lower your gun," a voice said softly.

Resigned to the idea I'd completely thrown away my life, I hesitated, contemplating pulling the trigger anyway. I didn't look over my shoulder at Brandan.

"He's scum, Julie. He's not worth this."

"Why do you want to debate what Rory's life is worth to me?" I argued. The gun wavered in my hand, and I finally let my arm drop to my side.

"Get this crazy bitch out of here," Rory squealed, taking a step forward only to be facing Brandan's gun instead.

"Back off or *I'll* shoot you," Brandan demanded, stopping him abruptly.

I handed Brandan my gun and the recorder. "His confession won't get him convicted for what he did to me," I said, "but maybe the prosecutor can use it for something else. At least it ought to be worth his job."

"She's psycho, man! She had a gun pointed at me the last ten minutes! There's nothing on that tape."

"If she recorded what I heard outside your door, Stewart, it's something. I'll make a deal with you. She and I walk out, and you forget we were here. I keep the tape, and you turn in your resignation on Monday morning. We let the chips fall where they may with the other charges."

"You can't make me resign!"

"Maybe not, but I think I can make you wish you had." Brandan countered, holding up the recorder. "You do all that or I'll sink you like the *Edmund Fitzgerald.* And if you even suggest entrapment, I promise that while you're cooling your jets in a cell, I'll turn her pitbull boyfriend loose with you till there's nothing left to identify but your DNA smeared on the walls."

CHAPTER

53

Brandan pulled me by the sleeve, directing me out the apartment door and toward the steps, following after a few seconds more with Rory Stewart, but saying nothing to me until I reached my truck.

"You're lucky he didn't shoot you!" Brandan's voice strained to maintain a whisper. "What the hell were you thinking?"

I turned away from him and looked up into the starless sky, seeing nothing. After the encounter, I'd expected my heart to be racing, to feel the jazz as the adrenaline burned through me. Instead, I was numb, like I had been most of the time since I'd left Zach at the Portland airport in January.

Dead but still walking.

"You really did beg him to kill you, didn't you?" Brandan said, running his hands over his face. "Damn it, Julie. I'm so sorry I got you involved in this."

I dismissed his revelation. "How'd you know I was here?"

"Zach said he thought you'd do this when I told him about Rory being parked down the street," Brandan explained. "That's why I didn't want to leave your house."

I shrugged.

He put his hand on my arm, turning me to face him. "Julie, I can't imagine what you've been through," he said. "Not this, not Bock. None of it. I don't know how you get up and go to work every morning. I don't think I could."

I had nothing to say. There were no words.

"Go home. Pick up the phone and call Zach. Work this out,

somehow. He can make you smile like I've never seen your face light up before. Stay, move, whatever gets you together, because the feeling you have when you're with him is something you shouldn't throw away. Nothing else in the world is worth that, in my opinion."

"What if he can't – if he doesn't –" I choked on the words.

What if he doesn't want me anymore?

"Can you imagine how hard it's been for someone like Zach to see the woman he loves get hurt? I didn't ask you to marry me, but I'm devastated by what's happened to you. You think he doesn't feel guilty about this? Or about Bock, or you getting cut up in Florida?"

I looked away.

"Julie, can't you forgive him for reacting like a man crazy out of his mind in love with you?"

I fought back tears.

"Forgiveness isn't a feeling, it's an action," he said. "Most important, you need to forgive yourself first."

He handed me the Glock and the ejected cartridge.

"Will you go home this time?" I asked.

"Yeah. If we keep hanging out like this in the middle of the night, people are gonna start to think I'm straight or something," he said with a wink, hugging me before he opened my truck door for me.

I went home and sat in the dark kitchen for a long time, unsure what I would say when I finally called Zach, but I did.

"Julie?" he said when the phone had barely rung in my ear.

"Yeah, Zach," I sighed. "I'm home."

"Are you okay?" he asked, anxiety thick in his voice.

"I will be, some day." I took a deep breath. "I'm sorry I dragged you through hell."

"Most of the time, I've followed along willingly, but this last few weeks, I've never been so scared of anything in my life."

"Of what?"

"Afraid of losing you."

"I was afraid you wouldn't want to touch me." I wiped away a tear.

"That's never been true, Julie. Ever," he said. "When Brandan told me that jerk was parked down the street watching, I knew you'd go after him. It was the ultimate prowl, the perfect dangerous place to go. I was terrified something would happen to you and the last words you'd heard me say were not 'I love you.'"

The only word to come out was, "Oh."

I hadn't even thought about it being like prowling, just vengeance.

How much more screwed up can I get?

"I don't blame you for what he did, but I'm angry someone else hurt you. It wouldn't have happened if . . . well, if I had done any of a lot of things differently. Maybe I shoulda pulled the trigger and shot him that night," he said, almost to himself. "Bottom line is I wasn't there to protect you. I've failed you over and over again."

"You didn't fail me. I've hurt you so much, Zach. Can you forgive me?" I asked quietly. "I know you can't forget any of this, but—"

"Oh, Julie. . ." he said in the same heart-breaking voice as the first night we'd made love. "I don't know what I'd possibly need to forgive, but yes, for anything. I didn't know if you'd trust me again for putting you in danger, but I swear I'm clean. I promise you I'll stay that way."

"I believe you. You've tried so hard to make this all perfect," I said, breaking into tears. "I don't understand why or how you love me like you do, but you're the best thing in my life."

"Baby, please come home," he asked again. "I know it's been a wild ride, but nothing else matters anymore except being together. What's happened doesn't change the way I feel. I love you. I want you."

"Forever?" I whispered.

"Always," he answered. "Will you marry me?"

I looked down at my bare left hand, where I'd worn the emerald and diamond ring those few days after he'd given it to me. I'd left it on the dresser when I packed to leave Washington in January.

"Zach, are you sure?"

"I'm absolutely positive."

"Yes."

I heard my front door close and turned around to find Zach standing there.

"Are *you* sure?" he asked, holding out the ring and turning off his phone. "Because I'm not letting go of you again."

CHAPTER

54

We stood in my foyer, Zach's arms wrapped around me so tight I could barely breathe. I clung to him even harder, but I felt alive again.

"We can be in Vegas by noon," he finally said, "or we can get married here or go to Albuquerque. I don't care where, but I don't want to wait a minute longer than I have to, Julie. There's nothing between us we can't fix, nothing we can't overcome. Will you be my wife, for better or worse? Forever?"

Words failed me. All I could do is nod my head.

◆

In the next two weeks, I quit my job again and put my house on the market, making plans to move to Washington.

One morning, I asked Zach to drive with me to Grand Rapids on an errand.

"I needed to pick up a few items before I leave Michigan," I explained as I pulled into the Harley-Davidson dealership.

It's the truth.

I left him browsing in the clothing section while I went to the counter and completed the transaction, presenting a cashier's check for the balance of the bike that had only arrived a few days before. I turned and watched Zach stroll through racks, making his way toward the bikes sitting on the showroom floor.

He considered them casually, but seeing him standing beside the silver and red Road King, similar to the one I'd chosen for him, I knew it was the right model. He reached out and slid a fingertip over the chrome mirror, unaware I was watching.

I could contain the surprise no longer, so I took the keys I'd been given and walked over to him.

"Done?" he asked.

"No, it'll be a few more minutes. See anything you like?"

He shook his head and followed me as I wandered through clothing aisles, trying on a leather jacket when he courteously held it for me to slip my arms in and then nodded his approval.

I didn't need one, though I wasn't sure if he might not. I shrugged and slipped it off, and he politely hung the jacket on the hanger and placed it on the rack.

"I think you'd look good on that bike," I said, nodding to the one he'd looked at. I picked up a lace-up boot to examine.

He shrugged. "Not red."

"Yeah, I thought black suited you better." I tried not to smile, which lasted about three seconds, so I tossed the keys to him. "Pick out a jacket and a helmet."

Speechless is not like Zach, and I delighted in seeing this rare glimpse.

"You didn't. . ."

I led him by the hand out into the service area where they were getting ready to roll the sleek black and chrome bike into the trailer I'd also bought.

As on the morning he finally took me to the cabin, there was a little trepidation about the gift. But when he swung his leg over it and settled into the seat, I knew it was the right choice.

He insisted on taking a quick spin before it was loaded. Even though it was bitterly cold, the roads were dry. When he returned after what could have been no more than a few minutes, his smile was a bright as a three-year-old's with a litter of puppies on Christmas morning.

♦

Leap Year Day seemed to fit everything unusual about us, so on February 29, 1996, Zach slipped the emerald and diamond ring back on my left hand, along with a matching band, and smiled an even bigger smile as we said vows in front of a gathering of friends and family.

We'd made more intimate promises to each other the night before our wedding – things most important to us but better left undisclosed to our guests.

I swore not to prowl. Ever again.

Zach declared he was then and forever drug-free.

We made a pact that the ghosts and demons of our past would stay there, even if not all the events from our past had been resolved – Brodenshot and several other law enforcement officers in Florida had yet to stand trial, but the corruption had been stopped cold.

Although Dr. Katz couldn't get away, Kimberly and Kayleigh flew down from Michigan with MaryAnne, who agreed to be my matron of honor. Eric and Samantha Rader came from Santa Fe with their new two-week-old bundle of joy, Eric, Jr. Domino Hurley, Zach's best man, brought his wife, Roni, who was nothing like what I'd imagined but who became a wonderful new friend nonetheless. Even my Uncle Jeff came from Chicago when my mother called him with the news, and he was delighted to give the bride away.

We had a lovely dinner after the wedding, explaining without the gory details how Zach and I ended up together. Having spent time in Hawaii before Christmas, we chose to stay in Albuquerque to visit with those who came to celebrate with us, rather than escaping on a so-called honeymoon. People came and went from my mother's house all weekend, with plenty of food and drink for all.

By Sunday evening, Zach and I were exhausted but married and at peace, and the ghosts and demons of our pasts held at bay by two gold rings and a promise. We had each other.

EPILOGUE

Two Weeks Later

Tears flooded my eyes.

Zach took my hand and kissed my palm, then held it to his cheek. "You don't know how much this is tearing me up. I pray to God I've made the right decisions today, but I know you'll be fine. I love you, Blue Eyes." He pulled my face close to his again and whispered, "Amber has another envelope for you with more instructions. I don't trust anyone but you. Trust Eric Rader or Nolan, but no one else. Especially anyone from the DEA. Take the money and disappear."

"How will I know when it's safe?"

"Eric will know. Don't come back for anyone else. Not even me, Julie," he said. "Do you understand?"

I didn't like it, but I understood. "I love you."

He stole one more soul-shattering kiss and wiped the tear that trickled down my cheek.

"Let me introduce you to Amber," he said and reached for the door. "I haven't told her that her grandmother died last night, either. Sorry."

"Is there anything about this I'm going to like?"

He leaned down to my ear and whispered again. "Yeah, going to Pauly Brodenshot's funeral."

In a small office area, two men stood guard next to a dark-headed girl who sat, reading a book in her lap.

"Amber?" Zach said from the doorway.

She looked up at him, a mirror of his green eyes. It was almost unreal how much she looked like Zach.

There was no doubt who her father was.

323

Thank you so much for reading one of
Val Conrad's *A Julie Madigan Thrillers.*
If you enjoyed the experience, please check out
the next book in the series!

Promises of Like Souls by Val Conrad

CPSIA information can be obtained
at www.ICGtesting.com
Printed in the USA
FSHW020243210220
67214FS